MICHELLE KIDD

The Phoenix Project

Copyright © 2018 by Michelle Kidd

All rights reserved. No part of this publication may be reproduced, stored or transmitted in any form or by any means, electronic, mechanical, photocopying, recording, scanning, or otherwise without written permission from the publisher. It is illegal to copy this book, post it to a website, or distribute it by any other means without permission.

This novel is entirely a work of fiction. The names, characters and incidents portrayed in it are the work of the author's imagination. Any resemblance to actual persons, living or dead, events or localities is entirely coincidental.

Michelle Kidd asserts the moral right to be identified as the author of this work.

First edition

This book was professionally typeset on Reedsy. Find out more at reedsy.com

Acknowledgement

Thank you to oliviaprodesign.com for the book cover!

The Phoenix Project

"We learn from failure - not from success"
Dracula - Bram Stoker

CHAPTER ONE

Time: 10.00am
 Date : 1st January 2008
 Location: La Vigne Rouge Chalet, Cote D'Azur, France

The fire had continued to rage for hours throughout the night, hungrily consuming everything in its path. The scorching flames quickly devouring the small, vine-covered cottage, leaving behind nothing but a smoking charred mountain of black ash which crumbled underneath the slightest touch.

Only after the heat had at last subsided could the bodies be removed. Both burnt beyond recognition.

Both unrecognisable.

Both unidentifiable?

He hoped so.

***

Time: 6.00pm
 Date: 4th November 2008
 Location: Paris

Boris Kreshniov sat at his desk and smiled. The time had come at last. He had waited so long for this day and now it was here he felt an almost unnerving sense of apprehension. Things were going to change. The world as everyone knew it was going to change. And Boris Kreshniov was going to be the one to change it.

He reached out and gently picked up the telephone receiver. He dialled the number, his fingers momentarily hovering over the keypad. He had not dialled this number in a long, long time – yet he still knew it by heart. The call was answered on the third ring.

"It's me." Kreshniov kept his voice low, even though he was certain no one else was in earshot. He swept his rooms daily for bugs, and knew that none existed. Not today at least. "It's all set up. Get yourself to the airport tomorrow morning. You're on the 13.45 flight to London." He paused, listening to the reply. "Call me when you make contact."

Kreshniov cut the call and poured himself a drink from the bottle he kept on his desk. He sipped, slowly, savouring the taste on his tongue.

And he smiled.

* * *

Time: 4.00pm
  Date: 5th November 2008
  Location: Metropolitan Police HQ, London

Detective Inspector Jack MacIntosh reached instinctively into his breast pocket, but found it empty – except for a fresh, unopened packet of chewing gum. It had been 37 days now – not bad for a first attempt. Instead, however, he drained the polystyrene cup of acrid black coffee sitting in front of him, grimacing at the bitter sweet taste. At least it took away the pangs of self-induced cravings – for the moment at least.

He glanced up at the clock on the wall in front of him. Four o'clock, almost exactly. A little late in the day for a briefing, but the Chief Superintendent had made it clear that he expected everyone to attend. And everyone included Jack MacIntosh.

The room was filling up with bodies. Those that arrived early enough were sitting at the rows of tables arranged in the centre of the room. The

CHAPTER ONE

latecomers perched on window ledges, edges of tables, or simply stood at the back by the windows that gave a not so impressive view of the rear staff car park.

"Hey, Jack," greeted a young red-haired detective dressed in a light, pale grey suit. The tie around his neck had obviously been knotted in a great hurry, or maybe in the dark. Or possibly both. "Mind if I?" DS Chris Cooper nodded at the corner of Jack's table and sat himself down on the edge.

"Sure, go ahead," replied Jack, shifting in his chair and leaning forwards onto the table. "So, any idea what this is all about?" Jack raised his eyebrows and nodded towards the rest of the congregation filing in behind them.

"No more than you, Jack," answered DS Cooper, shrugging his shoulders and attempting to straighten his tie, without much success.

"Been up long?" smiled Jack, noticing his colleague's ruffled hair and somewhat sleepy appearance.

"'Bout half an hour." DS Cooper yawned, noisily, rubbed his eyes and looked down at his wristwatch. "And even that was a struggle."

"Anyone I know?"

"I wish!" DS Cooper laughed, massaging his temples with his fingers. "Night shift on the Stavaros case. Spent all night outside a taxi cab office on the Mount Road. Waste of bloody time that was."

"Bonfire night tonight, you know. You planning to do the same again? Or taking the kids out?"

DS Cooper didn't have time to answer as both he and Jack heard distant footsteps echoing along the corridor outside. The footsteps grew louder and eventually the briefing room's door flew open and in breezed a tall, authoritative figure sporting a neat crop of ice-white hair.

Chief Superintendent Malcolm Liddell strode to the front of the room, and then turned to face the rows of expectant and rather inquisitive eyes trained on him. It wasn't often that the Chief Superintendent ordered a briefing with all available officers asked to attend. And for that reason, the room was packed to bursting point.

Chief Superintendent Liddell was a lithe 57-year-old. He had joined the force as a young man, fresh out of the Army, and had risen steadily through the ranks ever since, reaching the heights of Chief Superintendent at a very young forty. He was well liked and well respected amongst his peers – seen as a fair man, if somewhat old fashioned in his ideas and opinions.

"Gentleman," announced Liddell, his deep throaty voice booming out across the room, silencing any whispers in an instant. "And ladies," he added as an after thought, as he spied a couple of female detectives sitting together at the back of the room. One of the Chief Superintendent's old fashioned ideas included that of female police officers being restricted to positions of inferiority, and certainly not rising through the ranks of the CID. He gave the female officers his usual quizzical look before continuing.

"May I thank you all for turning up here this afternoon, as I'm sure you all have plenty of other seemingly more important places to be. Or at least, I hope you do." He smiled at his own joke, his tanned and lean face crinkling around the eyes and mouth. His deep set blue eyes stared out over the heads before him, finally focusing on Jack and DS Cooper sitting on the front row. "Especially you, DI MacIntosh, and you, DS Cooper. I take it we are at least a *little* bit closer to a result on the Stavaros case?"

Liddell's hard stare rested on Jack but it was DS Cooper who replied. "Yes, Sir. I was out on it last night, Sir." DS Cooper flashed a quick glance at Jack before carrying on. "Got some useful information – should bring the investigation forward quite a bit, Sir."

"Hmmmm," murmured Liddell, quickly taking in DS Cooper's somewhat dishevelled appearance. "So I see, Cooper, so I see."

Liddell looked away from Jack's table and again swept the room with his deeply penetrative stare. He stood tall, puffed out his chest and rocked slowly backwards and forwards on his well-polished heels. His close fitting, well-tailored dark grey suit stood out amongst the array of attire worn by the other detectives in the room. The predominant colour of the suits worn was a rather tired and washed out grey, often crumpled and mostly ill-fitting. Those that chose to wear a suit that was. Many opted for jeans and jackets, even a few short-sleeved t-shirts despite the inclement winter weather outside.

CHAPTER ONE

Even Liddell's tie pin shone out under the bright strip-lighting overhead.

"As I was saying," he continued," thank you for all coming here this afternoon. I would now like to take this opportunity to introduce you to Special Agent John Fleming here – from the United States FBI." Chief Superintendent Liddell swept a graceful arm towards the man standing slightly to his right. No one in the briefing room seemed to have taken much notice of the second man who had followed Liddell into the room only a few minutes before.

He was smaller in stature than Liddell, but of similar appearance. A neat and well-tailored pale grey suit, perfectly polished shoes, gleaming cuff-links and sparkling wristwatch. Jack guessed he was a little younger than Liddell, but both shared the same lean and lithe physique and the same air of quiet authority. Agent Fleming's short cropped, dark hair was only very slightly flecked with the same white which liberally covered Liddell's scalp.

"Good afternoon, everyone," greeted Agent Fleming, his pale lips parting momentarily to allow a glimpse of a perfectly straight row of perfectly white teeth. He stepped forwards slightly, and gave a small nod of the head towards his audience.

"Special Agent Fleming is over here in London investigating the whereabouts of an individual with dual American and Russian nationality." Liddell's eyes swept the room once again, checking to see that his officers were giving their utmost attention. "He is thought to have resided here in the UK recently, if only temporarily, and more specifically here in London. Whether or not he is still here is under investigation." Chief Superintendent Liddell opened a small black leather folder which he had tucked neatly under his arm. He pulled out a large photograph, blown up into A4 size, and pinned it to a large notice board on the wall behind him. "Agent Fleming?" Liddell motioned for Special Agent Fleming to step forwards once more and take the stage.

"As Chief Superintendent Liddell mentioned," began Fleming, his West Coast drawl cutting through the briefing room like a hot knife through butter, "this man has been on our wanted list back in the United States for some considerable time. We have reason to suspect that he has entered the UK recently, possibly en route to the Continent. He is not thought to be armed, but is declared to be a real threat to national security on both sides of the Atlantic. Hence our desire to apprehend him as soon as possible." Fleming paused and flashed another pearly white smile. "I am hoping that with the help of your good selves, we can wrap this up in record time." Fleming turned to face the notice board and pointed to the blown up photograph.

"This charming individual is adept at identification fraud and could be operating under any one of a variety of assumed names. He is approximately 45 years of age, and as far as we know he was last seen in your small town of Dover, Kent. He has no known family connections, but he has been known to frequent the UK and Western Europe. He is approximately 5 feet 9 inches tall, and weighs approximately 180 pounds.

"He is known to have dual Russian and US nationalities and due to his talent for identification fraud, he is likely to have passports in every nationality under the sun. The reason that we at the FBI and also the CIA are so keen to apprehend this man, is because of this."

Fleming took hold of Liddell's small black folder and pulled out another large colour photograph. He turned and pinned it on the notice board behind him, next to the photograph of the wanted man. He turned back to face the room, but paused momentarily, letting the effect of the photograph sink in.

The picture was a mixture of mangled metal, smashed concrete, and shattered bricks – with blood, broken bones and body parts scattered in between. It looked like something out of a horror movie.

"Details are set out more fully in the memos I have here." Fleming waved a sheaf of paper in the air. "I would be grateful if you could all take one before you leave. It contains all the information you need to know, including a list of his known aliases." He placed the papers down on the desk in front of him, directly in front of Jack.

"In short, ladies and gentleman, the FBI and CIA have good reason to believe that this man is part of a new European terror cell, planning atrocities across the western world, with specific targets in the UK, US and Western Europe. Maybe even further afield. We have intercepted very reliable intelligence which supports our suspicions that this individual is on the move and has every intention of recruiting others into his cause. I don't need to tell you that we need to stop him before this terror network grows beyond our capabilities."

Fleming paused and surveyed the room before him. Many of the detectives were still staring at the graphic photograph placed up on the notice board.

"I don't need to remind you all how important it is that we defeat this threat to our national and international security. We in the US are still coming to terms with the September 11th disaster – and you yourselves have had your own terrorist attacks here in July 2005, and other atrocities since. Many of you here, I understand, were on duty during these times, and witnessed the carnage that these people can cause."

Again he paused, letting his pale eyes sweep across the length and breadth of the room. Many of the detectives in the room had, indeed, been on duty on 7th July 2005 when the terrorist bombs had exploded on the London transport system. As they remembered that fateful day, eyes clouded over, faces dropped, stomachs tightened. Jack himself had not been far away from Tavistock Square, the scene of the double-decker bus explosion. He had rushed to the scene, like so many of his colleagues, only to be confronted with something that he had never seen before in his life. And never wanted to see again.

Fleming cleared his throat and continued. "The reason you are all being briefed in this way is so that if anyone, during the course of their own investigations, comes across any information in respect of the whereabouts of this individual, you can let me know immediately. There is every possibility that you may hear something, or see something while out on the streets, which may be useful in my investigation. But under no circumstances are you to approach him directly, or take the matter any further. Just report any information or sightings either directly to myself, or to the Chief Superintendent here. You are my eyes and ears out there –

I need you."

Fleming gave a brief nod to Chief Superintendent Liddell, indicating that his speech was over. Liddell took back the folder and stepped forwards.

"I have briefed the heads of both MI5 and MI6. They are working closely with us and Special Agent Fleming here on this." Liddell paused and carefully watched his officers' expressions. "If this man is indeed in our city, ladies and gentlemen, we need to flush him out."

A series of murmurs and nods of the head trickled around the room. Jack lowered his eyes and took a sneak preview of the stack of papers sitting in front of him. Smaller versions of the two photographs from the notice board were reproduced at the bottom of the front page.

DS Cooper stifled a yawn. The room was overly warm with all the extra bodies crammed inside, and the heating was still on full blast. The meeting soon broke up and the officers began filing out of the room, clutching their memos. Some studied them as they left, committing the facts and faces to memory – others, like Jack, scanned them quickly and then stuffed them inside their jacket pockets. As Jack neared the door, he glanced up at Fleming. Frowning slightly, he noted that for a West Coast FBI agent he had unusually pale skin. Wasn't it always sunny on the West Coast of the USA? Giving a small shrug, he nodded at DS Copper to head out the door in front of him.

Chief Superintendent Liddell waited until the last of the officers had left the briefing room, and then with the door safely shut he turned towards Special Agent Fleming.

"That's the one I was telling you about," he said, nodding towards the closed door and the departing officers. "DI MacIntosh."

Special Agent Fleming raised his perfectly manicured eyebrows, questioningly. "Yes?"

"Yes, you'll need to watch out for him."

"Consider me duly warned," smiled Agent Fleming, stacking up the rest of the unused and uncollected memos. "But I don't think he'll be a problem."

Chief Superintendent Liddell slowly shook his head, his face serious.

CHAPTER ONE

"You don't understand. You don't know Jack MacIntosh. He's like a dog with a bone – once he gets hold of something, there's no letting go. Are you sure you should have gone public with this? Does everyone else know?"

"Don't worry." Agent Fleming turned towards Liddell, again flashing his pearly white smile. "I know just how to deal with people like your Detective Inspector MacIntosh. Piece of cake."

* * *

Time: 14.15pm
 Date: 5th November 2008
 Location: Skies above London, England

"Excuse me, Sir."

Karl Poborski opened his eyes to see a smiling flight attendant leaning over and lifting up the shutters on the small cabin window next to him.

"Sorry to disturb you, Sir, but we are about to begin our descent." The flight attendant swiftly collected the empty plastic tumblers and half-eaten packets of cashew nuts from the in-flight table. "Can I ask you to return your seat to an upright position and fasten your seatbelt, please?"

Poborski nodded, and watched her move gracefully onto the next row of passengers. He straightened himself up in his seat, wincing at the stabbing pain shooting up the back of his legs. He yawned and checked his wristwatch. He was still on Moscow time, but could see that he must have been asleep for the best part of the last three hours. He raised his arms above his head, stretching towards the aircraft ceiling – he felt the bones in his neck and shoulders crunch and creak.

The fasten your seatbelt sign had illuminated overhead, and Poborski dutifully snapped the buckle into place. He peered out of the tiny window and watched as the aircraft began its bumpy descent through the thick grey cloud. Large droplets of moisture clung to the glass.

He wanted to call Kreshniov as soon as he landed, to check that everything was still on course, but he knew that he shouldn't. He knew that he mustn't. He wasn't supposed to call until the first stage of the plan was in motion. Boris had been most insistent on that. No calls. No contact. No nothing. Not until the plan was well underway. And even then, Poborski was only to call in an *extreme* emergency.

Boris Kreshniov didn't trust anyone. And at this precise moment in time, Poborski felt sure that he probably didn't even trust him.

And the feeling was mutual.

"Good afternoon, ladies and gentlemen," crackled the cockpit intercom. "Welcome to London Heathrow. I hope you enjoy your stay and thank you for flying British Airways."

Time: 4.25pm
Date: 5th November 2008
Location: Metropolitan Police HQ, London

Jack pulled open the door to his aged Ford Mondeo and slid into the driver's seat, noticing how the windscreen was already starting to ice up. It had been bitterly cold all day, and a severe frost was expected tonight. There was even talk of snow.

"Need a lift?" Jack caught DS Cooper's eye as the young detective pulled up the collar of his coat and wrapped a scarf around his neck.

"No, thanks, I'm fine boss," replied DS Cooper, lifting a gloved hand in acknowledgment. "I'm hopping on the bus to go and see the kids. Jane said I can take them to the fireworks display as long as I don't keep them out too late. No chance in this weather!" He thrust his hands inside his pockets, his breath billowing out in frozen puffs.

"Have fun," Jack smiled and closed the door. With the heating turned up full blast it didn't take long for the windscreen to clear, and Jack pulled out of the car park. He only lived a few streets away from Scotland Yard, and really didn't need to take his car to work, it often being quicker to walk than sit in the heavy afternoon traffic around Westminster.

While he crept towards Parliament Square, Jack rummaged in his jacket pocket for his mobile phone. A quick glance told him there had been no

CHAPTER ONE

calls or messages and he threw the handset onto the front passenger seat, next to the empty coffee takeaway cups and sandwich wrappers. Rubbing his tired eyes, Jack felt the all too familiar cravings begin to surface. Sitting in traffic was always a moment of weakness for him, as it was all too often the time when he would wind down the window and light up.

Drumming his fingers on the steering wheel, Jack reached back into his jacket pocket and brought out the unopened packet of nicotine chewing gum, along with the already crumpled memo from Chief Superintendent Liddell's briefing. Glancing momentarily at the memo and its photograph, Jack thrust the memo back into his pocket and ripped open the chewing gum. He winced as he chewed; the taste wasn't what he would call pleasant, but he knew it would take away the gnawing pangs of his cravings – for a while at least.

The traffic was moving more steadily now and it wasn't long before he could turn off the main street, and pull up outside his small flat. Kettles Yard Mews was a narrow, cobbled street with several whitewashed mews-style properties nestled snuggly together on both sides of the road. Jack's flat was at the very end of the street, and he skilfully managed to reverse park into a tight space outside.

With his keys in hand, Jack opened the front door and bent down to pick up the post from the doormat. After quickly flicking through and seeing nothing was for him, he placed the letters on the wooden cabinet at the side of the hall and made his way up the winding stairs to the second floor. The flat was perfect for Jack. It was small and compact, with not a lot of room for furniture, but Jack didn't take up much space. He had acquired few belongings in his 41 years, preferring the simple life without many trappings. The others at the station often mused how Jack could afford a place in such a select and central part of the city, even on a Detective Inspector's salary. Speculation was rife, many favouring there being a rich widow who was keeping Jack in the luxury he could ill afford himself. Such speculation made him smile, but Jack remained tight lipped.

Opening the door to his flat on the second floor, Jack snapped on the lights and sighed when he saw yesterday's washing up still piled up on the draining board by the sink, and the washing he had draped over the radiators. And there was a musty smell in the air, a mixture of damp clothes and last night's takeaway. A rich widow there was not.

As far as bachelor pads went, it wasn't the most enticing place to attract female company, but Jack didn't mind. Loosening his tie, he shrugged off his jacket and threw it onto the sagging sofa that sometimes doubled as his bed. Although only a little before 5pm, Jack spied the bottle of Glen Fiddich sitting on the low rise coffee table, remnants from the night before, and slowly chugged another few inches into the glass tumbler by its side.

As the night sky over London began to light up with brilliant, radiant explosions of colour, and bonfires filled the chilled air with wafts of burning wood and charcoal, Jack drew the heavy curtains and shut out the world. Tomorrow was Saturday and for once he wasn't on shift. The thought of switching off the alarm and having the day stretch out before him with nothing to do, made him smile with contentment.

And he poured another two inches of whisky into his glass.

CHAPTER TWO

Time: 2.30pm
Date: 6th November 2008
Location: Paris

Boris Kreshniov looked at his watch for the umpteenth time. He had slept only fitfully the night before and his eyes felt red and sore. He had risen early and taken an early morning stroll through the streets around his flat and down to the Seine; his favourite time of day, before the residents of the city awoke. Everything was calm. Everything was quiet. Everything was still. But it had done little to calm or quell his nerves.

Kreshniov thought about calling to check up on progress, but knew that he must not. Poborski would have called if there had been any problems, and he himself had told Poborski not to ring unless there was. He had to trust him. He had to. He didn't like it, but he had to.

The bottle of Jack Daniels sat within easy reach, but Kreshniov resisted. He needed to keep a clear head. He looked at the seemingly disorganised clutter weighing down his desk, but ignored the urge to tidy.

Instead, he sat and waited.

***

Time: 4.45pm

Date: 6th November 2008
Location: London

Simon Shafer's mobile phone started to ring. He placed the heavy briefcase and bulging bundle of papers down onto the taxi cab floor, and hurriedly fished the telephone out of his pocket. He recognised the number on the display panel of the phone straight away.

"Yes?" Shafer's voice sounded tense. He hoped Fleming didn't notice.

"Where are you?" barked the voice on the other end.

Shafer peered out of the taxi cab's window, squinting through the condensation which blurred his vision. Outside, the weak winter sun had quickly faded into nothing and night was already encroaching fast. The sky was a dark, inky blue, and it was starting to snow.

"Just passing St James' Park tube station," replied Shafer, his heart thumping loudly inside his chest. He ran a finger around the inside of his damp shirt collar, feeling sweat begin to form on his brow. "I should be with you in about five minutes."

"Make sure you are," growled Fleming. "We can't afford for there to be any mistakes."

Shafer opened his mouth to reply, but the phone went dead. Swallowing nervously, Shafer flipped the phone shut and placed it back in his pocket. Suddenly, the enormity of what he was doing, of what he was *about* to do, hit him like a freight train. He rubbed his eyes with the palms of his damp, sweating hands, then focused his mind on the briefcase sitting at his feet.

The briefcase.

It was all about the briefcase. And what was inside.

Shafer didn't know how long he had been staring down at the floor, but he was quickly jolted back into reality when the taxi swung to an abrupt stop.

"There you go, mate." The taxi driver tapped on the plastic safety glass behind him to gain Shafer's attention. "That'll be £13.30."

The taxi had stopped outside a tall, impressive building, looking out across the waters of the Thames. A building Shafer knew well. Taking

CHAPTER TWO

a quick glance out of the window, he saw the familiar rows of tinted windows rising higher and higher into the early evening sky. A lump formed in his throat as he fumbled for his wallet.

"Here, keep the change." Shafer handed over a crumpled £20 note and hurriedly gathered up the bundle of papers from the floor. The taxi driver took the money with a nod while Shafer scrambled out of the cab. He stood waiting by the side of the road for the taxi to pull away and disappear over the bridge before he turned and walked towards the front door of Vauxhall Cross, Headquarters of the Secret Intelligence Service. MI6. He gripped the papers tightly under his arm.

This was it.

It was done.

Now it was show time.

* * *

Time: 4.55pm
Date: 6th November 2008
Location: King's Street, Cambridge

The door to Taylor's Fine Art Supplies stuck just as Isabel tried to pull it shut. It was always the same in this kind of weather. The cold and damp made the antiquated woodwork swell, causing the door to stick like glue.

Just as she started to give the door one last tug, eager to get home, Isabel heard the telephone begin to ring from back inside the shop. She considered letting it ring for a moment – it was nearly five o'clock after all, closing time. But then, cursing silently under her breath, she pushed herself against the door and stepped back inside. The old brass bell jangled violently overhead.

Behind her a thick blanket of fog enveloped everything it touched. Isabel had been barely able to see the road outside the shop when she had glanced out of the window earlier. Every so often, hazy circles of soft light inched their way past her – cars trying to find their way home in the dense, impenetrable gloom.

It was a typical November evening. Cold, damp and foggy. The fog hadn't lifted all day and, if anything, had become deeper and thicker as the sun gratefully slunk down over the horizon and allowed the heavy night air to seep in and chill the bones. The air itself still had the faint smoky aroma of spent fireworks and slumbering bonfires from the night before.

Isabel slipped her coat off and hung it back on the coat stand. She walked over to the back of the shop, leant across the desk, and picked up the receiver. "Good afternoon, Taylor's Art Supplies. How can I help you?"

The voice on the other end of the telephone seemed to hesitate.

"Hello?" Isabel repeated. "Can I help you?"

Again there was silence. Isabel opened her mouth to speak again, but at last the voice answered.

"Oh, sorry, yes," replied the voice. "Having problems with this damn phone. I do apologise." The voice was warm and friendly.

Isabel smiled and sat down in the swivel chair behind the desk, automatically pulling a small notepad and pen across in front of her. "No problem," she said, absent mindedly tapping the notepad with the end of her pen. "How can I help?"

"My name is Cartwright. I was wondering if you had any viridian oil pastels in stock yet," said the voice. "I did telephone a couple of days ago, spoke to an elderly gentleman? He didn't have any at the time but was going to see if he could order some in."

Isabel scribbled the words "Cartwright" and "viridian" down onto the notepad. "That would be Mr Taylor," she replied. "He hasn't mentioned anything to me about it, but I'll just go and check out in the stock room for you. We had a delivery earlier today so we may have some in. I won't be a minute. Would you like to hold on, or shall I call you back?"

"I'll hold on," replied Mr Cartwright. "If it's no trouble," he added, pleasantly.

"No trouble at all. Won't be a sec." Isabel carefully placed the telephone down and headed out into the small stock room behind the desk. She snapped on the overhead light and a faint orangey glow illuminated the room. The stock room was only small, but filled from floor to ceiling with boxes and boxes of supplies – ranging from paint pots to acetate sheets, fine watercolour brushes to thick, chunky rollers. The shelves were bursting with a rainbow of colours.

Although crammed to the brim, Isabel knew exactly where everything was and immediately headed to the far left hand corner of the room. If they had any viridian oil pastels, then she would undoubtedly find them here.

Just at that moment, the familiar tinkling of the bell above the front door sounded again. Isabel frowned and glanced at her watch. It was 4.57pm. She remembered putting the "closed" sign up on the door when she had been getting ready to leave, just before putting on her coat, but she must have forgotten to lock the door behind her when she came back into the shop to answer the telephone.

"Sorry," she called out over her shoulder. "I'll be out in a minute." She pulled a large box of oil pastels off the shelf in front of her. A quick peek at the top of the box told her that they did now, indeed, have a shade of viridian.

Isabel tucked the box under her arm and made her way out of the stock room. She snapped off the light and went back to the desk. Placing the box of pastels down next to the telephone, she glanced quickly around the shop. It was empty. Whoever had just come in had obviously changed their mind again, and left. Shrugging to herself, Isabel picked up the telephone receiver.

"Hello? Mr Cartwright?" she said, seating herself back down in the chair. "Good news. I've found our delivery of oil pastels and…." Then she paused. There was silence on the other end of the line. "Mr Cartwright?"

Still more silence.

"Mr Cartwright? Are you still there?" Isabel held the receiver close to her ear. "Are you all right, Mr Cartwright? I have your oil pastels……."

The silence was now replaced by the long, continuous beeping sound of an empty telephone line. Mr Cartwright had hung up. Frowning to herself, Isabel quickly dialled 1471. She could always ring him back and let him know that they now had some viridian oil pastels in stock. It looked like Mr Taylor had ordered them in specially, as it wasn't a shade that they normally sold much of.

"You were called today at 16.56. The caller withheld their number." Isabel slowly replaced the receiver. Maybe Mr Cartwright would phone back again in the morning. She placed the box of oil pastels underneath the desk, and put the handwritten note with the words "Cartwright" and "viridian" on top of the desk to remind her about it when she got in the next day.

It was only then that Isabel noticed the front door of the shop had been left wide open. The customer who had come in whilst she had been in the stock room must have forgotten to shut it when they left. Consequently, the evening chill air was seeping into the warm shop, bringing with it a damp, foggy smell. Isabel made her way back over to the door and pushed it shut. As she did so she glanced down at the doormat under her feet. There, in the very centre of the mat, was a small, square piece of paper.

Isabel bent down and picked it up. Turning it over in her hand, she saw the word "Fizzy" written across the centre in small, neat, capital letters.

* * *

Time: 5.15pm
  Date: 6th November 2008
  Location: MI6, Secret Intelligence Service HQ, Vauxhall Cross, London

Shafer shifted nervously in his seat. Large damp patches of sweat made his shirt cling uncomfortably to his back. His hand shook slightly as he brought the coffee cup to his lips. He sipped the lukewarm, weak tasting liquid, then placed the cup back down on the saucer, china rattling on china.

Shafer was alone in the room. Fleming was making him wait. He looked at his watch for the millionth time. Time seemed to be standing still. Not that it made any difference. Fleming would only come when Fleming was

CHAPTER TWO

good and ready. That was the way it was.

The top floor of Vauxhall Cross afforded wide, breathtaking views across the River Thames and the London skyline beyond. On any other day, Shafer would be looking out over the horizon, drinking in the haphazard beauty of the buildings set out below him, the famous landmarks, the wonders of the world outside. Everything draped in a beautiful, shimmering carpet of white.

On any other day.

But not today.

Today, Shafer didn't so much as glance up at the floor-to-ceiling windows. He shifted his weight again in the deluxe leather chair, feeling himself sinking even further into its softness. The chair was facing the full length windows, but Shafer averted his gaze.

Suddenly, the door flew open, colliding noisily with the wall behind it. A tall, thin man entered, his pale eyes blazing from behind his equally pale-rimmed spectacles. His complexion was also pale – his skin taking on an almost translucent look. His lips were pulled into a tight line across his face, as pale as the rest of him.

He strode over to where Shafer was sitting and angrily threw a bulging manila folder down onto the coffee table, sending the china cup and saucer flying in its wake. The china splintered into tiny fragments as it hit the window, and thin rivers of coffee trickled down the panes like tears.

"You have a lot of explaining to do," roared Fleming, spit flying out of the corner of his mouth as he spoke. "And you'd better start now!"

* * *

Time: 12.30pm
   Date: 6th November 2008
   Location: Washington DC, USA

"The papers – they're on their way." His voice sounded tense.

"Good," the reply crackled down the long distance telephone line. "I want to know immediately the moment they are destroyed." Dimitri Federov's voice sounded much farther away than the 5,000 or so miles from Washington DC to Moscow.

"You have my word." Austin Edwards ample frame leant back in his chair, feeling the taut leather creak beneath his weight. He looked over to his right, gazing out of the window at the sun nestling behind the Lincoln Memorial. It was a view that he never tired of. "He won't let us down."

"You trust him this time?" Dimitri Federov's voice failed to hide his obvious scepticism.

"He won't let us down," repeated Edwards, simply. "I guarantee it."

"But if he does?" The question hung tantalisingly in the air.

Austin Edwards rubbed his tired and worn face with his bony fingers. He felt every single one of his 62 years, if not a good deal more. He licked his dry and cracked lips, and tilted his silver-haired head closer towards the receiver. "If he does, then you know what we must all do."

* * *

Time: 5.05pm
Date: 6th November 2008
Location: Taylor's Art Supplies, Kings Street, Cambridge

Isabel's eyes widened in surprise. Hesitating only briefly, she unfolded the piece of paper and saw the same neat handwriting spell out a message in the middle.

"Fizzy," it read. "Check the Evening News tonight....please xxx"

That was it.

Isabel frowned and turned the piece of paper over, but there was nothing else written on it. Nothing more than the one-line sentence she had just read. Isabel looked at the message again. Her heart began to quicken, and stepping forwards she pulled open the shop door, making the bell jangle loudly once again.

Isabel quickly looked up and down the street outside, searching for

CHAPTER TWO

who might have left the message on the doormat. It must have been whoever had come in whilst she was busy out in the stock room. It certainly hadn't been there when she had been trying to leave earlier, just before the telephone call from Mr Cartwright had brought her back inside the shop. If it had been there, she would have noticed it – stepped on it probably.

Isabel's eyes darted backwards and forwards, left and right, searching through the inky blackness. But the dense heavy fog made it impossible to see clearly. Whoever it had been, they had been able to easily slink away quietly into the night.

Isabel stared back down at the name written on the front of the piece of paper. Fizzy. Just Fizzy. Isabel instantly thought of one person – the one and *only* person that could have left such a message.

Miles.

It just had to be Miles. Miles was the only person who ever called her Fizzy. Some of her friends called her Izzy, or Izz. But never Fizzy. That had been Miles, and only Miles.

Isabel slowly stepped backwards into the shop, still searching with her eyes for any movement amongst the shadows outside. But there was nothing. Nothing but stillness. Nothing but blackness. Nothing but quietness. She pushed the door shut once more, the sound of the bell cutting though the silence.

Isabel's mind was racing. She hadn't seen Miles for the last six months, not since he decided to pack up and go trekking half way around the world. He had asked Isabel to go with him, pleaded with her to leave everything behind and explore the great unknown, just the two of them together. Isabel had been tempted, sorely tempted, and almost gave in – but she knew deep down that she would not go.

And Miles had known that too.

And that had been the end of their relationship…just like that. They had not spoken since they day he left. Isabel often thought about him, wondering what he was doing, where he was, who he was with. It often left her with an empty, raw feeling inside. Had she been right to stay behind? Or should she have thrown caution to the wind and gone along with him?

It was a question she had asked herself many, many times over the months since their parting. And most of the time she did not have any answer. When Isabel had politely, but firmly, refused to go with him, part of her had expected Miles to stay behind. To change his mind about leaving, to realise that he couldn't go without her, that he couldn't be separated from her, that he couldn't leave her behind.

But he could.

And he had.

Isabel clutched the note in her hand. Had it been Miles who had come into the shop whilst she was in the stock room? If so, why hadn't he stayed to see her? Or called out? If it was him, why would he just secretly leave a note and disappear?

Isabel looked down at the note once again.

Unless it wasn't him. Unless it wasn't Miles. The writing was small – with neat capital letters no more than a centimetre high. She had never known Miles to write like that. His handwriting was usually large and scruffy, unintelligible most of the time.

Isabel suddenly shivered, and not just because of the cold night air. She put the note into her jeans pocket. She wanted to get out of here. She wanted to get home. She felt uneasy, as if someone, somewhere, were watching her. She hurriedly dimmed the shop lights before grabbing her coat from the coat stand next to the door. She pulled the door firmly shut behind her and locked it with a large brass key. Slipping the key into the pocket of her coat, she turned and walked briskly into the deepening darkness of the night. She walked quickly, the only sound being her own soft tiny footsteps on the ice cold pavement.

The temperature was sinking, and Isabel's breath billowed out of her mouth in front of her like tiny puffs of smoke. Head down, and without looking behind her, Isabel headed for home. Across the road, directly opposite the entrance to the shop, obscured by the thick wisps of fog which hung like heavy curtains in the night air, the window of a sleek, coal-black Mercedes gently and silently lowered itself.

Inside, the driver picked up his telephone and held it to his ear, his face

CHAPTER TWO

obscured by a thick, black, woollen scarf and a black woollen hat pulled down firmly over his ears. Only his pale grey eyes and thin hooked nose were visible.

"Subject leaving building on foot," he said in a low, controlled voice. He smiled at the reply, gave a brief nod and clicked shut his phone. Then, silently, he drove off in the direction of Isabel's shadow.

* * *

Time: 8.15pm
  Date: 6th November 2008
  Location: Red Square, Moscow

Sergei Ivanov snatched at the telephone receiver as soon as it began to ring. He had been waiting for the call. He knew who it would be. "Ivanov," he barked, pouring himself another generous serving of vishnnyovka.

"It's me." Dimitri Federov's voice sounded small and distant, yet he was no more than 200 metres away around the corner of the adjacent building.

"And?" The warming cherry vodka had done nothing to loosen the tightness Ivanov felt in his throat and chest. His heart pounded like a wild beast begging to escape.

"It's done. The papers are on their way. I just got off the phone to Edwards." Federov paused. "It'll soon be over."

Ivanov grunted and took another large mouthful of the fiery vishnnyovka. He grimaced as the burning hot liquid hit the back of his throat. "I still don't like it," he mumbled. "I don't trust him."

"Who?" Federov asked the question but knew exactly who his friend was referring to. He felt the same misgivings gnawing at his insides.

"Edwards who else?" Ivanov swallowed the rest of the vodka and slammed the empty glass back down onto his cluttered desk. It wasn't his first drink of the day, and it wouldn't be his last either. "And that little runt he has working for him on the other side. I don't trust either of them."

"Edwards says nothing will go wrong. The papers will be destroyed."

Ivanov reached again for the bottle and took a long gulp. He didn't bother with the glass this time. He swallowed quickly and exhaled noisily, his throat seemingly now numbed to the searing pain. "With Kreshniov back from the dead, anything can go wrong."

"Kreshniov hasn't been seen – we don't know he's still alive for sure." Federov tried to make his voice sound sincere, and more convincing than he felt, but he knew that he had failed when he heard Ivanov's dry laughter crackling down the telephone line.

"You know why he called it the Phoenix Project?" Ivanov's voice was stern, his laughter having subsided. It wasn't a question, and Federov knew better than to profess an answer. "Because he'll rise from the ashes, my friend – one day, he will rise from the ashes – just like a Phoenix." Ivanov paused, and stared out of his window in the direction of Red Square. "This isn't over. Just you wait and see."

CHAPTER THREE

Time: 5.30pm
Date: 6th November 2008
Location: Green Park Parade, Cambridge

Isabel opened her front door, glad to feel the warm air greet her like an old friend. The November chill had seeped into her bones during the short walk home, numbing her fingers and toes, and giving her nose a pale pink tinge.

She quickly slammed the door shut behind her and snapped on the hallway light. She leant back, gratefully, against the door and closed her eyes. Although she lived only a short walk from the shop, tonight the journey had seemed to take an age. She had jumped at every slight noise, every bang of a dustbin, every screech of tyres, every sound of an engine. She had criss crossed the road dozens of times, glancing nervously over her shoulder in case she was being followed. But every time she looked, she saw nothing but foggy blackness.

Kicking off her shoes, Isabel walked down the length of the hallway and into the kitchen. She took off her coat and hung it on the back of the kitchen door, then made her way over to the sink and switched on the kettle.

Just then a fluffy white tail twirled its way around her ankles. Isabel looked down and smiled.

"Hello, Snowy," she murmured, softly. "Did you miss me?" Snowball purred rhythmically and began rubbing her soft head against Isabel's calves.

Then she turned and leapt onto the kitchen table behind Isabel, her usual cue that she wanted to be picked up and cuddled. Isabel turned and obliged, scooping the fluffy cat up into her arms and giving her a squeeze. She buried her head into the soft fur and let out a huge sigh.

"Oh, Snowy," she breathed. "You don't know how glad I am to be home."

The kettle had boiled and Isabel put Snowball back down on the floor while she made herself a strong cup of steaming tea. Carrying it through to the living room, with half a packet of chocolate chip cookies, Isabel heard the letterbox rattle. She paused in the hallway and looked down the passage towards the front door. There, on the mat, lay a neatly folded newspaper.

Isabel's stomach knotted once more. Balancing her mug of tea and packet of biscuits in one hand, she reached into her jeans pocket and brought out the carefully folded piece of paper. Then she glanced up at the newspaper which was still lying on the mat. The Evening News.

Isabel went to the front door and picked up the newspaper. Tucking it under her arm, she carried her tea and biscuits through to the living room where Snowball was already curled up on the sofa, purring happily. Isabel gently sat down beside the fluffy cat, placing her tea on the floor next to her feet.

She took the newspaper and lay it across her knees. If the note had been from Miles, she knew exactly where to look. She quickly turned the pages until she got to the classified ads section towards the back of the newspaper. Without pausing, she began to scan the messages in the personal section.

Oriental lady seeks fun and friendship. Professional male seeks companion for love and good times. Divorced mother of two looking for a kind and caring male. Escort services recruiting now – earn up to £500 per night. Isabel nervously chewed her bottom lip as her eyes flicked up and down the columns. If Miles had sent her a message, then it must be here. It was always here. Then, just as she was about to give up, she saw it nestling at the bottom of the final page.

"Fizzy. Meet me tonight. Usual place. 9.00pm. Please. I need to see you.

CHAPTER THREE

M xxx"

Isabel's heart skipped a beat. She hastily read the message again. There could be no mistake.

He was back.

Miles was really back.

* * *

Time: 6.05pm

Date: 6th November 2008

Location: MI6, Secret Intelligence Service HQ, Vauxhall Cross, London

Simon Shafer winced as Fleming slammed the door behind him. The meeting had been brief – and had gone just as Shafer had expected. Just as he had been told it would. He hoped he had been convincing. The dark coffee stains on the window pane were now dry. The china still lay in broken fragments on the plush red carpet.

Shafer exhaled slowly and reached into his suit jacket pocket, taking out his mobile phone. He quickly dialled the number, his eyes trained on the door, watching for any sign of Fleming returning.

His call was answered quickly.

"It's me. Fleming's just left. But he'll be back soon." Shafer listened to the reply and nodded. His eyes left the door for a moment or two and began to sweep around the walls of the room. Would this place be bugged? Maybe behind the picture frames on the walls? Behind the light switches? The pot plants? The lamp shades? Shafer wasn't sure, but he intended to take no risks. He would keep his conversation short and to the point. He had risked so much already. Too much. Again.

Shafer's eyes rested back on the doorway once again. Fleming would be back soon, he knew it. And then no doubt he would have to go through the whole explanation one more time. How he, a trusted and experienced secret service agent had managed to leave highly sensitive papers inside a London black cab.

"Are you sure you know what you're getting yourselves into?" he hissed, his voice low. "I'm in so much trouble I'll be lucky to keep my job beyond the end of today." Shafer paused and listened to the curt reply. "Well, just see that you do. Things are not what you think they are, believe me. There's stuff going on here you have *no* idea about – you need to be careful. I did exactly what you asked me to do – but I'm not risking it again."

Shafer snapped the phone shut and tucked it away inside his jacket pocket again. He glanced up at the large clock on the wall facing him. 6.05pm. Had he really been here that long? Shunted from room to room, explaining himself again and again, explaining how he, an experienced intelligence agent, had been so careless, so stupid, so irresponsible. Trying to give them good reason why he should not be dismissed on the spot for such lack lustre behaviour. And did they really believe that it had been an accident? A brief moment of incompetence? Or did they suspect more?

Shafer got to his feet and wandered over to the windows. It was dark outside, and London's skyline was a myriad of bright, flashing lights blinking and winking in the night air. The snow was coming down heavier now, leaving the streets carpeted in a soft blanket of white. Everything looked so calm, so quiet, so peaceful.

Shafer jumped as Fleming burst in through the door once again, looking angrier than ever. "I've just been speaking with your boss, Charles Tindleman." Fleming's cold eyes bore into Shafer. "And he's not a happy man. He and I have never seen such sheer downright incompetence from a security agent in all our days. You are going to help us clear this god dammed mess up, you understand?"

Shafer nodded, hesitantly.

"Are you sure that's all you have?" Fleming nodded curtly towards the manila folder he had flung across the room a few minutes earlier – its contents strewn across the coffee table and onto the floor. "Nothing else?"

Shafer shook his head. "No, that's all…I….." Fleming cut him dead.

"You seriously left top secret security documents in the back of a London black cab?" Fleming's temperature was visibly rising, his pale complexion tinged with pink.

CHAPTER THREE

"I..I'm sorry...I.."

"Because if I find out that you are holding out on me, Shafer, your life will not be worth living. That, I can promise you." Fleming's words hung threateningly in the air. "Now get out of my sight."

* * *

Time: 6.15pm
Date: 6th November 2008
Location: Kettle's Yard Mews, London

Jack stood back and scanned the living room of his flat and felt satisfied. He had woke early despite turning off the alarm, and spent the whole day cleaning and tidying. Wasn't that what they said – tidy house, tidy mind? He had started in the living room, folding away the clothes that seemed to live draped over radiators and backs of chairs and put them away in his wardrobe and chest of drawers in his bedroom. Next he had cleaned the windows and hoovered the carpet, wiped down the leather sofa and polished the coffee table. In the kitchen he had washed up, put everything away and bleached the sink. The air now smelt of a pleasant mixture of lemon and rose scent, instead of an accumulation of the week's takeaway offerings.

His bedroom had been easy – it housed only a bed, a single wardrobe and a chest of drawers. One wooden high backed chair sat in the corner, a tattered teddy bear making it his home. A change of bedclothes and a quick hoover had been all that was needed.

Jack glanced around the flat and smiled to himself. He would make someone a good wife one day. He almost laughed out loud at the thought of a wife – in all his 41 years on this earth he had never come close to attracting a wife. Or indeed anyone who might want to spend more than a passing acquaintance with him. He rubbed a hand over the stubble that covered his chin. It wasn't that he wasn't a bad catch, or at least he would like to think so. He had a good job, a nice flat in a very wealthy area of

London, no children, no baggage. And he wasn't all that bad looking. In a rugged, well-worn kind of way.

Well, maybe no baggage was not strictly true, but on the face of it Detective Inspector Jack MacIntosh was good marriage material. Or at least good co-habiting material. But Jack remained alone. And if Jack was truly honest with himself it was the way he preferred it. He couldn't visualise sharing his life with anyone, allowing someone to get that close to him, to share every minute of every day with him. The thought made him feel claustrophobic.

Jack pulled the living room curtains shut, noticing that everything had been dusted white by the day's snowfall. All the pretty chocolate-box mews cottages in the street looked to have been dusted with icing sugar, good enough to eat. The thought of food made Jack's stomach begin to rumble. He hadn't stopped for food all day, immersed in his cleaning routine. He considered for a moment what he might have in the fridge and cupboards but soon made the decision that a short jog to the Indian takeaway around the corner was in order. He had earned it after all.

* * *

Time: 6.15pm
Date: 6th November 2008
Location: MI6 Secret Intelligence Service HQ, Vauxhall Cross, London

"So, what exactly are we to do about this?" asked Charles Tindleman, his voice taut and clipped. The head of MI6 fixed Special Agent Fleming with a questioning look. "Where are those papers?"

"Well, Sir," began Fleming, clearing his throat. "I have made some calls already this evening, tracking down some of my own contacts, but no one seems to have heard anything about them. They don't seem to have

CHAPTER THREE

surfaced anywhere...yet." Fleming emphasised the word "yet".

"And they were left in the back of a black London taxi cab by..." Tindleman glanced back down at the paperwork in front of him, searching for the name. He raised his eyebrows. "Simon Shafer."

"Yes, Sir," nodded Fleming, clasping his hands tightly behind his back. "One of your intelligence agents."

"Yes, I know who he is, Fleming. I take it you've contacted all the London cab firms..?" Tindleman looked up at Fleming expectantly. "What did they have to say?"

Fleming nodded. "Yes, Sir. Nothing has come up. It would seem that the taxi cab in question picked up another fare straight after Shafer, Sir. The documents are no longer there."

"So, someone has taken them," nodded Tindleman. "From under your very nose, it would seem."

"The cab company seemed to think that they were picked up by a customer and then more than likely dumped when they didn't contain anything useful to them..." Fleming's voice tailed off and he bit his lip.

"You don't really believe that, do you?" Charles Tindleman's face was reddening by the second. "I think we both know that *he* has the documents. Or at least, that he's after them."

Fleming didn't reply, but gave a small nod.

"This is very damaging to us, you know that. If this kind of sloppiness were to leak out into the public domain, the press would have a field day. I don't know what it's like where you come from but in this country any indiscretions of the security services are reported to the media with a vengeance and the bones picked over for weeks and months to come. The current terrorist threat to this country means that every single mistake that we make leaves us open to public annihilation. Leaving top secret security documentation on the floor of a taxi cab..." Tindleman shook his head and exhaled loudly.

Fleming nodded again, lowering his eyes to the floor.

"This paperwork," continued Tindleman. "You will find it – and then destroy it?"

"Yes, Sir," replied Fleming, regaining eye contact with Tindleman once again. "As planned."

"And Kreshniov?" The word hung in the air as Tindleman's eyes flickered, waiting for a response.

"Nothing yet, Sir. No one's seen him."

"Of course no one's bloody seen him!" exploded Tindleman, his cheeks suddenly flushing scarlet. "He's been dead for the last twenty years!"

"I mean, he hasn't surfaced yet, Sir."

"Well, he will – you mark my words. He will. Now that these papers are floating about God knows where, sure as hell he will surface. And when he does, I want him dealt with. And I want you to do it."

Fleming nodded. "Yes, Sir."

"Then get on with it," snapped Tindleman, folding the report closed on his desk. He looked up at the clock on the wall, willing the day to end. He closed his weary eyes. "And God help you if those papers end up in the wrong hands."

* * *

Time: 7.15pm
    Date: 6th November 2008
    Location: Flat 7, Rue de Bougainvillea, Paris

Andre Baxter slowly scratched his head, and stared intently at his computer screen. His tired face was reflected back at him on the monitor. He lowered his eyes to the keyboard and tapped in another series of commands.

"Access denied," blinked the message in the centre of the screen.

"Damn," muttered Andre, resting his chin in his hands and leaning forwards on his elbows. He inched his face closer and closer to the monitor, a small smile curling across his face. "You are a clever one, aren't you?"

He continued to stare at the screen for several minutes, oblivious to anything else going on around him. He didn't hear the traffic passing outside his apartment window; nor the argument brewing in the middle of the road below between a middle aged man on a bicycle and a young Parisian on a scooter. Horns honked as the traffic backed up behind the fractious couple. Arms were flailing and voices were raised above the exhaust fumes. But Andre heard none of it.

There must be a way in, he thought to himself, slowly shaking his head. He ran a hand over his chin, feeling the day's faint stubble prickling at his fingers. His stomach rumbled, but he barely noticed.

Andre tried again, bringing up the password box and typing in a different set of numbers and commands. He hit the "enter" key and held his breath. Almost instantly the all too familiar "access denied" box winked back at him, teasing him, laughing at him.

Andre finally pushed his chair back and stood up, stretching his arms high above his head. He had been at this for five solid hours and was getting nowhere fast. The password was unbreakable. He yawned and went over to the window, pulling it open and letting the chilled Paris evening air drift inside. He poked his head out and saw the scooter boy and bicycle man had moved their argument onto the pavement, letting the traffic edge past them and head up towards the lights of the Champs Elysees. He sat down on the wide window ledge and reached into his shirt pocket for his packet of cigarettes. Lighting one, he leant his head back against the window frame and closed his tired, grey eyes. I'm getting too old for this, he thought to himself, taking a long drag and blowing the smoke out the window.

The apartment was small, but room enough for Andre. He had simple tastes. He didn't need much. He lived and worked mainly out of the one room. The walls were plastered with bookshelves from floor to ceiling. Each shelf visibly groaning under the sheer weight of so many books crammed together into such a small space. There were books on anything and everything. Dusty volumes stretching as high and as wide as you could see. Andre's book collection. His pride and joy.

Along the far wall sat Andre's desk, quickly disappearing under the weight of papers, files and folders on top; and the much loved bottle of Jack Daniels. His computer screen and keyboard barely visible amongst the mess. Not that Andre called it a "mess". Structured disorganisation he called it. He knew where everything was, and that was all that mattered.

Next to the large bay window, where Andre was now perched, stretched an old and battered sofa. This often doubled up as Andre's bed when he worked too long into the night and could not make it into the next room. Instead he would collapse here, waking up looking more worn and crumpled than the sofa he was lying on.

Suddenly there was a rap at the front door, which rapidly brought Andre back to his senses. He snapped open his eyes, flicked his cigarette out of the window and walked through to the short hallway.

"Monsieur Baxter?" greeted the late night courier as Andre pulled the door open. A small brown jiffy bag was instantly thrust into his outstretched hand. "I have this packet for you. Will you sign here please?" The courier looked tired, as if he wanted his shift to end and to go home.

Andre took the proffered pen and notepad, and scribbled his shaky signature in the box at the bottom. "Merci, Monsieur," he replied, returning the pen and book to the courier and glancing down at his package. The courier nodded quickly and was gone.

Andre shut the door and returned to his desk. His careworn face broke out into a grin and his tired eyes began to sparkle. He eagerly opened up the packet and tipped out a small CD rom.

"Now I've got you!" he remarked, pulling the computer keyboard towards him. The page he had been working on was still loaded – the "access denied" box still teasing him from the centre of the screen. He swiftly inserted the disc into the computer and waited a few seconds for the programme to boot up. "Now I most definitely…have.….got….you."

The programme loaded slowly. The wait was agonising. Andre moved his cursor up to the top of the screen where a small icon had now appeared. The icon was of a tiny red key. With the cursor hovering over the icon for a few seconds, Andre licked his lips, gave a small smile, then clicked the mouse.

The screen went dark for a few seconds, and then slowly a circular pattern began swirling in the centre of the monitor like a whirlpool, which

CHAPTER THREE

then grew larger and larger until it filled the whole screen. The swirls turned orange, then red, then yellow, then silver. Faster and faster they went, spreading out to all four corners of the screen until the swirls became just a blur.

Then the screen went black and, instantaneously, up popped the password box. Andre flexed his fingers and clicked into the box, which at that time was empty. With one click of the mouse the box filled with a series of numbers and letters.

The password.

Andre clicked the "submit" button and waited.

"Access authorised" winked the message this time.

"I'm in," thought Andre, unable to stop grinning. "I'm in."

* * *

Time: 6.30pm
    Date: 6th November 2008
    Location: Metropolitan Police HQ, London

"How long have you known?" Chief Superintendent Liddell shut the door to his office behind Fleming, and gestured for the FBI agent to follow him. When they reached his desk, Liddell nodded towards a vacant chair. Fleming did as he was bidden and sat down.

"I've had my suspicions for a while now," replied Fleming, watching as the Chief Superintendent lowered himself into his own chair, exhaling loudly. "But it was only confirmed a couple of weeks ago."

"And it's definite?" Liddell's face tensed. He already knew the answer, but needed to hear it for himself anyway. "There's no mistake?"

Fleming shook his head. "No mistake. Not this time. Boris Kreshniov is alive and well."

Liddell closed his eyes. His chest felt taught. He reached into one of his desk drawers for the indigestion tablets he kept there for moments like this. He popped a couple in his mouth and opened his cool ice-blue eyes, letting them drop to the paperwork on his desk. The desk was tidy and in an orderly fashion, empty except for a copy of the memo Special Agent Fleming had handed out at the team briefing earlier that evening.

"Do we know where?"

Fleming gave a small shrug. "My contacts tell me he's probably on the Continent – but we don't know for sure. My money is on Paris."

Liddell nodded. "And you think he's got the papers?" The words threatened to stick in his throat so he reached for a glass of water and took a sip.

"I don't think he's got them yet – but he'll have heard about their disappearance…..and he'll be after them. No doubt about it. I just got back from talking to that waste of space Shafer." Fleming gave an exasperated sigh.

"Then you need to get on his tail, and fast," Liddell snapped. "Go to Paris. And take Shafer with you. This is his mess, so he can sure as hell help to clear it up. He lost the damn things – he'll help to find them again if it's the last thing he ever does." Liddell paused and closed his weary eyes. His head was pounding, and his indigestion was getting worse. "Leaving them in a taxi cab of all places – the *stupidity* of it." He snapped his eyes open again and stared intently at Fleming. "I want you to stay close to him. Shafer. Watch him like a hawk. I'm not sure that I trust him."

Fleming nodded and made to get up from his chair. He sensed that the meeting was over.

"And when you do find him," added Liddell, continuing to fix Fleming with a hard stare as the pair of them stood up to face each other across the desk. "Kreshniov, that is. Because sure as hell, you *will* find him. Make sure he's dealt with properly this time. He was supposed to have died twenty years ago, but now I'm being told he's alive and kicking somewhere." Liddell paused and gripped hold of the edge of his desk to steady himself. He could feel himself starting to lose his temper. "I saw his bloody death certificate for Christ's sake! I even saw pictures of his coffin at his fucking funeral! If he's alive today, then he didn't die in 1987 and he's been laughing at us for the best part of two decades. You find him this time, and you

CHAPTER THREE

don't let him get away."

***

Time: 3.00pm
    Date: 26th June 1985
    Location: The Glade, Church Street, Albury, Surrey

"Princess?"

Her mother's voice sang out across the garden, carried towards her by the light summer breeze, but Isabel carried on climbing. She was nearly there. Just a few more steps. She'd never been this high before and her tiny stomach began to churn as she glanced down through the branches to the grass far below.

"Isabel!" The voice was much louder now, and more insistent. "Will you come down from that tree right now, young lady!" Her mother was now striding across the lawn, heading for the shady line of trees at the bottom of the garden by the summer house. Isabel's favourite place in the whole wide world.

Isabel looked through the dappled green leaves and saw her mother standing below her, wiping her hands on her flowery apron. Her hair was scraped back from her face, her cheeks looking shiny, her skin flushed pink. Small traces of flour peppered her hair.

"Your Uncle will be here any second, and here you are scratching yourself half to death up this tree!"

Isabel's eyes widened. "Will he bring a present?" Instantly, she dangled her legs down below the branches, ready to leap.

Elizabeth Faraday smiled and held out her arms so that Isabel could jump down. "Let's go and see shall we, birthday girl?" she laughed, ruffling Isabel's head and picking out pieces of broken twigs and leaves from her hair. "Look at the state of you!"

Isabel wrapped her legs around her mother's waist and clung to her neck as she was carried back across the lawn towards the house. She could smell freshly baked cakes and biscuits as they entered the back door into the kitchen. The kitchen table had rows upon rows of pretty little cupcakes decorated with pink and yellow icing, plates of homemade buttercream biscuits, tiny sausages on sticks and a wobbly pink jelly. Isabel's eyes danced with happiness and her little tummy began to rumble.

"Mummy, can I....?"

"Not until your Uncle gets here!" smiled Mrs Faraday, watching her daughter's small hand hovering by the side of the buttercream biscuits. "And speaking of which...."

Just at that moment there was the sound of a car horn beeping furiously from the front drive.

* * *

Time: 8.00pm
   Date: 6th November 2008
   Location: Green Park Parade, Cambridge

Isabel woke with a start at the sound of the car horn outside. The clock on the mantelpiece showed exactly 8.00pm. She must have dropped off. Her mug of cold tea and packet of uneaten biscuits still sat on the floor next to her, untouched.

She yawned and stretched her legs out across the rest of the sofa. Snowball seemed to have disappeared. The dream had been so real, as always. She could almost still smell the faint aroma of baked cupcakes and those wonderful buttercream biscuits her mother always made on special occasions. She could remember the birthday cake better than anything – her mother had spent all morning icing it to perfection. It had been in the shape of a star, with pale pink icing and little jelly sweets on top. Five large candles and the words "Happy Birthday Isabel, Our Little Star" were

CHAPTER THREE

piped carefully around the edge in yellow letters.

It was always the cake she remembered.

Isabel's gaze shifted away from the mantelpiece clock to a small framed photograph sitting next to it. She could see her own smiling face grinning out, sitting proudly astride her very first tricycle. It had been the day of her fifth birthday. In the background was the tree at the bottom of the garden – her favourite climbing tree that had caused her so many cuts, bumps and bruises.

Her mother was standing next to her, resting a comforting hand on her head. She was wearing her hair down now, letting the long, wavy tresses dance silkily over her slim shoulders. She had taken off her apron and dusted the flour from her hair. She looked happy. So very, very happy.

Isabel smiled, looking at the way her father was standing close behind – a protective, caring arm around her mother's shoulders. I must take some more flowers over on Sunday, she reminded herself, tearing her eyes away from the photograph and picking up the cold cup of tea and biscuits. She took them through to the kitchen and placed them on the worktop next to the sink. I really must. It was Dad's birthday at the weekend, after all. And it had been ages since she had last visited.

Isabel felt the familiar pangs of guilt well up inside her when she thought of the bunches of flowers which must look so dead and withered by now, lost and forgotten amongst all the other headstones. Visitors to the graves nearby must look at them and wonder who had forgotten the poor souls who lay beneath the earth. Who had ceased to remember them? Who had ceased to care for them? Who had ceased to love them? Isabel made a firm mental reminder to make the journey this coming weekend. A nice pot of winter pansies would be nice. Maybe she would pick out Mum's favourite colours. And maybe she would plant some snowdrops and crocus bulbs to bring some later winter cheer. Dad would like those.

Isabel then turned and saw the clock – it was now 8.15pm. Without a further thought, she grabbed her coat and keys and left to meet Miles.

CHAPTER FOUR

Time: 9.20pm
   Date: 6th November 2008
   Location: Flat 7, Rue de Bougainvillea, Paris

Andre grabbed his telephone and punched in the Premier Capital Bank telephone number.

"Good evening. Thank you for calling Premier Capital Bank. Our offices are at the moment closed. Our hours of business are Monday to Friday………"

Andre cursed silently under his breath and cut the connection. He glanced at his watch, only just realising it was way past ordinary office working hours. He had spent such a long time trying to crack the bank's security network he had completely lost track of time. Instead, he punched in a different telephone number and waited, smiling serenely to himself, almost unable to control his excitement.

"Julian? It's me, Andre," he announced, as soon as the call was answered.

"Andre!! How the devil are you?" roared a deep, booming voice. "I was just thinking about you."

"I'm fine, Julian," laughed Andre, twisting the coils of the telephone wire around his fingers as he spoke. "But after you hear what I've got to say, I don't think you'll be feeling so good."

"Oh." Julian Browlow, Chief Executive of the Premier Capital Bank, now sounded more sombre. "Bad news I take it?"

"Well, you put up a good fight, but I eventually got in." Andre held his breath.

"You got in?" breathed Julian. His voice sounded deflated. "You got right into our accounts system?"

"Your accounts system; your customer files; your personnel files. You name it, I can see it all." Andre began navigating the computer mouse over the computer screen before him. "I'm just scrolling through now, Julian. At the touch of a button I can find out all your company bank account transactions; any of your customers' account details held at any of your branches nationwide; personnel files and contact details for everyone within the organisation, ranging from yourself at the top right down to the tea lady. I've got access to contracts, dossiers, investigative reports, internal memos, meetings and conference reports. Basically anything you have logged onto your computer system anywhere in your company throughout the world, I can download in seconds." Andre paused while this information sunk in. "I can ruin you, Julian. I can bankrupt you and all your customers by the end of the day." Andre heard a groaning sound on the other end of the telephone and the triumphant smile faded from his lips. His initial euphoria at cracking the code and gaining access to one of the most powerful multi-national banking corporations in the world began to evaporate. Julian was a friend.

"I'm sorry," said Andre, quietly. "I know it's probably not what you wanted to hear. But it was what you paid me to do."

"I know, I know," sighed Julian. "I just don't know what I'm going to tell the Board. We spent millions on security controls for this computer system. It was supposed to be fail safe. Crack proof. Unable to be broken. Not even by the smartest hackers in the world."

"It's not quite as bad as you think," said Andre, optimistically.

"No?" Julian didn't sound convinced. "How's that?"

"I wasn't able to get inside even your outermost security checks on your systems with even my most advanced techniques. You have a very good ring-fencing security around the core areas of your system. I tried for days. Nothing worked."

"But if nothing worked, how did you get in?" Julian sounded perplexed.

"I had a little help. There is some software floating around at the moment. Only just started surfacing. Supposedly it can get you inside any security system anywhere in the world. Without exception. No matter what their security controls happen to be. I managed to get my hands on a copy today, ran it through and hey presto – it worked." Andre bit his lip, waiting for Julian's reply.

"Some software you say?"

Andre nodded, even though Julian couldn't see him. "Hot off the press."

"You'd better send it to me. I need my security guys to get onto it straight away. This could kill us."

"I know, I'm sorry," said Andre. "I'll send it right over."

"Thanks Andre," sighed Julian. "I mean it. I'll wire your fee right over to you now. I'll talk to you again later."

"Sure, no problem," replied Andre, removing the disc from the computer. "Any questions, just ask."

"Oh, and Andre?" added Julian, before hanging up. "Thanks. If there is ever anything I can do for you, anytime, you just call me up, you hear?"

Andre nodded and replaced the telephone receiver. He looked at the small disc in his hands. But instead of slipping it back inside the jiffy bag, ready to send to Julian, Andre slipped it inside his shirt pocket.

* * *

Time: 8.45pm
    Date: 6th November 2008
    Location: Silver Street, Cambridge

The taxi pulled up sharply at the side of the road and Isabel jumped out onto the icy pavement. She waited until the taxi had pulled away; slinking back into the foggy night, even the sound of its engine muffled by the dense gloom. Isabel crossed the road and headed in the direction of the restaurant. She glanced at her watch. It was 8.45pm. Thrusting her hands deep into the pockets of her heavy coat, she sunk her chin down inside

CHAPTER FOUR

her scarf. The temperature had continued to drop all evening and Isabel could now just faintly feel small specks of snow landing on her face as she walked.

When she reached the far side of the road she glanced back over her shoulder. She still felt a little uneasy, as if she were being watched or followed. It was the same feeling that had come over her back at the shop, and it was a feeling she had failed to shake off since. Was Miles already there? Was he on his way, or following her even?

Isabel felt the familiar butterflies fluttering inside her stomach. What would she say to him when she saw him? What was there left to say that hadn't already been said six months ago? Their parting had not been pleasant, and for many weeks had left a bitter, acrid taste in Isabel's mouth whenever she had thought of him. She had always known that Miles dreamed of travelling, taking off to see the world. He had been passionate about it from the minute they had met. He would spend hours on the internet, planning and researching where he would go, the best route to take. But as far as Isabel was aware, that was all it had been. A dream. Something to aim for, but something that was always that little bit too far out of reach.

Until one day, things changed. Miles changed. He told her that he had booked his flight to Melbourne and would not be coming back for a while, maybe not ever. He had been so cold, so distant towards her. It was as though nothing mattered to him anymore. As if Isabel didn't matter to him anymore. Isabel sighed and stopped at the corner of the market place, sheltering in the doorway of a bookshop. The snow was beginning to fall in much bigger flakes now, silently covering everything it touched in a gleaming, glittering white. The ground was already so cold and icy that the snowflakes lay where they fell. The air around was quickly turning into a blanket of white.

There had been one moment, just before he left, when Isabel thought he was going to change his mind. That he wasn't going to go and leave her behind after all. For the briefest of moments, it was as though the old Miles was back again – the coldness gone, the distance between them extinguished. The fire and warmth had returned to his eyes and he had asked her to come with him. Pleaded with her, even. Willed her to come away with him, to see the world. To leave everything and everyone behind them. But Isabel had hesitated – hesitated for far too long. And just like that, the moment was gone. And Miles had gone too. The coldness returned to his eyes and he had left. Six months had passed without a word.

Until now.

Now Miles was back.

Taking a deep breath, Isabel carried on through the snow towards their favourite restaurant, Ce Soir.

* * *

Time: 9.55pm
   Date: 6th November 2008
   Location: Flat 7, Rue de Bougainvillea, Paris

Andre sat down on the crumpled sofa, stretching his legs out in front of him. He looked at his watch. 9.55pm. He had closed the window, shutting out the sounds of a gently slumbering Paris. The news said it was snowing in London…..it wouldn't be long before the cold air sank southwards. Swirling a generous portion of Jack Daniels, he listened to the ice clunking comfortably against the sides of the lead crystal glass. He took a long sip and rested his head back against the softness of the sofa.

Paris life suited him just fine. He worked from home, earning a more than comfortable living from his security consultancy business. He was hired by some of the richest companies in the world, paid to try and hack into their internal computer security systems and access confidential information. Sometimes it worked, sometimes it didn't. More often than not, it did. Andre was very good at his work.

He lived in a one-bedroomed apartment, no more than a stone's throw from the Champs Elysees, the Arc de Triomphe and the Place

CHAPTER FOUR

de Concorde. There was a scrumptious delicatessen and boulangerie underneath his apartment – the early morning smell of baking croissants, pain au chocolate and fresh baguettes was to die for. Andre's French was more or less fluent and he was managing to blend in with the local Parisians as if he had lived there all his life. He was now accepted as one of the locals, one of the faces. He merged into street life and became invisible. Which was exactly why he came here in the first place.

To be invisible.

Andre opened his eyes to take another swig of his drink, relishing the warmth as it slid down his throat and spread out into his stomach. As he did so, his eye caught something blinking on his computer monitor. He reluctantly got to his feet and padded over to the desk, squinting through the near darkness at the screen. An icon was flashing at the bottom, telling him that he had a new message.

Andre clicked on the icon, expecting it to be a message from Julian congratulating him on almost destroying his company. But it wasn't from Julian. Andre's heart quickened as the message flashed up on the screen.

"The rubbish is ready to be moved. But rats have been sniffing around again. Are you ready?"

Andre's throat tightened. Suddenly the warmth of the Jack Daniels had transformed itself into a piercing artic freeze. Andre's mind started to race. The haziness that had been washing over him as he slumbered on the sofa had now been swept aside. Clarity quickly returned.

Andre quickly and deftly replied.

"Sorry to hear about the infestation of rats. Haven't seen any here. When are you bringing the rubbish?" He clicked "send" and waited. Another message appeared almost instantly.

"Will bring rubbish over ASAP. Can you store it for a while?"

Andre replied, his fingers dancing over the keyboard. "No problem. Rat-free here."

He leant back in his chair and stared at the screen. It was really happening. Finally, Mac was on his way. And the rats were sniffing around again. Andre suppressed a smile. He knew exactly who those rats would be, and they did not have little pink noses and long tails.

* * *

Time: 9.15pm
 Date: 6th November 2008
 Location: Ce Soir, Silver Street, Cambridge

Isabel looked around the restaurant, trying not to feel self-conscious. She was sitting at a small table for two, by the window. There was a crisp, white tablecloth, with heavy silver cutlery. In the centre was an elegant pale cream vase with a single red rose blooming out of the middle. The restaurant was almost full, most tables occupied by young couples out for a romantic meal together before an equally romantic walk home in the snow. The air was filled with soft murmurings, the occasional laugh, and the gentle clinking of wine glasses.

Isabel nursed the glass of white wine she had ordered, sipping at it occasionally as she looked around. She slowly glanced down at her lap, and tilted her watch towards her. 9.15pm. He was late. Isabel felt very conspicuous, as if all eyes were on her, feeling sorry for her as she had quite clearly been stood up. She avoided their gaze.

Why did I come, she asked herself as she tried to stare nonchalantly out of the window. There wasn't much to see as the snow had already begun to build up along the edges of the panes. Hadn't he hurt me enough the first time round? Do I really need to be humiliated in public as well?

When she had arrived at the restaurant the head waiter had shown her directly to the reserved window seat. She had given her own name and he had nodded affirmatively when looking in the reservations book. So she *was* supposed to be here. She hadn't got the message wrong. But someone else was supposed to be here too, with her. And he was late.

Isabel made a mental decision to give Miles until 9.30pm to turn up. If he wasn't here by then, she was going. Hopefully without bringing too

CHAPTER FOUR

much attention to herself. The thought of having to get up and walk out of a packed restaurant, in front of everyone, made her cheeks begin to turn rose pink.

Just then, the waiter appeared at her side. He was holding something in his hand.

"Miss Faraday?" he enquired, raising his eyebrows. Isabel merely nodded, unable to speak in case it turned her cheeks an even darker shade. "I have this note for you. The young gentleman sends his apologies. Your bill had been paid." He nodded at the now empty wine glass still being nursed in Isabel's hands, and passed her the folded note. With a polite smile and a small bow, he left.

Isabel sat for a second or two, holding the note between her thumb and forefinger. So it was true then. She *had* been stood up. How embarrassing. She slowly glanced around the room, but it seemed that no one was paying her the slightest piece of attention anymore. Gratefully, she lowered her eyes back down to the note in her hand. Carefully, unsure if she really wanted to read whatever excuse Miles had come up with this time, she opened the note. It was the same, neat handwriting as the one she had received in the shop.

"My most sincere apologies, Fizzy. I can't make it after all. I will tell you all about it later. Can you do me a special favour? Can you go to my place and wait for me there? Use the key. Thanks Fizzy. M xxx"

Isabel turned the note over and saw a small Yale key taped to the back. The key had an address tag attached.

Flat 4a. Hope Street.

CHAPTER FIVE

Time: 9.45pm
  Date: 6th November 2008
  Location: Hope Street, Cambridge

Flat 4a overlooked the river, in a quiet stretch of water towards the south of the city. Growing all along the banks were vast weeping willow trees, silently casting their swaying branches into the still, frozen water. Short wooden jetties protruded out every so often alongside, but all boats had been safely stored away for the winter. It was a tranquil setting, the river now motionless and sleeping.

  Isabel stood outside a group of sixteen apartments. She looked up and guessed that Flat 4a would be at the top. The whole building appeared to be bathed in darkness and completely deserted. She slowly walked up the pathway which led to the communal front door, glancing furtively over her shoulder as the outside security light suddenly sprang into action. There was no one about, no one except her. The snow had now stopped falling, but no one was venturing outside. Isabel's footsteps were muffled and quiet on the snow covered path, for which she was quietly thankful. She turned the small key over and over in her hand, wondering if she was doing the right thing.

  She had just been stood up by someone she hadn't seen for six months, and was now going to let herself into a strange flat. She hesitated at the front door, and almost turned back. It seemed such a crazy idea. Insane even. She wasn't even sure she actually wanted to see Miles now. The initial excitement and euphoria at him being back in the country and wanting to see her, had quickly evaporated, leaving only a sense of quiet discontent. But curiosity got the better of her, helped by the large glass of wine she had drunk in the restaurant, and she gently pushed at the front door. To her surprise it was unlocked, and opened easily. Isabel stepped inside and was immediately greeted by both warmth and light.

The communal hallway opened up in front of her, welcoming her inside from the coldness and bitterness of the night. Soft recessed lights were sunk into the low ceiling, casting elegant soft hues over the wide expanse of pure space set out before her. It was tranquil and calming. There were more recessed lights set into the walls, interspersed with framed pictures of what could only be described as abstract modern art. Odd, angular drawings, splashes of colour, faces without features.

The walls were a soft cream colour, the picture frames all in modern hues of mocha, chocolate and cappuccino. Along the far wall, facing her as she entered, was a long, comfortable looking plush leather sofa – again in soft cream with chocolate and coffee coloured scatter cushions. It looked inviting, but Isabel dared not sit down.

The room breathed class and good taste. And expense, thought Isabel, as she crossed over to the small alcove by the far wall which seemed to hide the stairs. Flats in the city were expensive enough at the best of times, but this group of apartments just oozed wealth. Lots of it.

She didn't fancy using the lift on her own, and so decided to take the stairs. Continuing the comfort and elegance of the communal hallway, the stairs were enveloped in a thick, deep pile of cream coloured carpet. Softly and quietly, she padded up to the next level. This contained the first level apartments, numbered flats 1a-1d. Isabel continued past them, stopping every now and again to listen and see if she could hear any signs of life. There were none. Either nobody was home or everyone was already tucked up in their warm cosy beds. Isabel headed for the next set of stairs, and then the next, until she soon arrived at the top level. Level 4. Flat 4a she could see was the last apartment in the row, at the very end of the corridor.

Isabel made her way along, past flats 4d, 4c and 4b. She paused in front of a heavy looking door with 4a written in large gold lettering, set in the centre. There was nothing else to indicate who lived there. No name plate. No letterbox. No nothing. Isabel brought the small silver key out of her pocket and again rolled it around in her hand, still unsure if she was doing the right thing. Should she knock first? In case Miles was home? Maybe he was springing a surprise for her? Isabel nervously bit her bottom lip, and again looked over her shoulder. Although she knew she was alone, she felt as though she was being watched. The hair on the back of her neck began to prickle and her heartbeat quickened. Make your mind up Izzy, she thought to herself. Are you staying, or are you going?

* * *

Time: 10.01pm
    Date: 6th November 2008
    Location: Kettles Yard Mews, London

Rain splattered against the windowpane, the soft rhythmical drumming sound of the raindrops echoing around the near empty room. Outside it was starting to get dark – swirls of intense blue and violet streaked across the stormy evening sky, the heavy black rain clouds being forced to scurry away by an ever freshening breeze.

Jack woke with a start. His eyes snapped open and he held his breath. He was sure he had heard something – a footstep, a creaky stair, the sound of the front door clicking shut.

He sat up in bed and glanced at the alarm clock on the bedside table. 10.01pm. It was always 10.01pm. He looked down and saw that he was still fully clothed. He must have fallen asleep before getting undressed. Again. Wearily, Jack swung his legs round onto the cold bedroom floor and stood up.

There it was again. Definitely a footstep. And voices now, too. And they were coming from further down the hall. Jack silently stepped across his bedroom floor, taking care to avoid the creaky floorboards – he knew which ones they were – and gently pulled the door open a few inches. The hallway was dark, save for a soft white light coming from the room at the far end. It was always that room.

Always 10.01, and always that room.

And it was always raining.

Jack knew what he had to do. He had done it so many times before. Without needing to think, he stepped out into the hallway and began walking towards the light. He could hear them more clearly now. Voices. Definitely voices. Whispering and laughing, coming from the room at the end of the hall. Always coming from the room at the end of the hall.

Jack walked steadily along the corridor, his feet making no sound, and the voices getting louder and clearer with every step. His breath was coming in short, sharp rasps now – his chest rising and falling in steady jumps. His stomach tightened and his heart quickened with every silent step he took. He already knew what he would find before he got there – he had found it so many times before. But each time it was as if he were entering the room for the first time. The fear, the shock, the horror – all so palpable he could almost taste the sweat dripping into his dry mouth.

He reached out with a shaking hand and grasped the door handle. It felt cold underneath his grip. Icy cold. He gently pulled the door, feeling its heaviness in his hand, and watched as it swung open without a sound.

It never made a sound.

And then he saw it.

Again.

***

Time: 9.45pm
 Date: 6th November 2008
 Location: Green Park Parade, Cambridge

The sleek black Mercedes pulled up outside Isabel's flat, its tyres making a soft, scrunching sound on the newly compacted snow. The engine cut out and the lights extinguished.

Silently, a figure emerged from the driver's side and noiselessly jogged up the front steps. Karl Poborski took a quick glance over his shoulder, then brought his mobile phone to his ear.

"I'm at the girl's flat now," he breathed, his cool grey eyes searching the street behind him. "Keep them inside until I get there. Don't let them out of your sight." He snapped the phone shut. Satisfied he was alone, he slid out a long, thin instrument from inside the sleeve of his jacket and deftly jabbed it at the window pane in the front door.

There was a soft tinkling sound of shattered glass, but it was lost just as quickly as it was made. He reached in through the jagged hole, careful not to snag himself on the rough glass, and silently unlocked the door.

* * *

Time: 10.00pm
   Date: 6th November 2008
   Location: Flat 4a Hope Street, Cambridge

Isabel thrust the small key into the lock and gave it a quick turn. It clicked easily and the door began to open. Taking a deep breath, Isabel cautiously pushed the door fully open and stepped inside. Feeling as though she was trespassing, entering somewhere uninvited, she quickly shut the door firmly behind her. It gave a heavy sounding click, which seemed to echo through the emptiness of the apartment.

The apartment's décor continued the theme of the downstairs hallway. A deep pile cream carpet was underfoot, with smooth cream walls and sunken spotlights. Each spotlight in the entrance lobby was on dim, casting only a very soft light around the walls. Isabel inched further into the apartment. Behind her the spotlights dimmed even more and then turned themselves off completely. But the ones ahead of her brightened up, illuminating her way. Isabel smiled. Sensor lighting. The lights came

CHAPTER FIVE

on when someone was near, and turned off when they had gone. Miles would have loved these.

On her right hand side an archway appeared which led into what Isabel assumed was the main living room. She tiptoed in, the cream plush pile carpet following her, as were the smooth walls and recessed spotlights. The living room spotlights sprang into life as she entered. A chocolate brown leather sofa graced the right hand wall, with a large glass-topped coffee table in the centre. Directly ahead of her were the huge floor-to-ceiling windows that she had seen from the outside. She wandered over and looked out over a small balcony.

Isabel peered through the glass, imagining Miles sitting out in the summer sunshine, watching the boats paddle up and down the river below. She wondered how long he had been living here. Had he even been here in the summer, when Isabel thought he was thousands of miles away on the other side of the world? Isabel pushed the questions from her mind and turning around, she surveyed the room again. It was so neat, so precise, so very well-coordinated. Everything in its place. So very stylish.

So very unlived in.

So very "un-Miles."

The coffee table sported a selection of coffee-table type magazines, displayed in a neat symmetrical fan shape. Isabel glanced down at them. A couple on interior design and home décor, a few on needlecraft, and even one about fishing. They looked as though they had never been read, maybe never even opened. And they certainly weren't the kind of magazines Miles would normally go for, Isabel felt sure. An uneasiness began to creep further inside her.

On the left-hand wall was a large shelving area, decorated with several sleek looking vases – sleek looking, but empty vases. There were picture frames without pictures, photo frames without photographs, candles which had never seen a match, books with obscure titles which had never been opened. Ornaments from places Isabel was certain Miles had never visited.

Isabel cast her eyes around the rest of the room. Where was the

TV? Where was the CD player? Where were the signs of human life and habitation? It looked and felt like a show room, a display feature, something you would see from the pages of one of the unread coffee-table magazines. Not somewhere she would have expected Miles to end up living in. It was so unlike him. At least, it had been. Maybe his many months of trekking and travelling had changed his perspective, changed his tastes, changed his personality completely. Maybe Miles was no longer the Miles who had loved her, and then left her. Isabel pushed the thought firmly from her mind.

Nonetheless, it was a beautiful apartment, and Isabel could not help smiling to herself as she looked around. She went over to the shelves and picked up some of the obscure ornaments, ran her fingers across the spines of the unread books, peered into some of the empty vases. Everything was so well-coordinated – the colours were either cream, coffee, chocolate, mocha or burnt orange. There were no other colours at all. Even the dust jackets on the books were in the correct colour scheme. Nothing was out of place. Nothing at all.

Isabel left the immaculate living room and crossed back into the hallway. The living room lights extinguished themselves behind her, leaving her in the illuminated passageway which appeared to lead down towards a small kitchen area. Glancing behind her at the front door, which still remained closed, Isabel walked into the kitchen and immediately saw another room that had just stepped off the pages of a kitchen planners brochure. Gleaming stainless steel work surfaces greeted her as she stepped in – an immaculately clean sink with nothing stacked or left to dry on the draining board. Nothing waiting to be washed. Nothing waiting to be put away.

She pulled open a large American-style fridge, suddenly bathing the whole kitchen in a bright, white light. It was empty, save for a bottle of water, a bottle of wine and a jar of salad dressing. Isabel shut the door, plunging the kitchen back into the soft hues cast from the ceiling lights.

She wandered over to the breakfast bar, pausing to perch on one of the two stools neatly tucked underneath. It didn't look like anyone had ever sat here before, even less likely to eat breakfast. Isabel retraced her steps and padded back out into the hallway, lights springing on to illuminate her way. This time she opened a door on the opposite side to the living room, which she presumed would be a bedroom.

The room was dark – no soft recessed spotlights snapped on this time. Isabel stepped further into the room and waited, but still she remained in pitch darkness. Maybe the lights aren't working in this room, she mused, and she began to fumble on the wall by the door for a light switch. Her hands swept over the smooth walls, but found nothing.

She inched further into the room, trying to see where there might be a lamp or light switch. Her eyes scanned the darkness and slowly started to become accustomed to the blackness. She could see dark shapes and dark outlines before her. Something that looked like a bed over by the far wall, with a small table next to it. There appeared to be a shape like a lampshade on the table, so Isabel began to slowly creep towards it, careful not to walk into anything in the near total blindness.

As she slowly crossed the room, something blinked out of the corner of her eye. She turned and saw, in what must be one of the corners of the room, a small green light winking on and off. Isabel changed direction and stepped over towards the light. As she neared it, she could see that it was a light flashing on a small dark box with a handset attached to the side. An answering machine, thought Isabel, her eyes slowly coming into focus.

She peered down at the light and saw that there was a small piece of paper propped up in front of it. In the glow of the green light, Isabel could make out some small, neat handwriting. Kneeling down, she reached out and tilted the paper towards the light, straining her eyes to read the message.

Two simple words were all that there was.

"Play me."

Isabel's stomach tightened. She withdrew her hand quickly from the note, as if she had touched something hot. The handwriting looked chillingly familiar. It was the same as the handwriting on the note in the shop, and on the note from the restaurant. Writing that Isabel was now convinced did not belong to Miles. And neither did this apartment. It was too clean, too tidy, too false. Nobody lived here, Isabel could see that now. It wasn't a home. And it certainly wasn't Miles' home.

Isabel stood up and turned to go. She had to get out, right now. She stepped towards the bedroom door, still faintly outlined by the lights outside in the hallway, but just as she did so the door slammed shut in front of her and the answering machine whirred into life.

The message began to play.

Isabel listened, horror struck, to the voice echoing around the room. It wasn't Miles. It definitely wasn't Miles.

"Isabel. You are in danger. There are people outside who want to kill you. I am a friend and I want to help you. You have to trust me."

The voice on the tape machine paused. All Isabel could hear was her own heartbeat pounding inside her chest, her own short gasps as she fought to control her fear. The voice continued. "I have something which places us both in extreme danger. There are people outside willing to kill for it – willing to kill me, and you. You must stay where you are and do as I say. If you leave this flat alone, you will be killed. Please erase this message."

The machine clicked to a stop and the blinking green light disappeared. Isabel held her breath, not daring to make a sound. A hot, sick feeling spread out through her stomach and she opened her mouth to cry out. But try as she might, no sound escaped.

"Please do as it says – erase the message." The low voice came out of the darkness behind her.

Isabel swung round, sharply, to where the voice had come from. Her feet felt clumsy and she stumbled forwards in the blackness. Just at that moment the spotlights came on in the room and, perched on the bed by the far wall, was a man. He held a small remote control device in his hand and pointed it at the answering machine.

"OK, I'll do it for you."

* * *

CHAPTER FIVE

Time: 10.01pm
Date: 6th November 2008
Location: Kettles Yard Mews, London

The body swung lifelessly from the light fitting in the centre of the room. The curtains were open, letting the last of the evening light creep through the window and cause its shadow to dance eerily back and forth over the bare floorboards.

Jack stood rooted to the spot, just like he always did, his hand still gripping the door handle. Then, from the corner of his eye, he saw a small child crawling across the shadows, his head turned upwards, gazing up at the sight dangling before him. Jack watched as the small child stopped beneath the body, reaching up with a tiny hand to touch the lifeless feet above his head. Then the eyes snapped open and the lifeless body began to speak.

"Look after him, my darling." The voice was gentle, with a richness like honey. "I'm sorry, so very sorry." Then the room began to fade, the hanging body and the small child becoming fuzzy, blurred images. They both turned at the same time to look at Jack through the fog. And then the most frightening, chilling laughter escaped their mouths. Their sound filled the room, bouncing off the walls. They stared and laughed, laughed and stared, until Jack could bear it no longer.

He crumpled against the doorframe, hugging his head with his arms, trying to block out the noise, block out the laughter, block out the pain.

"Stop it!" he screamed, his face contorted in pain. "Stop it now!"

But they only laughed even louder.

And louder.

And louder.

Jack woke with a start. His body was drenched with sweat – his hair clinging to his head in thick, matted clumps. The room was still dark, except for the light emanating from the TV screen which was still playing in the corner of the room. It was an old black and white comedy – the tinny, canned laughter filling the quietness of the room. Jack reached for the remote control and killed the sound, the laughter quickly subsiding into silence. He frowned at the remote control. He must have fallen asleep watching the television – again. It had been the laughter that had woken him from his dream. From his nightmare.

The laughter.

Jack shivered and rubbed his eyes with the backs of his hands, trying to rid himself of the vision of the body, the lifeless body swinging from the light fixing in the room at the end of the hall.

He glanced at the clock beside the bed. 10.01pm.

It was always 10.01pm.

* * *

Time: 10.02pm
   Date: 6th November 2008
   Location: Flat 4a Hope Street, Cambridge

Isabel scrambled to her feet and ran for the door. But the man was too quick for her. He leapt from the bed and reached the door before her, barring her way with a muscular arm. Isabel threw herself at him and began pummelling his chest with her fists, and screaming with all her might.

"Get out of my way!!" she yelled, throwing fist after fist at his body, trying to wrench him out of her way. "Leave me alone!" She fought, frantically, trying to smash her way past the stranger – but he was too strong for her. Her hands and fists made no impact on him at all. Instead he simply stepped behind her, slipped a powerful arm around her body and pinned her arms underneath his. He clamped his free hand tightly over her mouth and instantly stifled her screams.

Isabel's chest heaved up and down in rapid bursts, her eyes wide with fright. She continued to struggle, trying to free herself from the vice like grip the man had around her. She wriggled violently from side to side, trying to dig her elbows into his chest and stomach, but it was impossible.

CHAPTER FIVE

The more she struggled, the tighter his grip became.

She tried to wrestle her mouth away from underneath the hand which was still tightly clamped over it, hoping to be able to scream loudly enough to wake the neighbours, but the hand seemed to be stuck like glue. She tried to bite his fingers, but she couldn't even get her jaws open.

The man placed his mouth towards her ear and spoke softly. "It's OK, Isabel," he whispered. "I'm not here to hurt you."

Isabel's body began to shake. She gave up trying to fight her way out, knowing that was no use. The more she struggled, the tighter he held onto her. She felt her legs give way beneath her and she slid down towards the floor, still shaking. The stranger continued to hold her as her legs crumpled, but he relaxed his arms a little as they both slid down to the floor together.

Small whimpers began to escape from Isabel's mouth as the man loosened his hold, and tears began to roll down her panic-stricken face. Hesitantly, the man removed his hand from her mouth, seemingly unsure if she was about to start screaming again. Not that it would matter. He knew that there would be no one around to hear her cries for help. None of the other flats were occupied. Just like this one wasn't. He gently brushed away the tears that were trickling off the end of Isabel's chin.

"I'm not here to hurt you, Isabel," he repeated, quietly. "I promise you. I'm here to save your life."

* * *

Time: 10.02pm
Date: 6th November 2008
Location: Kettle's Yard Mews, London

Jack wrenched open the fridge and reached for a bottle of water. He drank heavily, letting dribbles stream down his face and splash onto his feet. The iciness of the water cleared his mind, lifting the heavy fog that seemed to be engulfing him.

The dream.

The nightmare.

They were coming more frequently now, and each time they came it drained him even more. They left him ragged, left his body in pieces. Jack closed the fridge door, plunging the room back into darkness. He padded back to his bedroom and lay down on the sweat ridden bedsheets. The sweat on his skin had dried and now he felt chilled, chilled to the bone. He wrapped himself up underneath the covers and stared out into the blackness of the room. The psychologist had said that the dreams would stop.

But she hadn't said when.

Although the room was dark, Jack reached out to his bedside table and took hold of a small photograph frame in his hands. Without looking, he carefully placed the frame face down on the table and turned his back. He could never quite manage to look at her smiling face after one of these dreams.

* * *

Time: 10.10pm
　　Date: 6th November 2008
　　Location: Flat 4a Hope Street, Cambridge

Isabel was now sitting on the bed, hugging her knees tightly to her chest, her shoulders jumping up every now and again as she fought to control her tears. Her face was cold, wet and blotchy.

The stranger brought her a warm mug of coffee handing it to her, gently, and then retreating to sit on the floor by the door. He was a slim man, but powerfully built. He was dressed completely in black – black jeans, black polo neck jumper and black jacket. He also had a black woollen hat on top of his head. But he had a kind face, and deeply penetrating blue eyes. Isabel looked up at him, her own eyes still full of watery tears.

"Why..why should I believe you?" she started, her voice small and shaky.

CHAPTER FIVE

"I don't even know who the hell you are."

The stranger smiled, his eyes crinkling, and nodded his head. "That's true, Isabel. You don't." He paused. "But I know you. And I'm here to protect you, and to help you."

"So you keep saying," replied Isabel, gruffly. She sipped her coffee and wiped her wet cheeks with her sleeve. "But I don't need protecting thank you." The cool sarcasm in her voice masked the fear she still felt inside. She was still trapped inside a strange apartment; with a man she had never met before – someone who was clearly capable of hurting her. Someone she would have slim chance of fighting off.

"I'm afraid you do, Isabel. It's just that you don't know it yet." The stranger then crawled over to Isabel on his knees and held out his hand. "My name is Mac – I'm here to tell you about your parents."

* * *

Time: 10.15pm
  Date: 6th November 2008
  Location: Metropolitan Police HQ, London

"I understand everything's underway?" Edwards' voice sounded light and airy, jovial even. "Soon the whole thing'll be dead and buried, and no one will ever know anything about the Phoenix Project."

Liddell's mouth was dry. Edwards obviously hadn't heard about Shafer's little mishap and the fact that the Phoenix Project documents were now somehow at large in London, or more than likely elsewhere by now. Liddell decided that he wasn't going to be the one to tell him.

"So they tell me," he replied, hoping that his voice didn't give him away. He paused for a moment. Now he had made the call he wasn't sure whether Edwards was the man to talk to. Edwards sensed his apprehension.

"Well, spit it out man!" Edwards gave a small laugh. "You sure as hell didn't call me up just to make small talk!"

Liddell pulled in a deep breath. "Do you trust him?"

"Who?"

"You know damn well who. Our so-called FBI friend. You think he's on the level?"

"Oh him!" Liddell could hear Edwards' laughing crackle along the telephone line and held the receiver further away from his ear. "I wouldn't worry about him if I were you. He's small fry. Trust me. It'll all be over real soon."

Liddell replaced the receiver. It'll all be over real soon.

That's exactly what I'm afraid of, he thought to himself.

CHAPTER SIX

Time: 11.10pm
  Date: 6th November 2008
  Location: Flat 7, Rue de Bougainvillea, Paris

Andre logged onto his computer and checked his email inbox. There was nothing more from Mac. Perhaps he was already on his way. Andre snapped off his computer and got to his feet. He had to be prepared this time – there could be no more mistakes. He went to his bulging bookcase and scanned the higher levels until he spied what he was looking for. Then, pulling over a small set of step ladders, he quickly climbed to the top. Reaching up, Andre took down a large, rusty-red leather bound book. Thick grey dust clung to the cover. He wiped his finger across the front to reveal the gold lettering of "Dracula by Bram Stoker." Tucking the book under his arm, Andre slipped back down the steps.

  He placed the book on his desk and then took a small key from around his neck. He always wore this necklace, never took it off, ever. But he had not opened this particular book for some 10 years, maybe even more. He hesitated for a moment, his hands slightly shaking, while memories flashed back and forth inside his head. After a moment or two his head cleared and he unlocked the small clasp on the side of the book. It opened up like an ordinary book should, and from the outside it looked just like a normal, age-worn literary masterpiece should. But it was not a book. It did not contain any pages. It was merely a hollow box made to look outwardly as if it were indeed a book, whereas in actual fact its hollow recess instead contained a variety of papers, cassettes and technical drawings. Andre leafed through them quickly, mentally checking that everything that should be there was, indeed, still there. Then, satisfied, he closed the book and carefully locked the clasp once again. Climbing back up the step ladder, he replaced the book from the spot where it had come from.

Andre stood back down on the floor and gazed up, To the untrained eye, the shelves contained old, dusty, careworn books that had long since been forgotten, and left to slumber in amongst the dust. Andre smiled, satisfied with his work, and then left his flat.

Although it was late, he had work to do.

* * *

Time: 10.20pm
   Date: 6th November 2008
   Location: Flat 4a Hope Street, Cambridge

Mac sat down on the edge of the bed, careful not to sit too close. He didn't want to scare her any more than he had already. Andre had warned him about that, warned him to go carefully. He noticed that she was no longer shaking or crying. He took that to be a good sign.

"I have some information about your parents, Isabel. Something you may not want to hear, something you may not want to believe." He paused, trying to catch her eye. "But you need to know – hopefully it may save your life."

"So tell me." Isabel fixed Mac with a cool stare. Her voice sounded more in control than she actually felt. "What is so important you need to cook up some half-baked wild goose chase, take me halfway across town, lure me into a strange apartment and scare me half to death? Ever heard of the telephone?"

Mac's lips flickered into a smile." They told me you were a little hot headed."

Isabel did not reply. Instead she stared into the now lukewarm coffee she was nursing in her lap.

"I have some information in my possession which is highly secretive." Mac looked around him before continuing. "I can't go into details...not here. It's not safe. This information has remained buried for years....until now." Mac reached up and gently began to unwind the scarf from around Isabel's neck.

"What information?" asked Isabel, watching Mac, somewhat warily, as he placed her scarf into his pocket.

"As I said, I can't go into details right now. But it is information that someone is trying to get back at any price. They will kill me to get at it, and they will most certainly kill you too. That is why I had to find you. I need to protect you from these people. You have no idea what they are capable of. They are assassins, hired to kill you. They will stop at nothing."

"Assassins?" Isabel slowly edged herself away from Mac. "What on earth have they got to do with me?" She watched as Mac reached over and picked up her handbag, turning it over and over in his hands. "You must have the wrong person......"

"They're watching us." Mac breathed in and held Isabel's gaze. "Just like they watched your parents. They're probably watching us right now from outside. We need to move. And soon."

"I'm not gong anywhere with you." Isabel moved further away from Mac. "I'm not involved in anything. You've got me mixed up with someone else. You let me go or I'll scream."

"You *are* involved, Isabel, whether you like it or not. Your parents were involved, and now you are, too. You have no choice but to come with me. These people want to kill you because of who you are – and because of who your parents are, too. Because you're a Faraday. *And* because of the Phoenix Project."

"The Phoenix *what*?" Isabel eyed Mac, suspiciously, edging further and further away until she was perched on the end of the bed. "Look, I don't know what the hell you're talking about. I've never heard of any Phoenix Project...and if you *really* knew my parents you would know that they're already dead." Isabel's voice sounded small and hollow once again. "So now you see why I don't believe you."

Mac opened his mouth to reply, but Isabel caught him off guard. She leapt from the bed and ran from the room, the spotlights in the hallway snapping on to light her way as she rushed past. Mac swore under his breath and jumped after her.

"Don't go out there!" he shouted after her, watching as she headed for the front door. "They'll be outside right now!"

But Isabel ignored his warnings and wrenched open the door of the apartment. She ran, blindly, down the corridor, heading back towards the stairs. She leapt down them, two at a time, quickly reaching the first floor apartments. They were all still quiet. Still deserted. She paused briefly, listening, and could faintly hear Mac's heavy footsteps running down the stairs from above. She carried on down the last flight of stairs, bursting out into the entrance lobby, running as fast as she could. She looked behind her, expecting to see Mac leaping down the last few stairs – but he was still far enough away to be out of sight.

Isabel fled towards the door. She had to get out, out of these damned apartments. As she ran, she turned to look back behind her, looking out for Mac in hot pursuit, so she wasn't watching when she tripped and fell over something soft.

She fell, heavily, onto the carpet below, her arms stretched out in front of her to break her fall. She could now hear Mac jumping down the last set of stairs behind her and running into the hall. Isabel pushed herself back onto her knees, only then noticing that her hands were covered in something warm and sticky. Looking down, she saw that a large pool of dark liquid was staining the plush carpet all around her. She turned to see Mac standing behind her, his face ashen. He was staring, not at her, not at her hands – but at the object Isabel had had the misfortune to trip over.

Isabel's eyes followed Mac's down to the carpet at her feet. The scream that then left her lungs was ear piercing.

"No!! No!! No!!" Isabel scrambled away from the furry mound lying prostrate before her. The thick, white, fluffy fur was now stained a stomach churning deep crimson. Mac knelt down and gingerly lifted up the limp,

CHAPTER SIX

furry body, so that its face and head could be seen.

"No!" sobbed Isabel. "No! Not Snowy! Not my Snowy!" She collapsed in a heap on the blood stained carpet, unable to look at Snowball's lifeless body in Mac's hands. Mac knelt down beside her, but she shrugged him off. "Leave me alone! How could you do this?!" She raised her head and looked up at him, her eyes filled with hatred. "Who are you? What do you want with me?"

"Isabel..I.." Mac reached out and tried to hold onto her arm to explain, but Isabel shied away from him, her eyes suddenly fearful.

"Keep away from me! Let me go!" she screamed, scrambling to her feet. She made a run for the door, desperate to get away, to get out of this place and away from the man standing next to her who had just killed her beloved Snowball.

* * *

Time: 5.20pm
   Date: 6th November 2008
   Location: Washington DC, USA

Austin Edwards waited for what seemed like an eternity for the call to be picked up. When it eventually was, his displeasure at being kept waiting was all too apparent.

"Where have you been?" he snapped, gripping the telephone receiver tightly. "I've been trying to get hold of you for over an hour."

"I'm sorting things out this end," came the curt reply, not impressed with Edwards' tone. "There's a lot to do if this is going to work properly."

"I've had Liddell on the phone. He's a worried man."

"He's always worrying, leave him to me. He'll not be any trouble."

"And the girl?" Edwards looked out of his office window, his eyes again resting on the Lincoln Memorial in the distance. "What about her?"

"It's all in hand."

"Everything to do with the Phoenix Project must be destroyed – that was what we agreed. And that includes her. She may not know anything about the Project now – but it won't be long before she does." Edwards paused only very slightly before continuing. His voice was cold, bereft of any emotion or feeling. "She must be erased. Permanently."

"It will be done," came the reply. "Just as soon as we get what we need from her. Then Isabel Faraday will be no more."

* * *

Time: 10.25pm
   Date: 6th November 2008
   Location: Flat 4a Hope Street, Cambridge

Mac leapt over Snowball's body and reached the communal door just as Isabel was fumbling for the handle to pull it open. He forced himself against it and slammed it shut, grabbing hold of Isabel as he did so. Once again, his powerful arms enveloped her from behind and held her firm.

Isabel struggled once again, fighting as much as she could, trying to kick out with her legs. But she felt so weak. All her energy and strength had now sapped away, leaving nothing behind. The more she struggled, the tighter Mac held on, until eventually Isabel stopped wriggling and just sobbed.

"My little Snowy," she wailed. Tears flowed thick and fast down her face. "My poor, poor little Snowy."

"I know," murmured Mac, his face close to hers. "I know." He tried to shield her face from the sickening sight stretched out on the carpet behind them. "Don't look, Isabel. Don't look."

"Why?" Isabel croaked. "Why her?" Slowly, she looked up into Mac's face, her eyes pleading for an explanation. "What did she ever do to you? To anyone?"

"You know it wasn't me, Isabel," said Mac, shaking his head. " She wasn't here when you came in, was she?"

Isabel considered for a moment, then slowly shook her head. The

CHAPTER SIX

entrance hall had been empty when she had walked in.

"I was up in the apartment waiting for you. I heard you come in. You went to the living room first. I saw the lights come on. You went over to the window, then looked around the shelves, picked up a few things." Mac stopped for a moment while Isabel nodded. "Then you came through to the kitchen, looked in the fridge, came back out and went into the bedroom…..where you found me." Mac relaxed his grip, but pulled Isabel towards him, still trying to comfort her. "It wasn't me, Isabel. It wasn't me."

Isabel sniffed and wiped her eyes on her sleeve. As she did so she caught another glimpse of Snowball's stricken body. Her face screwed up once again and tears flowed silently down her already wet cheeks.

"They did it to scare you," Mac carried on. He glanced over the top of Isabel's head, towards the front door, looking out through the small glass panel. "To make you run."

Mac gently released Isabel from his grip and stepped towards the door. He pressed his face up against the glass and peered out, searching through the frosty air for a sign….any sign.

"Come on, come on," he murmured to himself. "I know you're out there, somewhere. Let me see you. Let me see your face."

Isabel tore her eyes away from Snowball and followed Mac to the door. She opened her mouth but Mac immediately turned and placed a finger to his lips. He mouthed to Isabel to remain quiet. He took hold of her hand and pulled her gently over so that she was flat against the wall by the door. Then he gestured to her to look through the glass, holding her close to him all the time.

"Don't let them see you," he whispered.

Isabel raised her head and peeked out through the chilled glass window. All she could see was the short path winding down to the river ahead. There were a couple of bicycles chained to the railings by the water's edge, some small frost-covered bushes and shrubs growing alongside. Her eyes searched through the darkness, but saw nothing.

She was about to turn back to Mac when she noticed the pathway leading up to the front door. She remembered walking on it when she arrived, her footsteps crunching through the soft snow that had fallen. And she remembered there had only been one set of footprints on the snow – hers. But now, she saw several sets of footprints, all leading up to the door. And next to the footprints she could just make out a splattering of small, dark circles. Spots. Spots of blood. Snowball's blood.

A lump formed in Isabel's throat as she pictured whoever it had been carrying Snowball's limp body up the path, in through the front door, and then laying it down on the carpet. And then waiting….waiting for her to come down and discover it.

She felt sickened. That very same someone had been inside her home. She followed the footprints with her eyes, back down the path towards the river. She searched deeper into the dense shadows of the night until she saw it. A faint outline of a person – a man. He was standing next to a small weeping willow tree, next to the bicycle railings. He was hard to see as the night air very quickly faded to inky blackness towards the river's edge, but he was there. He was most definitely there. As she watched, the man shifted position slightly, and slunk back towards the trunk of the tree, almost out of sight. Almost, but not quite.

Mac gently pulled her away from the window. "We have to get out of here," he whispered, urgently. "And quickly." Before Isabel realised what he was doing, Mac had knelt down beside her and began to slip off her shoes. Seeing her quizzical look, he again placed a finger to his lips, nodding towards the front door. He then slipped off his own shoes and wrapped both pairs in a small cloth he produced from his pocket. "There'll be more of them, and they'll be waiting for us," he murmured. "We have to get out." He stood up and pulled her by the hand towards the stairs.

Isabel suddenly stopped in her tracks and jerked her hand out of his grip. "Why should I believe you?" she asked, warily. "I still have no idea who you are, or what you want with me. All this talk about some Project I've never heard of….."

"I will explain it all," interrupted Mac, trying to keep his voice low. "I promise. Just not now. You have to trust me." Mac was pleading with her

CHAPTER SIX

now, glancing every now and then over at the front door behind them. His eyes looked fearful. "If they come in here, we're finished. They'll kill us both. You think they'll just stop at your cat? They've been inside your house, Isabel. They mean business."

Isabel hesitated, thinking back to the silhouette of the man waiting outside. Then she looked back at Snowball's mutilated form on the floor next to them, and she shuddered. Nodding her head at Mac, she followed him across to the stairs and watched as he brought out a set of keys from his pocket. In front of them was a door.

"Quick, in here," he whispered. Ushering Isabel into the dark room. He followed and closed the door quietly behind him, the lock clicking snugly into place. Once inside, he set the shoes down on the floor and brought out a small torch. In the pale light, Isabel quickly looked around her. It was a small broom cupboard or store cupboard, full of brushes, brooms, boxes of cleaning cloths, toilet rolls and dusters. Everything was piled up high around the edges of the room, leaving only a small space in the middle.

"Here, take this." Mac handed Isabel the torch. "Shine it on the floor there, in the middle. Over those crates." He nodded and indicated to the space in the centre of the room where several wooden crates sat arranged haphazardly on the floor. "Quick, we haven't much time."

Isabel did as she was told, her hand shaking as she tried to hold the torch steady. She watched as Mac carefully and noiselessly slid one of the crates to the side. He then knelt down on the floor and took a small penknife out of his back pocket. Carefully, he deftly used the blade to lift up one edge of one of the floorboards that had been underneath the crate. It popped up and Mac gently placed it to the side. He then removed the next floorboard and placed it on top of the first.

The floorboards gave way to a narrow black hole. Mac looked up at Isabel and then nodded back down at the opening. "You first," he mouthed.

Isabel's mouth dropped open, aghast. "You have got to be kidding," she whispered.

Mac shook his head and gestured to her to get down the hole. "Come on, quickly. They'll be inside this building any minute. This is our only escape." Mac watched Isabel's facial expression change from sheer incredulousness to one of horror. "Unless," he continued, his voice firm, "you want to end up like your cat." Isabel shivered and instinctively moved towards the hole. It looked barely wide enough to slip through. She shined the torch down into the gap and saw the dusty floor below. It wasn't far. She sat down on the edge of the hole, dangling her legs through into the darkness below. Then, handing the torch to Mac, she gently slid her body down through the opening.

Mac swung his legs down through the hole and quickly jumped down, landing beside Isabel with a soft thud. He pulled over a small set of steps and climbing back up, he poked his head back into the store cupboard. He paused for a moment, listening for sounds from outside. He couldn't hear anything. Not yet. Their luck was holding. But they would be here soon. And they wouldn't leave before they found what they were searching for. Isabel.

He reached over to the bundle of shoes still sitting where he had left them by the door, and pulled them down into the hole. Then he tugged at the floorboards stacked nearby and pulled them back over the top of the hole. They fell neatly and seamlessly into place, looking as though they had never been moved. The crate would have to be left where it was.

Back underground, Mac quietly took hold of Isabel by the arm. He once again placed a finger to his lips and nodded at the ceiling above them. There were now muffled noises coming from above. Their luck had just run out.

* * *

CHAPTER SEVEN

Time: 10.30pm
Date: 6th November 2008
Location: Flat 4a Hope Street, Cambridge

Karl Poborski stood in the centre of the communal hallway and slowly looked around him. He glanced down at Snowball's mutilated form, taking in the smears and trails of blood that circled the animal's lifeless body. Two sets of bloody footprints led over towards the door, but nothing else. The footprints stopped dead in their tracks, and then just seemed to vanish into thin air. Poborski scratched his head, somewhat perplexed. No one had left through the front door, he was sure of that. He would have seen them. He had been waiting. Watching. And the back exit was covered too.

Again Poborski surveyed the carpet. A small, narrow set of footprints, and then a larger, broader set. Both sets tracked towards the front door, hovered there……..and then simply disappeared.

They must have gone back upstairs, he thought, pushing from his mind the fact that there were no footprints leading in that direction. Poborski swept his eyes around the deserted hallway once again. He shook his head, trying to clear the fog that had quickly descended. They must have. There was nowhere else to go, was there? He back tracked towards the stairs, leaping over Snowball's body as if it were no more than a bag of rubbish. Rushing up the four flights in a matter of seconds, he arrived outside Flat 4a , breathing heavily. He drew out a small black pistol from a leather holster underneath his jacket and, aiming it at the door lock, he rapidly fired off three shots, one after the other. The lock disintegrated on impact and the door swung open.

Poborski rushed inside, running from room to room, the automatic sensor lights flicking on and off as he did so. But it was soon very clear to him that there was nothing and no one in the apartment. The place was empty. Poborski entered the back bedroom and his eyes were instantly drawn towards the open window above the bed. He ran to it and thrust his head out into the cold night air. Facing him, directly outside the window, was a large tree – its thick gnarled branches almost touching the window ledge. Hanging on one of the branches was a small piece of cloth. Poborski reached out and grabbed it. It was a scarf. He lifted it to his nose. It smelt of perfume. Leaning back over the window ledge, Poborski peered down at the ground below. Something else now caught his eye. Something small and square.

"Petrov?!" he barked, whipping out his mobile phone. "Get your arse around to the back and check out what's on the floor, underneath the tree!"

Poborski waited for a moment, turning the scarf over and over in his hands. Soon a lumbering figure appeared below him, bending down to pick something up from the ground. Poborski put the phone back to his ear.

"Well, what is it?"

"It's a handbag, Sir," replied Petrov, growling into his phone. "A ladies' handbag."

"What's inside?" commanded Poborski, starting to screw the scarf up in his hands, wringing it like a wet cloth. His heart was racing. They were so close. They were so very very close. "Quickly!"

There was a short pause before Petrov replied. "A diary, Sir. Some pens. Packet of chewing gum. Small bottle of perfume and a credit card." Petrov paused, knowing his boss wasn't going to like what he was about to say. "A credit card in the name of Isabel Faraday."

"Damn!'" swore Poborski, snapping his phone shut and throwing the scarf on the floor. He clenched his fists with rage and leaned out of the window. "Vasiliev! Petrov! Get out there and bloody well look for them! They jumped! They fucking jumped from right underneath our noses!"

* * *

Time: 10.55pm
  Date: 6th November 2008
  Location: Flat 4a Hope Street, Cambridge

Mac gestured for Isabel to move backwards towards some stools which nestled around a small, square wooden table. As she sat down. Mac put a small touch control lamp onto the table top and snapped it on. Soft light filled the room, and Isabel could now see that she was sitting in a cellar. The floor was soft and dusty, the walls roughly hewn. Dampness clung to the still, musty air. And it was cold. Isabel shivered and hugged her arms around her body.

Mac sat down on a stool opposite her and slid off his black jacket. He silently placed it over Isabel's shoulders, and she nodded gratefully.

"What is this place?" she whispered.

"Just a little room I know of," Mac replied, smiling. "You never know when it might come in handy." His blue eyes twinkled in the soft light. He reached behind him and pulled over a large leather holdall bag, slipping the torch Isabel had been using into one of the side pockets.

They had both been huddled into one of the corners of the cellar for the last half an hour, neither of them daring to speak or make a sound – hardly even daring to breathe. They had stood, frozen to the spot, clinging onto each other in the darkness, listening to the sounds coming from above. There were gunshots at first, then the sound of running footsteps. They had then heard the front doors slam shut several times, and raised voices coming from outside. There were more footsteps, more slamming of doors, more urgent shouting before they heard the screech of tyres and roar of a car engine. And then there was nothing. Not a sound. But they had continued to stand in total silence, and near total darkness, for what seemed like an eternity. Just to be sure.

Satisfied that they were now alone, Mac got up and went over to a pile of boxes at the far end of the small cellar. He pulled out a briefcase, and brought it back to the table.

"I think you need an explanation."

Isabel raised her eyes to meet Mac's, but she said nothing.

"I have a file here which contains some extremely important information, and much sought after papers. I also have a disc that backs up what is contained in the file." He waved a flat disc in front of Isabel's face. "These papers were left in the back of a London taxi cab earlier today – for me to find. And what I am about to tell you will sound unbelievable – in fact, it *is* unbelievable. All I ask is that you just hear me out."

Isabel still said nothing, but nodded. She shivered under Mac's jacket and pulled it closer around her. Mac sat back down on his stool and took a deep breath.

"In 1982 NASA set up a committee called PRISM – a committee which stood for Primary Research into International Space Management. The Americans love a good acronym. Its function was to oversee space research being undertaken in the United States and to try and coordinate it with space research being conducted elsewhere in other countries. Particularly the Soviet Union, as it then was. The United States had always thought of themselves as being the front runner in space exploration – ever since sending the first man to the moon. But it was worried by the threat posed by other countries which were developing their own space programmes, seemingly at a faster rate than them. By 1982 space was big business. The first American space shuttle took off the year previously, and the programme was expanded just as PRISM was set up. But the Americans were worried. The Soviets had their own space programme, but it was being developed behind closed doors. The Americans thought that the best way to monitor the situation was to try and work *with* these other countries, glean what they were doing and find out what their objectives were. "Mac paused and gave a small shrug of his shoulders. "I guess some might call it spying."

CHAPTER SEVEN

He reached down in the holdall bag at his feet and removed a thin, sleek-looking laptop. Isabel didn't move or even register that she was listening. She stared at the wall, her eyes glazed and unfocused. Undeterred Mac carried on.

"PRISM was headed up by a man called Boris Kreshniov – a former Russian scientist and suspected ex-KGB agent who defected to the West in 1980. He was, by all accounts, an incredible scientist, a phenomenal mathematician, and was the perfect candidate for spear heading the new committee. But he had visions which didn't belong within the delicate confines of PRISM – that soon became all too apparent. He wanted to do more. He wanted to go outside the boundaries of PRISM, outside the constraints that NASA placed on them. NASA and the US Government were fully in control of PRISM and what its objectives were – but Kreshniov felt suffocated by the tight controls. He wanted more. So, he created what was later to become known as the Phoenix Project."

Mac noticed Isabel stir at the sound of the Project's name. But still she said nothing. Mac continued.

"The Phoenix Project was a highly secretive, almost secular, organisation and only a handful of PRISM members were involved. It was so secretive, in fact, that many people denied its very existence. Most considered it to be a myth, a figment of the imagination. NASA and the US Government flatly refuse to acknowledge its existence. But it was real.

"The Project itself was headed up by Kreshniov – with a man called Karl Poborski as his second in command."

Mac paused and looked at Isabel. Her blank face, still staring past him into the darkness, confirmed to him that she had never heard of either man before. Despite Isabel's apparent lack of interest, he carried on.

"Poborski was also a former Russian agent, who like Kreshniov had defected to the West in 1980. It wasn't known if the two had known each other before, back in their native country, but when they were both brought together on the PRISM committee they formed an unnervingly close partnership. Poborski still maintained useful contacts in the Soviet Union, and Kreshniov intended to exploit this. He knew that he needed a way of infiltrating the Russian space agency – and Poborski was his way in. Kreshniov quickly recruited Poborski into the Phoenix Project.

"Then there was the question of money. To achieve what it wanted to achieve, the Phoenix Project needed funds. Huge funds. PRISM only had access to a fraction of NASA's state funding, and none could be used for Kreshniov's own secret society. So, Kreshniov used Poborski's contacts to secure a steady, if not unorthodox, stream of Russian funding for the Project."

Mac paused again and switched on the laptop. He noticed Isabel stirring at the sound of the machine's whirring. She raised her eyes to meet his gaze. Mac knew he only had one shot at this – if he got it wrong, then she was most likely to get up and run as soon as she was able.

"For many decades' people have asked the same question – is there life outside our universe? Are we really alone? Is there anybody out there? The possibility of there being life on other planets, in other solar systems, in other parts of the universe, fascinated Kreshniov. He was convinced that the Earth could not be unique. That we could not be the only planet sustaining life. He believed that the Earth was only the beginning. The very tip of the iceberg. Just a stepping stone to what else lay beyond. He firmly believed that at some time or other, life did exist elsewhere in the solar system – and further beyond that. And where life once existed, life could exist once again.

"The Phoenix Project was born to push the boundaries of space exploration as far as they could go – far further than they had ever been pushed before. Boris Kreshniov didn't just want to prove that there *was* life in space – Boris Kreshniov wanted to prove that he could *create* life in space."

* * *

Time: 11.00pm
   Date: 6th November 2008
   Location: Flat 4a Hope Street, Cambridge

CHAPTER SEVEN

Karl Poborski sat in the back seat of the Mercedes and smiled, ruefully, his thin lips stretching over his perfectly white teeth. They had been smart – he hadn't been prepared for that. In a way, he was impressed. But the game wasn't over yet.

"What do we do now?" asked Petrov, turning round to face Poborski from the driver's seat. "Where will they have gone?"

"I don't know where they are, but I know where they'll be going." Poborski took out his mobile phone and scrolled through the contacts list. "They won't get far." He selected the number he needed and heard the call connect after the third ring. "It's me. We missed the girl."

"She needs to be taken care of," came the reply. "That was part of the deal."

"I know. And it will be done. Trust me."

Poborski snapped the phone shut and slipped it back inside his pocket. "Take me back to London."

* * *

Time: 11.00pm
   Date: 6th November 2008
   Location: Flat 4a Hope Street, Cambridge

"These papers contain the classified information regarding the experiments of the Phoenix Project during the 1980's." Mac tapped the bulging folder he had placed next to the laptop. "The people who killed your cat, the people who want to kill us, they are after these papers."

Mac sat himself back down next to Isabel and opened the folder.

"The Phoenix Project, using PRISM as a front, funded extra space missions to develop technology which they hoped would one day enable people to live in space for great lengths of time – maybe even indefinitely.

"We're talking about the early 1980's here – way before the International Space Station came into operation, and even before the Russians launched

79

MIR. NASA had nothing even remotely close to what the Phoenix Project required, what Kreshniov needed to get his ideas off the ground. They needed a base, somewhere they could conduct their tests and experiments in the correct environment. And this was where Poborski came in. Through his connections, he was able to secure the use of the Russian space station Salyut 7."

Mac stopped and looked up at Isabel. She hadn't moved; she was still staring blankly at the wall. She hadn't even acknowledged that she was listening. He continued nonetheless.

"Salyut 7 was the last of the Russian Salyut space stations and was a precursor to the MIR space station. It stayed in orbit for some 9 years and saw two world records broken for the longest duration spent in space for its Russian cosmonauts. Kreshniov thought it was the perfect place for the Phoenix Project.

"The original plan had been to wait until the Russians launched MIR, but Kreshniov was getting impatient. He was anxious to get the Project's experiments up and running, so he decided to go with Salyut 7 instead. The Salyut 7 module had a large living area, with each living quarter having its own artificially created air supply continuously pumped through. The Phoenix Project experiment was meant to be the first step along the long road to answering that age old question. Can humans ever live in space? Can humans ever live on another planet? Kreshniov wanted to be able to answer both of those questions with a "yes, they can."

"This is all mad." Isabel's quiet voice cut through the cold, damp air of the cellar. "All of it. Madness." She shook her head and shifted in her seat. Glancing around herself, peering through the dimness, she was conscious of there being only the one way in – and only the one way out.

Mac looked up and studied her face, intently. "I don't blame you," he said, simply, adjusting the computer screen so that it was now facing Isabel. "I'd be looking for a way out too."

"What do you mean?" replied Isabel, a little too quickly. Her voice sounded hoarse, her throat feeling dry and prickly. She felt her pulse begin to quicken, and the palms of her hands felt sweaty. She was trapped.

CHAPTER SEVEN

Mac raised his eyebrows and looked around the room. "Here – you're looking for a way out. A means of escape. You think I'm a madman holding you captive."

"And are you?" The words escaped Isabel's lips before she could stop them. Her heart thumped painfully against her ribs in an ever increasing crescendo.

Mac held her frightened gaze for a moment, but then a smile flickered across his lips. "No, I'm not a madman. But I don't expect you to believe me, not right away." He paused for a minute, still watching Isabel's tense face. "You're free to go any time you want" He raised his eyes towards the trapdoor overhead. "Just say the word and I'll open it up."

Isabel's eyes rested on the trapdoor above them once again. In the heavy silence of the cellar, she imagined hearing again the muffled footsteps and voices overhead, the gunshots, the fierce shouting. A vision of poor Snowball's mutilated body flooded into her head and she felt instantly nauseous. The sickly sweet smell of fresh blood filled her nostrils once again.

She shook her head to rid herself of the macabre thoughts circulating through her head. "Why are you doing this to me?" she breathed, swallowing back the nausea which was wallowing up inside her. "Why are you telling me all this? I've told you…I've never heard of this Phoenix Project. Why should I care about any of it?"

Mac noticed Isabel was no longer eyeing the trapdoor, and her hands were more loosely clasped in her lap. He knew that it was now, or never.

"Because something went wrong with the experiment. The Phoenix Project experiment." Mac's voice lowered. "It moved on. It started getting involved in things that it wasn't meant to. It began to get out of hand. The Project moved on from just seeking to prove that humans could survive for long periods in space. Kreshniov wanted more than that. Much more. The Russians were already setting new records for the amount of time their cosmonauts could spend in space. Kreshniov wanted some of that recognition, some of that glory. He wanted to prove that the human race can live, and reproduce, outside of the confines of the planet Earth."

Mac noticed Isabel's eyes widen a little. He knew she was listening.

"The Phoenix Project research culminated in one landmark experiment – the experiment Kreshniov had been planning for years. His ultimate goal. This experiment involved a man and a woman – and they were to produce the first human baby to be born in space."

Isabel's eyes widened even further, but she remained silent. Mac wasn't sure if that was a good sign or not, but, taking a deep breath, he carried on.

"That couple, Isabel – they were your parents."

***

Time: 11.15pm
Date: 6th November 2008
Location: Metropolitan Police HQ, London

Chief Superintendent Liddell sat in the darkness of his office. Everyone else had long since gone home. It had been over an hour since his conversation with Edwards – but Liddell had been unable to put his fears out of his mind. If anything, they were growing steadily with every minute that ticked by.

Edwards had not convinced him that everything was going to be all right. Quite the opposite, in fact. The American's apparent lack of concern, and blasé attitude to what was happening, only further fuelled Liddell's fears.

He had to do something.

Chief Superintendent Liddell rose from his desk, his mind made up. Despite assurances from Edwards, and Fleming himself, he still didn't feel comfortable. Something was bound to go wrong, he could feel it.

There was only one person he could turn to.

One person he could trust.

***

Time: 11.20pm

CHAPTER SEVEN

Date: 6th November 2008
Location: Flat 4a Hope Street, Cambridge

"Say something, then." Mac's voice sounded hollow. It was as if the cellar had suddenly grown larger, turning itself into a cavern hewn into the rocks deep underground. His voice bounced off the walls, sounding lost and empty.

Isabel's eyes stared through the blackness, searching for something to focus on. Eventually she found Mac's penetrating blue eyes. She felt her mouth open, but no words emerged. Mac edged closer, scraping his stool over the dusty floor.

"I know it sounds bizarre, and I don't expect you to believe me straight away…"

Isabel cut him dead. "Too right you bloody don't. I don't know what game you're trying to play here, but it's really starting to freak me out." Isabel's voice started to quiver. "Just let me out….let me out now! This has got nothing to do with me, or my parents. They're dead for Christ's sake! They have been for years!"

Isabel jumped to her feet. "I don't know anything about any bloody Phoenix Project, and I don't want to. Just let me out! Now!" Suddenly, she felt her legs buckle beneath her, and she began to sway violently from side to side as her head swam in and out of focus. Mac leapt forwards, grabbing hold of her arm and gently lowering her back onto her stool.

"Easy does it," he said, softly. "Put your head down between your knees." Mac gently pushed Isabel's head down so that it rested on her knees. She instantly felt her head begin to clear, the fuzziness melting away so that all that was left was a faint blurriness around the edges. "I assure you that everything I'm telling you is the truth." Mac's voice was slow and steady. "Just give me ten more minutes of your time. I've got something to show you. After that, you can do what you want."

Mac reached forwards and angled the computer screen further towards Isabel. The screen went black for a moment and then sprang into life. The words "Mission PP" flashed up in the middle, with the date 19th September

1985 underneath.

"Hello. My name is Boris Kreshniov. I work at the NASA scientific development laboratory in Washington DC." There was no face, no image on the screen, just a deep, calming voice speaking in the background. "I have been working on a project which, in time, I hope – we all hope – will be the saviour of all mankind. Today is an historic day for America and the people of the civilised world. Today, we here at the scientific development laboratory will show you something that until now you have only ever dreamed of, or maybe read in science fiction magazines. But what you witness here today, ladies and gentlemen, is not science fiction – this is science *fact*."

The screen then cut to a picture of a space shuttle. The body of the spacecraft looming up high into the air, stretching ever skywards. The sky above was a clear, azure blue, with only a handful of wispy white clouds to spoil the view. Around the shuttle's base several important looking individuals scurried about, evidently preparing last minute checks for the shuttle's next mission. The same deep voice continued its overtone.

"The Space Shuttle Explorer is due to take off from Cape Canaveral in two days' time, taking with it two young astronauts who are going to become the first human beings to produce a live infant whilst in orbit."

"I'm going to fast forward the next bit," said Mac, reaching forwards and tapping the keyboard. "It gets a bit technical. I can always rewind if you want."

Isabel shook her head, solemnly, and waved her agreement. She wasn't sure what she was doing, why she was even watching this macabre floorshow. All she knew was that she wanted it to end – and soon. The sooner it ended, the sooner she could leave.

Mac clicked the play button again and the familiar velvety tones of Boris Kreshniov filled the cellar.

"I would like to introduce the good people of America, and indeed the rest of the world, to two of the bravest people I have ever had the good fortune to meet. These two astronauts will soon be producing the first ever live infant birth in space. I can't describe how much of a privilege

CHAPTER SEVEN

and honour it is to be in the company of such wonderful people, dedicated to the furthering of space technology and space exploration, and indeed the human race as we know it, in such a momentous way. I am proud to call them not only my colleagues, but also my friends."

Isabel raised her eyes to the screen and instantly felt her stomach catapult its way towards the floor. She felt as though someone had just squeezed all the air out of her lungs, painfully wringing them out like a disused dishcloth until they were flat and lifeless. For there, right in front of her on the screen, right before her very eyes, were her mother and father. There could be no mistake. It was definitely them. She recognised them instantly from the treasured photographs she kept at home.

Isabel instinctively reached out towards Mac, and clung to his arm. He let her grip tighten, not even flinching when her nails began to press deeply into his skin. The rest of the film played without interruption. Isabel stared, unblinkingly, at the screen, and Mac hardly dared to breathe in case it broke the spell. Eventually the screen returned to an inky blackness and silence once again filled the cellar.

"Well?" Mac's voice was barely above a whisper. "What do you think?"

Isabel breathed in deeply, letting her eyes close as she filled her lungs with the cool air. As she exhaled, she relaxed her grip on Mac's arm and turned towards him, fixing him with a cold stare.

"What do I *think*?" She raised her eyebrows and snatched her hand away from Mac. "I think you're insane. You drag me all the way down here to show me some….some cruel, hoax film? What is it you want from me?" Strength had returned to Isabel's voice. She now felt calm. She now felt in control.

"It's no hoax, Isabel," replied Mac, shaking his head. "I swear. I know it's hard to believe, but when your parents…."

"Don't you *dare* talk about my parents like that!" Isabel exploded. "You never knew them. They're dead for God's sake! Don't you dare mention their names again!"

"They're not dead, Isabel….."

"You know that's a lie!" Isabel rose from her seat, not caring anymore if there was anyone above who could hear them. "They died when I was six years old!"

"Your parents are not dead, Isabel," repeated Mac, calmly, also rising to his feet. "They're still alive."

"Liar!" screamed Isabel, backing steadily away from Mac's advancing shadow. "Liar!" She stepped further and further away into the depths of the cellar, soon feeling herself bumping up against the back wall. Mac continued to move steadily towards her, his arms outstretched. "Get away from me!" she yelled, kicking out with her feet. "Get away from me or I'll scream!"

"I'm sorry, Isabel," said Mac, holding her frightened and angry eyes in his cool calm gaze. "Really I am. But I have to do this."

Mac reached out towards her, and then there was blackness.

* * *

CHAPTER EIGHT

Time: 7.27am
Date: 7th November 2008
Location: Kettles Yard Mews, London

Jack woke after a fitful night's sleep. He glanced at the clock on the bedside table and cursed under his breath. He was going to be late. He'd wanted to be in early today to try and clear some of the steady backlog of cases which threatened to overrun his already teeming desk. But last night's visitation had put pay to that idea.

Jack groaned and pulled himself out of bed, heading sleepy-eyed towards the bathroom. He turned the hot tap on full-blast and stood underneath the therapeutic drumming of the shower's spray until his head began to clear.

It was always the same after one of those dreams. Not that they could be called dreams, really. Not even nightmares came close. But whatever they were, they were coming more and more frequently now…..more frequently than they had ever done before.

Jack tried to shut the previous night's visions out of his head and snapped off the shower.

He needed to get himself together.

He had work to do.

*　*　*

Time: 9.15am
   Date: 7th November 2008
   Location: 35 miles north of Paris, France

The sunlight streamed in through the window, causing Isabel's eyes to flutter open. She turned her head away from the glare which seared through to her eyeballs like a burning spear. Her head was throbbing, the pain radiating out from her thumping temples and enveloping her skull like a pulsating blanket.

Peering through heavy-lidded eyes, Isabel could just make out that she was inside a car. She was on the back seat, her legs curled up underneath her, her shoulders pressed painfully against the passenger side door. She tried to move but a wave of intense pain shot up her spine and stabbed her between the shoulder blades. Her whole body ached. Her legs were numb from being crumpled beneath her for…for however long it was that she had been there.

With her eyes slowly becoming more accustomed to the light, Isabel looked around her. The car was empty. There seemed to be nobody else in sight. Without moving too much, Isabel turned her head to look out of the passenger side window. Condensation clung to the glass, making her view hazy. She didn't recognise anything outside. It looked like a car park. A large, deserted car park.

Something on the back seat caught her eye, making her heart leap up into her throat where it threatened to explode. A heavy coil of rope lay curled up next to her, together with a roll of masking tape and a cushion. Isabel instinctively brought her hands around into her lap. She rolled up her sleeves a little and saw that her wrists had deep red grooves eating into her pale skin. She gently touched the marks – they felt raw and scolded like fire. The red marks wove around her wrists in a spiral pattern – like rope lines. She slowly flexed her wrists backwards and forwards – they felt stiff and sore.

Isabel then raised a shaky hand to her mouth and dabbed her lips. The skin around them felt sticky. The masking tape. She caught her breath,

CHAPTER EIGHT

swinging her legs round to the floor of the car. She tried to ignore the pain which shot out from her feet. The pins and needles prickling at her legs from being curled up underneath her body for goodness knows how long was almost unbearable. Almost, but not quite. She had to get out.

It was only then that she noticed the rope still tied around her ankles. It was the same type as the rope lying next to her on the back seat – the same type that she guessed had been used to bind her wrists. Isabel began to pull frantically at the ends of the rope, but the knot was too tight. It wouldn't budge. Each time she tried, she only seemed to make it tighter. Abandoning her feet, Isabel began scrabbling at the door. She tried both rear doors but they were both locked. The windows were electronically controlled and would not open.

Feeling the fear and panic rise up inside her, Isabel began banging on the steamy windows with her fists.

"Help me!" she screamed, smacking the glass as hard as she could. "Get me out of here!"

But it was fruitless. Isabel's eyes scanned the car park outside and realised she was shouting at nothing, and no one. It was truly deserted. There was no one else around at all. No one to hear her screams, no one to hear her shouts.

Tears began to stream down her cheeks, and Isabel wiped them roughly away with the backs of her hands. She didn't even flinch when the salt water of her tears stung against the red wealds on her wrists. Pain meant nothing to her now. Thoughts raced around her head, hammering at her brain. What should she do? How could she get out? How much time did she have?

The sun had just crept up above the treetops, so Isabel guessed it was still morning. How long had she been here? Suddenly, she whirled around at the sound of the rear door opening behind her. She had been so wrapped up in looking out of the side window that she had not seen him approaching from behind.

Isabel opened her mouth to scream – but no sound escaped. It was as if someone had ripped out her voice box, leaving her mute and helpless.

The man leant inside the car, but Isabel didn't look at him. She didn't look at his face as he inched closer and closer towards her. All she could see was the glinting silver metal blade of the knife in his hand.

* * *

Time: 10.30am
  Date: 15th July 1973
  Location: Christchurch, Dorset

"Jack?" The voice was weak and uncertain. "What's happening, Jack?"

Jack looked up and saw a small boy, about his own age, maybe a little younger, standing in front of him on the damp grass, his face streaked with wet tears. The boy was clutching a soft brown teddy bear, hugging it tightly to his chest.

Behind the boy stood a man and a woman. They both had tired, careworn faces – both looking far older than their years. The man reached out and touched the boy's shoulder. It was a gentle, loving touch, but instantly the boy whirled around and began shouting.

"No! You can't make me! Tell them they can't make me go, Jack!"

The boy turned and faced Jack once again, his face panic-stricken, his eyes flashing with a heady cocktail of fear, anger and loathing. He tried to back away, but the man had already grabbed hold of his upper arm and had begun pulling him across the neatly mown lawn.

"No! Please!" screamed the boy, trying to dig the heels of his shoes into the soft grass, writhing and wriggling under the man's firm grip. "Jack! Help me, Jack! Tell them I'll be good! Please don't let them take me – please don't let them take me, Jack!"

Jack looked up and silently watched the scene being played out before him. He saw the boy's terror stricken face as he was dragged away towards a waiting car on the driveway. He saw the expression on the man's face – a mixture of pain and sadness, tinged perhaps with regret.

The woman hung back, unable to take part in the show. She was crying

CHAPTER EIGHT

now, small silent sobs sending steady tears pouring down her pale face. She buried her head in her hands, unable to watch as the boy was pushed towards the car, and fled back towards the house.

Jack watched as the boy was firmly placed, kicking and screaming, into the back of the car. Another woman emerged from the passenger seat and spoke briefly with the man before they exchanged a quick shake of hands.

And then they were gone.

The car sped off down the drive and all that was left was an eerie, empty silence. Jack noticed that, in the struggle, the boy had dropped his teddy bear. It lay, lost and forgotten, by the side of the gravel drive.

Jack turned away and continued to play with his trucks. He pushed the biggest and brightest truck he had as hard as he could, sending it careering down the garden steps to the patio below.

Bang! Bang! Bang! Sounded the truck's plastic wheels on the hard, concrete stonework.

Bang! Bang! Bang!

Bang! Bang! Bang!

Bang! Bang! Bang!

* * *

Time: 8.27am
    Date: 7th November 2008
    Location: Kettles Yard Mews, London

Jack woke with a start, his heart pounding.

Bang! Bang! Bang!

Bang! Bang! Bang!

It was the front door, downstairs – someone was knocking on it so hard they threatened to break through the woodwork into the hallway.

Bang! Bang! Bang!

Jack rolled off the bed and glanced at the clock.

08.27 blinked back at him.

He frowned, noticing that he was lying on the bed, dressed only in a damp towel. He remembered getting up for a shower, but then nothing. He yawned. He must have lain down whilst getting dry and fallen asleep – again.

Bang! Bang! Bang!

"All right, all right – I'm coming." Jack pulled on his dressing gown and walked out into the communal hallway. No one else from the flats on his level seemed to be stirring.

Bang! Bang! Bang!

Slowly, stifling a yawn, Jack jogged down the spiral staircase towards the front door. Pulling it open, he winced at the arctic blast of cold air that greeted him. The plunging temperatures overnight had encased everything in frost and ice; it was like standing in an ice-box. Jack stood on the threshold and looked out across the deserted street. Frowning and rubbing the sleep from his eyes, he peered up and down the road, left and right, but there was nothing. And no one.

Shrugging to himself, Jack made to shut the door. Maybe he had imagined the whole thing. Again. He shuddered from the cold, pulling the dressing gown more tightly around his waist. But then it caught his eye. If he hadn't glanced down at the pavement, he might never have found it. It was small, and barely visible underneath the empty milk bottle which was holding it down.

But it was there.

A small white envelope.

An envelope that bore Jack's name.

Jack bent down and opened the envelope, pulling out a small, square piece of paper. He looked up and down the street once again for any signs as to who had almost battered down his door to deliver it. But whoever it had been was long gone. Their job was done.

The wording on the note was short and simple. It contained merely two lines. Two dates.

January 28th 1986

February 25th 1986

CHAPTER EIGHT

* * *

Time: 9.17am
 Date: 7th November 2008
 Location: 35 miles north of Paris, France

The knife was razor sharp and cut through the rope threads like they were made of butter. Isabel flinched with each cut. Mac looked up and tried a smile.

"Sorry if I panicked you," he said, putting the knife down and gently pulling the coil of rope free from Isabel's ankles. "But I couldn't get the knot undone. I needed a knife to cut it with. Called in over there as soon as they opened."

Mac nodded out of the window behind them towards the small motorway services station nestled into the far end of the car park. Isabel could see the building now. Before, it had been obscured by the condensation and mist on the windows. She could now also hear the steady rumble of traffic passing by behind a row of trees.

"Got us something hot to drink while I was there, too," Mac continued, leaning back outside the car where he had left two hot, steaming cups of coffee on the ground. He handed one to Isabel. She took it, warily, without saying a word. She took a sip and flinched as the hot liquid burned her lips. But as she drank, its warmth loosened her throat.

"Where am I?" she whispered, her voice small and still edged with fear. She glanced back outside at the motorway service station. She didn't recognise anything. They could be anywhere.,

"A few kilometres outside Paris," replied Mac, shutting the car door behind him and seating himself next to Isabel on the back seat. He took the rope and masking tape and dropped them out of sight by his feet.

"Paris?!" Isabel's voice was much louder this time. Her surprise almost caused her to spill the scorching coffee into her lap. "In France?"

"The one and the same," smiled Mac, draining his own coffee and discarding the polystyrene cup. "We've been driving most of the night.

Should make it within the next hour or two."

"But.." Isabel frowned and gingerly touched her forehead with her fingers. Her head still ached and throbbed.

Mac eyed her carefully. "You don't remember? What I told you last night?"

Isabel's frown deepened. Her head seemed so fuzzy, her thoughts so blurred.

"You remember the apartment? The cellar?" Mac paused, watching Isabel's face as she tried to force her brain to make sense of the pictures dancing around inside it. Everything was so jumbled up, so mixed up and confused. "They were right above us. Looking for us. You could hear them."

Isabel closed her eyes as her memory swam in and out of focus, like she was swimming underneath the sea, the water dark and murky. She could see a building now – covered in snow. There were footprints outside. Fresh footprints. Her own footprints. And then there was blood. Blood in the snow. Blood next to the footprints. Blood on the floor. Blood on her shoes. Blood on her hands.

Then she heard muffled footsteps. Then shouting. And then gunshots. Isabel's eyes snapped open. Her mind had suddenly cleared. "Snowy!" she gasped, bringing a hand to her mouth in shock.

Mac nodded. "We got down to the cellar just in time. I made them think we had jumped through the upstairs window and climbed down the tree. It gave us some breathing space to get out."

Isabel slowly shook her head, unable to stop the mass of pictures flooding into her head. She saw Snowball's limp body lying on the carpet, the blood seeping into the pile at her feet. She saw the darkness outside, and the man lingering in the shadows….watching….waiting……for her.

"I don't remember getting out," she whispered, thinking back to the cold chill of the cellar. "I just remember…" Then she broke off. She remembered Mac coming at her when she was looking for a way out. Looking for the door, looking for an escape. But he had come towards her…and then there had been nothing but blackness and she remembered no more.

CHAPTER EIGHT

Isabel breathed in through her nose. She could detect a faint strange aroma around her nostrils. The smell was sweet, yet acrid. Then her mind opened up once more and she could see him this time – Mac coming towards her, holding out a piece of cloth, forcing it over her nose and mouth. She remembered the smell, the fuzziness, the blurriness. And then there was blackness once again.

"What was it?" she asked, simply, avoiding Mac's gaze.

Mac shrugged. "Something like chloroform, I suppose. I don't really know." He paused. "I had to do it."

"Sure you did." Isabel looked out of the window. The sun was a little higher in the sky now, and the condensation was clearing from the window. "And the rope? You had to do that too?"

"It was the only way. I needed to get you out of there without causing a scene. I didn't know when they would be back." Mac tried to catch Isabel's gaze, but she didn't turn to face him. "I needed to get you over here as soon as I could."

"Where did you put me? The boot?" Isabel gave a faint shudder at the thought of being bundled lifelessly into the boot of the car, trussed up like a dead body, ready to be dumped or discarded.

Mac hung his head. "I got you out again as soon as we crossed the channel. I couldn't take the risk of you waking up in the car. I didn't know how long the…the stuff would last."

Isabel didn't reply this time. Her attention was caught by the sound of an engine. She watched as an articulated lorry pulled into the service station car park, coming to a stop only a few metres away. It was a British lorry, with British number plates. Isabel's heart gave a small, involuntary leap.

Mac saw the connection. "Like I said before – I can't stop you if you want to go. The doors are unlocked." He paused, making sure Isabel was listening. She had half turned her head towards him to show that she was. "But if you do, you'll be a dead woman by sunset." Mac let the words hang in the air before continuing. "I have one more thing for you. Then, if you want, you can get out right now and take your chances. Hop in that lorry over there and see how far you get. But I can promise you that they'll find you. People like this always do."

Mac let his words hang in the air, then reached into his jacket pocket and brought out a small box, not unlike a ring box. It was covered in soft, black velvet, smooth to the touch. He held it out towards Isabel, nodding at her to take it.

Isabel hesitated, but then took the box – keeping one eye on the lorry parked outside. "Why are you giving me this? What is it?" She made no attempt to open it.

"It's not from me," replied Mac, simply. "I'm just the messenger. I was just told to give it to you."

Isabel let her forefinger stroke the top of the box, feeling the richness of the velvet beneath her skin. Then she snapped open the lid. Inside was a small silver object, no bigger than a 5p piece. It was solid looking, with several smooth sides meeting to a point at the bottom, not unlike an ice cream cone shape. Its top side was uneven and ragged, flagged with jagged edges.

Isabel frowned. Mac read her thoughts instantly.

"Take it out," he said. "Look at it properly."

Isabel lifted the object out of the box. It felt surprisingly heavy for something so small. She held it in the palm of her hand, and then saw something she hadn't expected. The sunlight from the rising sun streamed in through the window and caught the object in its glare. Its surface glinted, revealing a myriad of colours not unlike a rainbow.

Isabel felt her other hand rise instinctively towards her neck. She fumbled, unable to take her eyes off the object in her hand, until she found what she was looking for. She pulled her neck chain out from underneath her jumper and slowly lowered her eyes to see the small charm pendant hanging from it. She had always called it a charm, but she had never really known what it was. Looking at it again now, it had the same smooth exterior as the one now nestling in her hand. And the same show of rainbow colours when the sun hit its surface.

Although she had never seen it before, Isabel knew exactly what to do with the new pendant in her hand. She lifted it up towards her neck chain

CHAPTER EIGHT

and slotted the two pieces together. They fitted perfectly, even giving a tiny "snap" when they had clicked into place.

The two pieces had now become one.

One perfect prism.

* * *

Time: 8.45am
  Date: 7th November 2008
  Location: Kettle's Yard Mews, London

"Hey, are you driving in this morning?" Jack poured hot water into a mug of instant coffee and stirred the murky brown liquid. He cradled the telephone under his chin while he opened the fridge in search of milk.

"Yes, on my way in right now. Want me to swing by and pick you up?" DS Cooper's voice sounded faint and tinny.

"That'd be great, mate. I'm running a bit behind." Jack swore under his breath when he saw there wasn't any milk, and then remembered the empty milk bottle on the doorstep. And as it was Sunday, the milkman wouldn't be coming to help him in his predicament. He put the phone down and resorted to drinking it black, wincing at the bitterness and scalding temperature.

Taking the mug through to his bedroom, Jack sat on the edge of the rumpled bed and sighed. Taking another swig and feeling the heat spread as he swallowed, he closed his eyes and waited for the caffeine to hit, hopefully banishing the tiredness he felt to another part of his brain so he could at least pretend to function today. Placing the mug on the bedside table, Jack made to get up and sort out some clothes from the wardrobe. As he did so he saw the photo frame lying face down by the bedside lamp. His hand hovered momentarily beside the coffee cup, his mind now filling with memories from the fitful night's sleep he had had…..and the dream.

After a moment's pause, Jack reached across and flipped the photo frame back up, then headed to his wardrobe to get dressed.

***

Time: 9.30am
  Date: 7th November 2008
  Location: 35 miles north of Paris, France

"I went to their funeral," said Isabel, simply. "And I visit their graves…take them flowers sometimes." Isabel's eyes began to smart with fresh tears. "I even talk to them…." She bit her lip, her voice beginning to tremble.

Her hand gripped the pendant tightly, pressing it hard against her chest, close to her heart. She remembered her mother giving the necklace to her when she was small. Only four, maybe five years old. She had been obsessed with dressing up, just like other little girls all around the world. She would hunt through her mother's wardrobe in her bedroom and try on her shoes, scarves, gloves, dresses, anything she could find. But most of all she loved her mother's jewellery box. She would sit, perched up on top of the dressing table stool, and open the ornately decorated box which housed so many treasures. Inside she would find rings of sapphire and gold, bracelets of silver and diamonds, necklaces of rubies and shimmering emeralds.

A young Isabel would slip the rings onto her little fingers, wrap the bracelets around her wrists, and drape the necklaces around her delicate neck. She would be covered from head to toe in glittering, glistening beauty. Her mother would often take photographs of her – pictures of her little diamond princess as she would call her.

And then, one day, as Isabel again opened up her favourite box, she pulled out something different. It was a necklace which had never been there before. A necklace which looked so ordinary, so plain against all the others. It had been a simple silver chain, with a simple silver pendant. Except that the pendant looked to be broken, as if it had a piece missing.

Isabel had taken the necklace and held it up in front of the dressing table mirror. As it swung from her tiny fingers, it caught the light from the window. The plain silver pendant began to shimmer and sparkle with

CHAPTER EIGHT

secret, hidden beauty. The rainbow colours glimmered before her eyes and captivated the little diamond princess from that moment on.

Ever since that day, it had become Isabel's necklace. Her mother had fastened the chain around her neck and told her that it was hers. Forever. For keeps.

"What about the missing piece, Mummy?" Isabel had asked, gazing at the jagged edge of the pendant. "Where is it?"

And it was then that her mother had shown her an identical necklace, fastened around her own neck. From it dangled a similar coloured pendant, which even at the age of four or five, the young Isabel knew would fit perfectly. That the two pendants would fit together to become one.

Isabel looked out of the car window, watching as the British lorry started its engine and slowly pulled out of the car park. She made no attempt to follow it or to gain the driver's attention.

She now had the missing part of the necklace. Her mother's necklace.

And it could only have come from one place. From one person.

And that meant one thing, and one thing only.

They were alive.

"So what happens now?" Isabel was now sitting in the front passenger seat of the car, all thoughts and memories of the rope and masking tape banished from her mind. "Where are they?" She gently rolled the pendant between her fingers as she spoke. "I have to see them."

Mac swung the car onto the main road heading towards Paris. "We need to go and see a friend of mine. It's all arranged."

"And, they're there?"

Mac shook his head, slowly. "No, your parents won't be there. It's still too dangerous. They can't surface until all this…." He indicated with his head back towards the bulging folder of Phoenix Project papers now sitting on the back seat of the car. "…..is sorted."

"And how does it get "sorted" exactly?"

Mac shrugged. "Not part of my job. I was just meant to get you, and the papers, and bring you both over here. Keep you both together. Andre will have the rest figured out."

99

"Andre?"

"The friend we're going to see. He'll sort it. He's got it all planned."

* * *

Time: 9.00am
Date: 7th November 2008
Location: Kettles Yard Mews, London

"This was left on my doorstep." Jack handed DS Cooper the small white envelope. "Just a half hour ago. Whoever left it made damn sure I didn't see them."

Jack went over to his wardrobe and selected a fresh shirt and tie – yesterday's trousers would have to do. He hadn't managed to get to the launderette this week. Again.

DS Cooper read the note and frowned. "This is it? Just some dates?" He turned the note over, half expecting there to be more on the other side. But there wasn't.

Jack nodded, pulling on his shirt and hastily fastening the buttons. He ran a hand over his chin – rough, but he'd get away with it for another day. He didn't have time to shave, not today. "I need you to find out what they mean. Whatever happened on those dates, I need to know about it. Someone left them there for a reason."

DS Cooper nodded and handed the note back to Jack. As he did so, his eyes rested on a battered looking teddy bear sitting on top of a chair in the corner of the room. "I didn't have you down as a teddy bear man, Jack!" he remarked, nodding at the stuffed toy and smiling.

Jack's eyes darted towards the bear but he said nothing.

"You going soft in your old age?" laughed DS Cooper, his eyes twinkling.

Jack began to wind the tie around his neck. He stopped and stared thoughtfully over at the teddy bear. It was old, and tatty, and had been with him since before he could remember. Somehow he couldn't bring

CHAPTER EIGHT

himself to let it go.

"It was my brother's," he remarked, simply, resuming his tie fastening. "I've had it for years."

"Your brother's?" DS Cooper looked up at Jack and frowned. "I never knew you had a brother."

Jack shrugged and pulled on his jacket. "I haven't seen him in years. We were fostered out as kids when our mother....well, when she couldn't look after us anymore...." Jack left the sentence unfinished, his gaze locked on the battered teddy once again. "He left it behind."

"I'm sorry. I never knew."

Jack shrugged again. "It's OK. Not many people know about him. He went to a different foster family when we were small and we kind of lost touch. I only ever see him now and again – usually when he wants something."

"So, where is he now?"

Jack looked up at DS Cooper and swiped up his house keys from the bedside table. "I have absolutely no idea."

CHAPTER NINE

Time: 9.45am
   Date: 7th November 2008
   Location: Petrol station forecourt, 10 miles north of Paris, France

Mac shut the car door but let his hand hover, hesitantly, over the ignition key. He cast a sideways glance at Isabel who was merely staring out over the petrol station forecourt. She had been very quiet during their journey from the motorway service station, often just gazing out of the window, her hand clutching the prism pendant tightly to her chest.

"What are you thinking?" Mac tried to gain Isabel's attention, but she continued to look out of the window, her eyes glazed. She half turned towards him at his question, her mouth working up and down but failing to find any words. She merely shrugged in response.

Mac nodded. "It's OK. I understand. It's a lot to take in." He turned and reached behind him onto the back seat, pulling through the Phoenix Project folder into his lap. He rummaged through the papers before bringing out a small, battered photograph and handed it to Isabel. "Andre thought you might like this."

Isabel took the photograph and looked deeply into the faces of her mother and father. She ran her finger over their faces, trying to feel the contours of their skin beneath her own. They looked so young, so happy, so full of life.

"It was taken the day they left." Mac watched as Isabel continued to stare, unblinkingly, into her parents' eyes. "The Phoenix Project……."

CHAPTER NINE

"All this time I thought they were dead," interrupted Isabel, shaking her head and passing the photograph back to Mac. She could feel tears beginning to prick at her eyelids and she hurriedly rubbed them with her sleeves. "Why would they want to do that? Why would they want me to think they were dead?"

Mac shrugged. "I guess......I think they had no choice. The founders of the Phoenix Project wanted them silenced."

"Silenced?" Isabel whipped her head round to face Mac. "What do you mean silenced?"

"I mean *silenced*. Because of what they knew about what *really* happened on Salyut 7."

"You mean they…. they *went*?" Isabel's mouth gaped open in a mixture of horror and surprise, her eyes wide. "They actually……?"

Mac nodded. "The experiment went ahead as planned. And it was a success….to begin with."

"A success?" Isabel's eyes widened even further. "You mean they had…. a *baby*?"

"Yes, they did. A boy."

Isabel reached out and took back the photograph which was resting on Mac's knee. More tears pricked at her eyes now, but she let them fall. She wasn't sure if they were tears of joy or sorrow.

"But there's more…." continued Mac, gravely. "Andre is best placed to tell you the rest…."

"Tell me now." Isabel's voice was strong and firm. "I need to know now."

Mac sighed, shaking his head. "Your brother was born three months after they arrived on Salyut 7. Kreshniov's experiment had worked – the Phoenix Project was a success. At least, it was for a while. But not long afterwards, something went wrong. An accident."

"What kind of accident?"

Mac paused and watched Isabel continue to stare at the photograph in her hand. "An accident – Andre will fill you in on the details. But to cut a very long story short, the Project was aborted and everyone was ordered to return to base. The Phoenix Project founders were keen for the whole mess to be buried and forgotten. They couldn't risk news of the accident getting out into the public domain. They wanted your parents to live in the United States under assumed names, under their direct control. Your parents knew too much. They were a liability.

"But your parents refused. They wanted to come back to the UK, to come back to you. The founders of the Project made threats against their lives, so your parents went into hiding and Andre helped them to disappear. It's something he's good at – disappearing. At the time he had been involved in the Project as a senior technical advisor, and once the disaster had happened he, and your parents, disappeared."

Isabel looked up at Mac, her face awash with shock. *"Disappeared?"* she whispered, shaking her head. "What do you mean, *disappeared*?"

"Andre faked your parents' deaths, and his own, in order to stop the Phoenix Project founders from continuing to search for them. It was the only way to make the trail go cold. And it worked. Everyone thought your parents had died."

Isabel swallowed past the huge lump which had formed in her throat. "I know." Visions of her parents' graves filled her thoughts, and tears pricked at the corners of her eyes.

"But they've been in hiding ever since. So has Andre. When he disappeared, he took with him one set of Phoenix Project documents." Mac tapped the bulging paperwork in his lap. "This is the only other set in existence." He paused and caught Isabel's gaze. "And now the other members of the Project are after them…..and you."

"Why me?" Isabel's voice was small and faint. "What do they want with me?"

"You're a Faraday, Isabel. Simple as that. They still think your parents are dead, but they know that you are alive. And that the papers are missing. Your connection to the Phoenix Project makes you a target. A deadly target."

"So what do we do?" Isabel now looked truly frightened. She whipped her head round to look out of the window, wondering if anyone was watching them from the shadows of the petrol station forecourt.

CHAPTER NINE

"We go and see Andre." Mac started the ignition, and pulled away.

* * *

Time: 10.30am
Date: 7th November 2008
Location: Kings Street, Cambridge

Ronald Taylor walked as briskly as his 70 years would allow. He was careful to avoid the icy patches that had formed on the sheltered pavements overnight. The snowfall that had arrived during the night had now turned into a hardened ice-rink. He had already had one hip replaced and was in no hurry to get a matching pair.

The fog hadn't lifted and still clung to the chill air like a child's hand clings to its mother. He reached out and turned the handle to the front door of Taylor's' Artists' Supplies, but the door wouldn't budge. He paused, a small frown crossing his already well lined and creased forehead. He turned the handle once again, muttering under his breath, and heaved his whole body weight, such as it was, against the door – thinking that the old door was merely stuck again due to the cold and damp.

Again it failed to move. Ronald glanced up, adjusting his thick lensed spectacles perched on the end of his nose. The "closed" sign hung lopsidedly in the centre of the glass section of the door. He frowned once again, the lines on his forehead deepening. Peering closely through the door into the shop, with his nose pressed up against the glass panel, Ronald saw that the shop appeared to be empty. No sign of anything or anyone. And certainly no sign of Isabel.

He checked his pocket watch. 10.30am. Isabel should have been here hours ago. Not in all the time that Ronald had known her, had Isabel failed to turn up for work. And she was never, *ever* late. He checked over his shoulder and glanced down the road, almost expecting to see her jogging up the pavement through the fog towards him, breathlessly explaining that the bus had been late, the cat had spilt its milk, that she had lost her handbag. But the pavement was empty.

Ronald brought out his own set of keys from his pocket and quickly unlocked the door with a shaky hand. He pushed the door hard and then stepped inside the shop, the bell over his head jangling fiercely. He stepped over the pile of letters and envelopes which lay on the doormat and pulled the door shut behind him. Instinctively, he turned the "closed" sign over to "open."

"Isabel?" he called out, heading towards the back of the shop. "Are you there?" He peered into the stockroom and snapped on the light. It was empty.

He came back into the shop and sat down behind the desk. Picking up the phone, he quickly dialled Isabel's home number. He let it ring, and ring…..and ring. There was no answer. Maybe she's on her way, he thought, replacing the receiver thoughtfully.

Ronald then glanced down at the notepad in front of him. He immediately recognised Isabel's neat handwriting on the top sheet. "Mr Cartwright" the note said, "Viridian." Frowning once again., he looked back down at his pocket watch through squinted eyes.

"Isabel'" he muttered to himself, replacing the watch into his pocket. "Where the devil are you?"

*　*　*

Time: 12.15pm
Date: 7th November 2008
Location: Rue de Bougainvillea, Paris, France

Andre let his eyes wander, hungrily, over the rows and rows of breads, pastries and other mouth-watering delicacies lined up neatly on the counter in front of him.

"Monsieur Andre!" A slim girl appeared behind the counter, wiping her hands on her crisp white apron which was tied in a small, neat bow around her equally small, neat waist. It clung, suggestively, to her narrow hips.

CHAPTER NINE

She smiled at Andre, her perfect white teeth gleaming and her shining red lips parting. "It is good to see you again, no? What would you like today?"

"Hello, Marie," smiled Andre, his cheeks beginning to flush. "I….I'm not quite sure at the moment." He put a nervous hand up to his chin as he lowered his eyes back to the counter, away from Marie's inquisitive gaze.

"I 'ave not seen you for a while, Monsieur Andre," continued Marie, her chocolate brown eyes twinkling at him. Her jet black hair was pulled back from her face into a neat pony tail, tied with a delicate red ribbon which matched the hue of her lipstick. "I was beginning to think you were avoiding me, no?" She fixed Andre with her smouldering eyes, leaning forwards over the counter so that her face was only inches from his.

"I…I'm sorry, Marie," stammered Andre, quickly pulling himself back from the counter and moving down to the section holding the filled baguettes and rolls. He fidgeted awkwardly from one foot to the other, and cleared his throat which curiously felt very dry all of a sudden. "I've been…er…I've been a bit busy lately."

Marie pouted her lips and slid along the counter again so that she was directly in front of him once more. She spoke in a soft, low whisper. "I thought that after our last night together you had not liked me anymore, Monsieur Andre."

Andre's cheeks immediately flushed scarlet. He looked over his shoulder to see if they were being overheard. They were not. They were very much alone. "I..I…", he stammered once again.

"It's all right, Monsieur Andre! I am just…what do you English call it? Teasing with you?" Marie's laughter filled the small shop and Andre relaxed slightly, although his cheeks remained a burning hot red. Marie pushed herself back from the counter and waved a smooth, perfectly manicured hand towards her left – her long, elegant fingernails painted a deep shade of luscious red. "I have made some delicious fresh baguettes this morning, Monsieur Andre. With prawns, just the way you like them."

Andre looked longingly at the baguettes, and then back at the nails – remembering how they felt as they gently stroked his back, how they tickled and caressed. Andre shook his head and the vision vanished.

"Yes, yes – they look lovely, Marie." Andre nodded and cleared his throat, loudly. "I'll take two please."

Marie carefully picked up two large baguettes filled with prawns, lettuce and onions, and placed them onto the wooden chopping board in front of her. Deftly, she began to wrap them up in delicately thin greaseproof paper, then placed them inside a strong paper bag decorated with red, white and blue stripes.

"And I'll take another cheese salad baguette, please – and a ham salad one, too." Andre let his eyes wander over the length of the counter. "And four croissants and a large bowl of tuna salad."

Marie reached for the cheese and ham baguettes, looking up at Andre as she did so. "You are having friends to stay, no? Monsieur Andre?" Then she added, coyly. "Or have you worked up a very big appetite, you naughty boy."

Andre's already red cheeks flushed a deeper shade of crimson. "I…um..I have some friends who might pop by today, yes," he replied, lowering his head away from Marie's laughing gaze and concentrating on counting out the money in his pocket.

Marie continued to wrap the food and placed everything in the same large paper bag, sitting the tub of tuna salad on the top. She handed the package across the counter to Andre with another teasing smile.

"That will be 20 Euros and 25 cents, please, Monsieur Andre." She held out her hand, ready to take Andre's money. He handed her a 20 Euro note and some change, and as she took it she let her hand linger for a moment, letting her fingers glide slowly over Andre's outstretched hand.

"Keep…keep the change," he mumbled, quickly pulling his hand back and shoving it inside his pocket, safely out of the way. He took hold of the package with his other hand and turned to go.

"Thank you, Monsieur Andre," smiled Marie, placing the money inside the till and shutting the drawer. "Maybe I can see you again…sometime?" She cocked her head, playfully, to the side and pouted her full red lips. "Maybe we could go out? And then……?" Marie looked deeply into Andre's eyes, her own eyes dancing mischievously. She left the sentence unfinished.

CHAPTER NINE

Andre shuffled backwards towards the door. "Of..of course," he nodded, his voice trembling a little. "That would be….that would be nice. Can I…um..can I call you?"

"You can call me anytime you like, Monsieur Andre," Marie breathed. "Day or night."

Andre smiled sheepishly, and backed out of the shop, banging into the door frame as he did so. Marie gave a little giggle and another coy little wave as she watched him go.

* * *

Time: 12.15pm
Date: 7th November 2008
Location: Rue des Lyons, Paris, France

The sun was high in the sky when Mac pulled the car to a halt, its weak milky rays trying their best to warm the chilled Parisian air. He leant across Isabel and rummaged in the glove compartment above her knees. Inside there were street maps of all the major European cities, and Mac pulled out one for Paris and began to search.

"Where does he live?" asked Isabel, yawning. Although it hadn't been long since they had left the petrol station, she felt as though she must have dozed off. Her neck felt stiff and sore. She stretched her arms high above her head and peered across at the map now balanced on Mac's knees.

"I've no idea," replied Mac, slowly.

"But if…" Isabel frowned. "If you don't know where he lives, what are you looking for?" She watched as Mac's forefinger trailed over the streets of central Paris until he appeared to find what he was looking for and tapped the paper. "Can't you just phone him?"

Mac shook his head, re-folding and placing the map on the dashboard in front of him. "Too dangerous," he replied. "With telephones you can never tell who's listening in. Same with emails. Too easy to track and trace them." He glanced at his watch. "With any luck, we should just about make it though." He started the car's engine again and pulled back out into the Paris traffic.

"So," said Isabel, settling back into her seat again. "Are you going to tell me where we're going?"

"The library," replied Mac, swinging the car sharply to the left. "We should just about get there before it closes for the afternoon."

"The library?" frowned Isabel. "Why there?"

"Because," began Mac, glancing across at Isabel and half smiling. "That's how I find out things." Isabel's blank expression made Mac smile even more. "I'll show you when we get there."

All throughout the 15-minute journey into the centre of Paris, Mac regularly checked his rear view mirror and nervously glanced outside the side windows, searching for any signs that they were being followed. As far as he could tell, they weren't. So far, so good.

They arrived at the Rue de Lyon library, an impressive-looking building stretching high into the sky. Mac parked illegally on the opposite side of the road and jumped out.

"Quick." He gestured to Isabel to get out of the car. "We can't spend too long in here. And I can't leave this here for long either." He nodded at the car while grabbing Isabel's arm and pulling her across the road, dodging the early afternoon traffic. Car horns blared as they danced their way in and out between the bumpers.

Mac ran up the front steps of the library two at a time and pushed open the heavy front door. Inside it was warm and cosy, with a heavy smell of old musty books and parchment. Isabel followed, stopping to gaze up at the elegant high ceiling overhead, a look of instant awe melting onto her cold and frozen face. The walls of the library were wood panelled, with elegant carvings and inscriptions chiselled deep into their grain. Huge thick concrete columns lined the main thoroughfare through the library's ground floor, each bearing yet more intricate inscriptions and carvings around their trunks. Isabel stepped forwards to take a closer look, running her fingers across the deeply chiselled grooves. Gazing up, she followed the columns as they stretched up into the rafters of the ceiling above.

CHAPTER NINE

Behind the columns lining the ground floor were rows upon rows of shelving, crammed full to bursting with books and papers. Small wooden tables and benches sat in front of each row of shelving, inviting visitors to take the weight off their feet and immerse themselves in one of the many literary offerings the shelves provided.

Inside the library there was a deathly hush, the only sound being a gentle tap tapping noise coming from the information desk at the front. A young woman was sitting before a computer screen, intently entering data into the library computer terminal. She barely glanced up as Isabel and Mac silently padded past her, returning to her work without pausing.

"Quick," whispered Mac, still glancing nervously around him. "We haven't got time to stop and look at the architecture. This way." He again pulled at Isabel's arm and dragged her towards the lifts and staircase at the rear of the ground floor.

Beside the lifts was a huge plaque attached to the wall, detailing the various floors of the library and what book sections could be found on each. Mac's eyes darted from one section to the other before he found what he was looking for. "Deuxieme floor," he murmured to Isabel, holding up two fingers. "Second floor." Grabbing hold of Isabel yet again, he began to jog up the wide staircase.

"What are we...?" But Isabel didn't have time to finish her sentence. Mac held his finger up to his lips and continued to drag her up the steps.

"Sssshhhhh," he hushed. "I'll explain when we get out. Just follow me, and don't run off."

At the top of the staircase, Mac turned to his left and skirted the second floor, glancing quickly at the shelving as he passed by. About halfway down the aisle he stopped, glanced back over his shoulder to see if anybody was about, and then side stepped closer to the shelving. Isabel followed, obediently, watching as Mac began scouring the titles of the books on show. He lightly ran his finger over the spines of the books, searching, searching, searching. Isabel glanced up at the sign overhead.

"Jardinage," it said. Isabel's schoolgirl French was not too great but even she understood this to mean that they were in the gardening section.

Mac suddenly breathed in sharply, and his finger came to a rest on a large, fat book on the very bottom shelf. It was hidden right in the corner, almost out of sight. Mac gently pulled out the book and placed it on the floor at his feet. Kneeling down he opened the book and began flicking through the pages. Isabel peered curiously over his shoulder, noticing that the title of the book was "Un Jardin Parisian Chalet" by someone called Pierre Bateaux.

It only took a few seconds. Mac stopped skimming through the pages and let the book fall open. Tucked into the middle of the book was a small piece of paper. Mac slid the paper out and shut the book, returning it to the shelf where he had found it. He pushed himself back to his feet and turned to face Isabel, holding up the piece of paper in front of her so that she could read it.

"Flat 7, Rue de Bougainvillea."

Isabel looked questioningly at Mac. "Is that…?"

Mac nodded and pocketed the piece of paper. "Andre's address, yes."

"But how did you know it was there?"

Mac smiled as they both turned and headed back towards the staircase. "It's just a little game of Andre's. He's been doing it for years. Whenever we want to send sensitive messages or information to each other, we leave a message inside one of the books at the local library. Easy."

Isabel was still frowning as they exited the library and jogged back down the steps towards the car. "But…how do you know which book to look at? Is it always the same one?"

Mac snatched up Isabel's hand and guided her across the increasingly busy road once again, relieved to see that the car was still parked where they had left it. And there was no parking ticket. "No, it's always a different book. We'll text or email each other with the title of the book – even if someone intercepts it, it won't mean anything to them."

Mac opened the door for Isabel, and waited while she slipped inside, grateful to be out of the biting wind.

"But…" Isabel was still frowning as Mac got into the driver's seat. "But what happens if someone comes in and takes out the book you're looking

CHAPTER NINE

for?"

Mac laughed. "That's the clever bit. The messages are always left in books that can't be taken out on loan. Just reference only books. Andre is a whiz with computers, and he can hack into any computer network in the world. He just gets himself into the library's computer system, finds out what titles are reference only books, and bingo." Mac started the engine and pulled out into a steady stream of traffic. "He will have nipped in here earlier today and slipped the note inside."

"But.." Isabel cast her mind back to the young woman who was sitting behind the information desk when they first went inside. She had been tapping information into her computer, no doubt oblivious to the fact that someone like Andre could be doing exactly the same thing somewhere else, possibly even at the same time.

"It's a bit like you and your personal columns, in the newspaper," said Mac. "A way of communicating that no one else knows about – something secret."

Isabel thought back to the message columns in the newspapers that she and Miles would use. She gave a half smile as she remembered, but then stopped. She turned to Mac, her eyes narrowing. "But they weren't so secret after all, were they?"

"What do you mean?"

"Well, *you* knew about them, didn't you?" Isabel looked inquisitively at Mac. "How did you find out about that anyway? I take it that it was you who placed the ad in the paper. As far as I was aware, no one else knew about it."

Mac laughed and swung the car into a side street. "I wondered how long it would be before you asked me that."

"Well? How did you know?"

"That's one for Andre. He'll have to explain it to you."

"Very convenient," sniffed Isabel, staring again out of the passenger window. She watched as they headed down a wide avenue, lined with pavement cafés and restaurants already open for the afternoon trade. Chairs and tables sat on the pavements, hopeful that a few plucky souls would brave the weather and sit outside on a cold November day.

They sat in silence for the rest of the journey. Mac successfully negotiated the enormous roundabout at the Arc de Triomphe and headed down the Champs Elysees. About half way along, he took a right hand turn across the traffic and headed down into a smaller, narrower side street, Rue de Bougainvillea. He parked at the side of the road behind several small dusty looking motor scooters, and a bright yellow Smart car.

Mac nodded across the road towards a boulangerie and delicatessen. "It's over there. Just above that bakery." Isabel leaned across and looked out of Mac's side window. "I'll get out first and go over. If it's OK I'll wave you across, all right?"

Mac got out of the car and jogged silently across the deserted street. The bakery was open and doing a brisk lunchtime business. Inside a queue of hungry Parisians snaked their way from the counter towards the door, which was firmly shut to keep out the chilly November air. No one paid any attention to Mac as he hovered outside.

Isabel watched from the car as Mac pressed a small button at the side of the door next to the bakery. A few seconds later she saw him bend his head towards the intercom, give a brief nod, and then beckon her over with his hand.

* * *

Time: 11.45am
   Date: 7th November 2008
   Location: Green Park Parade, Cambridge

"Cambridgeshire Police, how can I help you?"

"I'd...I'd like to report a missing person." Ronald's voice was small and quavering. He had to hold the telephone receiver in both hands to stop them shaking. He had waited in the shop for Isabel to appear, but she

CHAPTER NINE

hadn't. Time ticked away slowly, and still she didn't arrive or call – so he had walked over to her flat, hoping to find her tucked up on the sofa watching a black and white movie, having forgotten she was meant to be opening the shop today. Ronald knew that was unlikely, as Isabel never forgot the days she was opening up, but he clung to the thought just the same.

"What's the name please?"

"Um…her name is Isabel….Isabel Faraday."

"And you are?"

"I'm Mr Taylor – Ronald Taylor. She works for me. Except she didn't turn up for work today…." Ronald's voice tailed off.

"OK, Mr Taylor. Try not to worry. Does she have any family she lives with? Husband? Boyfriend? Parents?"

"No..no." Ronald swallowed, trying to dislodge the hard lump that had formed in his throat. "She doesn't have anyone."

"All right then, Mr Taylor. I'm sure she'll be fine. But I'll get an officer to come out and see you, take down some more details. Where are you, Mr Taylor?"

Ronald Taylor glanced around the room, his eyes wide open and frightened. His hands began to tremble. "I'm…I'm in Isabel's flat. Someone's been in here…broken in. The place is a mess. I think someone must have taken her."

CHAPTER TEN

Time: 1.00pm
   Date: 7th November 2008
   Location: Flat 7, Rue de Bougainvillea, Paris, France

Andre handed Isabel a steaming hot cup of coffee and then perched himself on the end of his computer desk. He smiled at her while she sipped.

"It's good to see you at last, Isabel," he said. "Good to see you here, safe and sound."

Isabel drank deeply from the cup, grateful for the warmth now spreading through her body. She hadn't realised how cold she had become in the car, but now felt her fingers and toes tingling in Andre's warm front room. She hesitated before answering.

"I'm still not quite sure why I'm here," she said, looking up at Andre, questioningly.

"Hasn't Mac…?" Andre darted a quick look over at Mac, who had collapsed onto the sofa next to Isabel and was resting his head back against the cushions, his eyes closed. He replied without opening them.

"I've told her everything about the Project, Andre, don't worry. She's been told it all."

"Doesn't mean to say I believe it though," Isabel muttered, taking several more gulps from her coffee.

"Of course," continued Andre, nodding and watching Isabel carefully. "It's a lot to take in. But you're here. That's the important thing." He paused. "Mac showed you the papers?"

CHAPTER TEN

Isabel nodded. "He showed me something, yes." She faltered, and stared down into the bottom of her now empty coffee cup. "Not sure I really understand it all though." She absentmindedly squeezed the prism charm between her fingers.

Andre nodded. "And you have the necklace – the Prism. Out of which was born the Phoenix Project. All members of the Project were given one." He caught Isabel's eye and beckoned her over to his desk. "Come over here. I've got something else to show you."

Isabel hesitated momentarily before getting to her feet. "Where are they? When can I see them?" Her eyes bore into Andre's, and he could see they had been rubbed red from tears. He smiled comfortingly.

"Soon…soon," he murmured, softly. "But I need to show you this first." He nodded to a chair in front of the computer screen, and Isabel slid herself into it. Andre then went over to his sagging bookshelf and climbed back up the small step ladder to reach the top level. He pulled down the fat leather book once again and brought it over to Isabel, placing it on the desk in front of her. She watched as he again took the small silver key from around his neck and snapped open the lock. Isabel's eyes widened with surprise when she saw the large compartment inside the book and not the pages and pages of literature she had been expecting. Andre took out a disc from a thin, red sleeve and quickly slid it into the computer's disc drive. It took a few seconds for the disc to load – the only sound in the room being the whirring from the computer and deep, heavy breathing coming from Mac now fast asleep on the sofa.

"I've been keeping these," explained Andre, in a low voice. "Just in case."

Isabel looked at the screen and visibly stiffened. "Are they………..?" Her voice cut off as she saw image after image flickering before her.

Andre nodded. "Yes. They are your parents. Some pictures are from before you were born, others after."

Isabel took control of the mouse and scrolled through the pictures before her, clicking on each one in turn to enlarge them. She instantly saw pictures of her parents' happy, smiling faces beaming out at her – she saw them relaxing on holiday, working in the garden, pottering around at home. Instinctively, Isabel brought her hand up and gently touched their faces, running her fingers down the screen as if she could feel them. It was the closest she had been to them in twenty years.

"You knew them?" she asked, her voice sounding small and lost. "My parents?"

Andre nodded slowly and brought another chair over to sit next to her. He sat down and removed the disc from the computer. "I was the Senior Technical Advisor for the Phoenix Project. I got to know your parents very well – they became good friends of mine."

"This…this Phoenix Project…?" muttered Isabel, slowly, still touching the blank computer screen as if her parents' images were still visible. "It really existed? They really were a part of it?"

Andre nodded and leant forwards in his chair, resting his elbows on his knees. He clasped his fingers together, tightly, as if in solemn prayer. "It existed, yes. Very much so. Despite all the attempts to cover it up. At the time, we all thought we were on the threshold of a discovery which would change the world as we knew it. To open up the universe to something which had only ever been dreamt of before. Survival in space was to become a reality – no longer just a fantasy. No longer something you read about in a science fiction magazine. We had hard, concrete evidence that it could work – that it *would* work. It was to be the answer to so many problems – overcrowded planets, war, disease, famine. The possibilities were endless. As endless as the Universe itself."

Andre paused, his eyes becoming glassy. He stared out, vacantly, far into the corner of the room. "It could be done," his voice now a whisper. "People could actually live in space, in specially designed capsules continuously pumped through with breathable air, all waste materials removed. It was perfect. If the planet was ever compromised through war or disease, life would be possible somewhere else. And who knew where that could eventually lead to. It was a stepping stone – a step towards the discovery of life on other planets."

Isabel broke her gaze from the blank computer screen. There was a heavy silence in the air. Andre's hands were still clasped tightly together,

CHAPTER TEN

so tightly that Isabel could see the whites of his knuckles showing through.

"Why didn't I know anything about it?" Isabel eventually broke the silence. "How could my parents have disappeared…..with my *brother*…..and I never knew about it until now?"

Andre sat perfectly still, continuing to stare unblinkingly into the far reaches of his front room. Isabel watched him, wondering if he had heard her. He appeared to be in some kind of trance-like state, his mind detached. After what seemed like an eternity, Andre leant back in his chair and unclenched his fingers. His voice was low, almost inaudible to begin with.

"What you have to appreciate is that, at the time, it sounded so fantastic. Everyone was caught up in the frenzy of being on the brink of the greatest discovery known to man." He paused and turned to Isabel, managing a half smile. "Is there life on other planets, Isabel? Some people believe there must be, others don't. Some don't give a damn either way. But just supposing there was, sometime in the future, the discovery that another planet in the solar system could support life." Andre paused again, leaning further forward towards Isabel, his eyes no longer glassy. He no longer had a dazed, vacant, trance-like expression on his face – his eyes now burned with a fire, a fire fuelled by passion.

"If we had already developed the technology to enable our species to live in space, we would be one step closer to proving what had *never* been proved before. Life *could* really exist outside of planet Earth." Andre's voice was louder now, his tone urgent and excited. "When PRISM set up the Phoenix Project, the results started coming in thick and fast. The Project was a small unit, a handpicked team. But it was not something that could become common knowledge, not at that time. Not until we were sure. More field tests were undertaken, and teams sent up to Salyut 7 to live inside the prototype capsule that had been developed. The initial results were breathtaking. It was working. It really *was* working.

"Your parents were recruited and the experiment took on a new focus. When the time was right, they joined our technicians on Salyut 7 and everything worked perfectly. The Phoenix Project really was a success. Your brother was born and……"

Andre stopped suddenly and shifted in his seat. He turned to Isabel, and she noticed that the fiery passion that had been burning so fiercely in his eyes had somehow died – replaced by a haunted, empty look.

"But then things changed. Three of our technicians were doing a routine check of the airflow system. Everything was computerised on board the module – airflow, air content, waste product readings, humidity, everything. And any abnormalities would show up on the system, detected *before* they became a problem. The computers were showing that everything was fine, no problems, so the technicians went into one of the capsules to do some routine maintenance. They became trapped inside – the locking mechanism of the sealing door had frozen fast and wouldn't let them back out." Andre paused, forcing himself to swallow past the lump in his throat. "There had been some kind of electrical short circuit, and nothing would make it budge. The door was sealed tight. The short circuit also affected the airflow to the capsule, effectively paralysing it. No air was getting in, and no waste products getting out." Andre's voice cracked slightly as he held Isabel's gaze. "The three of them suffocated.

"Everyone was ordered to return - your parents included. A space craft was sent up to remove them as soon as news of the accident reached the Project's headquarters."

"And then they disappeared," finished Isabel, quietly.

"Yes," nodded Andre. "Then they disappeared."

* * *

Time: 2.00pm
   Date: 7th November 2008
   Location: Metropolitan Police HQ, London

"Don't forget those dates." Jack slammed the passenger door shut and headed for the station's front door. He pulled his suit jacket firmly around himself as the chilly early afternoon breeze threatened to slice through him like a sword. He half turned to see DS Cooper following in his wake.

CHAPTER TEN

"I need to know what they mean."

"I'm onto it," nodded DS Cooper, jogging up the steps behind Jack. "What are you going to be doing now? Calling it a day? I can write up the notes on Stavaros; such as they are."

Jack hesitated at the door, and instinctively reached up into his breast pocket. His head was still throbbing, and his body aching like anything after his fitful night's sleep. And he had only felt worse as the day had progressed and now needed something to take his mind off it.

"That's not the answer, Jack." DS Cooper watched as Jack's fingers slipped inside his breast pocket, and shook his head. "How many days has it been now?"

"Thirty-eight – not that I'm counting."

"Well, don't ruin it now. Come on." DS Cooper grabbed hold of Jack's arm and pulled him inside. "I'm going to get you a strong cup of coffee to banish those cravings."

"And then you're gonna look at those dates for me," replied Jack, allowing himself to be dragged towards the canteen.

"And then I'll look at those dates – promise."

* * *

Time: 3.00pm
Date: 7th November 2008
Location: MI6 Secret Intelligence Service HQ, Vauxhall Cross, London

Charles Tindleman sat behind his desk and eyed the manila folder in front of him. Simon Shafer shifted nervously in his seat opposite.

"Remind me, Simon, "spoke Tindleman, raising his gaze from the folder up into Shafer's wide eyes. "How long have you worked for MI6?"

Shafer cleared his throat before replying. "About 15, 16 years, Sir." Shafer watched as Tindleman nodded, thoughtfully, and once again lowered his eyes to the desk behind which his ample frame nestled. Shafer had been inside his boss's office quite regularly, and always viewed the man as a fair and approachable person. They had never crossed swords before…..until now.

"Yes, yes, "murmured Tindleman, letting his hand rest on the manila folder. "That's what I thought. An experienced officer of some 16 years' service, Simon. 16 years' exemplary service, I might add." He paused and raised his piercing blue eyes to meet Shafer's once again. "So what went wrong?"

Shafer tried to quietly clear his throat again, but failed and just made a strangled gurgling sound. "I…I don't know what to say, Sir. I'm really sorry. I'll..I'll do anything to help put it right."

"And that you will," concurred Tindleman, standing up and walking over to a large, metal filing cabinet that stood next to the floor to ceiling windows. Wrenching open one of the drawers, Tindleman reached in and pulled out a single sheet of paper. "You are on the next Eurostar service to Paris. Working with Special Agent John Fleming. These are your instructions."

Tindleman returned to his desk and handed the sheet of paper to Shafer, who had already risen from his seat. "I want you to find those papers you so carelessly lost, and bring them back to me. Here. Do I make myself clear?"

Shafer took the paper and nodded. "Crystal, Sir. Crystal."

With a curt nod of the head, Shafer was dismissed.

* * *

Time: 3.20pm
   Date: 7th November 2008
   Location: Metropolitan Police HQ, London

"Don't worry." Chief Superintendent Liddell nodded his head slowly to himself as he spoke. "I know just the person. Just wait a minute." Liddell listened to the reply and then placed the call on hold. Pausing for just a second, he pressed the intercom button which connected him through to

CHAPTER TEN

his secretary's office outside. "Penny? Could you page DI MacIntosh for me, please? Ask him to come to my office right away."

Liddell released the intercom button and leant back in his chair. Lacing his fingers underneath his immaculately shaven chin, he let his eyes fall upon his personal diary which was still lying open on the desk in front of him. He reached forward and closed the pages, returning the book to the central drawer.

Liddell then returned to his telephone call, pressing down the hold button and resuming the connection.

"I'll brief him as soon as he gets here," said Liddell, leaning forwards and resting his elbows on the leather bound desk. He had rolled up his shirt sleeves and loosened his collar a little. He was beginning to feel warm. "And yes, I'll only tell him as much as he needs to know. What do you take me for?"

A hint of exasperation entered Liddell's voice, and he slowly rubbed his tired eyes. He listened to the sarcastic response from the other end of the telephone, but did not take the bait. He was too tired. He did not have the energy to argue.

"Look, none of this mess was my doing if you care to remember," he continued, his voice gruff. "I didn't ask to be involved in the Phoenix Project or any part of it. They came to me." Liddell paused, collecting his thoughts. "Salyut 7 was a mistake, and you know it. They should have waited for MIR and then maybe none of this would have happened. I thought they were going to wait for MIR – that's what I agreed to. I never agreed to bloody Salyut 7." The words were beginning to stick in Liddell's throat and he poured himself a glass of water from the decanter sitting on the corner of his desk. He savoured the cool taste as it slipped down the back of his throat, but wished he had something stronger. "But hell no – they had to rush ahead and use something not fully designed for the job." Liddell paused once again and listened to the chaste reply. He started to shake his head. "No, that's not true. That's damn well not true. The experiment was meant to be on MIR. End of story. There was no talk of Salyut 7 – bloody hell, I'd never even *heard* of the thing before. You were there the whole time. You know that."

Liddell drained his glass. "It haunts me, you know." A heavy weariness entered his voice, and he sighed as he spoke. "I go to bed thinking about the bloody Phoenix Project, and I wake up thinking about the bloody Phoenix Project. I wish I'd never got involved. And I wish I'd never heard of the damn Faradays."

Liddell closed his eyes and exhaled deeply. "It has to stop. Now. It has to." The voice on the other end of the line attempted a response, but Liddell wasn't convinced by what he heard. "So you keep saying, so you keep saying. But how can I believe that? It should never have come to this in the first place. We should never have been put in this position. *Never.*"

Liddell paused and immediately his cheeks flushed red. "This is *not* about the money, damn you! This is about bloody Salyut 7 being used when it shouldn't have been! Plain and simple. Everything stems from that. The accident, Kreshniov, everything. Have you spoken to Charles about this yet? Well, see that you do, because he's even madder than I am!"

Liddell's outburst was broken by a firm tapping on his office door. The door opened and Jack walked in, his face unable to disguise the sense of intrigue he felt at having been summonsed to see the big boss. It wasn't often you were specifically called for, ordered to attend. And it was a bit like being sent for by the school headmaster.

Jack had only been inside Liddell's office on three occasions – and all of those had been for raps on the knuckles and one very severe dressing down. The room did not exactly hold happy memories for him, and it was with some degree of trepidation that he slowly walked over to Liddell's desk.

"You wanted to see me, Sir?" Jack hovered behind the chair, making no attempt to sit down. He wasn't sure whether or not he was supposed to be making himself comfortable. He watched as Liddell hastily returned the telephone receiver to its cradle and began straightening his tie.

"Yes, MacIntosh, yes I did," replied Liddell, clearing his throat and gesturing with his hands for Jack to take a seat. "Please sit down."

Jack hesitated briefly before lowering himself down into the vacant chair

CHAPTER TEN

directly opposite his superior. The seat was hard and very uncomfortable. Jack perched on the edge and awaited his fate.

"I have a rather...how can I put it... a rather delicate situation on which I would like your assistance."

Jack raised his eyebrows but remained silent.

"A young woman has gone missing in Cambridge – failed to show up for work this morning. Her employer checked her home address – looks like someone has been there, torn the place apart. And no one's seen her since."

Jack nodded, slowly. "OK."

"I'm getting all the information on the case fed through to me here. I'd like you to manage the case from this end."

"A missing person?" Jack frowned and shifted, uncomfortably, on the hard chair. "Surely someone from uniform could......?"

Liddell held up his hand to cut Jack short. "I realise that, but I'm doing this as a kind of favour for a friend. I used to know the family quite well, so I feel like I should be involved in some way. Call it a sense of duty, whatever. I would just like to try and find out what happened to her. And quickly."

Jack nodded, slowly. "And she went missing from Cambridge? Surely that's a bit off our patch?"

Liddell passed Jack a thin manila coloured folder. "The Cambridgeshire force are happy to hand it over – all the paperwork gathered so far is right here. She's a woman by the name of Faraday. Isabel Faraday."

Jack glanced down at the file he now held in his hands. It was thin – very thin. There could be no more than two or three pieces of paper inside.

"Are they sure it's a suspicious disappearance?" Jack opened the file and quickly scanned the meagre contents. "She's not just upped and gone away for a couple of days? Left her flat in a bit of a mess?"

Liddell shook his head and nodded towards the folder. "Sadly not. It's all in the file there. She was due to report for work this morning, but never showed up. Completely out of character according to her employer. He went over to her flat and was convinced the place had been ransacked."

Jack shrugged and tucked the folder under his arm. "Ok. I'll see what I can come up with."

Liddell nodded and rose from his chair, indicating that the impromptu meeting was now at an end. He walked with Jack across the room towards the door.

"Keep me informed, won't you?" said Liddell as Jack turned to go. "I'd like to know what you come up with, however small."

Jack nodded and waved the folder in the air as a kind of salute before disappearing. Liddell closed the door behind him and leant heavily against it, momentarily shutting his eyes. He took a deep breath and pulled out his mobile phone. He hit the keypad and waited for the call to be answered.

"It's done," he said, curtly, keeping his voice low. "I just hope you know what you're doing."

* * *

Time: 4.15pm
    Date: 7th November 2008
    Location: MI6 Secret Intelligence Service HQ, Vauxhall Cross, London

Simon Shafer closed the door to his office on the top floor of Vauxhall Cross and hurried over to his desk. Lifting the telephone receiver, he paused and listened for any movements outside in the corridor or in neighbouring offices. There was none. It was deathly quiet. Sundays were always a quiet day, and for that Shafer was thankful. He dialled the number from memory and it was answered on the first ring.

"It's me." Shafer kept his voice low even though the upper floor of the building appeared to be deserted. "I'm coming to Paris. Tindleman is sending me." Shafer paused as he listened to the voice on the other end of the phone. "How do I know? He seemed to buy the fact that I was just a stupid bumbling idiot who left top secret files in a taxi cab…..but I have no idea what he really thinks. He's a smart man." Again Shafer paused, and nodded slowly. "OK, well, I'll catch up with you when I arrive. But I won't

CHAPTER TEN

be alone. Fleming is coming with me."

Shafer put the telephone receiver down and checked his watch. He should be getting on the tube to catch the Eurostar. But what he needed to do would only take a few minutes. Quickly waking up his computer from sleep mode, he accessed his personal email file and began the process of deleting its contents.

Time: 10.30pm
Date: 7th November 2008
Location: Flat 7, Rue de Bougainvillea, Paris, France

Mac yawned and stretched out across the sofa. He had no idea how long he had been asleep, but Andre's apartment was now dark and quiet. He felt his legs aching painfully from being crumpled underneath his body for so long. As he looked up through half closed eyes, he noticed a light on from the direction of the kitchen.

Isabel was sitting at the kitchen table nursing a tall glass of water. A smile flickered over her lips as she saw Mac's dishevelled figure appearing in the doorway.

"Good sleep?" she enquired, as Mac slumped into the chair opposite her. He yawned again and ran a hand through his unkempt hair.

"Mmmmmmm," he mumbled. "You?"

Isabel shook her head. "No – too much going on up here." She tapped the front of her forehead. "Couldn't sleep."

Mac nodded and poured himself a glass of water from the jug in front of them. "Did Andre…..explain everything?"

Isabel nodded her head, slowly. "I think so….most of it. Some of it." She shrugged and sighed, deeply. "I don't know. There's so much to take in."

Mac gulped down his water and poured himself another glass. "He obviously didn't quite tell you all of it then. I didn't think he would."

Isabel frowned. "What do you mean?"

"The technicians? He told you about the ones who were trapped in the capsule? The ones that died?" Mac paused, holding the glass of water in front of his lips. "One of them was his fiancé."

"His fiancé?" Isabel's' voice was barely a whisper. "But he never said………."

Mac nodded. "It's not something he likes to talk about much. He only told me recently. I think he feels guilty, responsible in some way."

"How could he be responsible?"

Mac gave a shrug. "He was in charge of the technical data for the Project. He felt he must have missed something, made a mistake somewhere along the line."

"But surely he couldn't have known what was going to happen – it was an accident, right?"

Mac nodded again, draining the last of his water from the glass. "I know. But he still feels responsible all the same. And it didn't help that the rest of the Phoenix Project members were quick to blame him too. Along with Poborski. They need a scapegoat, someone to pin all the blame onto as to why the experiment went so disastrously wrong. Don't forget, most of the money invested in the Project came from the Soviet Union, via Karl Poborski's contacts. The Soviets were demanding answers as to why they had just seen their investment go up in smoke."

"But even so………."

"Andre left PRISM and the Phoenix Project pretty soon after the accident. Just disappeared one day, along with your parents. Kreshniov himself went not long afterwards. Andre left it all behind, came to Europe, and lost himself."

"Lost himself? How do you lose yourself?"

Mac's tired face managed a small smile. "When you're Andre, losing yourself is the easiest thing in the world. There's not much that he doesn't know about computers – he can hack into the most secure networks anywhere in the globe and within minutes create a false identity. Up until then, André Baxter didn't even exist. Up until then he was Gustav Friedman. But after he ran from the Phoenix Project, Gustav was no more, and Andre was created."

Isabel merely shook her head. "I had no idea…"

CHAPTER TEN

"Andre is a very private man. He doesn't open up very easily, especially about this. But the protection of the Project and the evidence surrounding it meant everything to him. The rest of the Phoenix Project wanted the whole sorry mess dead and buried, destroyed – treated as though it had never happened at all. Like it had never existed. They were frightened of what would happen if any of it got made public. They wanted it erased, forever; deleted from memory. But Andre wouldn't and won't ever let that happen. If the evidence of the project is destroyed, then memories of what happened there are also destroyed. And memories, I suppose, are all he has left."

"So what now?" asked Isabel. "What do we do?"

"Andre knows a newspaper editor here in Paris, someone who owes him a few favours. He's willing to talk to us, off the record. We'll go and see him, take him the papers, and see if he'll print the story."

"You think that's wise?" Isabel raised her eyebrows. "Making it public like that?"

"Why not?" frowned Mac, rubbing his chin with his fingers, feeling the prickle of two days' growth of stubble. "What other choice is there? There are people searching for us, Isabel. Trained killers. They'll kill whoever they have to, to get to the documents. People searching for you, searching for a true Faraday. We can't just sit on them and hope they'll go away. Because they won't. If we bring it all out into the open, it's the best protection we can get."

"And my parents? Are they safe? Where are they?"

Mac shrugged. "I'm not sure. I haven't actually seen them myself, but Andre's got it all sorted. He told me you'd see them soon."

Isabel's face took on a downcast expression. "OK." She gave herself a rueful smile. "I guess I can wait a little longer," she sighed. "Look, I'm going to go and lie down for a while. My head's banging." She rubbed her forehead, only just realising how tired she felt.

Mac nodded as Isabel got up and left the tiny kitchen, padding back towards the front room. She noticed that Andre was standing by the window, curtains pulled back, gazing up at the night sky. She quietly crept into the room, lurking in the shadows by the bookcase, not wanting to disturb. She spied her cardigan draped over the sofa, and gently tip toed towards it.

"Beautiful, isn't it?" Andre turned around and held Isabel in his gaze, his face bathed in the moonlight shining through the window. "The night sky. Beautiful, don't you think?" He turned back towards the night and continued to stare up at the inky black sky, everywhere littered with hundreds and hundreds of shiny, sparkling stars winking down at them.

Isabel retrieved her cardigan and edged over to join Andre at the window. She followed his gaze, taking in the array of twinkling, blinking spots of light dancing before her. The night was cold and clear, perfect for star gazing. She glanced down and saw that Andre was holding something in his hand – a picture, a small photograph, slightly worn around the edges. Angling her head to one side, Isabel saw that it was the picture of a young woman with long, sleek jet-black hair tied back off her face, with a perfect white smile.

Andre noticed her look. "She's my Stephanie." He carried on looking intently up into the night sky. "I often just stand here and look up at the sky…look up into the night. Into the darkness." He paused and then pointed with his hand at a star directly ahead of them which seemed to be shining far brighter than the rest of them. "See that star? That's my Steph looking down on me, watching over me. That's her star." Andre's voice tailed off, as both he and Isabel gazed at the star. The longer they looked at it, the brighter it seemed to burn. "When the sun shines in the morning, that's my Stephanie laughing. She had such a warm laugh, brought a glow to anyone who heard it." Andre smiled and glanced back down at the photograph in his hand. "And when it rains, that's my Stephanie's tears."

With one last long look up at the bright night sky, André turned and left the room, stopping only to slip a small silver key on a chain into the desk drawer, and Stephanie's picture back inside his pocket.

CHAPTER ELEVEN

Time: 8.12am
   Date: 8th November 2008
   Location: Flat 7, Rue de Bougainvillea, Paris, France

"You need to be careful," warned Andre, keeping his voice low. He edged closer to Mac, keen for Isabel not to overhear. "You're being followed."

"Followed?" Mac looked up sharply, his mouth full. He dropped the croissant he had been eating back down onto his plate and licked his lips. "Who the hell by?"

"I'm told its FBI – someone by the name of Fleming. John Fleming. Special Agent out of the Washington DC field office."

"*FBI?*" Mac's eyes widened. "How the hell did they get involved in this?"

Andre shrugged. "I guess the Project founders are getting nervous. Probably Edwards putting his feelers out. He has contacts in all sorts of places. I'll bet that news of the lost documents had filtered through by now." He paused for a second. "They'll need to hush this up, and quick. They need to get their hands on those papers and destroy them – before it destroys them. And they'll need all the help they can get. Edwards has a lot of contacts in Washington. I'm not surprised the FBI are in on it."

"So, are we safe here?" Mac looked instinctively over his shoulder at the door. "Do they know where we are?"

Andre shook his head. "I think you're safe enough here for the moment. But it won't take long for them to catch up. Go ahead with the meeting this morning, then we'll figure out what to do about Special Agent Fleming."

THE PHOENIX PROJECT

* * *

Time: 9.27am
   Date: 8th November 2008
   Location: Metropolitan Police HQ, London

Jack quickly scanned the tables in the canteen. It didn't take long before he found what he was looking for. He poured himself a cup of coffee from the self-service machine by the counter, grabbed a packet of digestive biscuits, and indicated to the woman standing by the till that he would settle up with her later.

The woman smiled a knowing smile and rolled her eyes towards the fluorescent strip lighting overhead. Detective Inspector Jack MacIntosh was well known in the station's canteen. His inability to pay for anything he selected was legendary. He ran up quite a tab on occasions.

Jack quietly slipped into the vacant seat next to DS Cooper, who he found was nursing a mug of steaming tea and a hot, bacon sandwich. DS Cooper looked up as he sunk his teeth into the soft white bread, a thin trickle of red tomato sauce oozing out of the corner and dripping down his chin.

"Good?" enquired Jack, watching as his colleague wiped away the sauce with the back of his hand. He nodded towards the sandwich DS Cooper had just dropped back onto his plate.

"Mmmmm," murmured DS Cooper. "Not bad."

Jack took a sip of his coffee and grimaced. He had forgotten the sugar. Coffee without sugar made his cigarette cravings ten times worse.

"What did the boss want you for?" asked DS Cooper, taking a long gulp of his tea and picking up the sandwich again. "I heard on the grapevine that you'd been summonsed upstairs."

"I'm not sure exactly," frowned Jack, thinking back to his conversation with Chief Superintendent Liddell. "Something about a missing person case, but…I don't know." Jack shrugged and sipped at the bitter coffee once again.

CHAPTER ELEVEN

"So what can I do for you?" DS Cooper eyes Jack, knowingly. "I'm pretty sure you didn't come in here just to sample the coffee and watch me eat my breakfast."

Jack managed a smile. "I need you to do something for me."

"I thought as much," replied DS Cooper, smiling as he chewed. "What do you want this time?"

"If I were to say Salyut 7 to you, what would spring to mind?"

"Sally, what?"

"Seven – Salyut 7," repeated Jack. "Not sure of the spelling. Ever heard of it?"

DS Cooper shook his head. "Nope. Never. What's it to do with?"

"I'm not sure." Jack rubbed his chin, thoughtfully. "It's just something I overheard. I need you to do some digging around for me – look up a few things and see what you come up with."

"OK. About this sally thing?"

Jack nodded and reached into his jacket pocket, bringing out a folded piece of paper. He slid it across the table towards DS Cooper. "It's all on there. Salyut 7, plus some other stuff. See what you can find out – and don't forget those dates I told you about, either."

DS Cooper took the piece of paper and nodded. "OK, sure. You think they're all connected? This sally whatsit, and the dates?"

Jack shrugged. "No idea, but keep it to yourself. Don't let anyone find out what you're doing – especially Liddell.

* * *

Time: 11.26am
    Date: 8th November 2008
    Location: Eiffel Tower, Paris, France

"So, who is he?" Isabel's voice was breathless as she jogged to try and keep up with Mac, who was striding out purposefully in front of her.

"Albert Dupont," replied Mac, glancing back over his shoulder at regular intervals as they headed up the slight incline of the Champs Elysees. "Editor in Chief of the Paris Tribune. Covers major international stories, mostly with US or British perspectives. Has a huge circulation and reputation here in Paris and throughout France. A bit like the Times back home."

"And he believes us?" questioned Isabel, raising her eyebrows. "Just like that?"

"Well, maybe not exactly," admitted Mac, pulling his black woollen hat down firmly over his ears to keep out the chill of the early November air. He steered Isabel across the road. "Andre says he doesn't know the exact details of the story yet. But he's a good friend of Andre's, and Andre has fed him many a good story over the years so he kind of trusts his instincts."

"You think he'll print it?" asked Isabel, burying her chin into the thick black scarf Mac had insisted she wear before they set out.

"I'm banking on it," replied Mac. "I don't think Andre knows who else to turn to if this doesn't work out. He won't want to risk going back to the UK with this again." He patted the outside of his puffer jacket, behind which he had concealed the folder containing the Phoenix Project documents. "Kind of makes me a bit of a target, carrying this around with me." He looked nervously over his shoulder once again. "You don't have to come with me, you know," he said, looking up at Isabel and seeing the fear in her eyes. "You could have stayed back at the apartment with Andre."

"No," said Isabel, firmly. "This is about me and my family. I'm coming with you."

"OK," said Mac, nodding quietly. He leant his head closer to Isabel and slowed down his pace so that she could catch up with him. "But if I say run, you run, OK?" His voice had an edge of urgency to it. "You run, and you don't stop, OK? Don't follow me unless I tell you to. Just keep on running. You promise?"

Isabel nodded, her stomach suddenly tightening. They turned down Rue de Bourdonnais and quickened their pace. Andre had said Dupont would be under the South entrance to the Eiffel Tower at 11.30am. And

CHAPTER ELEVEN

apparently he was *always* punctual. With the meeting in such a public place, there would be enough tourists around to give them cover and prevent them from looking too conspicuous. At least, that was the plan.

The cold clear night had dawned into a cold crisp day. The sky was a deep azure blue, with only the occasional wispy white cloud floating by in the strong freshening breeze. The milky white sun was low in the sky, its rays stabbing weakly through the bare trees that surrounded the gardens around the Tower.

Mac and Isabel crossed the main road behind the Tower and headed underneath the huge metallic structure. Isabel couldn't help but stare up in awe at its sheer size, stretching up high into the sky above them. Although the square plaza beneath the Tower was busy with holidaying tourists, everyone shrouded in thick scarves, hats and gloves, taking pictures and posing for photographs, there was a calmness and serenity about the place too. Although she could hear people's chattering voices and shrieks of laughter, in varying languages, all around her, Isabel felt distant and removed from it all. It was almost as though she were in a different world.

Mac jolted her back into the present by grabbing hold of her arm and tugging her further underneath the Tower. "Come on," he said, briskly. "No time for sightseeing. The South Entrance is over there." He nodded his head in front of them towards a large, snaking queue of Japanese tourists waiting patiently to gain entrance to the Tower's southern entrance. The queue extended across the plaza, mingling with people casually strolling amongst the pigeons, many nursing hot cups of coffee or chocolate bought from the Tower snack vendors selling their wares around the perimeter.

Mac and Isabel continued walking, hurriedly, heading towards a series of concrete benches facing the weak sun. Mac's eyes quickly scanned the area, then he squeezed Isabel's hand and nodded over towards a bench where one solitary figure was sitting all alone. The figure had his back to them, and was dressed in a long navy blue woollen coat, flat navy beret and a distinctive scarlet red scarf wound around his neck. Next to him sat a small, brown leather briefcase with a neatly folded newspaper on top.

"That's him," whispered Mac, anxiously looking back over his shoulder and letting his eyes sweep across the crowds of people underneath the Tower. "That's Dupont."

"You sure?" replied Isabel, finding herself whispering as well.

"Positive," said Mac, taking one last cursory glance around him before continuing towards Dupont's bench. "Let's go. Let me do the talking, OK?"

Isabel nodded and let Mac hurry her forwards towards the bench. They approached Dupont from behind, but he didn't seem to hear them above the noise and chatter around them. Mac hesitated briefly and then leaned forwards, bending his head down towards Dupont's, and saying in a low voice. "Monsieur Dupont? Albert Dupont? I'm Mac...."

Mac paused, waiting for Dupont to turn around and acknowledge them. But there was no reply. Mac edged slightly closer towards Dupont's rounded frame and gently placed a hand on his shoulder. "Monsieur Dupont?"

As Mac's hand lightly rested on him, Albert Dupont's body listed to the side and fell against his neatly folded newspaper. The man's face was now upturned towards the sun, and Mac found himself staring directly down into two empty, lifeless blue eyes. Dupont's mouth was slightly open, and a small ribbon of blood seeped out of one corner, trickling down his chin. Mac reached out and pulled the scarlet scarf away from Dupont's neck to reveal a gaping slit across the jugular, with warm wet blood flowing down his chest.

"Jesus Christ!" Mac turned wildly around and stepped away from the bench. He scanned the plaza behind him. His heart was pounding inside his chest, the blood pulsating in his eardrums. Someone had got to Dupont first.

Isabel stood frozen to the spot, her face drained of all colour. Her mouth opened but she uttered no sound, her face paralysed with fear. Gingerly she reached out and steadied herself against a nearby lamp post, fighting the overwhelming feeling of nausea filling up inside her.

"Quick – we have to run!" Mac rolled Dupont back onto his front and grabbed Isabel's shaking hand. "Now!"

CHAPTER ELEVEN

* * *

Time: 12.30pm
　Date: 8th November 2008
　Location: Jardin des Champs-Elysees, Paris, France.

The cold wind whipped into his face, but Shafer barely noticed. He sat on the edge of the park bench and nervously looked around him. He was being watched, or followed he knew that much. He just didn't know by whom.

It was lunchtime, but the park was almost deserted. Almost. Shafer eyed the bench opposite him on the other side of the small lake. A man was sitting reading an early morning edition of the Paris Tribune and eating what looked like a croissant from a white greaseproof paper bag. Two joggers sped past on their pre-lunch workout, circling the lake before heading off towards the trees. Over towards the entrance gates, two dog walkers entered the park and began strolling around the perimeter, struggling to keep control of their excitable dogs.

It could be any one of them, though Shafer. It could be all of them. It could be none of them. He felt uneasy, even out in the openness of the public park. He had left his hotel room just after sunrise thinking he would feel better out in the open air. And he had walked almost continuously ever since, pounding the streets, covering mile upon mile of Parisian pavement.

The man reading the newspaper opposite him changed position and reached over to deposit his empty paper bag into the rubbish bin. Shafer froze, wondering if the man would catch his eye and give the game away. But he didn't. He didn't seem to be paying Shafer the slightest bit of attention at all, and returned to reading his newspaper. The joggers had disappeared from sight, as had the dog walkers.

Fleming had been on his back ever since they had arrived in Paris, wanting to know his every move, demanding to know what he was going to do to help track down the missing papers. The papers he had so carelessly left unguarded.

And then there was Tindleman. Shafer was under strict instructions to telephone Tindleman every morning and evening, with an update on the situation. Shafer glanced at his watch. 1.28pm. Tindleman would be waiting for his call.

But Shafer wasn't ready. Tindleman would have to wait. He needed to do something first. He reached inside his jacket pocket and brought out a small flash drive. He needed to act fast. Every second that he delayed could mean the difference between life and death, not just for himself, but for the others too. If he was being followed, then whoever it was was doing a good job. For no matter how hard Shafer searched the trees and shrubs around him, he saw no one.

Conscious of what he was holding in his hand, and what would happen if it found its way into the wrong hands, Shafer pushed himself up off the park bench and strode purposefully out of the gates.

It was time.

* * *

Time: 12.30pm
Date: 8th November 2008
Location: Rue du Carnaval, Paris, France

Isabel's legs were burning. They had run for what seemed to her like miles, not stopping for even a second. Mac had led the way, taking Isabel's hand in a vice like grip and practically dragging her in his wake. He didn't know where he was running, or where he was going, but all he knew was they had to keep moving.

Someone had found out about their meeting with Dupont. The meeting had only been arranged last night, so it had to be someone close by. Maybe someone who was still here, watching, following. Mac's heart continued to race, but he daren't slow down even for a moment. Every so often he would glance backwards to check if they were being followed. Someone was bound to have found Dupont's body by now – there were too many

CHAPTER ELEVEN

people around the plaza for him to go unnoticed for too long. And the police would no doubt be called. They had to get themselves as far away from the scene as they could.........and they had to warn Andre.

They had run so far and so fast that they had very quickly left the busy streets around the Tower far behind. Now they were in a quiet residential area, Mac began to slow down to a jog.

"Please," gasped Isabel, stopping to bend over to catch her breath. "Please! I have to stop!" She wrenched her hand out of Mac's grasp and fell to her knees, gasping for air. Her body heaved up and down as her lungs greedily sucked in as much air as they could muster. Mac stopped and knelt down by her side, himself breathing heavily.

"OK," he panted, resting a hand on Isabel's back. "OK. I think we're all right now. Just move to the side here, out of the way." He guided her crumpled body towards the side of the pavement where there was a small alleyway between two apartment blocks. Mac gently pushed Isabel into the gap and then slid in after her. He looked at Isabel, watching her clutching at her sides and wheezing painfully. "You OK?"

Isabel nodded in between breaths, unable to utter a sound. She steadied herself with one hand against the wall, her breaths becoming longer and deeper, and more controlled. She shut her eyes and rested her head against the wall.

"Sorry about that," breathed Mac, wincing himself at the pain in his chest. "I just panicked and ran. We couldn't afford to stay there a moment longer. Not after....."

"I know, I know," mouthed Isabel, her voice barely audible.

"We have to warn Andre," continued Mac, his mind beginning to race. "Someone's onto us. They might even know where Andre is......then they'll get to us, and the papers. And then you." He pulled out his mobile phone and started punching in Andre's number.

Isabel looked at him, frowning. "I thought you said that using the phone was too dangerous? People might be listening in?"

Mac shook his head as he held the phone close to his ear. "We have no choice. Whoever killed Dupont already knows we're here, probably already knows where Andre is, too. It's not going to make any difference, not now."

Isabel closed her eyes and sank exhaustedly to the floor, while Mac briefly filled Andre in on what had happened to Dupont. It was a quick phone call. Mac flipped his phone shut and slipped it back in his pocket.

"Come on." He held out a hand and pulled Isabel to her feet. "We have to go back to Andre's."

"Are you sure?" Isabel's stomach tightened as she recalled the horrifying look on Albert Dupont's face – those lifeless eyes, the blood seeping through the gaping slit in his throat. "It's safe?"

"I don't know. We'll just have to be as careful as we can. If it looks dangerous I'll tell you to run, OK?" Mac studied Isabel's face and tried to give her a reassuring smile. "Andre's fixing us up somewhere to go. Somewhere safe. Somewhere they can't find us."

* * *

Time: 12.30pm
Date: 8th November 2008
Location: Flat 7, Rue de Bougainvillea, Paris, France

Andre hastily yanked open the drawers of his desk and hurriedly tipped the contents onto the floor. He had to be quick. With Dupont now dead, the police would be swarming all over the city. He wasn't sure if they would be able to connect him with Dupont – but he couldn't take the risk. All it would take would be an entry in Dupont's diary, a message on his desk at work – something which connected him to Andre. And then the trail towards him would begin.

Andre rummaged through the contents of the drawer and soon found what he was searching for. The small silver key he had thrown there only last night. He slipped it into the back pocket of his jeans and looked up at the top row of the bookshelf behind him. Bram Stoker's Dracula sat, inconspicuously, at the far end of the shelf. Whatever happened now, that book had to remain safe. And the safest place at the moment was right here.

Andre had already packed his laptop, spare battery, change of clothes, and several mobile phones. He hoisted the holdall over his shoulder and made for the front door. He glanced at his watch and had a last look around the living room. There was nothing else he needed – nothing else that mattered anyway. As he passed his desk, he stopped and reached into his back pocket. He pulled out Stephanie's photograph, and then with a slight smile on his face he threw the picture into the wastepaper basket underneath the desk.

Andre reached for the front door, pulling it open. Immediately he jumped several feet backwards, feeling his heart leap into his mouth. Marie was standing directly in front of him, her slender wrist raised as if about to knock on the door.

"Oh!" Marie was herself somewhat startled. She quickly lowered her hand and placed it on her chest. "Monsieur Andre! You frightened me!" Her eyes moved to the side and came to rest on the holdall hanging over Andre's right shoulder. She looked up, questioningly. "Are you going somewhere?"

Andre glanced at the bag, then dropped it to the floor by his feet. He felt for his keys inside his jacket pocket and started to close the door behind him.

"But this is all so sudden," continued Marie. "You did not say you were leaving. Is it a holiday?" Marie looked up at Andre, her deep chocolate brown eyes beginning to melt in his gaze.

"Um, well," muttered Andre, edging forward and turning the key in the lock. "Sort of. Not really." He could feel his temperature rising as he stood close to Marie. He could feel her breath tickling his cheek. He looked away, feeling his face begin to flush. "Did you, er, want me for something?" He bent down and picked up the holdall once again.

Marie's expression took on a concerned look and she glanced backwards over her shoulder, down the staircase which led to the communal front door. She nodded. "Yes, Monsieur Andre. I came to warn you."

"Warn me?" Andre looked sideways at Marie, who had now taken a step away from him. He could no longer feel her breath or smell her delicate perfume. "Warn me about what?"

Marie leant forwards and lightly touched Andre's forearm. "There have been some people…a man…looking for you downstairs. Asking questions about you."

"When was this?" Andre's throat tightened. Maybe he had been right. Maybe the police had already made the connection between himself and Dupont.

"A few minutes ago," continued Marie, her eyes full of concern. "I was taking a delivery of bread from the front of the shop, when I saw this man standing over on the pavement outside. He was watching me. Watching the shop." Andre thought he saw Marie's slight frame give a small shudder. "I went back inside the shop, and when I turned around he was there. Right in front of me. Inside the shop."

"What did he look like?"

"He was about this tall," said Marie, holding up her arm and placing her hand a little above Andre's head. "And he had very…how do you say it? Smooth skin? On his face. And very small lips. And he was wearing dark sunglasses. His hair was dark, and very short." Marie placed her hands on her head to show the man's hairstyle. "And it looked, how do you say it? Greasy?" Marie frowned. Andre nodded for her to continue. "He wore a light suit, but no coat. Do you think he was the police?"

"What did he say?" Andre felt his heart quicken a little. "Did he speak to you?"

Marie nodded. "He showed me a picture…a picture of you. And he asked me if I'd seen you."

"And what did you say?" Andre's mouth turned dry.

"I…I spoke French to him. I told him that I didn't understand English."

"Did he say anything else?"

"He carried on for a while – in English. I don't think he understood me. He didn't speak any French. He asked me again, very slowly, if I had seen you before. If you lived upstairs above my shop. He pointed at the ceiling

CHAPTER ELEVEN

with his finger to try and make me understand." Marie gave a little smile as she recalled. "He pointed at the photograph and then at the ceiling. I kept shaking my head and speaking French to him. After that, he left."

Andre leant against the wall of the hallway, his mind racing.

"I hope I did the right thing, Monsieur Andre." Marie's voice was small. "I didn't...he didn't look like a very nice man."

Andre opened his eyes and managed a half smile. He leant forwards and lightly touched Marie on the shoulder. "You did fine, Marie. Thank you."

"Is this why you are going away?" Marie nodded at the holdall bag. "Because of this man? What does he want from you?"

Andre let out a deep sigh and shook his head. "Sorry, Marie. I can't tell you. But yes, I do need to get away. If that man turns up again, or anyone else asking about me, just tell them...just tell them..." Andre broke off. He couldn't ask Marie to lie for him, that wouldn't be fair. "Just tell them you don't know where I am."

Andre made to walk past Marie and head down the stairs. Mac and Isabel should be on their way back by now. Once they arrived, they needed to move fast.

"Where are you going?" Marie stepped into Andre's path, blocking his passage to the stairs. "Do you have somewhere to stay?" Her eyes searched his, a deep frown developing on her forehead as she spoke.

"I'm working on it," mumbled Andre, keen to get past. "I have a few friends, we'll be OK."

Marie stood her ground, pursing her lips. "You don't know where you're going, do you?" She folded her arms across her chest. "And your friends? Are they going with you too?"

Andre shot a quick look at Marie. "What friends?"

"It's OK," smiled Marie, her face relaxing. "I saw them leaving this morning. Are you all looking for somewhere to stay together?"

Andre felt himself drawn in towards her stare, almost mesmerising him, and found himself nodding.

"Well, if you have nowhere to stay, I have a small flat that you could use."

"You do?" Andre frowned. "But I thought you..." He nodded down the hallway towards a door where he thought Marie lived. "I thought you lived above the shop?"

"Oh, I do," she replied, her eyes twinkling. "But I only stay here during the week. I like to go back to my flat on a Sunday, or when I have some free time from the shop. It's empty at the moment, so you are quite welcome to stay there if you would like."

Andre hesitated. It was true. He didn't know where they were going to go. All he knew was that they needed to get away from here, away from this flat, away from this street. Somewhere. Anywhere.

Slowly, he felt himself nodding. "OK, that would be great, Marie. Thanks. We won't be there long."

Marie shrugged. "It's OK. You may stay as long as you wish, Monsieur Andre. I am not using it at the moment. I haven't been there for a while. Wait downstairs and I'll get you the keys." Marie stepped past Andre and headed down the corridor towards her own flat, leaving a waft of sweet perfume in her wake.

CHAPTER TWELVE

Time: 3.10pm
 Date: 8th November 2008
 Location: Marie's bakery, Rue de Bougainvillea, Paris, France

Isabel and Mac were seated just inside the bakery door, nestled in behind the doorway, keeping out of sight as much as possible. Luckily, there had been no passing traffic, and no one had called into the shop. It was Isabel who first spotted Andre emerging from the entrance to the flats next door. She gently tapped on the window until she caught his gaze, and he hurried inside.

"You made it OK?" he said in a low voice. "No one followed you?" He quickly sat down next to Mac, ducking out of sight from the window. He swung the holdall underneath the table.

"We didn't see anything, or anyone," replied Mac, looking down at the bag. "You have everything?"

Andre nodded. "I've also found us somewhere to stay – for the moment at least."

"Where?" said Mac, in a loud whisper.

"Marie, the girl who works here. She's offered us her flat for as long as we need it."

"Why would she do that?" asked Mac, quickly. His face took on a concerned expression. "You didn't tell her….?"

Andre quickly shook his head and held up his hands. "No, no, nothing like that. She just offered. She…." Andre checked back over his shoulder, noticing that one of the other shop assistants had come into the room and was busily wiping down some tables in the far corner. She didn't appear to be paying them any attention. "She says that someone was here earlier…looking for me."

"Kreshniov?" Mac said the word as more of a statement than a question.

Andre shrugged. "Maybe…or maybe the police. With Dupont dead only a short way up the road, they might have managed to connect him to me. But she sent them away, and so far they haven't been back."

"It's only a matter of time," grimaced Mac, his face darkening. "We need to get out of here."

Just at that moment, Marie slipped into the shop and smiled at the assistant still cleaning down the tables. Then she turned to Andre and pressed a set of keys into his hand. She clasped her own hands around his for a few seconds before releasing them. She bent down and whispered close to Andre's ear.

"The address is on the key tag. It's about a 20-minute drive. I've already called you a taxi – they'll be here in five minutes." Marie held her hand up to indicate the number five. Then, with a last smile at Andre, she turned away and returned behind the counter to serve the customers who had just walked in.

"There's someone I need to call," said Andre, pulling out his phone. "Shafer. He needs to know what's happening. I'll take it outside." Andre got up and walked to the door. "I'll tap on the window when the taxi arrives."

* * *

Time: 2.15pm
   Date: 8th November 2008
   Location: Metropolitan Police HQ, London

Jack closed the door to the office and picked up the telephone from DS Cooper's desk. He would need to be quick. Opening the thin folder

CHAPTER TWELVE

Liddell had given him, he quickly located the direct dial number for Cambridgeshire Police. He dialled it quickly, and watched the door for any sounds of people returning from lunch. The call was quickly answered.

"Good afternoon, Cambridgeshire CID, how may I help?"

CID? Jack paused, a frown growing on his forehead. CID? This was meant to be a missing person enquiry.

"Hello, Cambridgeshire CID?" repeated the voice from the other end of the phone.

"Yes, sorry, technical issues this end." Jack brushed aside the growing feeling of disquiet that was spreading through his body. "My name is Detective Inspector Jack MacIntosh. From the Met. I've been passed a file by Chief Superintendent Malcolm Liddell – to look into the disappearance of a woman from your patch."

"OK, do you have a name? I'll look it up on the computer."

"Faraday. Isabel Faraday." Jack's eyes continued to watch the door.

"Right, bear with me. I'll see if I can locate any details. What was it you were after?"

"Anything really, I have very little to go on here." Jack cast his eyes back down to the manila folder in front of him and the scanty notes that had been supplied. "I have nothing more than her name, date of birth and address. And when she was last seen."

"OK. So…..we have an Isabel Faraday, date of birth 26th June 1980, reported missing on 7th November by her employer…….a Mr Ronald Taylor."

"That's the one. Do you have any other information about her?"

"Not that I can see…….it seems that the case was requisitioned by our Assistant Chief Constable and passed over to yourselves."

Jack closed his eyes and exhaled. It seemed like he had hit the proverbial brick wall. "Any details as to why? I mean, it's a bit off our patch."

"No, no details. Just an immediate transfer – requested to be handled personally by your Chief Superintendent Liddell. No one else was to investigate, only him. That was it, nothing more from this end."

Jack expressed his thanks and hung up.

Isabel Faraday. Just who are you, he mused?

***

Time: 4.05pm
   Date: 8th November 2008
   Location: Paris suburbs, France

The taxi cab sped along the outer ring road, heading in the direction of Marie's flat. The taxi driver had nodded when Mac had showed him the address on the key fob, and merely mumbled that the fare would be 50 euros.

The journey passed in relative silence. Isabel rested her head up against the passenger side window and closed her eyes. Mac and Andre took turns in glancing out of the rear window to make sure that no one was following them through the late afternoon dimness.

Eventually the taxi cab left the ring road and entered a more residential looking area. The driver swung the cab around to the left and headed down a long tree-lined avenue with expensive looking apartments hugging both sides of the street. The driver slowed down and pulled over outside an impressive looking building with smooth yellow sandstone walls and green wooden shuttered windows.

"L'Avenue du Soleil" stated the taxi driver, nodding at the sandstone apartment block. "L'Apartament Blancos." He held his hand out for the 50 euro note.

Isabel stirred at the sound of Mac opening the taxi cab door, and taking only a few moments to collect herself, she followed him out onto the pavement. As soon as the door was shut behind them, the taxi cab moved off into the late afternoon gloom. The street lights were on above them, casting a faint orange glow through the still frosty air. Condensation billowed from their mouths as they breathed.

The avenue was broad and long – huge trees lining the sides of the pavements, mirroring each other across the road as far as the eye could see.

CHAPTER TWELVE

Fallen leaves cushioned the ground like a soft golden blanket, deadening the sound of their footfalls as they moved towards the apartment block entrance.

Mac had the apartment keys in his hand – Apartment 3a. Standing outside the main entrance, he looked up at the shuttered windows and guessed that apartment 3a would be up on the third floor.

"Come on," he said, keeping his voice low even though there wasn't a soul around to hear them. "Now we're here, let's get inside."

Just as they stepped forwards towards the communal entrance, a terrible crashing sound came from behind them. All three whirled round to see a figure stumbling out of the shadows, arms flailing towards them. Isabel stifled a scream and hid behind Andre, as a man lumbered unsteadily towards them, falling to the ground at their feet.

"Simon!" yelled Mac, dropping down to his knees and pulling the man over onto his back. "Jesus, Simon! What the fuck's happened?!"

The man on the ground was smartly dressed in a charcoal grey suit, pale grey tie and tan coloured full-length raincoat. His face was hideously contorted in equal amounts of pain and fear, his eyes bulging fiercely, as though they were about to pop out of their sockets. His hair was plastered to his head in heavily matted clumps with what looked and felt like sweat. He was taking short, sharp, painful breaths, finding it increasingly hard to talk – his lips quivered and his whole body began to shake uncontrollably.

"Shit, Shafer, who did this to you?" Andre dropped to his knees next to Mac, the pair of them trying to prop the stricken man up. Grasping him around the chest, Andre heaved him up into a sitting position, but the man screamed so violently he immediately let go. Instead he rested the man's head back down onto the thick bed of leaves behind him. Andre's forearm was now heavily stained with something warm and sticky.

Quickly, Mac unbuttoned the man's raincoat and pulled it aside. Blood was seeping steadily out of a deep wound to his chest, staining his suit a deep maroon colour. Without thinking, Mac pressed his hands against the open wound, frantically trying in vain to halt the seamless and never-ending flow of blood.

"Simon!" croaked Mac, shaking his head slowly from side to side, his face shocked and wide-eyed. "Simon!"

Simon Shafer gazed up, his eyes wide and seared with pain and shock – first looking at Andre who was sat on the pavement, shielding Isabel from the gruesome sight, and then at Mac who was still hunched over his chest, his hands still trying to damn the flow of thick, warm blood. Mac was still whispering his name in a stunned voice, willing the blood to stop flowing.

Finally, Shafer's eyes searched and came to rest on Isabel, who was cowering behind Andre, her quivering hands covering her face.

"Is…Is.." spluttered Shafer, blood stained sputum dripping from his mouth as he spoke. "Far…a….day." His words were almost inaudible.

Mac leant closer to Shafer's stricken body, trying to get close enough to hear. "Simon?"

Suddenly, Shafer's body became rigid, his teeth clenched together in agony. From somewhere he found the strength to grab hold of Mac's upper arm and pull him forwards, so that he was no more than inches from his own face. "Far…a….day," he croaked again, gripping Mac's arm even tighter as another wave of pain and nausea enveloped him. Gritting his teeth, a mixture of saliva and blood sprayed from the sides of his mouth as he spoke. "Who…knows…what…is…possible…..who …..knows….what…..is….poss…..poss……possible."

The dying man's back then arched violently and his grip on Mac's arm fell away. His chest rose and fell for the last time, the rasping noise of the air finally escaping from his lungs being the only sound they could hear in the cool frosty air. After that, there was silence.

Mac looked frantically into the dead man's eyes, willing him to speak, willing him to breathe – but all they did was stare back at him, utterly devoid of feeling, utterly devoid of life. Andre leant forwards pulled Shafer's raincoat closed, covering up the mass of blood that now stained his chest. Then slowly, and gently, with only the faintest shaking of the hand, he closed his eyelids and wiped away the smears of blood from his face.

Both Mac and Andre continued to stare in silence at the body in front

CHAPTER TWELVE

of them, their faces frozen in fear and shock, neither of them uttering a word. It was Isabel who broke the silence.

"Who…who was he?" She was sitting down amongst a pile of damp leaves, hugging her knees to her chest to stop herself from shaking. This was the second dead body she had seen in less than 12 hours.

Andre wiped his forehead with the back of his hand and closed his eyes. This couldn't be happening. This really could not be happening. Not here. Not now.

"His name was Simon," replied Mac, his voice hollow and empty. "Simon Shafer. And he was my friend."

* * *

Time: 3.10pm
Date: 8th November 2008
Location: Metropolitan Police HQ, London

"That list you gave me?" DS Cooper waved the small piece of paper at Jack as they both sat down in the station canteen. The canteen was virtually empty, so they had the pick of the seats available, choosing one in the far corner where no one would overhear them. "Not getting very far, I'm afraid."

Jack nodded. "I thought you might say that." He placed two bottles of water down on the table in front of them, having noticed the coffee machine was playing up on the way in.

"All I have on Faraday is Michael Faraday – and the Faraday Cage."

"The Faraday what?"

"Cage."

"What on earth is a Faraday Cage?" Jack took a swig from his water bottle and grimaced. He needed a caffeine fix. That, or a cigarette.

DS Cooper smiled. "I take it you didn't pay attention during your physics lessons at school, then?"

"Obviously not," remarked Jack, replacing the lid on his water bottle and pushing it away. "So enlighten me."

"Well, it's kind of beyond me too, to tell you the truth. Basically its an enclosure made of conducting material which blocks out external static and electrical fields." He paused. "Was that what you wanted me to find out about?"

"No." Jack shook his head. "I don't think it's Michael Faraday that I'm after. There weren't any other famous Faradays then, other than him?"

It was DS Cooper's turn to shake his head. "None. Sorry."

"What about the rest of the list? Anything else?"

DS Cooper cocked his head to one side and eyed Jack, curiously. "The rest were, well, kind of intriguing. I just never had you down as a space freak."

"A what freak?" Jack frowned, ignoring his partner's inquisitive look.

"A Space freak. The Universe. The "one small step for man" brigade. The final frontier."

A confused look spread across Jack's already tired face. He rubbed his eyes and sighed heavily. "I have no idea what you mean."

"The other words you had me look up? They all had a common theme." DS Cooper paused, a small smile flickering to his lips. "Space."

* * *

Time: 4.20pm

Date: 8th November 2008

Location: L'Apartament Blancos, L'Avenue du Soleil, Paris

Mac turned the key in the lock of the apartment door, his hand trembling. He didn't dare look back at Shafer's body, still visible from across the road. It looked like a mound in the middle of the alleyway, a pile of old clothes, a pile of forgotten rubbish. waiting to be collected. Mac hoped he would be found soon. The idea of leaving him out there in the cold didn't rest easy with him. But they daren't call the police. Not themselves. Not yet.

They had dragged Shafer's body out of sight of prying eyes, away from

CHAPTER TWELVE

the path, away from the apartment block – away from anyone who might stumble across him. Over the road there was a small alleyway, and Mac and Andre had half carried, half dragged the limp, lifeless body across the street and hidden it in the safety of the approaching darkness. They couldn't risk him being found, not like this. Instead, they laid him down in the shadows of the alleyway covering his body with his coat.

Andre had hastily brushed the bloodstained leaves into a pile, using his feet, and left it in the gutter beneath one of the sprawling trees. Looking up and down the deserted street, he was thankful that no one in any of the surrounding apartments seemed to have heard or seen anything. There were no shouts, no screams, no cries for help. No commotion at all. Nothing. And no one.

Just darkness.

And death.

* * *

Time: 3.20pm
Date: 8th November 2008
Location: Metropolitan Police HQ, London

"Salyut 7 was easy." DS Cooper brought out a bundle of papers where he had hurriedly scribbled down his findings. "From what I can gather it was some kind of space station built by the Russians. A kind of fore-runner to MIR and the International Space Station."

Jack nodded, carefully eyeing the notes DS Cooper had made. "And?"

"Prism – that was trickier. Apart from the obvious references to geometric shapes, the only other reference I found that made any sense referred to a sub-division of NASA. Some kind of acronym."

"Go on." Jack moved his chair closer to his partner. "Anything else?"

"Well, the Phoenix Project was a dead end. Plenty of references to the phoenix – the dictionary definition is of a mythological bird that consumed itself by fire and then rose renewed from its ashes. And then obviously plenty of Harry Potter connections – the Order of the Phoenix. I think that was my favourite film out of all of them. But nothing with "project" on the end."

"I see." Jack slowly rubbed his chin and stared, thoughtfully, out of the canteen window. "So, we have an old space station, a division of NASA and a bird that bursts into flames."

"I'll keep digging but……..are you going to tell me what any of this is all about?" DS Cooper reached for his bottle of water and took a long sip, eyeing Jack carefully as he did so.

Jack returned his gaze to the canteen, looking about him to make sure he wouldn't be overheard. Leaning forwards in his chair, placing both elbows on the table, he beckoned DS Cooper closer. "When I was summonsed to Liddell's office earlier, I overheard an interesting telephone conversation while I was hovering outside." Jack paused and lowered his voice even further. "He mentioned the Phoenix Project, this Salyut 7 thing, and the name Faraday. I have no idea who he was talking to, but he was as mad as hell. And now here I am chasing a woman named Faraday. And when I phoned Cambridgeshire Police for any other information they had on her, they had nothing. Just told me it had been requisitioned by their Assistant Chief Constable and passed to Liddell. No questions. No investigations. No one was to investigate her disappearance except him."

"And now you."

"And now me."

* * *

Time: 4.25pm
    Date: 8th November 2008
    Location: L'Apartament Blancos, L'Avenue du Soleil, Paris

The apartment was on the third floor, up three flights of clean, well-kept stairs. Mac fumbled for the apartment keys, hoping none of the other residents of the block came out into the hallway to greet the new

CHAPTER TWELVE

bloodstained arrivals. They needed to keep out of sight. Now more than ever.

Marie's apartment was spacious and tastefully furnished. It was obvious she had excellent, but somewhat expensive Parisian tastes. The apartment door opened into a wide, expansive living room with a tall, high ceiling. A huge bay window adorned the left hand wall, giving views out over the street they had just crossed…..and over to the alleyway opposite. Mac quickly strode over to the window and pulled the heavy velvet drapes shut. This was one view they could do without tonight.

The floor was made of dark, almost plum-red, hardwood floorboards, with a luxurious deep-pile rug in the very centre. Around it were three soft leather sofas, nestling around a low glass topped coffee table. Overhead hung an ornate golden chandelier, decorated with hanging droplets of pure crystal and glass. They twinkled as they caught the light from the open doorway.

The walls surrounding the room had vast oil paintings in ornate golden frames, depicting urban scenes with an angular and clinical feel. Great swirls of charcoal black, silvery grey and burnt orange gave the room a modern, futuristic look. Along the back wall were two doors, one leading into a bedroom, and a second door leading off into a small, but well-equipped, kitchen.

Isabel perched uncomfortably on the edge of one of the sofas, wringing her hands rhythmically in her lap. She rocked slowly backwards and forwards, her face looking pale and drawn. Her eyes had a fixed, glazed look, as she stared silently into space. She took in none of her surroundings, none of the paintings, pictures or furnishings – nothing. She looked at nothing. She saw nothing. She felt nothing.

Andre paced up and down in front of the window, deliberately forcing his eyes to stop straying towards the plum coloured velvet drapes, knowing full well what view was lurking behind them. He paced quickly up and down, his mind racing almost as fast as his footsteps.

"What was he doing here?" said Mac, quietly, leaning against a huge mahogany sideboard beneath one of the oil paintings on the back wall.

"Why was he waiting for us?"

Andre grasped his head with his hands, almost willing his brain to give him an answer. Any answer. He continued to pace back and forth, his footsteps on the hardwood floor being the only sound in the room.

"It must have been Kreshniov," Mac carried on. "He must have known about Dupont, and got to him before we did. The he did the same with Simon. He must have tracked them both down and…and then…" He didn't finish the sentence.

"Shafer was no idiot!" barked Andre, anger welling up in his voice. "He would never have made a mistake like that. He would never have let anyone get within a mile of him. He was too good for that."

"But he's dead! *Someone* bloody well got to him!" Mac's voice was unable to mask the bitterness he felt. "And my money's on Kreshniov."

"I know he's dead, Mac!" yelled Andre, fiercely. "I just saw his fucking dead body, and held his fucking hand as he fucking well died!"

Isabel started to sob, small inaudible sobs to begin with, which then became louder with every breath. "Please," she whispered. *"Please* don't."

Andre and Mac stopped their angry exchange and glanced up at Isabel as she let herself sink back into one of the sofas, clutching a velvet cushion to her chest and burying her tear stained face into its softness. She looked so fragile, so helpless. The anger in Andre's eyes instantly faded and he silently stepped over towards the sofa. He bent down beside her and placed a hand on her trembling shoulder.

"I'm sorry." He wiped a stray tear away from Isabel's cheek. "Shafer…Simon was a good friend of mine. "He glanced up at Mac, meeting his gaze. "A good friend of us both. I think he was trying to help us."

Andre gave Isabel's shoulder a squeeze and returned to the window, his eyes once again drawn towards the curtain.

"What was he doing here?" Mac swept an angry hand towards the velvet curtain. "Why was he out there? He shouldn't have been within a million miles of here." Mac fixed Andre with an angry, penetrative stare. "What was he doing here?" he repeated.

Andre shook his head. "I don't know. No one knew we were coming

CHAPTER TWELVE

here."

"Well someone clearly did," muttered Mac, his face darkening.

Andre resumed his pacing once again, thrusting his hands in his pockets to stop the urge he felt to pull the curtains apart and look out into the Paris night.

"It's Kreshniov," repeated Mac. "It's got to be. We need to move on – we can't stay here now."

Andre shook his head as he continued to pace. "Too risky. Whoever did this, he wouldn't want to be seen around here with a dead body lying in the street." The words "dead body" hung emptily in the air. "If it was him, then he'll be long gone by now."

* * *

Time: 6.00pm
Date: 8th November 2008
Location: Metropolitan Police HQ, London

"So, what are you up to exactly, Detective Inspector?" DS Cooper hurried after Jack as they left the building and jogged down the stone steps into the reserved car park. It was dark and only a few cars were left. The frosty ground crunched beneath their feet as if they were walking on crushed glass. "What does any of this mean?"

"No idea," replied Jack, heading briskly through the darkness towards his battered Ford.

"No idea what it all means, or no idea what you're up to?"

"Both." Jack hesitated before unlocking the driver's door. "But thanks for what you've done so far, anyway."

"No problem," replied DS Cooper, fastening up the buttons on his overcoat to keep out the early evening chill. More snow was forecast for later that night. "But if you really want to know anything about all that stuff, you need to speak to Trevor Daniels."

"Who the hell is Trevor Daniels?" Jack frowned, pulled open the car door and slid himself into the driver's seat. He threw the thin manila folder containing the papers in relation to the Isabel Faraday missing person investigation onto the passenger seat.

"PC Daniels – works in the traffic section." DS Cooper leant in the driver's side and handed Jack a piece of paper. "I took the liberty of getting his number."

Jack took the piece of paper and gave it a glance before throwing it onto the Faraday folder. "Thanks. Maybe I'll give him a call."

"You do that. There's not much Daniels doesn't know. And he's an interesting character." DS Cooper gave a smile, stepped backwards and closed the driver's door.

Jack pulled out of the car park, setting his heaters on to full blast. The short distance he had to drive home would mean the car would barely have warmed up by the time he got there. Glancing at the clock, Jack made the decision to take a detour – not only to give the car, and therefore himself, a chance to warm up, but he knew of an off licence and takeaway pizza place a few streets away. His stomach rumbled at the thought.

CHAPTER THIRTEEN

Time: 9.00pm
 Date: 8th November 2008
 Location: L'Apartament Blancos, L'Avenue du Soleil, Paris

Night began to fall and a heavy dampness descended into the room like a curtain. No one had thought to put on the heating, so the room chilled quickly. Isabel sat curled up on the largest sofa, burying herself as best she could beneath a blanket she had found underneath the one and only bed in the apartment. Her eyes were closed and her breathing slow and rhythmical.

Mac leant against the side of the huge bay window and rubbed his eyes with his fingers. He hadn't managed to sleep. Whenever he closed his eyes all he could see was Shafer's body – its lifeless form slumped in the gutter of the alleyway, cold and alone.

"We need to get out," he said in a low voice. He glanced over his shoulder at Isabel – she continued slumbering. "Kreshniov is getting too close. For all we know, he's sitting outside, waiting."

Andre shook his head. "No. He won't be out there." Andre stood beside the curtains and slowly pulled back one of the drapes a few inches. The street lighting was dim, so much of the pavement was bathed in darkness. Andre felt his eyes flicker across towards the alleyway, drawn towards it like a magnet. He slowly searched the gloom, but Shafer's body was still hidden from sight. There had been no rush of police. No emergency services. Nothing. Shafer was still lying outside in the cold, undetected….for now. Andre sighed and pulled the curtains back shut. "We don't even know he's alive for sure."

"Of course he's bloody well alive!" exploded Mac. "We both know that!"

Andre stepped away from the curtain. "OK, so maybe we do. But he won't be outside. He won't be waiting. He'll have put as much distance between himself and this mess as he could."

"Well, it still doesn't feel right," said Mac, shortly. "None of this feels right. We need to get out of here – find somewhere else."

"And where exactly did you have in mind?" replied Andre, unable to stop a hint of sarcasm entering his tone.

"Well, I don't bloody know do I?" retorted Mac. "Just anywhere. Look, has someone blown your cover? Found out Andre Baxter doesn't truly exist?"

Andre paused, grim faced. He began pacing once again, up and down rhythmically in front of the closed drapes. Things were not going to plan. This was not how it was meant to be. No one was supposed to get hurt. No one was supposed to die. And certainly not Simon.

"I think we're OK here for a bit," he said, eventually. "There's no way the police or Kreshniov could have found out about this place – not from Marie. She said that whoever came to the bakery this morning went away, and didn't come back. She didn't tell them anything."

"You sure? Shafer seemed to know where we were going to be. Who can say who else knows?" Mac grimaced. "We need to get further away. How much cash do we have?"

Andre shrugged. "Not a lot on us. A few hundred euro. I can get some money transferred online, then withdraw it first thing in the morning. There must be a bank around here somewhere."

Andre went over to the door where he had left his holdall, unzipped it and pulled out his laptop. "I still think we're safe here for a few days, but if it makes you happy I'll get the money transferred and we can decide in the morning what we want to do." He sat down, gently, on the end of one of the sofas, careful not to wake or disturb Isabel. He flipped open the laptop and started it up. The light from the screen cast an eerie glow in

CHAPTER THIRTEEN

the otherwise dark room. No one had dared to turn on the lights.

Mac edged over towards the sofa where Isabel still lay curled up underneath the blanket. He saw the rhythmical rise and fall of her slumbering body and secretly envied her ability to sleep. His own body craved sleep, demanded it, ached for it. But it never came. He still couldn't close his eyes without seeing Shafer's body shaking as it grasped with its last breaths. Mac had managed to wash the blood from his hands, but it had stained his memory.

"Jesus Christ!" swore Andre, his voice tearing Mac away from his macabre thoughts. "The bastard!" He continued tapping the keyboard, more urgently this time, then paused and swore again.

Mac's eyes darted across the coffee table towards Andre. "What? What's up?"

Andre mouthed another expletive and then simply nodded at the computer screen, turning it around so that it faced Mac across the table. Mac could see that Andre had logged into the United World Bank website and up on the screen was a bank account for Mr Andre Baxter – an instant access deposit account. At the very bottom of the screen was the figure for the total funds available. Zero.

Mac stared at the screen and frowned. "How...?"

Andre closed his eyes and mouthed yet more obscenities under his breath. Mac moved closer to the computer and squinted at the screen.

"It says here you withdrew 156,798 euros....yesterday." Mac paused and looked up. "You didn't, did you?"

"Of course I bloody well didn't!" retorted Andre, jumping to his feet and snapping the computer screen shut. "What do you take me for?"

"Then how...." The uneasy feeling in Mac's stomach quickly spread through the rest of his body like the damp, pervading mist on a bleak and desolate moor. "Kreshniov," he said, flatly. "Bloody Kreshniov."

Andre walked over to the window but resisted the urge to draw back the curtains once again.

"It's him, isn't it?" breathed Mac, still staring at the closed laptop in front of him. "Kreshniov. It's him. He's cleaned us out. He knows we have the papers, and he's coming after us."

"Fuck!" swore Andre, slamming a clenched fist into the wall next to the window. He knocked a gold edged picture frame with his hand, sending it crashing to the ground. "Fuck! Fuck! Fuck!" With every expletive he thumped the wall, each time harder than the last.

"What about the other accounts?" said Mac, reaching for the laptop. "Did you check them? Maybe they're OK. Maybe he didn't……"

Andre marched over to the table and snatched the laptop out of Mac's hands. "You think he's that stupid?! There'll be nothing left – the bastard will have taken it all! You think he'd just stop at the one?" Andre flung the laptop down, angrily, into his open holdall. "He knows exactly what he's doing. The bastard!" He strode over to the bay window and this time forcefully yanked back the drapes, almost pulling them from their curtain rings in his anger. Shoving the huge window open, he yelled out into the chilled frosty night air. "Come on then! Where are you?!" Spit flew out of the corners of his mouth as he screamed, his eyes burning a hot, fiery red. "Come and get me, you spineless bastard! Come on, I'm right here! You know I am! Come in and fucking get me, you fucking arsehole!"

Mac leapt over the coffee table and grabbed Andre from behind, pulling him back into the room.

"Andre! Shut the fuck up!" Mac tried to get his arms around Andre's body and wrestle him to the ground. "What the bloody hell do you think you're doing?! You want the whole world to know we're in here?" He clamped his arms around Andre's chest and pulled him backwards, away from the open window. Twisting his body violently, Andre pushed Mac away from him and the two men stood facing each other, breathing hard, faces contorted in anger and hatred, fists clenched by their side.

"He already fucking knows where we fucking are!" shouted Andre, his chest heaving. "Or haven't you been listening to a word I've just said! We're cleaned out! Fucking hundred thousand euros, just gone!"

Just then a whimpering sound came from behind them and they both turned towards the sofa. Isabel was sitting up wide-eyed and rigid, clutching the blanket towards her, her face sickeningly pale. Andre looked

CHAPTER THIRTEEN

into Isabel's eyes and saw the pain and panic etched deep within them. He clenched and unclenched his fists, letting the sea of rage wash over him. His breathing began to slow and his hardened face softened slightly.

"Sorry," he murmured, wiping his mouth on his sleeves. "You didn't need to hear that."

Mac turned away and closed the window, taking a brief moment to glance up and down the road outside to check whether Andre's outburst had awoken anyone in the otherwise slumbering street. There was nothing. No movement, no sound, nothing at all. Pulling the drapes firmly shut once again., Mac took a deep breath and went to sit down next to Isabel. She flinched as soon as he came near her, pulling the blanket up around her neck protectively.

"It's OK, we just got carried away." Mac tried his best at a reassuring smile, but failed. He flashed an angry look up at Andre. "It won't happen again." Isabel merely shrank back further into the sofa.

Andre opened his mouth to attempt an explanation, but the sound of a police siren cutting through the dead night air, and getting steadily closer, silenced him.

* * *

Time: 8.00pm
　Date:8th November 2008
　Location: Kettles Yard Mews, London

Jack opened the thin folder and sighed. He grimaced as he slowly sipped a strong coffee and flicked through the meagre pages. The unopened bottle of Glenmorangie he had picked up in the off licence sat within range but Jack felt he needed to keep a clear head on this one. He had managed to demolish most of the large Tandoori Hot pizza he had brought home, the rest looked promising for breakfast.

Jack let his head rest against the back of the sofa and closed the file.

Isabel Faraday.

Faraday.

The Cambridgeshire force had given them the bare minimum of information – name, address, work details, family contacts. But that was it. No one had done any follow up enquiries with friends or family. The file had merely been passed over.

At the Chief Superintendent's request.

Jack frowned and asked himself the same question he had asked a million times that evening. Why was Liddell getting himself involved in a seemingly run of the mill missing person case which was so far off his patch? And why him? Why had he asked Jack to "handle it personally"? Those had been his words. Personally.

And the name Faraday.

I *wish I'd never heard of the damn Faradays*? Wasn't that what Liddell had said? Jack had arrived quickly at Liddell's office once he had been summoned by Penny, and had caught snippets of Liddell's conversation behind his closed door. "I wish I'd never heard of the damn Faradays…"

It meant something, Jack was sure – and he could bet it wasn't anything to do with a missing person. Taking another long swig of coffee, Jack swung his legs down from where they had been resting on the low coffee table and opened the Faraday file again. Nestling in the corner was the piece of paper Cooper had given him as they had left the station. After pausing for only a moment, Jack reached for his mobile phone.

* * *

Time: 9.20pm
   Date: 8th November 2008
   Location: L'Apartament Blancos, L'Avenue du Soleil, Paris

"I'll give you the money."

   Isabel handed a mug of coffee to Andre and seated herself back down on the sofa. They gratefully sipped the hot liquid, barely wincing at the bitter aftertaste. Isabel had managed to find a jar of coffee in the small kitchen, but there was no milk or sugar that she could see.

The police car which had sped past the apartment had continued on its course and disappeared deep into the night. They heard nothing further.

"You can't do that, Isabel." Mac pressed his fingers around his hot mug, letting the heat scold his skin. He welcomed the pain. It comforted him to know that despite the numbness inside his body he could still feel something. He could still feel pain.

"Yes, I can," replied Isabel, her voice hard. "I'm involved in this too, in case you hadn't noticed. They're my parents, and I need to see them again. If it's money you need then you can have it. All of it."

"Andre, tell her she can't," said Mac, wearily. "We can't take her money."

Andre remained silent, taking a long sip from his coffee and letting the warmth slip down his throat.

"Andre?" Mac looked up and studied his friend's face, frowning slightly. "Tell her. Tell her we can't take her money."

Again, Andre said nothing.

"Look, I've got a trust fund," carried on Isabel. "I've never touched it. You can use that….whatever you need. And I've got some other savings accounts…and then there's the house…"

"The house?" Mac looked up, sharply. "What house?"

"My parents' house, in Surrey. It was left to me. I didn't want to live in it so I've been renting it out." Isabel paused as she thought back to the family home she hadn't seen for such a long time. The sprawling garden, the cool summer house, the cluster of trees at the bottom of the garden that she would hide and play in – much to her mother's discontent. "I suppose, if it was necessary, we could sell that. It must be worth £500,000, maybe more."

"Whoa! Slow down, Isabel!" said Mac, holding up his hands and staring at Andre. "Tell her, Andre! We don't need any of this. We'll work something out. Tell her we don't need it."

Again, Andre paused, the heavy silence hanging in the air like a dead weight.

"Andre?" Mac looked from his friend to Isabel, and then back again. "Surely you can't be thinking……?"

"Have you got a better idea?" snapped Andre, firing an angry glance up at Mac. "Face it. We're cornered. If we want to get out of here in one piece, we need money. And right now, we don't have a penny."

"I know, but…" Mac shook his head, slowly. "Surely there's another way."

Andre slammed his coffee cup back down onto the table with such force that the remnants of cold coffee splashed across its glass surface.

"Yes, there is another way, Mac. You just go on out there and give yourself up. Take Isabel and the papers with you. Then all of this will have been for nothing. Simon…." Andre stopped for a moment as he mentioned his dead friend's name, his voice catching. He swallowed to regain some composure. "Simon, lying out there, would have all been for *nothing*."

Mac held his hands up in defeat. "OK, OK. I'm just trying to think of other options."

"Well, right now, there aren't any," said Andre, flatly, focusing his eyes on Isabel. "And if Isabel has the money to help, then…."

"I want to do it," said Isabel. "I want to help. They're my parents. If I can help, I want to. If there's just the smallest chance that I can get to see them again, then I'll give you everything that I've got."

Andre resumed pacing up and down in front of the window. All that could be heard was the faint ticking of the clock on the mantelpiece and Andre's footsteps on the floorboards.

"How much do you need?" Isabel tried to catch Andre's eye as he paced back and forth. "If you can get me to a bank, I can get whatever you need."

Andre stopped, mid pace, and looked over at Isabel. His eyes searched hers. "You'll get it all back – every penny. I promise."

Isabel shrugged. "It's no problem. I want to do it."

"In that case, we can do it right here, right now."

Andre strode over to his holdall and retrieved his laptop.

CHAPTER THIRTEEN

* * *

Time: 9.45pm
Date: 8th November 2008
Location: Metropolitan Police HQ, London

Jack sat down opposite PC Trevor Daniels and took a bite out of the late-night round of toast he had obtained from the self-service toaster in the staff canteen. The canteen was almost deserted at this hour, only one other table was occupied by three tired looking PCs on the night shift.

"So," he mumbled, crumbs falling from his lips as he chewed. "Cooper said you might have something for me."

PC Daniels looked up and nodded, pushing his spectacles back up onto the bridge of his nose as he did so. He was young, only just out of probation, with a thin, wiry frame. He put down his coffee cup and pulled over a thick leather bound folder which had been resting on the table next to him. "He said you were interested in PRISM? And Salyut 7?"

"Mmmm, did he?" replied Jack, taking another bite out of the toast and crunching, noisily. A dribble of melted butter trickled down his chin. "That was good of him."

Jack didn't know PC Daniels very well. He had seen him around the station, more often than not with his nose in a book of some sort. He had earned himself the nickname "the nerd" very quickly after joining as a probationer – he was small, thin, and had the remnants of his spotty teenage years still haunting his face. Thick rimmed, thick lensed spectacles completed the picture.

"How far do you want to go back?" continued Daniels, ignoring Jack's overt lack of enthusiasm. He opened the leather folder and looked up expectantly at Jack through his glasses.

"Eh?" frowned Jack, taking a gulp of lukewarm tea to wash down the dry toast.

"How far do you want to go back?" repeated Daniels, nodding at the opened folder. "I've got everything from the 1950's to the present day."

Jack glanced down at the pages in front of PC Daniels. The first page appeared to be some sort of chronology or contents page, separated into various colour coded sections. Cross reference information was noted neatly in the margin.

"I update it every month, when the new publications come out – so it should be pretty up to date." PC Daniels let his forefinger trail down the contents list. "You want to start with Salyut 7?"

Jack nodded, and edged closer to the folder. He pulled it towards him slightly, and began flicking through the pages. There were hundreds of newspaper cuttings and magazine articles, all carefully cut out and stuck in chronological order. There were handwritten notes, pictures and diagrams in Daniels' own neat handwriting, all carefully annotated with explanations written in colour coded pens, cross referenced to other sections in the folder.

"Where on earth do you get the time to do all this?" Jack looked up at the young fresh-faced probationer. "I'm impressed. It's all so......"

PC Daniels shrugged and took a sip from his coffee. "I guess I'm just interested in it, that's all. Have been ever since I was a kid and my dad bought me my first space rocket."

"I know, but...there's interested, and there's *interested*," continued Jack, shaking his head. "This goes way beyond a childhood hobby. This is....this is *obsessive*."

PC Daniels' cheeks began to darken, and he again rearranged his glasses on the bridge of his nose. "Well, if you would like to tell me exactly what you want to know, DI MacIntosh, then I won't waste any more of your clearly valuable time." His tone was short and sharp. "If all you've come to do is ridicule me, like everybody else seems to do, then I'll be on my way."

Jack realised he had hit a painful nerve and held up his hands, apologetically. "Sorry, sorry. I'm not making fun of you. Honest. It's just that, I've never seen anything like this before. It's amazing. Truly, it is. You must be very proud of yourself." Jack nodded down at the folder.

PC Daniels caught his gaze and gave a short nod. "It's a hobby, DI MacIntosh. An interest. Unlike you, my job doesn't rule my life. I have

CHAPTER THIRTEEN

other interests outside these four walls." He paused for a moment, and then gave a small clearing of the throat. "Maybe you should try it sometime."

Jack nodded, acceptingly. The kid had a point. What else did he have in his life apart from this job? Nothing. No outside interests, unless you count the odd evening sat in an empty pub, drinking warm beer and picking at a packet of salt and vinegar crisps, all alone. He had no hobbies, no real friends outside the job. Nothing. Any women who were unfortunate enough to meet his acquaintance usually never hung around for very long, and he couldn't really blame them. He couldn't actually remember the last time he had taken anyone out on a date. It wasn't that he was bad looking – he had aged quite well; his body was still in good shape. But at 41 years of age, his job was his life, and his life was his job. End of. Not a lot of room for much else.

"So," said Jack, pushing the lonely thoughts from his mind. "Salyut 7. What can you tell me?"

PC Daniels flicked through the pages of his folder. "Salyut 7 was a Russian space station – the last in a series which began back in 1971 with the launch of Salyut 1. Very sophisticated pieces of kit – Salyut 7 was the precursor to the Russian MIR space station, which was launched in April 1982."

"And Prism? What was that?"

PC Daniels flicked further through the file. "PRISM was an acronym – stood for Primary Research into International Space Management. It was a US state-funded NASA sub-committee, set up in 1981 in conjunction with the first ever American space shuttle launch. Its job was to oversee space exploration programmes throughout the world, to find out what stages their rivals had got to in their space development – especially the Russians - and then try to integrate them with the US space programme, so everyone was effectively working at the same pace."

Jack raised his eyebrows. "So NASA was spying on the others to make sure they weren't getting left behind?"

PC Daniels shrugged his shoulders. "I suppose you could interpret it that way if you wanted to."

THE PHOENIX PROJECT

"And did it work? Did NASA get to the front of the space race?"

"Difficult to tell," replied Daniels, closing the folder and taking another sip of coffee. "Prism was suspended after the Challenger disaster in January 1986 – so whatever ground they had made up before then was effectively lost as the US space programme was placed on hold after the explosion. Up until then they'd had a pretty good run. The first US Space Shuttle, Columbia, was launched in 1981, had several further launches in 1982- then the Americans first tested space walking in 1984, with the Challenger space shuttle, which was a huge advance for space exploration. In 1985 NASA had a busy year with 9 shuttle missions alone that year – the space race was gathering momentum at an incredible speed, with talk even at that time of sending citizens into space. But Challenger brought an end to it all."

"1986 you say?" Jack shot a quick look at PC Daniels. "The Challenger disaster was January 1986?"

"Yes," nodded Daniels, draining his coffee cup. "January 28th 1986."

January 28th 1986. Jack immediately thought of the note underneath the milk bottle. *January 28th 1986.* It couldn't just be a coincidence, surely.

"It exploded over Cape Canaveral, shortly after lift-off, killing all 7 crew members on board, "continued Daniels, "including a civilian teacher. That single incident caused the US space programme to be suspended indefinitely. The Space Shuttle didn't fly again until 1988."

"What about the Phoenix Project?"

"The Phoenix Project?" PC Daniels stood up, slipping his uniform jacket over his shoulders and picking up his empty coffee mug. "How do you know about that?"

Jack merely shrugged. "Just something I overheard."

PC Daniels smiled and picked up his folder, tucking it under his arm "Well, you won't find anything about any Phoenix Project in here."

"No?"

PC Daniels shook his head and started walking towards the doors. "No. You'll struggle to find anything anywhere about about the Phoenix Project. It doesn't exist."

CHAPTER FOURTEEN

Time: 1.00am
  Date: 9th November 2008
  Location: L'Apartament Blancos, L'Avenue du Soleil, Paris

"So, how did you know him?" Isabel hugged her knees towards her chest and pulled the blanket further up around her shoulders. The temperature of the room had dropped, and sleep still felt a long way off. She was curled up at one end of the sofa, feet tucked up underneath her and sharing a cup of warming coffee with Mac. Andre had disappeared into one of the bedrooms some time earlier, waving off any offers of joining them for coffee.

"Simon?" Mac buried his hands deep inside his pockets, trying to keep warm.

Isabel nodded. "Yes, Simon."

"God, that goes way back…………………"

***

Time: 5.25am
  Date: August 6th 1986
  Location: 6th Floor, MI6 Secret Intelligence Service HQ, London

The trolley was heavy and awkward to push. Its wheels were in need of a good oiling, getting habitually stuck in the contours of the carpet as it made its repetitive and laborious journey through the corridors of the building. Day after day after day.

Mac paused and looked at his watch. It was early, and most of the staff on this floor had not yet turned up for work – which was exactly the way he preferred it. He grabbed a handful of letters and tossed them in through an open doorway to his left, watching them land in a heap on the centre of the desk inside.

He continued further down the corridor, pushing the heavily laden post trolley, distributing various parcels, letters, and internal documentation as he went. Thankfully the trolley was becoming lighter and easier to push the further he went.

Soon he reached the very end of the corridor and paused outside the final door on this floor on his early morning post round. The nameplate on the outside glinted as it caught the harsh light from the artificial strobes on the ceiling overhead – Mr Simon Shafer. The door itself was pulled shut, but Mac could see that it was not closed completely. A small chink of light from within the room crept around the door frame. Mac glanced over his shoulder along the deserted corridor behind him, and gently pushed at the door with his fingers.

The door swung open. The room was empty.

The desk light was on, casting its glow across Shafer's paper strewn desk. Mac noticed several polystyrene cups of half-drunk coffee in amongst the mass of paperwork. There was also a half-eaten doughnut discarded in the wastepaper basket, together with a copy of the early morning edition of the Financial Times. Mac smiled to himself – doughnuts for breakfast and the early edition of the Financial Times. That was so Simon.

But Simon Shafer himself was nowhere to be seen.

Mac knew Shafer had been coming into the office earlier and earlier for the best part of the last month. Sometimes he was even here before Mac turned up for his early post shift at 5.00am. And he was staying later and later into the evening as well, often the last person to leave the building, if he even left at all. Mac suspected that on more than one occasion the young MI6 officer worked through the night. Mac had also noticed that

CHAPTER FOURTEEN

lately he had become more distant, withdrawn, his mind clearly focused on something else. His face had a permanently troubled look etched onto it, but whenever Mac had voiced his concerns for his friend, Shafer had just waved him away with a wan smile and a promise to go for a beer with him.

Simon was his friend. They had met soon after Mac landed the post room job – instantly clicking and easing into a genuine friendship. Mac could honestly say, hand on heart, that Simon was the only person in the whole building who ever gave him the time of day. Mac the Post Man. Mac the Invisible.

Mac edged further into the office and reached for a piece of paper next to the telephone. He picked up a nearby pen and scribbled a message in his own scrawly, spidery handwriting.

"Birthday drinks tonight 7pm. The Fox and Hounds. Don't be late! Mac."

Mac picked up the message and went to prop it up in the middle of Shafer's desk, somewhere where he couldn't fail to find it. He moved a few pieces of paper out of the way, accidentally brushing a few of them onto the floor. It was then that Mac saw it. A large, blown up photograph of a man, just his face, staring out at him from the centre of the desk. Below the photograph was a small caption giving details as to the man's name, age, weight, height, hair colour, last known addresses and family contact details.

Mac moved the photograph to the side, but found an identical one underneath. And then another. And another. And another. The whole desk was littered with pictures of the same man, the same face, the same eyes. Mac pushed the photographs aside until he came to a piece of paper buried at the very bottom. It was an internal memo addressed to Shafer. Mac pulled it out and his eyes were immediately drawn to the large red TOP SECRET stamp emblazoned across the centre of the page.

He should have stopped there. He knew that. He knew that he should have replaced the memo back where he had found it as soon as he saw the top secret stamp. But Mac being Mac, he didn't.

As he began to read the memo, Mac saw a slight movement out of the corner of his eye. Assuming it was Shafer returning to his desk, Mac turned around, memo in hand, ready to greet his friend.

It was only then, as he turned around to speak, that he noticed it wasn't Shafer in the doorway at all. It was Charles Tindleman; Head of MI6.

* * *

Time: 1.15am
   Date: 9th November 2008
   Location: L'Apartament Blancos, L'Avenue du Soleil, Paris

The clock on the mantelpiece showed 1.15 am. Mac shifted wearily in his seat; sleep continuing to taunt him, to punish him and evade him.

"Needless to say, I got the sack," he muttered, rubbing his eyes and letting out an exhausted sigh. "Accessing classified information without authorisation they called it."

"Snooping," commented Isabel, simply.

Mac nodded. "The boss removed me from the building immediately. Never set foot in the place again." Mac let his mind wander back in time – he hadn't thought about those days for such a long time. It seemed like a lifetime ago, a different time and place altogether. A different world. He could remember clearly the man's face which had stared back at him from the many photographs strewn over Shafer's desk.

It had been Andre.

"The memo was from somewhere in the United States. It wasn't clear exactly where. But it was asking Simon to track down this man – Andre - find him, and report back. Andre had disappeared from Prism and the Phoenix Project by this time and there were many people desperate to find him. He had taken with him a copy of the Project's papers, papers which if ever made public could bring America crashing to its knees. Andre was a liability, and had to be found."

"So what did he do? Your friend, Simon?"

CHAPTER FOURTEEN

Mac sighed. "Simon wasn't stupid. He knew what the memo really meant. He knew that Andre – or Gustav Friedman as he still was at the time – was a dead man walking. So, he did exactly as he was told. He tracked Gustav down to a remote part of Switzerland."

"And then?"

"And then Gustav died, and Andre Baxter was born. Like I said to you before, Andre can create a false identity in minutes. It was easy. Just like that, Gustav had a death certificate. There was even a funeral and cremation service. Gustav Friedman's ashes lie peacefully in a small churchyard in southern Switzerland."

"And no one ever found out?" Isabel's eyes widened. "Really?"

Mac shrugged and shook his head. "Andre's too good. When he creates a new identity, it's watertight. The search for Gustav Friedman led to a dead end every time, literally. Simon went back to MI6 and reported what he had found, making sure that the trail ended there, with Gustav's death. He created surveillance reports, witness statements, even photographic evidence of the funeral. All extremely convincing. His actions helped to save Andre's life, and Andre has never forgotten that."

"Why did he do it?" Isabel hugged her knees even more closely to her chest, the chill of the room continuing to permeate her bones. "Why would he go to such lengths to help him disappear?"

Mac shrugged again. "That I don't know. Simon was a good guy, and an excellent intelligence officer. He didn't speak about his work. And….well I guess now we will never get to ask him."

"So what happened next?"

"Everything went to sleep for years. The remaining Phoenix Project members thought Gustav was dead, and news was also coming in that Kreshniov had committed suicide in the Soviet Union. They were no longer worried about the missing papers. They just assumed they had been lost along with Gustav's life.

"But then, out of the blue, Simon received an assignment from Charles Tindleman, head of MI6. And as soon as Simon saw the assignment's codename, Operation Faraday, he knew that the past was coming back to haunt him. He was being asked to take possession of a number of classified documents at Heathrow Airport and bring them to MI6 headquarters, guarding them with his life.

"It didn't take Simon long to realise what the classified documents would be. They had to be the Phoenix Project papers. He contacted me and, together with Andre, we hatched the plan to intercept the papers while they were en route to MI6. There was no way he could let them enter the building. I was told to hail a black taxi cab from Vauxhall Bridge and pick up whatever had been left on the floor. It worked like clockwork. I saw the cab arrive and pull up outside Vauxhall Cross. I saw Simon get out of the cab, and as soon as he left I jumped in. There was a briefcase on the floor which I just picked up. I let the cab carry me a few minutes up the road, then I jumped out and was gone."

Isabel nodded, and stifled a yawn. "And those are the papers you showed me?"

Mac nodded. "And now Andre has both sets. Finally, he now holds all the evidence of the Phoenix Project and can prevent them from being destroyed."

"How long have you known him?"

"Andre?" Mac shrugged. "When I got the sack from the post job, I struggled to find work. I couldn't get a reference, for obvious reasons, and my job history was pretty shaky to say the least. I got into a bit of trouble – nothing major. Just mixing with the wrong crowd, that kind of thing. I used to be a bit of a handful when I was young, spent a bit of time in a borstal facility." Mac looked up and quickly caught Isabel's eye. "I'm not proud of it. I wasn't a good person to be around for a while. My mother, well, she wasn't around when I was growing up and I spent a lot of time in foster care. I never knew my Dad. I ended up drifting around in gangs where I lived." Mac paused as he thought back. "So, I wasn't the most employable person as you can imagine. It was my probation officer who got me the postal job at the MI6 building. Christ knows how he managed it, with my track record. But they agreed to take me on and give me a chance. Guess I kind of blew that, though." Mac smiled, ruefully. "It was

CHAPTER FOURTEEN

Simon that suggested I go and see Andre. After I got the sack from the post job, Simon and I stayed in touch. I think he felt a bit guilty about what happened, said he should have locked his door when he went out. But it wasn't his fault; I ruined my chances at that job all by myself. But as Gustav had just died, and Andre had been reborn in France, Simon suggested I relocate for a while. Simon and Andre had become good friends, so I went to stay with him in France, and ended up helping him out in his security business. Andre gave me a chance to prove myself. I'll always be grateful to him for that. And to Simon."

Isabel shivered, and not just because of the cold. "Who do you think killed him?"

Mac's head filled once again with images of Shafer's lifeless body. "Kreshniov. It has to be. There's no one else. Deceive a man like Kreshniov and you'll end up looking over your shoulder for the rest of your life. He doesn't forget. If he found out that Simon double crossed him all those years ago, and helped Andre escape, then this would have been his revenge. Even after all this time. Deception has no time frame. "

Mac could see the warm blood drenching Shafer's shirt. The look of fear and horror in his eyes as he faced death head on. His face slowly draining of colour as his life trickled and ebbed away, clutching at Mac, clutching at whatever final piece of life he could grasp, struggling to find his voice. Mac could hear Shafer's final rasping words echoing around his head, time and time again, round and round in a never ending circle.

"Who knows what is possible…..who knows what is possible….."

Mac tilted his head back against the cushions of the sofa and closed his eyes once again. He could still see the blood. He could still see and feel its sticky warmth trickling through his fingers as he tried in vain to stop the life seeping out from the gaping wound in front of him. Simon's vice like grip on his arm. The tightening of his fingers, the blood in his mouth, his words echoing around and around.

Mac's eyes snapped open. He sat bolt upright, staring directly ahead of him. Something had just occurred to him, something that they should have noticed before. Straight ahead of him, in the centre of the mantelpiece, was a simple china vase. It looked harmless enough – tall and cream coloured, with an abundance of fresh red carnations and ivory coloured lilies tumbling over the sides. They gave off a calm, peaceful scent.

Mac's heart quickened its pace and he felt his stomach tighten.

Fresh flowers.

The vase held fresh flowers.

But hadn't Andre told them Marie hadn't been here for a while? That she hadn't used the flat in ages? Yet these flowers were fresh enough to have been placed there that very day.

Mac slowly got up from the sofa and edged over towards the vase. He could feel Isabel's eyes following him as he did so. He peered closely into the foliage, gently moving some of the leafy stems away.

"What the...?" started Isabel, but Mac quickly looked across and placed a finger to his lips to silence her. Isabel closed her mouth and continued to watch as Mac peered even closer into the vase.

It wasn't long before he spied it. It hadn't been concealed very well, if at all. Whoever had put it there had been in a rush. Gently, Mac reached into the vase and touched the small, round, metallic looking object which had been attached to a carnation stem. Then, holding his finger to his lips once again, Mac edged backwards out of the room to wake Andre.

* * *

Time: 12.45am
    Date: 9th November 2008
    Location: Kettles Yard Mews, London

Jack threw back the covers and gave up.

Sleep was not happening tonight.

Or any night, come to think of it, he mused, as he opened his bedroom door and padded through to the living room. He had forgotten to close the living room curtains and the faint amber hues from the street lighting outside his window gave the room a gentle, warm glow.

CHAPTER FOURTEEN

Jack headed for the fridge and pulled out the milk, snapping on the kettle as he passed. He glanced over at the bottle of Glen Fiddich on the coffee table, but knew that would be a bad idea. As he waited for the kettle to boil, Jack thought back to his chat over toast with PC Trevor Daniels. The man was a genius. A total nerd, clearly, but a genius nonetheless. Jack felt the faint tickle of envy infiltrate his bloodstream as he thought about PC Daniels and his hobby. To have something you cared about that much; something that interested you that much. Jack felt inadequate in comparison. His interests? He glanced around the room. It was devoid of anything really – apart from the bottle of Glen Fiddich.

After tipping a generous portion of milk into his mug, Jack took his coffee back through to the bedroom. A warm, milky drink? Wasn't that what they said would aid a restful night's sleep? Jack wasn't sure it was meant to be a caffeine laden mug of coffee, but he knew sleep would be a precious commodity tonight anyway. He would watch the clock steadily creep towards dawn, much as he did most nights, and then would begin a new day.

At least if he stayed awake he wouldn't dream.

***

Time: 1.30am
   Date: 9th November 2008
   Location: Paris

Karl Poborski looked at the screen of his mobile phone and recognised the number straight away. He had been waiting for this call, and flipped open the handset.

"Yes?" His voice was low and curt. He paused while listening to the voice on the other end. "You're sure?" Again another pause, followed by a nod of the head. "It will be done. I'm on my way."

Poborski snapped the phone shut and glanced at his wristwatch. 1.30am. It would be dark for some time yet; the perfect cover for the next part of the plan. With a thin smile on his lips, he flicked open the screen once again and dialled. The person on the other end was clearly waiting for his call, as it was answered immediately.

"I just got the call. They're all at the flat, just like she promised. I'll meet you there. 2 hours."

* * *

Time: 1.45am
   Date : 9th November 2008
   Location: L'Apartament Blancos, L'Avenue du Soleil, Paris

Mac motioned for André to sit down. He pulled a pad of paper out of his pocket and began scribbling feverishly. Andre lowered himself into the sofa next to Isabel, and opened his mouth to speak. Mac held up a hand and shook his head, violently. He held up the pad so that Andre and Isabel could see what he had written.

"We're being bugged. Device in vase of flowers on mantelpiece. DO NOT SAY ANYTHING. Act normally. We need to get out FAST."

Both Andre and Isabel read the note, a look of alarm reaching their faces only momentarily before being overtaken by a look of fear. Mac pulled the paper back towards him and scribbled some more. He held the pad up in the air, his hand shaking.

"We pack up our stuff. Leave it by the door. Keep talking as normally as possible. They mustn't know we have found the bug. We leave as soon as we are ready. Head for the Swiss border."

Both Isabel and Andre nodded and began to move. Mac was the first one to speak.

"I'm tired. I think I'll go and have a lie down on the bed." He began folding away the laptop which was still sitting on the coffee table, and handed it to Andre.

"I think I'll watch some TV," said Andre, loudly. "I can't sleep just yet." He went over and switched on the television, turning it to a French news

CHAPTER FOURTEEN

channel. He stared, warily, at the vase of flowers as he passed.

Mac nodded, approvingly. "We ought to stay here, lie low for another day at least. Maybe more. Then we need to think where we go next. My thoughts are that we head back to the UK. There's nothing out here for us now."

"I agree," said Andre, packing up the last of his things and placing his holdall by the door, draping his jacket over the top. "The safest place for us, and Isabel, will be back home."

Andre then bent down and picked up the bundle of Phoenix Project papers and stared at them. They felt heavy in his hands. He caught Mac watching him and hurriedly scribbled on the message pad.

"We need to get rid of these papers. Not safe to keep them on us."

Mac frowned and shrugged, then watched as Andre slipped them inside a large brown envelope and quickly scribbled a name and address on the front. Then he dropped the package on top of his holdall bag and turned away. He saw Mac still watching him.

Andre held up the notepad. "We need to keep them safe. There is only one place I know – now Shafer is gone. Trust me."

Mac grabbed the pen and scribbled frantically. "Do you think there are any more bugs?"

Andre read the note, held up his hands and shook his head. Both he and Mac then began scanning the room for likely bugging stations. There were plenty. Light fittings. Picture frames. Ornaments.

Mac scribbled once again. "Kreshniov???"

Again Andre just shrugged.

Mac scribbled another message. "How did he know we would end up here? How did he know about Dupont, and Shafer?"

Once more, Andre could only shrug.

Mac held Andre in his gaze for a several long seconds, then scribbled once more on the pad. "Give me your phone."

Andre frowned, but pulled his phone out of his pocket and handed it to Mac. Mac grabbed it and began pulling it apart. The plastic back came off easily, exposing the battery and SIM card. He removed both and held them up to the light, inspecting them closely. Nothing. Now it was Mac's turn to frown. He looked closely at the face of the phone, then turned it over and scoured the insides. Still nothing. Everything looked exactly as it should. The phone hadn't been touched. Andre's phone hadn't been bugged.

Mac shook his head. There had to be something. There just had to be. It didn't make sense. He replaced the battery and SIM card and then handed Andre his phone back. Andre reached out and took it, and as he did so Mac saw a glint from Andre's wrist. It had come from a large wristwatch around Andre's right wrist. Mac's eyes remained fixed on the watch.

Flashbacks coursed through his brain. Andre on the telephone to Dupont, holding the phone in his right hand. His wristwatch on his right wrist. Andre on the telephone to Shafer, again with the phone in his right hand. Andre talking to Marie about the flat, his wristwatch in full view.

Mac's features darkened. Slowly he held his arm out towards Andre and tapped his wrist with his forefinger. Andre frowned. Again, Mac tapped his wrist with his finger and nodded towards Andre's watch.

The same flashbacks filled Andre's head as they had Mac's only moments before. He was talking to Mac on the phone, holding the receiver up to his ear with his right hand. His wristwatch clearly visible. The he was talking to Albert Dupont. Then to Shafer. Then to Marie. Every time his watch was on his wrist.

Andre fumbled for the pad and pen. "How?" he scribbled, and thrust the pad at Mac.

Mac went to shrug, then changed his mind. He thought for a moment, then wrote one single word on the pad and handed it back to Andre. "Marie."

Andre shook his head, slowly. He mouthed the word "no way."

Mac scribbled some more. "Has she been inside your apartment?"

Andre shook his head firmly. She hadn't.

"Has she had any chance to get hold of that watch without you knowing?"

Again, Andre shook his head, more urgently this time. It was impossible. Not Marie. She couldn't have. In any case, he never took the watch off.

CHAPTER FOURTEEN

Never.

But then he hesitated. His heart thundered inside his chest as he remembered. His stomach suddenly felt as though a huge hole had been blasted through its walls. It had been that night. The night they had spent together in her apartment. Slowly, and surely, the awful realisation hit him. He remembered taking off his watch, just before Marie had turned towards him and began to stroke her long painted fingernails all the way down his back……Andre swallowed, his heart racing. Afterwards, he had fallen asleep in her bed, waking in the early hours of the morning and silently dressing before slipping out of her flat unnoticed.

But he had forgotten his watch. He had forgotten to take his watch with him in his haste to leave.

Andre frowned slightly as he recounted the events of that night. That wasn't entirely true. That wasn't how it had been. He hadn't *forgotten* to take it with him – it hadn't been there to take. He remembered looking for it on the bedside table, where he thought he had left it – where he *knew* he had left it. But the watch had disappeared. He looked underneath the bed, in case it had been knocked off the table and onto the floor, but nothing.

It had completely vanished.

So – Andre had gone back to his apartment without it. Marie had knocked at his front door later that day, handing him back the watch with a sheepish smile.

"You left this behind, Monsieur Andre," she had said, in her soft, sultry tone. Her eyes smouldered as she spoke. She handed him back the watch, and he had placed it back on his wrist without a second thought. Until now.

Realisation dawned on Andre thick and fast. Anger, mixed with shame, welled up inside him and he threw the note pad angrily across the room. Mac nodded at the watch and held his palm open for Andre to hand it over. Andre slipped it off his wrist, holding it between his thumb and forefinger as if it were contaminated. Carefully, Mac eased the back off the watch with his pocket knife. Inside, amongst the workings of the watch, sat a small, black, rectangular device. Two small wires connected it to the watch battery. Mac tipped the watch towards Andre, letting him see the bug for himself. Andre peered closer, taking the watch back into his own hands. It was then that he noticed something else. There wasn't just the one device – there was another. The second device was circular, with a small red blinking light

* * *

CHAPTER FIFTEEN

Time: 4.15am
Date: 9th November 2008
Location: Outside L'Apartament Blancos, L'Avenue du Soleil, Paris

The car pulled up outside the front entrance to Marie's apartment block. The engine idled silently for a while, and then died. The driver flipped open his mobile phone and dialled the number.

"It's me," he said, as soon as the call was answered. "I'm in position." His voice was cold and hard. Listening to the reply, he nodded and broke out into a small, thin smile which stretched across his equally small, thin lips. "Yes, all three still inside."

Karl Poborski cast a quick look out of the rear view mirror, and despite the darkness he could see the back-up car pulling into the kerb behind him. Inside he knew would be the rest of his team, dressed in dark grey suits and heavy woollen overcoats, each wearing an earpiece and holding a semi-automatic weapon close to their sides. "And the others are here too. We're ready to go in."

Poborski snapped the phone shut and slipped it back inside his overcoat. Silently, he slid out from behind the wheel and glanced back at the car behind him. He locked eye contact with the driver and, without the need for words, he nodded curtly and turned to cross the road. The men inside the back-up vehicle remained inside, watching and waiting for the call.

Poborski paused outside the communal entrance, standing underneath one of the huge trees which lined the avenue on both sides. His feet were cushioned in amongst a soft bed of autumn leaves. He didn't notice Shafer's bloodstains that were hidden underneath, or if he did he paid them no heed.

The streetlight overhead barely gave off a faint glow, so he brought out a small torch from inside his overcoat. At the same time, he brought out a small, black box and flipped open the built-in screen. He used a small control to zoom in on the tiny red blinking light which was winking at him from the centre of the monitor. The words "Flat 3a, L'Apartament Blancos, L'Avenue du Soleil scrolled across the bottom.

A cold, cruel smile teased Poborski's thin lips. He snapped the screen shut on the tracking device receiver and slipped it back inside his pocket. They were still inside. He felt like a wild animal cornering his prey, waiting to pounce, knowing that he was about to make a kill. And it felt good.

Turning off the torchlight, he then brought out a small hand-sized pistol and held it up next to his chest. He could feel his heart beating fast beneath his heavy overcoat. His leather gloved fingers curled even more tightly around the shaft of the gun. It felt good.

* * *

Time: 4.15am
    Date: 9th November 2008
    Location: L'Apartament Blancos, L'Avenue du Soleil, Paris

Mac gently opened the apartment door a tiny crack, and waited for any signs of movement on the landing outside. There were none. He opened the door a fraction further, and again waited for movement. Still nothing. The landing was silent and still. The only sounds were their own breaths, arriving in short, sharp rasps. Mac glanced over his shoulder towards André and gave a swift, silent nod.

Slowly Mac edged out into the corridor, his back hugging the cold, stone wall. He stepped sideways in carefully controlled steps, with Andre and Isabel following in his wake. All three then stood deathly still, backs hard

CHAPTER FIFTEEN

against the cold concrete of the corridor wall.

"This way," mouthed Mac, and he slowly crept along the corridor away from the main stairs. Andre and Isabel followed, ever watchful for signs of movement, but the whole apartment block appeared to be in a peaceful slumber. They arrived outside a fire escape at the very end of the corridor. Mac leant forwards and placed both hands against it. Taking a deep breath, and hoping the door was not alarmed, he pushed, heaving the heavy fire door open into an inky black cavernous space.

A chill breeze blew up and slapped them in the face. They were looking directly out into the dark Parisian night. Andre handed Mac a small penlight, which cast a faint, eerie glow into the pitch darkness before them. Without waiting any longer, Mac swung himself over the barrier and out onto the metal steps that hugged the outside wall and stretched down to the rear carpark below. Without the need for words, Andre nodded to Isabel to follow. They had no idea how much time they had, or if indeed time had already run out. One by one they climbed slowly and silently down the fire escape steps, hoping their luck would hold.

***

Time: 10.15pm
   Date: 8th November 2008
   Location: Washington DC, USA

Austin Edwards pushed his heavy frame up from his desk and went over to the drinks cabinet. The decanter on top was virtually empty. Edwards tipped the last of the amber liquid into the thick, crystal glass tumbler and brought it to his lips.

He could hear his doctor tutting in disagreement already. But Edwards shut him out. One more couldn't hurt, surely? And then the one after that. And the one after that. Edwards closed his eyes and drained his glass. Cirrhosis. Fibrosis. At risk of acute liver failure if he continued. He had heard all the warnings many times over, and was choosing to ignore them.

For now. When all this was over, maybe he would consider a lifestyle change. Maybe move out to the hills. To the mountains. Take up hiking. Or fishing.

He put the empty tumbler back down on the drinks cabinet and glanced at the clock on the wall above. 10.15pm. It would be early morning in Paris, and the deed should be underway. And hopefully then, the end.

**

Time:4.20am
   Date: 9th November 2008
   Location: L'Apartament Blancos, L'Avenue du Soleil, Paris

Special Agent Fleming gripped his pistol and slowly edged his way closer to the apartment door. His body hugged the corridor wall, the only sound being the soft scraping of the material of his overcoat on the cold concrete wall. His soft-soled shoes silently slid over the tiled floor, making no sound. He paused at the door to Apartment 3a, immediately noticing that it was slightly ajar. Bright light seeped through the gap around the door frame.

Frowning, Fleming stretched out his hand, holding his pistol steadily in front of him, and gently pushed open the door. It swung open easily, bathing the corridor in light. Fleming quickly slipped into the room, gun ready. He held the weapon with both hands, arms locked out in front of him, his eyes quickly sweeping the room.

He could tell that the main room was deserted. He noticed the vase of flowers lay smashed on the carpet, ceramic shards littering the deep pile. Two high-backed chairs lay overturned in the centre of the room, and two paintings lay askew on the walls. He stepped further into the room, and quickly checked both the bathroom and bedroom. There was nothing to see, except an unmade bed. Fleming dropped to his knees and checked underneath. Nothing. He opened the wardrobe. Still nothing.

Fleming returned to the main room, stowing his pistol back inside the

CHAPTER FIFTEEN

holster beneath his jacket. He pulled out his mobile phone and tapped in a series of numbers. He waited, anxiously, for the call to be answered.

"It's me," he said, sharply. "I'm in the apartment. There's no sign of them."

"Are you sure they were even there?" came the reply. "Maybe your tip off was a hoax?"

Fleming looked up, his eyes scanning the room, and began to wander over to the centre. And it was there that he saw it. A small, red blinking light coming from on top of the coffee table. He reached down and picked up Andre's watch, which had been dismantled to display its inner workings, the bug and the tracking device. Fleming turned the watch over in his hands and then carefully placed it back down next to a few strands from the bugged flowers. Next to the flowers was a small piece of paper.

"Nice try," it read, simply, in Mac's scribbled handwriting.

"Did you hear me?" barked the voice from the other end of the phone. "Maybe they were never there in the first place."

"No, they were here all right," replied Fleming, nodding to himself and placing Andre's watch into his pocket. "They were most definitely here." He glanced back over his shoulder at the two upturned chairs. "But I think maybe someone else got here before us."

"Are you sure?" Liddell's voice sounded tense. "Kreshniov?"

Fleming shrugged to himself. "Maybe, who knows. But I think they might have left in time."

"Well, you need to get out there and find them. I want the girl safe….and alive."

Fleming nodded once again. "I'm onto it. They won't have got far. My team is downstairs; we'll search until we find them."

"Make sure you do. And call me the minute you have a location." Liddell's voice paused. "And where's Shafer? He was supposed to have reported in this morning and this evening. Charles says he hasn't heard from him and his phone is switched off."

"I don't know. I didn't see him this morning. He left the hotel early and he's not answering his calls."

"Damn!" swore Liddell, his temperature rising. "Find me Shafer, and find me the girl. Fast!"

Fleming burst out of the front doors and dashed straight across the road to a waiting car. The three men inside instantly jumped out, flinging the doors wide open, pistols at hand. Fleming held up his hands and shook his head. "It's no go, guys. The place is empty. They've gone."

The three men hesitated, their eyes flickering towards the communal doors, checking for signs of anyone rushing out in pursuit, but there were none. Cautiously, they relaxed and lowered their guns to their sides.

"There's no one inside." Fleming was a little breathless after running down three flights of stairs and he held his sides, breathing in deeply. "But they were there. Someone's been in before us. Whoever it was has been bugging them, and tracking them." Fleming reached into his pocket and pulled out Andre's watch. "Two small devices in the back of this watch. One a listening device, one a location device. Liddell wants us to find them, and fast."

The three men nodded but remained silent. Fleming made eye contact with each of them before continuing. "We'll search on foot. Heading out this way first." He nodded along the deserted street in front of them. "Two on one side, two on the other. Backman and Dodds – you take the right. Carter, you come with me, we'll take the left."

The four of them started to move off into the shadows.

"And keep your eyes out for Shafer," added Fleming, crossing the road. "He's gone and disappeared on us as well."

***

Time: 4.30am
Date: 9th November 2008
Location: Outside L'Apartament Blancos, L'Avenue du Soleil, Paris

They hunched together in the darkness. Although they had made it out of the apartment, they had only got as far as the rear car park. It had been too

CHAPTER FIFTEEN

risky to attempt to go any further. As soon as they had reached the bottom of the fire exit steps, they were met by a torrent of shouting, slamming of car doors, barked instructions and commands coming from the front of the apartment block.

But now, all there was was an eerie silence.

"What now?" whispered Mac, leaning in towards Andre. "The place seems deserted."

Andre nodded, slowly. "I think they've all moved off. Looking for us probably." He paused and peered out around the car they were sheltering behind. He now had a clear view out into the road beyond, and all he could see was blackness. "I think we need to split up."

Isabel and Mac glanced at each other, and Andre noticed their apprehensive expression.

"It's the best way." Andre shuffled forwards. "They may have gone for now, but they'll be back. If we all move off together, we've more chance of getting caught. We need to get some money, and a car. There's no way we can make it to the Swiss border on foot. We'll need some wheels." Andre attempted a half smile. "Mac and I will go, find a car, and come back for you. You'll be fine, if you just stay still."

With a frightened look in her eyes, Isabel glanced warily around the car park, and shivered. Andre took off his jacket and slipped it over her shoulders. "You'll be fine. We'll be back before you know it." With that, Andre crept out into the car park, gesturing for Mac to follow on behind. Mac turned to go, but hesitated, taking a final look over his shoulder at Isabel.

"Don't move," he whispered. "We'll come back for you, I promise." He gently squeezed her arm before following Andre out into the car park, edging around the shadows until they disappeared into the dark.

Isabel was finally alone.

The hours crawled by and Isabel remained hidden in the shadows of the deserted car park. Dawn was now breaking and the sky lightened to reveal a clear, crisp morning with only a few high, streaky clouds. A pale white sun rose low in the sky, causing the shadows of the car park to shrink further and further back until they had vanished completely.

During the night, Isabel had heard a few shouts, the sound of a few cars screeching past, but nothing else. The silence was unnerving. She shivered and pulled Andre's jacket further around her shoulders, burying herself deep inside. Her fingers were frozen and numb, and she had lost all feeling in her feet and toes.

Mac and Andre had been gone for hours now. There had been no sign of them since they had slunk away into the heavy darkness. She glanced at her watch – it was 7.35am. How long did it take to reach a cash machine and find a car? They must have been gone for 3 hours or so by now. Isabel's stomach tightened and she began to fear the worst. What if they didn't come back? She was in a foreign country, with no money, no passport, and no idea where she was or where she was going.

A coldness that had nothing to do with the freezing temperatures around her, gripped her heart. Surely they should have been back by now?

Unless.

Unless they weren't coming back.

But surely they would not abandon her like this? They had told her they would be back, promised her they would come back. But three hours later, there was still no sign of them.

A wave of panic engulfed Isabel. She started to scramble out from her hiding place, trying to force her frozen limbs to move and support her weight – but failing. She fell heavily to her knees, being forced to crawl across the frozen ground on knees and elbows. Slowly, she inched forwards, scraping along the ground, ignoring the pain from the tiny gravel stones as they bit angrily into her skin. She crawled past the shadow of the car that had shielded her throughout the night, and peered around the bumper out into the car park and beyond. Everything seemed quiet. The same old cars in the same old places.

The same cars.

"We need to get some money and a car." Those had been Andre's words. *"We need some wheels."* The words echoed around Isabel's head, taunting her, teasing her. *"We need some wheels....we need some wheels."*

CHAPTER FIFTEEN

There were at least half a dozen cars parked around the edge of the car park. And in the street outside, more were parked nose to tail along each side. Why hadn't they just taken one of those? Isabel's mouth went dry.

She continued to crawl across the rest of the car park, her feet and hands still numb to the cold, gravel tearing into her skin. She reached the rear of the apartment block, turned around, and leant against the wall, breathing hard. She blew on her fingers, trying to will them to move and regain some feeling. She picked out the tiny gravel stones that were embedded in her palms, not feeling the stinging from the cuts and scrapes. Slowly, her ankles and feet began to feel more mobile, and she gingerly stood up, using the wall for support.

Looking around the edge of the apartment block, Isabel saw there was no one outside the entrance, and no one along the deserted street. No one was waiting. No one was watching. She was completely alone. She had no idea where she was going, or what she was doing, but she knew she had to get away from here. It wasn't safe. Not anymore. Not now she was on her own.

Again, Isabel glanced back at the vehicles parked in the car park where she had spent the night, and the rows upon rows of cars lining the street ahead. There could be only one reason why Mac and Andre had left her alone, and it was not to go and find a car. They had gone, quite simply, and left her, with no intention of coming back.

Isabel made up her mind. With one last look up and down the road ahead she made a dash for the alleyway opposite. She almost reached the pavement on the other side of the road, when she heard a car door slam behind her. Her heart jumped into her mouth and she whirled around to see four men in smart, tailored suits and overcoats moving towards her, each brandishing a sleek, gleaming black pistol in her direction.

Isabel froze to the spot. The ear piecing scream bubbling up inside her found its way no further than the base of her throat. She felt the insides of her stomach give way and her legs crumpled beneath her, sending her body crashing into the leaf-strewn gutter.

The four men quickly advanced on her, and all Isabel could think to do was curl up into a ball and hide her head underneath her arms. She tried to scream. She tried to shout. But she had no voice. She could barely breathe. She squeezed her eyes tightly shut and waited for what seemed to her like an eternity – waiting for the shot. The shot that would end it all.

She waited.

And waited.

And waited.

Then she felt a hand on her shoulder.

"Miss Faraday?" said a voice. The hand began to gently squeeze and shake her. "Are you Miss Isabel Faraday?"

Isabel's body stiffened under the man's touch. Where was the shot? Why wasn't she dead? The man's hand remained on her shoulder. It felt warm to the touch, comforting. Slowly, Isabel unclenched her eyes and peered out from underneath her arms that were still wrapped tightly around her head.

She could see someone kneeling down at her side. Someone in a smart, light grey suit. Shiny shoes. A gleaming silver watch and cufflinks dangled from his sleeve. The man's other hand emerged from his pocket and thrust a small, square object into her line of vision.

"Miss Faraday?" he repeated. "I'm Special Agent John Fleming. I'm from the FBI." He paused to let this information sink in. "You're safe now."

* * *

CHAPTER SIXTEEN

Time: 8.15am
 Date: 9th November 2008
 Location: Metropolitan Police HQ, London

"I need you to go to Paris," announced Chief Superintendent Liddell, turning away from the window and returning to his desk.

Jack was standing next to the visitors' chairs – he had not been offered a seat so had not sat down. "Paris?" he enquired, raising his eyebrows.

"Yes, Paris. I received a call a few moments ago," Liddell carried on, easing himself back into his chair and picking up the telephone. "That missing woman, from Cambridge? She's been found – in Paris. I need you to go and escort her home."

"Escort her?" Jack frowned, watching as Liddell pressed the zero button which connected him to his secretary Penny's office outside.

"Yes," nodded Liddell, holding the receiver up to his ear. "As I explained to you before – I promised I would look after this case personally. Give it my best officers and resources. Now she's been found, I want her personally escorted back home."

Jack gave a small shrug. "OK, Sir. Who found her?"

"I..oh, Penny…can you book DI MacIntosh here onto the next available Eurostar service to Paris, please? That's right. Thank you." Liddell replaced the receiver and looked back up at Jack. "I don't want there to be any mistakes, Inspector. You get over there and bring her back here, safe and sound."

Jack nodded, slowly. "OK. So, who found her?" he repeated.

Liddell's eyes met his. "Special Agent Fleming found her. It would appear that his own investigations crossed paths with our missing person case."

"Crossed paths?" Jack failed to hide the look of scepticism on his face.

"Yes, crossed paths," confirmed Liddell. "By coincidence."

"Mmmm, coincidence," muttered Jack. "Sure."

Liddell sighed. "Look, I don't know the exact details but from what I'm being told our Miss Faraday has been in the company of two men who have been under FBI and CIA surveillance for some considerable time." He paused before continuing. "But it looks like they took off, leaving her behind. Agent Fleming came across her outside an apartment block in a Paris suburb early this morning."

"That's some coincidence," commented Jack, looking down at Liddell's orderly, army-regulation tidy desk, avoiding his superior officer's penetrating stare.

Liddell's voice became strained. "Whatever the circumstances, she is alive and well – and I want you to go and get her. That's an order, Inspector."

"Why can't Fleming bring her home?" enquired Jack, shrugging his shoulders. "Surely if he's already there with her…….."

"Because I've asked *you* to do it, Inspector!" barked Liddell, his eyes darkening. "Special Agent Fleming is still conducting an ongoing investigation. And I don't want Miss Faraday hanging around there any longer than is absolutely necessary. You will go to Paris on the next available service and personally escort her home. Do I make myself clear, Inspector?"

"Crystal," replied Jack, giving a curt nod of the head.

"Penny will have your travel details by now. I'll see you when you get back."

Jack turned and walked towards the door, clearly having been dismissed from the Chief Superintendent's presence. As he reached for the handle, Liddell's voice cut through the air.

CHAPTER SIXTEEN

"And Inspector – you guard that woman with your life. Let no one and nothing come between you."

Jack closed the door behind him and hesitated for a moment. Paris? He was being sent to Paris to pick up a missing person who was no longer missing. Why? Penny looked up, sympathetically, from her typing and handed him a sheet of paper.

"You're on the 09.36 from St Pancras. The tickets will be at the Information Kiosk on the platform. "

Jack nodded his thanks and took the sheet of paper, stuffing it in his jacket pocket. "Thanks, Penny. See you later." He made his way out of Penny's office and headed out into the corridor. He rubbed his temples with his fingers, attempting to massage away the intense tiredness his fitful night's sleep had provoked. Having lain awake until 3 or 4am, Jack had only managed a couple of hours of drifting in and out of a very light slumber. And going to Paris? He felt the weight of another long day sag onto his shoulders.

Just at the moment, DS Cooper rounded the corner.

"Ah, Cooper, just the fella."

DS Cooper raised his eyebrows and stopped. "You been summoned to the headmaster again?" he joked, nodding at the closed door behind Jack.

Jack nodded. "Hmmm. He's sending me to Paris. They've found that missing girl – Faraday – she's in Paris. Apparently I've got to go and hold her hand and bring her back."

"Why?" DS Cooper frowned, and followed Jack as they moved down the corridor away from Liddell's office. "No disrespect, boss, but what does it have to do with you?"

"My thoughts exactly, Cooper, my thoughts exactly." As they neared the stairs, with DS Cooper heading up to their office, and Jack heading towards the car park, Jack stopped. "Keep digging on that list I gave you….while I'm gone. Especially the dates."

DS Cooper nodded and gave a wave over his shoulder and he disappeared up the stairs. With a frown, Jack headed towards the car park to pick up a pool car to make his way to St Pancras.

***

Time: 8.20am
 Date: 9th November 2008
 Location: Metropolitan Police HQ, London

"I can handle it," insisted Fleming, his voice sounding stern. "She's safe enough with me."

"I'm sending DI MacIntosh over to get her, and that's the end of it," snapped Liddell, gripping the telephone receiver so tightly that his knuckles began to turn white. "You have too much else going on. You still need to find those papers."

Liddell could hear Fleming exhale noisily on the other end of the telephone. "I would just like to keep her within my sights, that's all," he remarked. "Bearing in mind the lengths I've gone to in tracking her down. I've got it all planned."

"You don't need her." Liddell's voice was firm. "She's coming back with DI MacIntosh, and that's my final word on the subject."

"But, I....."

"Look, Shafer's already gone missing. He's not been seen or heard of since the day before yesterday, and he's not reported in to either myself or Tindleman." Liddell paused, trying to keep his voice steady. "I think he's close by."

"Who?"

"Kreshniov." The word almost stuck in Liddell's throat.

"You think Kreshniov is in Paris?"

Liddell nodded at the receiver. "It makes sense. It has to be him. He's not dead, we all know that now – and if he is after the papers then he's after Isabel as well. We need to get her as far away from those documents as possible. And fast."

"But Kreshniov......" Fleming's reply was instantly cut short.

"That's my final word! Let DI MacIntosh bring the girl home, and you concentrate on finding those damn papers!"

CHAPTER SIXTEEN

* * *

Time: 9.35am
 Date: 9th November 2008
 Location: St Pancras, London

Jack's telephone began to chirp as he boarded the Eurostar direct service to Paris Gare du Nord. He answered it on the second ring, just as he lowered himself into his window seat.

"Yes? Detective Inspector MacIntosh speaking."

"Sir? Special Agent Fleming here, Sir." Fleming's voice crackled down the telephone line. "Are you on your way?"

"Yes," replied Jack, glancing down at his watch. "I'm on the 09.36 from St Pancras. Should be arriving in Paris about 12.00 UK time. Is everything OK?"

"Of course, Sir," answered Fleming. "Miss Faraday is fine – cold, but fine. She has received a brief check up from a local doctor, but she's all right." He paused for a second. "I was just wondering if I could speak with her while we are waiting for your arrival. She could hold some vital information as to the whereabouts of the men she has been with for the last few days. She was the last person to see them. I really need to talk to her, find out what she knows, so that my guys can carry on with their search." Fleming paused again. "It would really help my investigation, Sir."

Jack didn't reply straight away. He glanced out of the train window and felt the carriage shudder into life and begin to move. He would like to be with Isabel before she was questioned by anybody, get her properly debriefed before she was put under any further strain. Make sure she was up to it physically, and mentally. But then again, Fleming and his team *had* been the ones to find her. Without them, they might still be searching. And without them, this may have had a very different ending. As much as it pained him to admit, he did owe Fleming a favour.

"You sure she was with them? The guys you're after?"

"Positive," replied Fleming. "There's no question. They abducted her from the UK, smuggled her into Paris. She's been with them constantly ever since."

"Abducted?"

"Well, I don't believe she left voluntarily…..do you?"

"OK, Fleming," breathed Jack, nodding to himself as the train began to pick up speed. "You can speak with her. But go gently. If you're right, she's been through a great ordeal. Treat her kindly."

"With kid gloves," replied Fleming.

"I'll be there as soon as I can."

"Thank you, Sir. It's much appreciated. I'll see you at the police station later on today."

Jack ended the call and closed his eyes.

* * *

Time: 10.45am
 Date: 9th November 2008
 Location: MI6 Secret Intelligence Service HQ, London

Chief Superintendent Liddell quietly closed the door behind him. "Have you heard from him yet?"

Charles Tindleman turned his ample frame away from the window and nodded at Liddell to take a seat. But Liddell remained standing. He felt unnerved – it wasn't often he visited the top echelons of the MI6 building. But this couldn't wait.

"Has he called in?" repeated Liddell, his face looked haggard and drawn.

"Not today, no. Or yesterday." Tindleman tried to keep his voice low. "But I wouldn't worry."

"You wouldn't worry?" Liddell tried hard to keep the anxiety out of his voice. "You wouldn't *worry?*"

"I'm sure everything is all right. It'll just be an oversight, that's all" Tindleman's calmness did nothing to placate the Chief Superintendent.

"Shafer, an experienced MI6 officer, out in the field, hasn't been seen or

CHAPTER SIXTEEN

heard from in the last 36 hours. What is there not to worry about?"

"Everything will be fine, I'm sure of it. We would have heard by now if it wasn't."

"Well, I don't like it," said Liddell, gruffly. "Shafer doesn't just disappear like that. It's not like him."

"Look, I'll try him again. Don't get yourself all worked up." Tindleman heaved himself wearily back down into his chair, the leather creaking noisily as he did so. "I'm sure he'll pick up this time." He lifted the desktop telephone and dialled Shafer's mobile number.

He let it ring.

And ring.

And ring.

The empty ringing sound echoed around Charles Tindleman's office. Liddell stared intently at the telephone receiver, willing it to connect. Willing it to show him he was wrong.

* * *

Time: 10.30am
    Date: 9th November 2008
    Location: Commissariat Central, Rue Louis Blanc, Paris

Fleming tapped lightly on the door before quietly slipping inside. Isabel was sitting at a small, worn-looking wooden table, her hands curled around a hot cup of steaming coffee. The vapour from the hot drink rose in wisps and curls up towards her tired, ashen face. She breathed in deeply, grateful for the warmth it gave. She looked up as soon as Fleming entered, her pale blue eyes, normally so crisp and clear, had taken on a muted, misty appearance. Fleming smiled, warmly, and sat down in a chair opposite, placing a thick grey folder on the table between them.

"How are you doing?" he asked, searching into Isabel's eyes with his own. "Bearing up OK, I hope?" He continued to fix her with his gaze, his eyes burning deeply like a hot probe.

Isabel nodded, but remained silent. She pulled the mug of coffee closer towards her and let herself be shrouded by the misty vapour.

"I'm Special Agent John Fleming." Fleming held out a thin, pale hand over the wooden table. "I'm with the FBI." Isabel looked up – and not knowing what else to do, she slowly took the proffered hand. It felt a little cold and clammy. She frowned, and returned her hand to the warmth of the mug.

"FBI?" she muttered.

Fleming smiled once again, returning his hand to his side. "I guess you're wondering why the FBI are so keen to talk to you, Miss Faraday…..or may I call you Isabel?"

Isabel shrugged, cradling the mug even closer.

"I need some information from you, Isabel," continued Fleming, resting his hands on the grey folder in front of them. "You are a very important witness to an ongoing investigation of mine."

"A witness?" Isabel felt her frown deepening." A witness to what?"

Fleming paused before opening the folder, slipping two photographs out onto the table before them. He turned them both over and slowly pushed them towards Isabel, stopping only when they were both directly in front of her. He watched as she glanced down at them, carefully monitoring her changing expression.

"I believe you know these two men?" Fleming placed his well-manicured hands next to the photographs. He tapped the picture on Isabel's right hand side. "This one I believe you know to be a Mr Andre Baxter?"

Isabel looked down at the photograph and saw Andre's features staring right back up at her from the table. Slowly and hesitantly, she nodded.

"And this one?" Fleming tapped the second photograph. "You know him as Mac? Or maybe Mackenzie?" Again, Isabel nodded slowly, not taking her eyes from the photographs.

"My department over in Washington has been searching for these two individuals for quite some time, Isabel," continued Fleming, opening up the folder once again. "For several years, in fact. They have proved very difficult to track down…..until now."

CHAPTER SIXTEEN

Isabel tore her tired eyes away from the photographs and looked back up at Fleming. She watched silently as he took out a thick bundle of papers and rested them on top of the folder. He paused briefly before giving a faint, but audible, sigh.

"Isabel, you may know these people as Andre Baxter and Mackenzie, or Mac." He watched as Isabel lowered her eyes once more to the photographs on the table. "However, the FBI and CIA know them as William Hastings….Robert Carson…Phillipe Ducon….Maxwell Stander….Oscar Lyons……" With each name, Fleming threw down a fresh photograph in front of Isabel. "Matthew McMilligan….Sean Raithman….Simon Bach….William Bester….Anthony Saint-Cloud……" Fleming continued to place photograph after photograph down in front of Isabel, each one slightly different but all unmistakably either Andre or Mac.

Fleming paused and picked up the last photograph on top of the pile. "Anthony Saint-Cloud." He waved the picture on Andre in front of Isabel and started to read from the typed sheet attached to it. "April 2004, Michigan, Ohio – stole or attempted to steal the sum of $3000 from a 27-year-old student by posing as an attorney." Fleming placed the picture of Anthony Saint-Cloud back down onto the table, and picked up another. This time it was a picture of Mac. "Matthew McMilligan, in October 2002, Dallas, Texas, conned a 35-year-old female out of $35,000 worth of jewellery." The picture was returned to the table. "Phillipe Ducon, in December 2002, Denver, Colorado swindled $49,000 out of two elderly sisters…..Oscar Lyons, in August 2003, stole over $100,000 from an elderly couple in Washington DC in an insurance scam." Fleming lay the photographs back down on the table and looked up at Isabel.

If it were possible, her already ashen face seemed to have drained of even more colour. She gripped the mug in her hands even more tightly than before, unable to drag her eyes away from the photographs littering the table before her. Everywhere she looked, Mac or Andre's eyes stared back out at her. Her vision began to swim in and out of focus.

"I could go on, Isabel," continued Fleming, his tone soft and even. "These two men have had more aliases than I care to mention…. They have tricked and conned their way across the length and breadth of the United States, managing to net themselves over $2 million at the last count. I have been on their tail for the last five years, and I have never, ever, come this close to catching them."

Isabel frantically licked her lips. Her mouth had suddenly become as dry as the burning hot sun. She searched for the words that were struggling to get out. "But…but they said…. They can't be…..I…I…"

"I know all about them, Isabel. I'm sorry." Fleming lowered his gaze. "And I know what they said to you…. About your parents." Fleming could instantly feel Isabel's body tense from across the table. "I'm sorry, but it was all a lie. A scam. A swindle. All made up. These people are conmen, Isabel. Nothing more than that. Just dirty, evil, conmen."

Isabel's hands began to shake, her grip on the mug lessening. She shook her head, slowly, from side to side. "No. No, no, no. They can't be. They said…..they said….."

Fleming nodded. "I know what they said, Isabel. And I know that you believed them. That was exactly what they wanted you to do. I've had them under surveillance for the last couple of weeks. I know what they said to you, what they said happened to your parents. But it was all a lie, Isabel. There was no secret project. There was no conspiracy. No accident. No cover up. It was all just an elaborate ploy to get to you….and to get to your money."

"My…my money?" Isabel's head jerked up. "No…that can't be true."

"No?" Fleming raised his eyebrows. "They never asked you for money? They never asked if you had any savings? Any property?" Fleming looked questioningly at Isabel, but he already knew the answer. "You're sure about that?"

Isabel's mind flashed back to their time in Marie's apartment, and her face tensed. When she spoke, her voice was small and weak. "I said I would sell the house…..I said I would give them everything……." But then she paused, frowning, and raised her head to meet Fleming's gaze. "But they didn't *ask* me for any money. It was me….I *told* them I had some savings, and the house. They didn't ask me for any of it, they didn't know I had

CHAPTER SIXTEEN

anything until I told them. I offered it to them."

Fleming reached out and grabbed hold of Isabel's shaking hands. He clasped them together inside his own. Isabel noticed they still felt cold and clammy. "They already knew about the money, Isabel. And the house. They already knew about your bank accounts…and your Trust Fund. They just acted like they didn't. They knew you had money. They knew from the very beginning. That was why they chose you. They wanted to make it look like you had offered it to them…..not that they had asked for it. It's what they do…. It's what they're good at. It's exactly how they have managed to con so many people out of so much money."

"But…but how?" Isabel's tired eyes began to prick. "Why?"

"The how is easy," replied Fleming. "The why is a little trickier. Your house back in England was nearly broken into about six months ago, wasn't it?" Fleming looked up and saw that Isabel was nodding, whilst dabbing at her wet eyes. "And your rubbish bins…. Outside your house?"

"They were turned upside down," whispered Isabel, hoarsely. She remembered it clearly. The day had been scorching hot and Isabel remembered chastising herself as she walked home that she hadn't left any of her windows open when leaving for work that morning. The place is going to be like an oven, she had told herself crossly. Poor Snowy would be hiding under her bed, trying to find the coolest, shadiest part of the house in which to sleep.

When she had arrived back home, she noticed that her two dustbins which were normally stowed neatly away underneath her front steps in a small basement area, had been dragged out and turned upside down on the pavement outside. Litter was strewn everywhere. Magazines, pieces of paper, empty cartons and boxes, tubes and plastic bags. Luckily the bin with her food waste had been emptied by the refuse lorry the day before.

Isabel had sprinted up the steps to her front door and noticed that the wood around the edge of the keyhole was worn and splintered. Someone had clearly tried to break in, trying to force the door open. Hurriedly, Isabel unlocked the door and rushed into her flat, running frantically from room to room. After five minutes she concluded that nothing was missing, and no one had been inside. The place was exactly as she had left it that morning.

She had reported the incident to the police and they had sent a young constable round to check that everything was all right. When he arrived and saw the upturned rubbish bins he suggested that it had been kids, or someone looking for a spare key. Some people still left spare keys outside their houses, he said ruefully, underneath rubbish bins or flowerpots. Always the first place a prospective burglar would look, he told her kindly. But it looked as though she had gotten off lightly, with no real damage and nothing disturbed.

Although the incident had shaken Isabel at the time, she had quickly forgotten all about it, putting it to the back of her mind.

"You didn't think they had stolen anything," continued Fleming, who had been watching Isabel carefully as the images of the attempted break-in had been flashing through her mind. "But in fact, they had stolen exactly what they had been looking for. The damage to your front door was just a ruse, something to put you off the scent. They had no intention of breaking into your house. They didn't need to go inside for what they wanted. Everything they needed was right there in front of them…in your garbage bin."

* * *

Time: 10.00am
   Date: 9th November 2008
   Location: London to Paris Eurostar line, Kent countryside

Jack sat back in his seat as the Eurostar began its gentle descent underground. He knew that he only had a few minutes before his mobile phone reception would be lost as they travelled deep underneath the English Channel, heading towards France. He pulled out his phone and quickly dialled the number.

The nagging doubts he had had before leaving had now doubled. Trebled

CHAPTER SIXTEEN

even.

"Cooper?" Jack peered out of the window, seeing nothing but blackness. "I need you to do something for me. I only have a minute. But first, can you get Penny on the line for me?"

***

CHAPTER SEVENTEEN

Time: 11.20am
 Date: 9th November 2008
 Location: Commissariat Central, Rue Louis Blanc, Paris

Isabel rubbed her damp eyes with the backs of her hands, still shaking her head, slowly. She accepted the fresh mug of Parisian coffee brought in by a pleasant looking young French policewoman, and gratefully cupped it in her hands.

"They stole details of your identity," continued Fleming. "Your bank account details were on bank letters, statements, old cheque books. They found your address, date of birth, full name and national insurance number, and your employment details, all from your pay slips. They would even have found out about your assets, your savings, your parents' house. Everything they needed was right there. Right there in the stuff you threw out with the trash."

Isabel held her head in her hands, feeling the damp tears trickle between her fingers. She could see it all now so clearly. Her bin had been full to overflowing. She had had a major clearout the week before – going through everything in her flat, throwing away everything and anything that had accumulated over the last twelve months. She could see herself doing it – rounding up all the bank statements and credit card statements that were normally just stuffed inside the desk drawer. Putting them all together inside a plastic bag. She watched herself as she threw it all out into the rubbish bin. Then there were the piles and piles of payslips, P60's, tax returns, council tax statements, telephone bills. She could again see herself scooping them all up and depositing them in exactly the same way as before – straight into the bin. Then there was the house – her parents' house. She had regular rental statements from the estate agents who were letting the property for her – and they went in the same place as everything else.

"How could I have been so stupid?" she whispered, more to herself than anyone else.

"Don't blame yourself," replied Fleming, sympathetically. "You're not the first one to be hoodwinked by these two. And you sure as hell won't be the last unless I catch them. They have this down to a fine art." Fleming took a small packet of tissues out of his pocket and offered them across the table to Isabel. "They can be very convincing."

"But why? Why did I believe it all?" Isabel took the proffered tissues and dabbed her eyes with one. "Why was I so…so…?" Isabel shook her head, unable to grasp the word she was looking for.

"Because they always go for the heart, not the head. That's how they get inside someone. They always invent a story, an idea, to capture someone's heart. Before you know it, common sense goes out of the window. In your case, they knew your history, they knew about your family. They knew about your parents and what happened to them. It was easy enough to find out – it was no secret. And they fed on that. They tapped into your feelings for them – and it made you an easy target."

"But why……why invent such a…such a….?"

"Such an elaborate story?" Fleming chuckled softly to himself and shook his head. "Well, it certainly was a good one, I'll give them that. Probably their best yet. But they needed something to hook into you, and they knew it had to be something big. You're an intelligent woman, Isabel. You were going to be a hard nut to crack. They had to invent something which was so unbelievable that it just had to be true. A kind of reverse psychology, if you like. They picked on a subject most people know little or nothing about. Space. The Universe. We all know it's up there. We all know rockets take off every so often…. but that's about it. We know very little else about what happens. All the information that we are allowed to know is fed to us through designated news channels. And we all just take that to be the truth. No one ever questions it. No one ever asks if it's correct. And why would they? The thought just doesn't occur to anyone. And even if you did want to question it, how would you go about doing it? How would you check what was really happening up there? Who would you turn to? The answer is simple. You don't and you can't. You take the official news as being the truth, end of story. But there is always that niggling feeling, that little question in the back of your mind – what if there is more to it? What if I'm not being told the whole truth? What if? What if? What if? You see what I mean?"

Isabel nodded slowly.

Fleming continued. "So, they very quickly found out – through the contents of your trash can – that you were a very wealthy young lady. You were left a lot of money and property after your parents died. All they had to do after that was make contact."

Isabel let her eyes scan the photographs in front of her once again. She stared at each one in turn, letting their eyes bore into hers. Their eyes. Their eyes. She had been so sure, so convinced. She had really believed them. Yet all the time, they had been lying to her.

"The photographs," murmured Isabel, flatly.

"Sorry, the what?"

"The photographs. They showed me photographs – of my parents. They were real. I held them in my hands."

Fleming shook his head, and again reached out to grasp Isabel's hands. "It was all part of the scam, Isabel. They weren't real."

"But they *were* real! I saw them! I did!"

"I know you did," nodded Fleming, squeezing Isabel's hands. "I know you did. But the photographs weren't real, Isabel. They were fake."

Releasing Isabel's hands from his grip, Fleming pulled a small laptop computer from his briefcase and switched it on, quickly bringing up a piece of software entitled PhotoMixer.

"This is a highly sophisticated piece of software, but surprisingly easy to

CHAPTER SEVENTEEN

use. It lets you do almost anything you want to any picture or photograph you can find. I can pretty much guarantee that they would have used something similar to this, maybe even something more advanced. Andre, as you knew him, would most definitely have had access to software like this on his computer. He has created so many different identities in so many different countries over the last few years……" Fleming let his voice tail off as he saw Isabel wince at the mention of Andre's name.

"All you do is scan in the photograph or picture you want to use – in your case, a picture of your parents." Fleming paused and opened up the grey folder once again, pulling out a folded newspaper. The newspaper was old – dated September 26th 1986. Fleming unfolded the newspaper, carefully, opening it up at page 7.

Isabel gasped. Staring out at her from the pages of ageing newsprint were two happy, smiling faces. Faces she instantly recognised, for she had similar faces in the photographs on her mantelpiece at home. Faces she knew and loved. The article was about the accident the previous day that had killed her parents. A full page spread concerning the particularly treacherous stretch of road upon which it had happened, and recounting the numerous other accidents that had happened there over the preceding years.

Isabel scanned the first few paragraphs. It detailed how her father's vehicle had unexpectedly left the road in otherwise clear and dry conditions, tumbled down a ravine, then collided with a tree and killing both occupants instantly. Isabel let her eyes wander across the page and gaze into the two faces staring out at her. She felt her own eyes mist over.

"Before I came here I took the liberty of scanning that picture into the computer." Fleming turned the flat screen of the computer towards Isabel. The newspaper picture of her parents was now looking out at her from the flat monitor, perfect copies, as clear as day. "From this, it is simple to concoct any picture that you want. You can mix it or superimpose it onto another picture that you have already scanned in, or you can choose one of the many thousands of bank pictures already stored on the programme." Fleming paused and then typed the word "astronaut" into the search option of the programme. Immediately, pages and pages of space related pictures and photographs filled the screen. Fleming scrolled through the pictures until he found what he was searching for. He highlighted a photograph of two astronauts, dressed in full spacesuit regalia, standing in front of the space shuttle. With a few swift key strokes, Fleming had removed their smiling faces, and pausing only slightly to watch Isabel's expression, he dragged the faces of Mr and Mrs Faraday into their place.

Before them now sat a photograph of Mr and Mrs Faraday – space astronauts, happily posing before their space craft. Fleming let the effect of the picture sink in before he spoke.

"You see – easy as pie." His voice was gentle. "All they would then need to do was print it out onto photo quality paper, rough it up a bit to make it look aged, and bingo……"

Isabel's cheeks were damp with tears as she gently pushed the laptop screen away from her.

"I'm sorry, Isabel," murmured Fleming, closing the programme and slipping the laptop back inside his briefcase. "I just thought it was best that you knew."

Isabel nodded and managed a weak smile. "Thank you, Mr Fleming," she whispered, her voice cracked and broken. "I appreciate it. I do, really. I'm glad…I'm glad that you showed me." She swallowed, forcefully, past a large lump that had formed in her throat. "I just feel so stupid."

"Stupid?" Fleming swung his briefcase up onto the table in front of them, and began packing away the grey folder. "Tell me about it. These guys have been running rings around me for longer than I care to remember. Anytime I get close to them, when I think that maybe this time I've got them, they just slip through my fingers and disappear. It's like trying to catch water. So don't you go blaming yourself for any of this, or thinking that you're stupid or silly for believing them. Because they make a career out of it, I'm telling you." Fleming paused and grimaced. "I've been made a fool of far too many times."

Gathering up the last of the photographs of Mac and Andre, Fleming slipped them back inside his briefcase. Snapping the locks shut, he checked

CHAPTER SEVENTEEN

his watch. "You have nothing to feel ashamed of, Isabel. You believed them because you wanted to. And they wanted you to. They've done this so many times before, to so many different people..." Fleming broke off. "Which is why I really need to act fast if I'm going to catch them and stop them before they do this again to somebody else. Did they tell you where they were heading?"

Isabel nodded, still looking down at the open newspaper. "Switzerland," she murmured, without looking up.

Fleming smiled and jumped to his feet. "That sounds promising. I have contacts in Geneva. We'll be waiting for them this time." He picked up his briefcase and turned away towards the door. "If you like...you can keep the newspaper." He inclined his head towards the table where Isabel was still gazing down at the article about her parents' death.

Isabel paused before looking up at Fleming. She slowly let her finger trail across the contours of her parents' faces. "Thanks. I'd like that."

"OK. Well, Detective Inspector MacIntosh should be here soon to do whatever it is he needs to do. In the meantime, I need to go and make a few calls. Will you be all right here on your own?" Fleming noticed a small nod of Isabel's head. "I'll only be a few minutes. And then, if it's OK with you, after you've had a bit of a freshen up and while we are waiting for DI MacIntosh to arrive, I'd like you to come with me to Andre's flat – just to make sure we've got the right place. Would you do that for me?"

Isabel nodded, weakly, brushing a fresh set of tears from her cheeks. She didn't look up but heard Agent Fleming's footsteps slip out of the door. Alone in the room at last, Isabel let her tears splash down onto the newspaper in front of her, bathing her parents' faces in her sorrow.

* * *

Time: 12.10pm
    Date: 9th November 2008
    Location: Rue de Plateau, Paris

Andre shivered against the cold and rubbed his icy hands up and down his arms to try and force some warmth into them. Every part of him ached. Every part of him was numb with cold. They had been curled up out of sight for the best part of the morning, listening to the steady drone of police cars passing by.

But now it had stopped. Now it was quiet.

Mac shifted position and stretched out his stiff legs, wincing at the pains which stabbed at his muscles. "We need to move. They're bound to be back soon. They'll have found Isabel by now – and she'll have realised we're not coming back."

Andre nodded and checked his wrist for his watch – but then remembered he had left it back at Marie's apartment. "What time is it?"

Mac shrugged. "No idea. Does it matter?"

Andre blew onto his frozen fingers. "I'd just like to know, that's all." Although he had a mobile phone on him, both he and Mac had switched them off so that they couldn't be traced. He was thankful that he had the foresight to get rid of the papers – the courier had turned up as asked and swiftly taken the envelope away. It would be safely on its way out of the country by now – probably even having reached its destination already. Andre just hoped that he had chosen wisely.

Mac frowned at Andre, then fumbled inside his back pocket. He pulled out a small stopwatch and threw it at Andre's chest. Andre caught the watch, glanced at the time, then placed it down next to him on the frozen ground. "How long do you think we were bugged for?" he asked, quietly, rubbing his wrist absent-mindedly.

Again Mac shrugged. "I think the only person who knew that was Simon." Mac tried to shake the image of Shafer's body out of his mind, but it refused to go, swimming in and out of focus. He saw Shafer's last gasping breaths being squeezed out of him, playing over and over in his head like a film on continuous loop – constantly replaying the horrifying moment when the life was finally, and so violently, ripped from his friend's body. Mac watched once more as the colour drained from Shafer's face, leaving a pallid, grey, deathly shade in its wake. His eyes turning from a vivid blue

CHAPTER SEVENTEEN

to a dull, lifeless opaqueness. The hands gripping his, clutching at him, clutching at life, drawing him near, dragging him in closer, and closer, and closer. And then he heard Shafer's voice, hard and rasping….. "who knows what is possible." The words echoed around Mac's head in a never ending sequence, getting louder and louder until Mac had to clamp his frostbitten fingers over his ears to try and block it out. "Who knows what is possible…..who knows what is possible….who knows what is possible."

Suddenly Mac shot bolt upright. "Who knows what is possible," he murmured. "Who knows what is possible!!"

Andre flinched at his friend's sudden movement next to him. He watched as Mac turned towards him, eyes wide open. "That's it!! It's Faraday!!"

Andre frowned. "What's Faraday?"

"Shafer," said Mac, scrambling to his feet and tugging at Andre's arm. "The words he said. What he was trying to tell me. Who knows what is possible!" He quickly hauled Andre to his feet and pulled him towards the road. "Quick! We have to go now – we may already be too late!"

* * *

Time: 1.25pm
    Date: 9th November 2008
    Location: Commissariat Central, Rue Louis Blanc, Paris

Detective Inspector Jack MacIntosh ran up the steps to the police station two at a time and checked his watch. He had made good time. It was a little before 1.30pm, French time, it had taken him less than 15 minutes to jog from the Gare du Nord train station to the police station on Rue Louis Blanc. Isabel shouldn't have been waiting too long. Just a quick chat and he could get the poor girl home again. His stomach rumbled, but lunch would have to wait.

He pushed open the heavy oak panelled door and entered the entrance lobby.

"Monsieur?" A French police officer, whom Jack assumed to be the desk sergeant, came out from behind his desk as soon as Jack stepped inside. Jack reached into his jacket pocket and brought out his ID wallet.

"Detective Inspector MacIntosh," he announced, still a little breathless from the jog. He held out his hand in greeting, speaking slowly, unsure whether the desk sergeant had enough of a command of English to understand him. He flipped open his warrant card. "I'm here to see Isabel Faraday? She was brought here a few hours ago, I believe."

The desk sergeant quickly shook Jack's hand, and glanced momentarily at the warrant card.

"Please wait a moment, Inspector," he replied, his English polite and well-spoken. "I will ask one of my colleagues to help you." He gave a small nod, and almost a bow, before leaving and disappearing through a door directly behind him.

Jack leant against the front desk and looked around him. The police station was old and antiquated, but seemed to be in the process of being dragged kicking and screaming into the 21st century. The walls surrounding the entrance lobby were panelled in a rough, heavy, dark wood, and Jack didn't want to hazard a guess as to how old they were, and how many secrets they held within them. But their aged quality was now being engulfed by a multitude of modern plastic notice boards, posters and wall charts. Their history and beauty disappearing beneath a plethora of drawing pins and sticky tape.

Jack looked up and noticed the ceiling was high, with ornate carvings and picture rails hugging the walls. Yet even that was now spoilt by the bright, incessant humming of the fluorescent strip lighting attached at regular intervals across the lobby.

Jack's eyes now rested on the desk he was leaning against – again made of the same, heavy dark wood as the wood panelling on the walls. Jack guessed the desk housed many a story to tell from the etchings, score marks and cigarette burns that littered its surface – secrets and lies embedded in its grain. Yet now it also played host to a modern touch telephone, a computer terminal and what looked like a series of police radios and pagers.

CHAPTER SEVENTEEN

Suddenly the door behind the desk opened and the desk sergeant emerged once again.

"My colleague, Sergeant Boutin, will be with you shortly," he announced. "He saw Miss Faraday and will fill you in on all the details. One moment please."

* * *

Time: 1.05pm
Date: 9th November 2008
Location: Rue de Londres library, Paris

Mac sprinted up the steps to the Rue de Londres library three at a time, almost tripping and crashing to his knees in his haste. He burst through the revolving doors into the entrance area. Andre followed a few paces behind, averting his gaze from the questioning looks thrown at them by their hasty entrance from the young woman behind the information desk.

Andre made a grab for Mac's arm, and firmly guided him down the central aisle towards the rear of the building, away from prying eyes.

"Don't cause such a scene," he hissed, increasing his grip on Mac's arm. "We need to be in and out of here without being seen, or have you forgotten that half of Paris is looking for us right now?"

Mac wrenched his arm free but remained at Andre's side, his eyes darting from side to side as they passed shelves upon shelves crammed full of books and publications on all manner of topics. "Down here," he growled, peeling off to the right and heading towards the science section.

Andre glanced, furtively, behind them, but no one seemed to be taking any further notice of them despite the initial commotion their entrance had caused. The woman at the information desk appeared to be busying herself once again with cataloguing a large pile of books, staring intently at her computer monitor. She now seemed oblivious to the library's two newest visitors.

Andre turned back in time to see that Mac was already on his knees, scanning the lower levels of the science and physics sections.

"It's got to be here, it's got to be here," he muttered to himself, trailing a shaking finger along the spines as he scanned them. "Where are you? Where the hell are you?"

Andre stepped over and began looking at the books along the middle section of the shelving.

"It won't be up there," said Mac, irritably. "Down on the bottom shelf – always on the bottom shelf, you know that." Mac's voice was cold and harsh, but Andre said nothing in return and merely dropped to his knees and began searching the titles on the bottom shelf as instructed.

"I've already done that bit," barked Mac, impatiently. "Try over there." He waved a hand to his right and flashed an annoyed look in Andre's direction.

Andre shook his head and pushed roughly past his friend. "Get over it," he hissed, dropping back down to the carpet and checking a fresh selection of books. "Stop acting like a spoilt child."

Mac visibly stiffened, his face instantly darkening. He opened his mouth to spit out a reply, his eyes burning fiercely into Andre's cool gaze, but instead he lowered his head and rubbed his temples with his hand. It was a while before he spoke.

"I just should've known, that's all. I should've realised what he was trying to say. What he was trying to tell me." Shafer's ghostly voice filled Mac's head. "Who knows what is possible? Why didn't I realise what he meant? If I'd have worked it out quicker, we wouldn't be....and Isabel wouldn't have...." Mac broke off and went back to searching through the books in front of him.

"Let's just concentrate on finding it now," replied Andre, simply.

Mac shook his head and sighed, pushing himself up against the shelving. "It's not here." He looked down at Andre, his eyes glassy. "It's just not here."

"Maybe we missed it," said Andre, crawling back to the beginning of the shelf and retracing their steps. "It's got to be here. You said so yourself."

CHAPTER SEVENTEEN

"Do you think they'll hurt her?" Mac's voice sounded hollow.

Andre froze, his hand hovering in mid-air over a selection of books about electro magnetism. He shook his head. "Of course not. She'll be fine."

"How can you be so sure? They've killed before….Kreshniov could….." Mac's voice tailed off, leaving the sentence unfinished.

"She'll be fine, OK?" barked Andre, his temper rising. "She'll be fine."

"But Kreshniov's after her…. She's a Faraday…..you said so yourself…"

"For God's sake, Mac, just shut up about bloody Kreshniov!!" Andre's voice rose and echoed eerily around the walls. "He's nowhere near her, I promise. It's us he wants, right? And the documents? She hasn't got them, so she'll be fine."

"Dupont didn't have the documents…. Neither did Simon. He still killed them."

Andre jumped to his feet and grabbed Mac roughly by the arm, pulling him round the other side of the shelving, out of sight. "For fuck's sake, Mac, stop talking like that! Isabel will be OK. Dupont was killed because of what he could print in his newspaper. And Simon…." Andre broke off and considered for a while. "Simon was killed because he was about to tell us something he shouldn't."

"I don't know why we couldn't go back for her," muttered Mac, shrugging off Andre's grip. "We could have gone back for her. I wanted to."

"It was too risky," snapped Andre. "The police were everywhere, you heard them. We had to lie low, stay where we were, otherwise they would have found us."

"Well, the book's still not here," mumbled Mac, turning away and heading back down the central aisle towards the exit. The book had gone, and so had whatever information Shafer had left inside. With Shafer gone as well, whatever he had found out, whatever information he had tried so vainly to pass on, that had also died with him in the damp Parisian gutter.

Mac started the long walk back to the front doors. If only he had worked it out sooner, the book might still have been there. But who could have removed it? The books they chose were never for public lending, always just reference only. So why wasn't it there? Maybe they had the wrong library.

Mac's thoughts were interrupted by Andre rushing past him, walking quickly and purposefully towards the study area to the right hand side of the front doors. There were six people sitting around one large square table, studiously scribbling down information or leafing through pages and pages of text. The area was deathly quiet. The only sound being the occasional scratch of pen on paper, or the gently flicking of pages as they turned.

Andre strode into the study area and silently took a book from a nearby shelf. He sat down in a vacant seat and pretended to read.

* * *

Time: 1.35pm
   Date: 9th November 2008
   Location: Commissariat Central, Rue Louis Blanc, Paris

"Detective Inspector MacIntosh?" A tall, rather thin man emerged from a side door and walked briskly over towards Jack. Jack had been filling in time by leafing through some of the notices on the notice board behind him. Everything in French, of course. He couldn't understand a word.

Jack turned round to find the tall, thin police officer, with a classic French dark moustache adorning his smooth skin, standing behind him, outstretched hand ready to greet his new visitor. "I am Sergeant Boutin. How may I help you?"

"Pleased to meet you, Sergeant," replied Jack, quickly shaking the proffered hand. "I'm here to speak with Miss Isabel Faraday, and take her home?" Jack opened his wallet once again and showed his warrant card. "She was brought in earlier this morning? I believe you have been in touch with my base back in the UK."

Sergeant Boutin glanced down curiously at the warrant card in Jack's hand, and then back up again. "I am afraid Miss Faraday is no longer with

CHAPTER SEVENTEEN

us," he replied. "She was signed out approximately 45 minutes ago."

Jack frowned. "She was *what?*"

"Signed out, Inspector. Approximately 45 minutes ago."

"Yes, I heard that bit. But how? She was supposed to have been waiting for me."

Sergeant Boutin looked down at the clipboard that he held in his hands, and scanned the top piece of paper. "After interview she was allowed to go. You signed her out yourself, Inspector."

Jack's eyes widened in surprise. "I did what?"

"Signed her out, Inspector. I have the details right here." Sergeant Boutin turned the clipboard round to face Jack. With the end of his pen, he pointed to the entry under Isabel's name.

"Interview terminated 12.31pm," read Jack, his voice a little shaky. "Signed out 12. 46pm. Conducting Officer Detective Inspector Mac-Intosh."

Sergeant Boutin tucked the clipboard back under his arm and eyed Jack warily. "So, you see, Inspector. She is no longer here."

Jack frowned and rubbed his eyes with his fingers. "But I..I've only just arrived. You've just seen me walk through the front door. I haven't even seen her yet, let alone interviewed her! There must be some mistake."

"I can show you the release form as well, Inspector." Sergeant Boutin flipped over the top piece of paper to reveal another identical one underneath. "She would have signed the release folder before she left."

Again the clipboard was turned towards Jack.

"Here. 12.46pm. Miss Isabel Faraday. There is her signature right there." Sergeant Boutin again pointed with the end of his pen at Isabel's neat signature. "And here's the conducting officer's details who confirmed the release." The pen moved slightly to the right and rested on the name Detective Inspector J MacIntosh.

It was followed by a signature. Jack's signature.

"Look that's not me…and that's definitely not my signature!" Jack stabbed at the entry in the folder with his finger and shook his head, his voice firm. "I haven't seen her. And I certainly haven't signed her out!"

Sergeant Boutin tucked the clipboard back underneath his arm and shrugged. "I am sorry, Inspector. I don't see what else I can do for you."

"Wait a minute....did anyone see her leave?"

CHAPTER EIGHTEEN

Time: 1.20pm
 Date: 9th November 2008
 Location: Rue de Londres library, Paris

Andre opened his book of medieval history and pretended to read, occasionally lifting his head to watch the others seated at the table. Two were clearly students, each with a pile of books at least three feet deep next to them. They looked tired, and overworked, staring intently at the text in front of them and scribbling down as much information as they could glean to complete that week's assignment. Neither of them looked up.

Andre shifted in his seat so that he could see the spines of the books they were studying from. The girl was a textiles student, Andre mused. Most of her books were about clothes designs, materials. Tapestries. The boy was clearly a history student – he was absorbing information from heavy tomes covering the French Revolution and the two World Wars.

Andre immediately scrubbed them off his mental checklist. He then turned his attention to an elderly gentleman sitting directly opposite him, reading from one solitary book. Andre cocked his head to the side and strained to read the title. "Claude Monet 1840-1926."

Two mature ladies were sitting together by Andre's right hand side. Both had books to do with cookery and appeared to be copying down recipes. Again Andre ticked them off his checklist and turned his attention to who was left.

There was only one more person left on the table. A young man to Andre's left, who had a pile of books towering up in front of him, but none of the spines were facing Andre. Andre had no idea what the man could be studying, as he couldn't see the titles, but as he quickly scanned the other people sitting at the table once again instinct told him it had to be him. It just had to be. There was no one left.

Suddenly Andre sensed a movement behind him. Out of the corner of his eye he saw that Mac was crossing over from the central aisle, heading towards the study area. Andre turned a little in his seat and caught his eye, then nodded slowly and discreetly towards the young man sitting to his left. Mac blinked purposefully, and then continued his journey towards the table.

"Excuse-moi?" he said, in his best French accent.

The young man looked up from his books and raised his eyebrows, questioningly. "Oui?"

"Parlez-vous Anglais?" said Mac, silently praying that the answer would be yes.

"A little, yes," nodded the young man, frowning, somewhat irritated at the interruption.

"Good. The lady at the information desk says she has some more books for you." Mac glanced over his shoulder and nodded towards the young woman seated behind them. While the young man's gaze was momentarily distracted over towards the desk, Mac leant forwards a little to try and catch a glimpse of what books lay on the desk. But the young man turned back quickly, and Mac hurriedly straightened up. "If you would like to go over to the counter, she will give them to you."

"Merci, Monsieur," replied the young man, getting to his feet. Placing the book he was studying from face down on the table, he turned and began to walk over to the information desk.

Both Mac and Andre glanced down at the book's spine, and met each other's gaze for a split-second.

It wasn't the one.

With the young man still over at the front desk, Mac made a dive for the

CHAPTER EIGHTEEN

table and began to rifle through the stack of text books towering neatly at the side of the man's workspace. He knew that he only had a matter of seconds before the man would realise that the lady at the information desk had no such books for him at all.

Mac knocked the pile over and the books spread out in front of him. He hurriedly turned them over, checking the titles in a blind panic. It had to be here, it just had to be here. Andre glanced nervously over his shoulder. The man was within a few feet of the information desk…..any second now….and second now…..

Mac threw the rejected books aside, causing the other occupants of the table to throw him disapproving glances and make discreet tutting noises under their breath. He ignored their looks and continued his search. Beads of sweat were popping up on his forehead, his heart pounding so hard it was almost bursting through his chest wall.

It had to be here. It just had to be.

Book after book was tossed aside. More and more angry looks were thrown in his direction, but he ignored them all.

Until.

Faraday's Diary edited by T Martin. The book stared up at him from the very bottom of the pile. Mac grabbed it and ran.

* * *

Time: 1.45pm
    Date: 9th November 2008
    Location: Commissariat Central, Rue Louis Blanc, Paris

Jack sat on a small, uncomfortably hard wooden chair whilst he waited for yet another French police officer. His head was swimming. His mind racing. Where was Isabel? How could she have just disappeared like that? He began to feel a gnawing sensation in the very pit of his stomach while Chief Superintendent Liddell's last words to him echoed round and round his head.

"Guard her with your life…. let no one and nothing come between you……guard her with your life……guard her with your life."

Jack's thoughts were thankfully interrupted when the door to the small, stuffy room swung open and Sergeant Boutin breezed in.

"Detective Inspector MacIntosh?" Sergeant Boutin closed the door noiselessly behind him. "This is Sergeant Matteau – he was on the front desk when Miss Faraday was signed out."

"Inspector?" Sergeant Matteau stepped forwards. He was a small man in his late forties, with a small head, a small brown beard and small round spectacles encasing his small round blue eyes. Everything about him appeared to be small. "I understand you want information about Miss Faraday?"

"I'll say," replied Jack, gruffly. "Your paperwork here has me down as interviewing her, then signing her out. Yet I've clearly only just arrived, and we've never met. It clearly wasn't me."

"I see." Sergeant Matteau perched his small frame on a vacant chair opposite Jack. He opened a thin black folder, held by Sergeant Boutin, and balanced it on his knees. With a small sniff, he placed a small, neatly manicured fingernail on the entry pertaining to Isabel. "It says here that she arrived at 08.16. Was checked over by the police surgeon, then taken to the interview room at 10.01am. And she was then signed out at……"

"12.46pm, yes I know," finished Jack, irritably. "Did you see who interviewed her, and who signed her out?"

"Well, yes," replied Sergeant Matteau, glancing at Jack's warrant card which was lying open on the table in front of them. "She was interviewed by……" His voice tailed off as he read the ID. Sergeant Matteau's small, beady eyes flashed up at Jack.

"By me, right?" finished Jack, once again. "Except it wasn't me, was it? I've been on a train from London for the last 3 hours, and we've never met before, have we? I telephoned to let you know I was coming."

Sergeant Matteau nodded, quickly. "Yes, yes, I remember. The front desk sent up a message to say that you would be arriving….."

CHAPTER EIGHTEEN

Suddenly, Jack cut him off. "What happened to Special Agent Fleming?"

"Agent Fleming?" Sergeant Matteau looked quizzically from Jack up to Sergeant Boutin, and then back again. "I don't remember there being an Agent Fleming."

Jack sighed heavily and closed his eyes. "When I telephoned I said that I would be coming to speak with Miss Faraday, and take her home, but in the meantime a Special Agent Fleming from the United States FBI would have my authorisation to speak with her…. before I arrived." Jack looked up, straight into Sergeant Matteau's gaze. "So what happened to him?"

"Mr Fleming?"

Jack nodded. "Yes, Mr Fleming. What happened to him? Did he show up?"

Sergeant Matteau swallowed nervously. "Well, when you…. when Detective Inspector Macintosh arrived he said that he had managed to arrive earlier than planned and that Agent Fleming wouldn't be coming after all. We didn't think anything of it….." Sergeant Matteau's voice trailed off into nothing and he looked awkwardly down into his lap, avoiding Jack's stare.

"What did he look like?" Jack's voice was bathed in urgency. The gnawing feeling at the pit of his stomach was now spreading like fire throughout his body. "The man who came to see Isabel. What did he look like?"

Sergeant Matteau replied without looking up. "He was about the same height as yourself, short hair, very short hair, dark with a few grey pieces. He had pale skin, very pale skin, was quite thin, wearing a light grey suit……"

"And he had ID?"

Sergeant Matteau nodded. "Yes, he had ID, He showed it to me. It had…."

"It had my name on it," finished Jack. "Yes, I realise that. And they both left together?"

Sergeant Matteau nodded and again looked at the papers in the black folder. "Yes, they left at 12.46pm. Both signed out and left the building together."

Jack leant forwards and sighed deeply. "OK. I need to get your CCTV footage from this corridor for the whole morning, and also from the front entrance. And I need a computer. And I need them now."

Sergeant Matteau nodded once more and turned to leave. As he did so, Sergeant Boutin stepped forwards. "While we get you a room sorted, Inspector, I have received a call concerning a body of a British man having been found this morning."

"A body?" Jack's headed whipped round. "Who?"

Sergeant Boutin glanced down at a piece of paper in his hand. "The wallet in his pocket said he was a Mr Simon Shafer."

Jack shook his head. The name didn't ring a bell. "Did the wallet give any next of kin details? I'm sure this is something that the British Embassy could help you with." He started to walk towards the door, anxious to get hold of the CCTV footage and a computer.

"Inspector. I think you may wish to know. Your Mr Shafer? He was a member of your MI6."

***

Time: 1.30pm
   Date: 9th November 2008
   Location: Rue de Londres library, Paris

Mac burst out of the front doors of the library, flew down the steps, turned left and ran full pelt along the pavement. The electronic anti-theft device attached to the inside of the book cover triggered the library alarm system as soon as Mac left the building, sending out an ear-piercing whistling noise.

Andre followed closely, not daring to look behind him at the startled gaze of the woman at the information desk. He, too, careered out of the front doors, down the steps and began the chase. Mac was a good hundred metres ahead of him, and Andre only just managed to catch a glimpse of him darting to the left before he disappeared out of sight completely.

Andre ran blindly on, only snatching the briefest of glimpses behind him

CHAPTER EIGHTEEN

– the path appeared to be clear. No one seemed to be following them. Not yet anyway. He ran on and on, holding the straps of his rucksack tightly in his hands to stop it bouncing painfully against his shoulder blades. He continued running until he reached the alleyway where he had lost sight of Mac, and turned to find him curled up behind a large commercial refuse bin.

Mac was already holding the book open on his lap. Andre slowed to a jog and stopped in front of him, his lungs feeling as though they were about to burst open. He leant forwards with his hands on his knees, breathing hard.

"Jesus Christ Mac!" he gasped. "Give me a warning next time you're going to try something like that!"

Mac merely blinked, and tipped the book in Andre's direction. Between gasps, Andre looked down into his friend's lap and saw that inside the back cover, attached with a small piece of tape, was a rectangular flash drive. Mac gently lifted it out and nodded at Andre's rucksack.

"Let's see what he has to say for himself then."

* * *

Time: 1.55pm
Date: 9th November 2008
Location: Commissariat Central, Rue Louis Blanc, Paris

Jack logged into the FBI website and very quickly found the information he needed. Picking up the telephone he glanced at his watch. It was early in the States, but he couldn't wait. He needed to know what he was up against.

The phone was answered after just two rings.

"Federal Bureau of Investigations, Sandy speaking. How may I help you today?"

"Good morning," replied Jack. "My name is Detective Inspector MacIntosh with the London Metropolitan Police in the UK. I need some help to trace one of your Agents who is over here at the moment."

"One moment please," replied Sandy in her West Coast drawl. "I'll transfer you."

It took nine minutes and several transfers until Jack spoke to someone who could help him.

"I need some details on one of your Agents," repeated Jack. "He's over here doing some case work at the moment, but I need to track him down urgently."

There was a slight pause on the other end of the phone before a man said, "Can you give me the Agent's details please and I'll have a look for you."

"His name is Special Agent Fleming. F L E M I N G." Jack spelt out the surname letter by letter. "First name is John."

"OK," replied the man on the other end of the line. Jack could hear him typing at a keyboard as he spoke. "And he was working on which case?"

Jack hesitated. Which case? He wasn't sure what case Fleming was supposed to have been working on. In retrospect, Fleming had never actually given any concrete details. "I'm, er, I'm not sure of the exact case name, but I have a copy of a memo sent to our department about it."

Jack started rummaging in his jacket and trouser pockets. After bringing out various crumpled notes, train tickets and a handful of change, he found it. The original memo from Chief Superintendent Liddell, looking more than a little worse for wear. He smoothed it out on the table in front of him.

"OK, well if you could let me have any case numbers, or reference numbers, on that document please?" continued the man, still tapping at is keyboard.

Jack scanned the memo. There were no case numbers, no reference numbers, no nothing. "Um, the only information it has is Agent Fleming's badge number, his ID number, and contact numbers for the supervising Agents back in the US."

CHAPTER EIGHTEEN

"Could you give me those details please and I'll log them into the computer and see what we come up with."

Jack read out the badge and ID numbers. There was a long pause.

"Could you confirm those numbers for me again please, Detective?"

Jack read out the numbers once again, feeling a dull gnawing sensation creeping into the pit of his stomach as he did so.

"And the contact telephone numbers please?" came the curt reply.

Jack read out the two telephone numbers given at the top of the page, plus the supervising officer's direct line. There was yet another long pause, and Jack nervously began to chew at his bottom lip. Something wasn't right, he could feel it.

"Detective? I'm sorry to tell you that we don't have a Special Agent John Fleming listed as active at present. The last Agent Fleming we have on record died in 1990 – and his first name was Robert. There is nothing else on file. And those contact telephone numbers you gave me? They are for a real estate company in Boston, and a dry cleaning service in West Virginia."

Jack felt as though a large stone had sunk into the very pit of his bowels. "S..sorry? Can you say that again, please?" Jack's throat felt dry, his voice hoarse.

"Of course. We do not have a Special Agent John Fleming listed as on active service. He is not on any of our files. He doesn't exist, Detective. And those contact telephone numbers are bogus."

"So…he's not an FBI Agent?"

"No, Sir. He's not."

Jack nodded to himself. He understood everything perfectly.

"I'm very sorry, Detective, but it looks like you've been slam dunked."

Jack replaced the telephone receiver with a shaky hand and stared at the memo in his hand. "You bastard," he muttered, starting the screw the paper up in his hand. "You bloody bast….."

Just then the door flew open and Sergeant Boutin walked in holding the CCTV video tapes in his hand.

"I have a room available for you, Inspector." He motioned for Jack to follow him. "And there is a call for you at the front desk."

* * *

Time: 2.05pm
 Date: 9th November 2008
 Location: Café Bleu, Rue Saint Pierre, Paris

The café was busy for a weekday afternoon. Mac had chosen a table right at the back in the corner, where hopefully they would not be disturbed. Andre brought over a tray with a pot of hot coffee and two croissants.

Mac angled the computer away from prying eyes and the pair of them sat together facing the screen. Mac retrieved the small flash drive from his jacket pocket and carefully slotted it into the computer's USB port. The computer whirred into action for a few seconds as it began to recognise the new hardware. Andre took a sip of the hot coffee, unable to take his eyes away from the screen – unaware that the coffee was scalding his tongue. He saw Mac glance nervously at him before opening up the one and only file contained on the flash drive.

It seemed to be a letter of some sort – a long letter – written by Simon. As Mac and Andre began to read the document they both felt uneasy. It was a letter from a dead man. A voice from the grave.

"By the time you read this I will be dead. That much I know. I just hope I'm in time to stop the same fate from happening to you. And to Isabel. There is so much that you don't know, and much that you don't need to know. And even more that you don't want to know.

"Fleming is out to get me. Because you are reading this, he will have already found me and killed me. Of that I am sure. And then he will come after you. He wants the Phoenix Project data, and he will kill for it. He already has."

Mac caught Andre's eye. "Why does he want the Phoenix Project data?", he whispered.

Andre merely shrugged and carried on reading.

CHAPTER EIGHTEEN

"There are two things you need to know. Firstly, Fleming is not who he says he is. That's not even his name. And secondly, there are things about Chief Superintendent Liddell which you need to be aware of."

* * *

Time: 2.15pm
Date: 9th November 2008
Location: Commissariat Central, Rue Louis Blanc, Paris

Jack was seated in a hastily arranged office suite. Sergeant Boutin had given him access to their entire video screening system and seemed eager to provide anything Jack wanted. Jack quickly inserted the first tape – the one covering the front entrance to the police station. He flicked the fast forward button and made the people starring in this macabre plot flash across the screen as if in some early black and white silent movie. All that was missing was the tinny, out of tune piano music.

At precisely 08.15am Jack paused the tape. Emerging through the front doors was Isabel. Although Jack had never met her before, he knew it was her. He used the mouse and keypad to home in on her face, bringing it closer and closer until it almost filled the screen. She looked tired, exhausted. And drawn. Her eyes looked frightened and confused.

Jack slowly tapped the play button and let the video move on at a slow speed. Isabel inched forwards through the police station front doors – and behind her, three other figures came into view. One had his hand on her elbow, guiding her forwards, the other two following several steps behind.

Isabel carried on walking forwards, towards the front desk. Jack turned his attention to the man at her side. Again he magnified the face, bringing his features up close until the whole face filled the screen. It was him. It was Fleming. The thin face. The thin nose. The cold eyes. It was definitely him.

Jack studied Fleming's face even more closely, and was convinced he could see a small smile curling at the edges of his thin lips. He played the tape forwards and watched as Fleming guided Isabel by the elbow up to the front desk, while the other two figures behind them slunk away back through the doors, presumably to wait outside. Jack then saw Fleming produce some ID, no doubt his own fake ID, and speak at some length to the desk officer. A piece of paper was placed before him, and Jack watched as Fleming began to fill in the details.

After checking the time on the screen, Jack ejected the tape and inserted another. This time it was the tape from the corridor outside the interview room. He fast forwarded the tape until he saw Isabel and Fleming enter the screen and walk into the interview room at 10.01am. They did not emerge until 12.32pm. Jack watched again as Fleming guided Isabel by the elbow out of the interview room and out of sight.

Again Jack switched tapes. He inserted the first tape, showing the entrance lobby, back into the machine. He hit the fast forward button and sped through the tape until 12.43pm when he saw Fleming move into the screen and immediately go up to the front desk and begin to fill out more details on a piece of paper attached to Sergeant Matteau's clipboard. Jack saw that Isabel went to sit down at the side of the lobby, underneath an array of posters. Her hands were clasped together in her lap, nursing what looked like a tissue. Occasionally, she would dab her eyes and cheeks.

Jack cast his attention back towards Fleming at the desk. He appeared to have finished filling out the paperwork and had handed the clipboard back to Sergeant Matteau. Fleming then turned to go, reaching inside his jacket pocket as he did so. He pulled out a mobile phone, looked at it, and then turned back towards the desk. Several seconds of conversation then ensued between him and Sergeant Matteau, the small spectacled police officer giving a curt nod and waving him towards the end of the desk where a single telephone sat. Fleming moved over and picked up the receiver.

Jack's eyes flickered. He paused momentarily before switching off the TV monitor and leaping to his feet.

CHAPTER NINETEEN

Time: 2.15pm
Date: 9th November 2008
Location: Café Bleu, Rue Saint Pierre, Paris

"We need to call the police," said Mac, urgently, watching as Andre slipped the laptop back into his holdall. "We can't deal with this on our own."

"No police," hissed Andre, safely stowing the bag underneath the table. "And keep your voice down!"

The two of them locked eyes across the table, but said nothing further for several minutes. It was Mac who eventually broke the silence.

"And what about the rest of the letter? We didn't get to read it all." Mac's eyes darted nervously around the café which was now filling up with customers for the afternoon trade. "He was going to tell us more; I know he was. He was going to tell us about Kreshniov."

"We can't read it all," replied Andre, keeping his voice low. "There are too many people in here. It's not safe." He drained the last dregs from his coffee cup and set down his cup. "We read the important bit – about Fleming."

"And Liddell," added Mac.

"If we can believe that," muttered Andre. "Shafer might have got it wrong."

"Well, someone thought he got it right. They killed him for it." Mac paused and grabbed hold of his friend's arm across the table. "We need to go to the police. Shafer has just told us that Fleming's not FBI. Never has been. I think that's something that the police need to know about."

"I said no police!" repeated Andre, firmly, shaking off Mac's grip. He looked around the rapidly filling café, and felt uneasy. He felt unsafe. "Not yet. Not until we're out of here. We've got two dead bodies linked to us already. We call the police in now and we're just asking for trouble."

"And Isabel?" asked Mac, hotly. "What about her? We've just left her out there on her own…. with Fleming, or whoever it is he's supposed to be."

"Fleming's after the papers," said Andre, flatly. "You just read that for yourself. And we have those." He tapped the holdall under the table with his foot. "Isabel is in no danger."

"How can you be so sure? Until five minutes ago we thought the FBI were after us. How can you be sure of anything? I bet Fleming wouldn't think twice about double crossing his own mother."

"I'm sure of it, OK! Can we just leave it now? We need to concentrate on how we get out of here." Andre nodded his head towards the mass of people queuing up at the service counter, blocking the exit.

"Shafer seemed pretty sure," Mac pressed on. "Fleming's not FBI, Liddell's bent. And he said that Isabel's life was in danger. It's obvious Fleming's after her and not just the damn papers."

Andre jumped up out of his chair, sending it scraping noisily backwards over the tiled floor. Several heads turned towards them. "Look, Shafer's wrong, OK? Isabel will be all right. He got it wrong. Now, are you coming or not?"

Mac got to his feet but made no attempt to follow Andre. "I think there's more to Fleming than you realise. If he's not FBI, who the bloody hell is he? And if he was just after the papers why isn't he here? Why isn't he following us?!" Mac paused and caught Andre's eyes. "We have to help her, Andre. We can't just leave her out there on her own. We brought her over her. We owe it to her."

Andre sighed and closed his eyes. "I know," he muttered. "I know."

"She put her trust in us. And what have we done in return? Everything is going belly up and we just cut and run. We have to help her."

"No one can help her now, Mac," sighed Andre, opening his eyes and

CHAPTER NINETEEN

fixing his friend with a hard stare. "No one at all."

* * *

Time: 2.30pm
Date: 9th November 2008
Location: Commissariat Central, Rue Louis Blanc, Paris

Jack burst through the set of double doors and headed towards the front desk. In one hand he gripped the phoney memo from Liddell, in the other he clamped his mobile phone to his ear and waited to be connected.

"Superintendent Liddell speaking," came the response.

"Sir? It's DI MacIntosh here," barked Jack. "There's been a development. Something you need to know. That FBI agent, Fleming? Well, it turns out he's no more FBI than you or I am. We've been set up. It's all a con. I don't know what his game is, or what he wants, but he's not who he says he is." Jack paused.

"Go on," breathed Liddell, his voice sounding old and tired.

"It's Isabel. He's after her. I don't know why, but he's after her. That's what all this has been about. He's just sprung her from the police station, impersonating me in the process. I don't know where he is, or where she is, or where they're heading. All I do know is that we need to get a full alert issued to all stations, ports and airports, everywhere, the works. Her picture is on my desk. Get DS Cooper to help you – we need to fax it round to make sure that if she does re-enter the country then we know about it first."

Jack paused for breath. He could feel his heart thumping manically inside his chest and his skin felt cold and clammy. He listened but there was no response from the other end of the line.

"Superintendent?" Jack waited, listening to the continuing silence. "Did you hear me?" More silence. "Sir? Are you still there?" Still more silence. "We need to act fast. We need to find her."

"I need you to tell me everything you know….and fast," ordered Liddell.

His voice stern. "Where do you think they'll head for?"

"Maybe the Eurostar – less chance of being spotted than at an airport. I'll get the French officers from here at the station to go over to the Gare du Nord straight away. See if we can't head them off. And…. Sir?" Jack paused for a moment. "An MI6 agent has been found dead, Sir. Found in an alleyway. Name of Simon Shafer. Does that name mean anything to you? Is he caught up in this too? If so, my money's on Fleming."

Jack heard Liddell exhale noisily. "Ok, Ok, let me think. Let me handle things from here. I'll get the girl's picture out to all ports and airports. Put out an alert. Don't you worry about getting anyone over to the Eurostar, I'll handle that. I'll telephone them direct and fax them a picture. You stay at the station and get hold of any CCTV they might have. Get this guy's picture. But stay there. I'll handle all the alerts, leave it to me."

Chief Superintendent Liddell then cut the call.

* * *

Time: 2.30pm
   Date: 9th November 2008
   Location: Rue Saint Pierre, Paris

Mac and Andre hurriedly left the café and walked quickly along the pavement edge, heads down, avoiding the heavy stream of pedestrians coming towards them from the other direction.

"How do we know where she's going to be?" Mac jogged quickly behind Andre, trying to keep up with the pace. "She could be anywhere in this whole city. She could be…." He broke off as the word stuck in his throat.

Andre quickened his pace even more. He felt his backpack containing the laptop banging up and down on his back, but he ignored the discomfort. "She's not dead, Mac. She can't be. He still needs her alive."

Andre looked down at his watch and frowned.

There was still time.

They could still get there in time.

CHAPTER NINETEEN

"Come on, quick. I think I know where they might be heading."

Mac opened his mouth to ask where this might be, but Andre quickened the pace even more and disappeared down a side street. With a quick glance behind him, Mac followed suit and followed in Andre's wake. But as he was running, he couldn't quite shake off what they had both just been reading.

"I need to tell you something....."

"This whole situation is fucked up...."

"No one is who you think they are..."

"Be careful...."

Shafer's words of warning were echoing around Mac's head as he continued to jog down the side street after Andre.

"Be careful...."

Mac felt a gnawing sensation start to grow in the pit of his stomach, alongside the fast developing stitch.

***

Time: 1.30pm
Date: 9th November 2008
Location: Metropolitan Police HQ, London

Liddell exhaled slowly, replacing the telephone receiver back into its cradle. He rubbed his eyes with the backs of his hands. How he wished his headache would go away, just disappear, so that he could think straight for a moment, so that he could see exactly what it was he should do. They would be expecting him to do something. Something right now, this very minute.

He jumped as Penny opened his office door and peered around the corner, glasses perched on the end of her long nose, a small notepad and pen in hand.

"Sorry, Sir," she said, hovering by the door. "But when Detective Inspector MacIntosh was on the line he said that he needed you to act urgently on something." She edged a little further into the room, hand poised over the notepad. "Would you like me to do anything? He mentioned some telephone calls? Airports? Railway stations? If you give me the details, Sir, I can make them straightaway."

Liddell looked up and smiled. "What would I do without you, Penny?" he breathed, his careworn face softening slightly. But he slowly shook his head. "It's OK – I'm going to make the calls personally. In fact,……" Chief Superintendent Liddell turned his wrist towards him and glanced at his expensive Rolex watch. "Why don't you take the rest of the afternoon off? I can finish up here."

Penny let her arms relax, the notepad and pen dropping to her side. She frowned a little "Are…. are you sure, Sir? Because it's no trouble, I can……"

But Liddell held up his hands and cut her short. "No, Penny, I insist. Isn't it your sister's birthday or something at the weekend? Why don't you take yourself off and buy her something nice? Honestly, it's no problem. I'm going to be tied up here for a while, so you may as well."

Penny hesitated, and then broke out into a small, nervous smile. "Well, yes….I suppose I could go and get her something. It would save me having to do it at the weekend. If you're sure?"

Liddell nodded and returned the smile. "Absolutely."

"And the calls?" Penny nodded at the telephone on Chief Superintendent Liddell's desk.

"I'll do them right away," he replied, picking up the receiver and letting his hand hover over the keypad. "Go on now, shoo!"

Penny smiled again, pushed her glasses back onto the bridge of her nose and quietly closed the door behind her. Liddell waited a few seconds and then stabbed at the telephone keypad in front of him. He held the receiver to his ear and waited. The call was answered immediately. "It's me," he said, instantly, his face darkening. "What the hell is going on?" He paused and listened to the reply, starting to shake his head in frustration. "I've just had MacIntosh on the phone asking me to alert all ports and airports to a suspected fugitive who has abducted a British citizen. Tell me this is not happening?"

CHAPTER NINETEEN

Again there was a lengthy pause. Liddell's face darkened even further at the reply.

"And impersonating a police officer?! What in God's name were you thinking of?!" Liddell leant back in his chair and massaged his right temple with his fingers. His headache was worsening by the minute. "And the girl? You still have her? Well, that's something at least. But what the hell do you need her for? We agreed that DI MacIntosh would be coming to take her back home. You don't need her to do the job. It's the papers we want, not her!"

Liddell gripped the telephone receiver even more tightly in his hand, the whites of his knuckles beginning to show. He gritted his teeth, angrily. "And the rest of Prism? The Project? You told me this was going to be easy. You told me this couldn't go wrong. Do you have any idea what will happen if *any* of this gets out?" He paused momentarily for the reply. "Well you'd better start sorting it out…and fast! Get the Phoenix Project data like we agreed, and destroy it!"

Liddell threw the receiver back in its cradle, sprung to his feet and stormed out of his office. Penny's desk was deserted, her bag and coat gone. Liddell headed past the desk but something caught his eye and he stopped dead in his tracks. His heart froze. As he looked down onto his secretary's desk, he could almost feel the colour physically draining from his cheeks. His eyes were fixed on Penny's telephone. The telephone receiver was out of its cradle, lying on its side in the centre of the desk. The small red light on the control panel showed that the line was connected to Liddell's office– and lying next to the ear of the receiver was a mobile telephone.

Liddell snatched up the mobile phone and held it to his ear. Whoever had been eavesdropping on his conversation was long gone – but they would have heard everything they needed to hear. Frantically he began scrolling down through the telephone's menus. He had to find out who it was.

* * *

Time: 2.35pm
Date: 9th November 2008
Location: Commissariat Central, Rue Louis Blanc, Paris

Jack marched over to Sergeant Boutin who was still manning the front desk.

"I need to know who Fleming spoke to from this telephone. Can you trace the calls from here?" Jack stabbed a finger towards the small telephone sitting at the far end of the information desk.

Sergeant Boutin paused for a moment or two, glancing sideways at the telephone. "The gentleman who said he was you? He made a call from this telephone?"

"Yes," breathed Jack. "Just before he left with the young lady, he stopped and made a call from that telephone. I've just seen the pictures on your CCTV cameras. Can you trace the calls made on that phone? I need to know who he spoke to."

Sergeant Boutin turned to speak to his colleague, Sergeant Matteau, who had appeared behind him. The pair exchanged a heated discussion in rapid French. The young spectacled officer shook his head, frantically, and gesticulated towards the telephone with animated hands.

Sergeant Boutin turned back towards Jack and shook his head. "Unfortunately no, we won't be able to trace the calls, as it is an internal phone…"

Jack's shoulders sagged. "But, I really need….."

"But do not despair Detective Inspector," continued Sergeant Boutin, a smile on his lips. "It seems that no one else has used that telephone today. Apart from your gentleman. So……" He raised his eyebrows and nodded at the phone.

Jack allowed himself a small smile. "So, if I just press redial……?"

* * *

CHAPTER TWENTY

Time: 1.45pm
Date: 9th November 2008
Location: Metropolitan Police HQ, London

Chief Superintendent Liddell locked his office door behind him. It was lunchtime and most of the office staff had left the building – for that, he was thankful. Penny hadn't been back, but then again he hadn't expected her to be. Everywhere was quiet.

He sat back down behind his desk and pulled open the top drawer. He removed a small, beige folder and placed it in front of him. Opening it up, he stared intently at the photograph. Isabel Faraday's warm features smiled back at him.

Reaching out, Liddell took a small piece of paper from the jotter pad next to his phone. As he did so, his eyes rested on another photograph – this time of his wife and two small children. All three were laughing and smiling, seemingly without a care in the world. They had been on holiday, that he knew, but where had it been? The Mediterranean? The Caribbean? He could no longer remember. Somewhere with golden sandy beaches and a deep blue sky. But it could have been anywhere.

Liddell's bottom lip faintly began to tremble. He tipped the photograph over so that it lay face down on his desk. He didn't want to see them, not now. Not this time. He didn't want their laughing, smiling eyes looking at him when he did what he knew he had to do.

He wasn't going to wait for the call. He knew it would come. It had to come. There could be no other outcome and he had known that all along. He had always known that one day it would end like this. And in a way, he felt strangely at peace.

He pulled the piece of paper over towards him and placed it on top of Isabel's picture. Picking up his fountain pen, he wrote three simple words. Then placing the pen back in its holder he reached back inside the drawer.

* * *

Time: 2.35pm
Date: 9th November 2008
Location: La Premiere Banque National, Rue de Picard, Paris

Fleming opened the car door allowing Isabel to slip out. He quickly rapped on the roof of the Mercedes. "Wait here," he commanded. "Make sure you are ready when we come out." He glanced down at his watch. 2.35pm.

In the driver's seat, Petrov nodded, curtly, but barely blinked. As Fleming and Isabel turned away he reached down into the pocket of his overcoat and removed a sleek, black pistol. He placed it in his lap and returned to staring, vacantly, out of the window. His partner, Vasiliev, sitting in the passenger seat, sported the same blank expression.

Fleming gently, but firmly, took Isabel by the hand and pulled her towards an impressive looking building with towering smoke glass windows.

"Where are we going?" she asked, as Fleming pulled her up the steps of the La Premiere Banque Nationale. Looking up she saw the building stretching high up into the Parisian sky. "I thought you wanted to see Andre's apartment…………"

"Just a small stop, I promise," smiled Fleming, his cold, grey eyes shining. "You need to safeguard the money in your Trust Fund. Your two friends know too much about you and what you have, and could easily access that money if you don't do something about it first. It'll only take a minute or two."

CHAPTER TWENTY

Isabel hesitated for a moment and then shrugged, while Fleming took a hold of her elbow and guided her up the remaining steps towards the entrance. He reached out and pushed open the heavy glass fronted doors, holding them open for Isabel to step through. They entered a dimly lit foyer, which was completely bare except for a small hatch in the far wall, the size of a large letterbox. As soon as they entered, the hatch snapped open to reveal a pair of inquisitive eyes.

"Pouvoir je vous aide?" spoke the eyes, blinking slowly.

Fleming walked quickly over to the hatch but stopped when he came to a thick red line painted on the floor in front of them. Isabel was too busy gazing up at the dizzyingly high ceiling above her and didn't notice the line approaching. Fleming pulled her roughly back to prevent her crossing over it.

"We mustn't cross the line," he whispered, nodding down at the floor. "If we do...." He looked up and nodded at the thin red laser beams criss crossing the airspace before them. "The whole place will go up. It's security. Best if you let me do all the talking – we'll be out of here in no time."

"Pouvoir je vous aide?" repeated the eyes from the hatch.

Fleming then spoke quickly and precisely in French, making only the briefest of indications towards Isabel as he did so. The eyes blinked twice, then nodded curtly. After another quick, short sentence in French, the hatch slammed shut.

Fleming stepped backwards and pulled Isabel after him. "Come on, over this way." He nodded towards the left hand side of the foyer where there were a series of armoured doors set securely into the wall. Fleming stopped outside door number 5. The door looked as though it were reinforced with steel, or some such other metal. It had raised bumps, not unlike a bullet proof vest, and with no door handle there was no obvious means of opening it. Almost immediately there was a low, hissing sound, and an eerie green light emanated from around the edges of the door.

Isabel flinched and edged backwards. Fleming, on the other hand, seemed to know what he was doing and reached forwards, gently pushing the door. It opened slowly in front of them and, without hesitating,

Fleming stepped over the threshold dragging Isabel with him.

As soon as they were both inside, the door closed itself, accompanied by another low sounding hiss, and the green light was extinguished. Isabel glanced behind her, warily, and noticed that there was no door handle on the inside either. No obvious means of getting in, and no obvious means of getting out.

They were now standing inside a small 12' x 8' space, no bigger than an average sized broom cupboard. It was ominously dark, the only light coming from three faint spotlights recessed into the low ceiling above.

"Do you know your account number?" asked Fleming, nodding at the wall in front of them which housed a computer keyboard. "You need it to access your account."

Isabel shook her head. "No, I never needed it. I….."

Fleming held up a hand. "No matter. There is another way." He guided Isabel through the darkness towards the wall in front of them. He tapped a few keys on the keyboard and then took Isabel's right hand. He placed it on top of a small square a green glass set into the wall next to the keyboard and pressed it down, firmly. Isabel gasped when she saw a thin green line sweep across the glass from top to bottom, and then from bottom to top, scanning her hand. After her hand had been processed twice, Fleming swiftly removed it and took hold of Isabel's index finger. Before she knew what was happening, he had inserted her finger into a small round hole next to the scanner.

"Ouch!" Isabel yelped and snatched her finger back out of the hole. With her eyes now becoming accustomed to the dark, she could see a small, red dot of blood forming on the tip. "What the…?" She stared incredulously from her bleeding finger to Fleming, and then back again.

"Fingerprints and DNA – if you don't know your account number or password then that's the only way to access your account." Fleming smiled and gave a small chuckle. "It's very secure."

Just then, on the right hand side of the wall, a section of the armoured plating began to slide out. When the opening was big enough a smooth sided grey metallic box slid out. It looked like a briefcase, although much

CHAPTER TWENTY

wider and deeper, and with a large metal handle on the top. Fleming took hold of the box and as soon as he did so the opening in the wall snapped shut.

Without being prompted, the door behind them began to hiss once again.

* * *

Time: 2.40pm
 Date: 9th November 2008
 Location: Rue Louis Blanc, Paris

Jack hijacked a French police officer's car outside the Commissariat Central police station and, in his best pigeon French, ordered him to drive as fast as was humanly possible…..and then faster still. They didn't need to go far; the police officer driving had told him. Only a few streets away. With any luck there would still be time. On the way he pulled out his mobile phone and dialled the office number. It was answered on the second ring.

"Cooper?" Jack barked into the phone. "Is that you?"

"Jack! Where the hell are you?!" DS Cooper jumped out of his chair and waved at a couple of officers who were about to leave the room. He beckoned them back over towards the desk. "We were just trying to get hold of you…..we just heard about this MI6 agent…"

"Yes, I know. I just heard myself. Killed in the street, apparently." Jack grabbed hold of the dashboard as the car hurtled round a sharp bend. "I've been at the station trying to see Isabel, like Liddell wanted. But now I'm on my way to the Premiere Banque Nationale. Fleming's on his way there with Isabel; he's taken her. There's no time to explain, but he's not FBI. Never has been. They've never even heard of him. And he just impersonated me to get to Isabel."

"Jesus, Jack, why ….?"

"That, I am about to find out." Jack braced himself against the passenger door as the car swung out violently to avoid a parked car. "But I need you to do something for me. It's about Chief Superintendent Liddell. He's been on the phone to Fleming, and I'm sure he already knew he wasn't FBI. I need you to get hold of Penny for me. I spoke to her earlier, but she's not answering her phone. Now."

"OK boss, I'm on it."

"Get her to call me. It's important." Jack snapped his phone shut and braced himself against the door once again as the police car swerved across two lanes of traffic, sirens blaring.

* * *

Time: 2.45pm
　Date: 9th November 2008
　Location: La Premiere Banque National, Rue de Picard, Paris

Fleming helped Isabel back into the rear seat of the waiting car, and then slid in beside her. He rested the metal briefcase on top of his knees and caressed it like a newborn baby. As soon as the door was shut, Petrov inched the car out into the early afternoon traffic.

Just as the car had left the kerbside, Fleming glanced out of his side window and allowed a thin smile to spread out over his lips. The plan was almost at an end. Just a few lose ends to tie up, and then it would all be over. He glanced over at Isabel before returning his gaze to the view from the window.

But as he did so, the newly formed smile froze on his lips. A figure shot past him on the pavement, heading back towards the Premiere Banque Nationale – quickly followed by a second. Fleming pressed his face up against the glass window. "Stop the car!" he yelled, spit flying out of his mouth and landing on the window pane. "Stop this bloody car, now!"

Petrov glanced fearfully in his rear view mirror and brought the car to a swift and sudden stop. He glanced across at Vasiliev, but neither man spoke. Car horns immediately started blaring at them from all directions.

CHAPTER TWENTY

Oblivious to the chaos his sudden halt was causing, Fleming quickly shoved the passenger door open and stepped out into the road. Angry drivers were now gesticulating at him through their windscreens, but he took no notice. He stared back down the street towards the Premiere Banque Nationale. Narrowing his gaze, he saw two figures jogging up the steps, just as he and Isabel had done only minutes before. The figures turned round, gazing out into the streams and streams of traffic behind them, searching for something…hunting for something…. Hunting for someone.

It was then that Fleming saw him.

One of the figures turned round and glanced up the street towards the Mercedes. And, despite the distance, instantly their eyes locked hard. Fleming returned the man's gaze, holding it steady, hardly moving, hardly breathing.

As he stared, Fleming gripped the briefcase in his hand even more tightly. With a final menacing look, he raised his free hand to his throat and drew a thin finger across his neck from one side to the other – then, he turned and slipped back inside the waiting car.

"Drive!" yelled Fleming, as he slammed the door behind him. "Now!"

Andre was frozen to the spot, staring after the sleek black Mercedes as it inched its way back into the traffic and pulled away from them. Mac had already pushed the door to the building open, but seeing that there was nothing and no one inside had come straight back out again.

"There's no one here, Andre," he panted, stopping to stand by Andre's side. "Where the bloody hell are we anyway?"

Andre was silent, his mind racing. He continued to stare after the Mercedes, unwilling to break his gaze.

"What shall we….?" But Mac was cut short by the sound of a screeching police siren cutting through the air towards them. A police car skidded to a halt beside them and two figures jumped out, one from the front and one from the back. Both ran up the steps towards them.

"Police!" Jack flashed his warrant card at Andre and shot past him into the building. He re-emerged seconds later, having found the place completely deserted in much the same way Mac had moments before. It was then that Jack turned to face Andre, and thrust a picture of Isabel in front of his face. "How long have you been here? Have you seen this woman?!"

"Hello, Jack."

Jack momentarily froze at the sound of the voice behind him. Slowly he turned around and the two men locked eyes. He felt winded, as though someone had just thrown a heavy punch to the depths of his stomach.

"Hello, Jack", repeated Mac, his voice steady but guarded.

Jack looked from Mac to Andre, and then back again, his eyes wide. "What on earth are you doing here?" he finally managed to blurt out.

Mac glanced at Andre, who remained silent. "It's a long story."

Jack tore his bewildered eyes away from Mac and focused once again on Andre. The man's face looked familiar. Strikingly familiar. He'd seen those eyes somewhere before. Those crystal clear, pale grey eyes, eyes that penetrated your soul. The loosely cropped beard. The slightly receding hairline.

And then it hit him.

Not taking his eyes off Andre for a second, Jack rummaged inside his jacket pocket and brought out a fistful of loose, crumpled papers. He briefly glanced down, flicking through the sheets until he reached the one he wanted. He pulled out the torn memo Fleming had given them all at the first briefing. At the bottom of the paper there was a photograph – a picture Jack had taken very little notice of…. until now.

Jack held up the picture of Andre for Mac to see.

"What the *hell* are you doing with this man?!" Jack turned towards his brother, his eyes wide. "And I want the truth."

Mac glanced at the photograph, then sideways at Andre, but said nothing.

"This man is wanted by the FBI," Jack carried on, returning the memo to his pocket. "How in God's name…..."

"Fleming's not FBI, and you damn well know it," retorted Andre, finding his voice and turning towards Jack. "And who the hell are you if you don't mind me asking?"

"I'm the one asking the questions," replied Jack, gruffly, thrusting his

CHAPTER TWENTY

warrant card inches from Andre's face. "Detective Inspector MacIntosh. What the fuck are you doing with my brother?"

"Brother?" Andre frowned and looked across at Mac. "You never said you had a policeman in the family."

Mac merely shrugged.

"What the hell are you doing here, Stu? What the *hell* is going on?" Jack's eyes bore into his brother.

"Look, this isn't the time or place for a family reunion," said Andre, hotly. "Isabel is in the back of that car." He pointed into the Paris traffic. "The black Mercedes. Fleming's in the back with about 1 million Euros and Isabel. And if I'm right, I think he's going to kill her."

* * *

Time: 1.45pm
 Date: 9th November 2008
 Location: Metropolitan Police HQ, London

DS Cooper clamped the telephone receiver to his ear, willing Jack to pick up.

"Come on Jack, where the hell are you?" The phone continued to ring and eventually went to voicemail. "Jack, call me when you get this, its urgent. It's all hitting the fan right now. I just went to find Penny like you asked, and you'll never guess what's just happened." DS Cooper paused. "It's Chief Superintendent Liddell…..he's been found dead at his desk. Shot himself."

* * *

CHAPTER TWENTY-ONE

Time: 2.45pm
Date: 9th November 2008
Location: La Premiere Banque National, Rue de Picard, Paris

The three of them squeezed themselves into the back of the police car and, with the aid of blue flashing lights and a deafening siren, they pushed their way out into the slow flow of Parisian traffic. Fleming's black Mercedes was still in view, the sheer volume of cars halting their getaway and turning it into a mere crawl.

The French police officers had radioed through for additional back up, and armed police together with a police helicopter were being despatched. Jack just hoped it was going to be enough. He got out his mobile phone and punched in the office number, noticing there was a voicemail message waiting for him. Ignoring it, he put the receiver to his ear.

"Cooper? I'm following Isabel. Fleming's with her. He's just accessed her private safety deposit box." Jack paused and cast a glance at Andre who was sitting in the middle of the three of them. "Apparently, he's going to kill her."

"Jack! Where the hell have you been?! We've been trying to get hold of you. Did you get my message?"

Jack frowned. "Message? What message?" Again he looked at his mobile phone screen and the small envelope blinking at him indicating there was a message waiting.

DS Cooper let out a long whistle at the other end of the telephone. "Jesus

CHAPTER TWENTY-ONE

Jack. This place is in chaos. Liddell's shot himself in his office. Poor Penny found him. Literally just minutes ago. We're all on lockdown."

Jack eyes widened. "Seriously? Jesus, Cooper. I'll try and get back as soon as I can. He *shot* himself?"

"From what we can gather, yes. Penny is distraught. The whole place is sealed off."

"OK, well I'll be back as soon as I can. In the meantime, I need you to run an all systems check on Isabel Faraday," Jack continued. "I need to know who she is and what I'm dealing with over here."

"But I thought we already had run a check on her?"

"Well *we* didn't, did we? Liddell did. We only had the information Liddell fed us. What I need you to do now is run a full check on her, and let me know what you come up with. This was never just a missing persons case. I need to know who she is and why Liddell took such a personal interest in her. And bearing in mind what's just happened….."

"Will do, Boss," replied DS Cooper, cutting the call and pulling the computer screen over towards him. "So, Miss Faraday – let's see who you really are."

* * *

Time: 2.50pm
Date: 9th November 2008
Location: Rue de Picard, Paris

Fleming glanced nervously over his shoulder back through the car's rear window. He could see the flashing blue lights of a police car about eight vehicles behind them, but thankfully the grid locked streets were keeping them from making up any real ground. They were coming up to a junction and Fleming's heart sank when he saw yet more flashing blue lights waiting to join the traffic from both sides of the road.

As if that wasn't enough, he could now hear the unmistakeable thud-thud-thud of helicopter blades sweeping low somewhere overhead. Beads of sweat formed on his brow and he wiped them away with a quivering hand. This wasn't part of the plan. He loosened the tie around his neck and closed his eyes, gripping the briefcase tightly on his lap. The sound of the sirens and the helicopter blades were getting louder and louder, circulating inside his head on a seemingly never ending merry-go-round.

The time had come.

They had failed. They had all failed.

He had to make the call.

He *needed* to make the call.

The call to end it all.

With one last glance out of the rear window, Fleming pulled out his mobile phone and began to dial.

* * *

Time: 1.50pm

Date: 9th November 2008

Location: Metropolitan Police HQ, London

DS Cooper typed in the name Isabel Faraday into the search engine and hit the enter button. Instantly, his monitor showed "Access Denied. Security Clearance Level 1 required."

Frowning, Cooper looked back down at the paperwork he had in front of him and scanned the details one again. He re-entered the information, making sure he had spelt the name correctly.

"Access Denied, Security Clearance Level 1 required." The same message flashed up once again.

DS Cooper exhaled loudly, his frown deepening. He ran his fingers through his unruly red hair, leaving it in messy tufts. He glanced up from his desk and spied a female DC sitting over in the far corner of the room.

"Hey, Amanda?" he called out, trying to catch her eye. "You still seeing that guy from over at Vauxhall House?"

DC Amanda Cassidy raised her head and looked over. "I might be, "she

CHAPTER TWENTY-ONE

replied, cautiously. "Depends who wants to know."

"Thing is," he smiled, "I need a favour."

* * *

Time: 4.55pm
  Date: 9th November 2008
  Location: Red Square, Moscow, Russia

Dimitri Federov carefully replaced the telephone receiver. He looked up from his desk and slowly pulled himself to his feet. Walking over to the window, he looked out across the rooftops towards Red Square. It was a fantastic view. The best in the whole of Moscow. Fitting really, that it should happen here. That it should all end here.

He had been expecting it, of course. One day he knew the call would come. And in a way, it was welcomed. He could, at last, let go – bring an end to the uncertainty that had tainted his life, once and for all. Twenty years of looking over his shoulder, wondering.

Casting a final look out towards the Square, drinking in its beauty bathed in the late afternoon darkness, Federov turned and walked back to his desk. Taking a small silver key from a chain around his neck, he unlocked a side drawer. Reaching inside, he pulled out a tiny, fragile-looking, clear glass vial. His hand quivered. Stopping only briefly to straighten his tie and button up his jacket, he removed the top of the vial and shook the small pill out into the centre of his palm. Closing his eyes and taking a single deep breath, Federov placed the pill onto the end of his tongue – and swallowed.

Time: 4.59pm
  Date: 9th November 2008
  Location: Red Square, Moscow, Russia

Sergei Ivanov let the telephone fall from his hand. It crashed down onto the desk in front of him, knocking over the half empty glass of cherry vodka. He barely noticed the liquid seeping into his notepad or trickling off the end of the table and onto the floor. The sweet aroma filled his nostrils as he breathed in deeply, eyes closed.

He had been standing behind his desk when he took the call. Now, he leant forwards and used both of his hands to steady himself. His legs, usually thick and sturdy, felt like buckling beneath him as if made of cotton wool. He took several deeper breaths, filling his lungs to steady his rasping breaths.

Reaching forward, he made a grab for the rest of the bottle of vodka which was standing next to the upturned glass. He drank deeply straight from the bottle, screwing up his eyes as the burning liquid scorched his throat and made him shudder. When he had finished, he hurled the empty bottle across the room, hearing it smash against the wall but seeing nothing.

His eyes were streaming now, clouding his vision. Steadying himself once again, he leant down and reached inside his desk drawer – he had to do it now before he lost his nerve. He frantically rummaged through the contents, sending books and papers flying until his hand closed around what he was searching for. Bringing it out, he clenched it tightly inside his shaking fist.

Pausing only momentarily, wondering if he should make any last minute calls, Ivanov forced the top from the small vial and shook the contents out onto the desk top in front of him. He considered calling Dimitri, but quickly cast the thought aside. He would have received the same call. Or was about to. It would make no difference to what they had to do. Before he lost his nerve completely, Ivanov reached forwards and swept the pill up into his dry mouth and forcefully held his lips shut with his fingers until he could do nothing but swallow.

And wait.

***

CHAPTER TWENTY-ONE

Time: 2.05pm
 Date: 9th November 2008
 Location: M16 HQ, London

Charles Tindleman leant back in his chair and smiled at the telephone in his hand. He closed his eyes and gave a small, tired laugh. Pulling his chair closer to the desk, he replaced the receiver and reactivated the screensaver on his desktop computer. Isabel Faraday's picture stared out at him from the centre of the monitor. He tapped a few keys and the picture disappeared. A small message box popped up in the centre of the screen. "Are you sure you wish to delete this file?" Charles Tindleman clicked on the "yes" box, and almost instantaneously was replaced with "file deleted."

He tapped a few more keys and went through the same process three more times, each time clicking "yes" for the files to be deleted. When he was finished, he opened his desk drawer and pulled out a thick brown envelope and a small glass vial.

He stood the glass vial in the middle of the desk, staring at it without taking a breath. He then turned his attention to the envelope. It had arrived earlier that morning – special delivery by courier. He had not needed to look inside. He knew what it would be, but he had looked anyway.

It was thick, and crammed full of papers and photographs. Bending down he retrieved a metal waste paper bin from underneath the desk, bringing it up onto his lap. Tipping the envelope upside down, he let a few pieces of paper fall into the bin. Before he had time to change his mind, he then picked up a nearby box of matches and quickly struck a match. Hesitating for only for the briefest of seconds, Charles Tindleman dropped the lit match into the bin and ignited the papers. They crumpled under the flames, quickly starting to turn black and disintegrate into charcoal ash. He dropped more papers into the bin, followed by more struck matches.

By the time he had finished he had used up an entire box of matches, and the envelope was empty. But he didn't mind. He wouldn't be needing them now. He put the empty match box down and picked up the glass vial.

***

Time: 10.00am
   Date: 9th November 2008
   Location: Washington DC, United States of America

Austin Edwards smiled to himself. He and just taken the call, the call he had been waiting for. The call they had *all* been waiting for.

He wondered who had received the call first.

Not that it mattered.

It was the call that had always been coming.

And he felt strangely at peace.

***

Time: 2.55pm
   Date: 9th November 2008
   Location: Rue de Chateau Rouge, Paris

Petrov stamped hard on the accelerator and the car lurched forwards at speed. They had managed to snake their way through the grid locked procession of vehicles and for the time being appeared to have lost their travelling companions. Fleming returned his mobile phone to his pocket, and continued to maintain a watchful eye from the back seat of the car – but now all he could see was the glare of the headlights behind him.

The Mercedes swung hard right, tyres screeching as they sped away from the main road. Petrov knew the traffic would be lighter this way and he roared down the street, skilfully manoeuvring the car through pedestrian crossings and T junctions, ignoring red lights as if they were no more than a minor irritation.

The flashing blue lights had vanished from behind, yet Fleming could still hear their faint sirens floating through the air. The sounds came and went, and it was difficult, if not impossible, to know if they were still in

CHAPTER TWENTY-ONE

pursuit or not. For the moment, the thud-thud-thud of the helicopter overhead had disappeared into the Parisian sky.

Fleming's heart began to beat faster. He was now on the final leg of the journey, after all this time. He kept glancing out of the back window, but still no lights could be seen.

Isabel had remained silent since their visit to the Premiere Banque Nationale. She eyed Fleming, warily, out of the corner of her eye, noticing how he was cradling the briefcase in his lap – grasping its handle firmly, unable or unwilling to let it out of his grip.

The streets were becoming quieter by the second. Petrov pointed the car towards the industrial part of the suburbs, where everyone had already shut up shop for the day and headed home. There were no residential flats or apartments in this part of the city – just offices, shops and warehouses. And at the moment, all appeared to be quiet and deserted.

Petrov swung the car violently to the left, momentarily throwing Isabel off balance. She put out her hand to steady herself, reaching out and pressing hard against the briefcase on Fleming's lap next to her. Fleming's cold eyes darted towards her hands, and he instantly snatched the briefcase out from under her grasp, placing it down on the floor, safely between his feet.

The car was now entering a small industrial complex and, as they passed by, Isabel looked out and saw a taxi cab firm, a motorbike showroom and what appeared to be a builder's merchants. All abandoned. No signs of life anywhere. As they reached the end of the road the small units began to change into larger warehouses – again, all of them empty and deserted.

Except for one.

The last warehouse loomed up dark and foreboding. The front doors were unlocked, the heavy padlock and chain lying loosely discarded on the ground outside. One door was slightly ajar, and a car was parked outside on the forecourt, its engine and lights extinguished.

Petrov drew up alongside the parked car, then reversed to slip in behind it. Isabel glanced nervously out of her side of the window. Fleming made to get out of the car. But as he did so he stopped and turned to face her.

"You stay here, and don't move," he commanded, his voice cold. "Don't even breathe."

Isabel shrank back into her seat, saying nothing. Her mouth felt dry and scratchy, her heart thumping inside her chest like a hammer on an anvil. She watched as Fleming stepped out of the car, taking the briefcase with him. As he passed Petrov's window, he rapped on the glass with his knuckles. Petrov slowly wound the widow down and turned his face towards the outside air.

"Give me your gun," ordered Fleming, bending down slightly and peering inside the car. He held out his hand, expectantly.

Petrov hesitated, a faint look of bewilderment crossing his face. He remained seated with both hands firmly on the steering wheel.

"I said, give me your gun," hissed Fleming, trying to keep his voice low. "Now!" He glanced quickly over at the parked car in front of them. There was the faint sound of a door clicking open. Someone was making a move to get out.

Petrov looked down into his lap where his pistol still sat. He made a move towards it, but wasn't quick enough. Fleming had leant in through the open window and grabbed it before Petrov's hand had even left the steering wheel. Cursing under his breath, Fleming stuffed the pistol into his overcoat and headed towards the other car.

The doors to the car had flown open before Fleming reached them. A tall, broad shouldered man stepped out of the driver's side, followed by a smaller, shorter man from the passenger side. Both wore their customary dark, tailored suits, but they now had long, woollen black overcoats on and were wearing sleek coal-black leather gloves. Immediately, they both eyed the gleaming metal briefcase hanging from Fleming's hand.

"Why don't we get back inside," smiled Fleming, nodding his head at the car the two men had just vacated. "It's much warmer in there….and we can talk."

The two men hesitated, glancing warily at each other and then up at Fleming. They then returned their gaze to the briefcase. But they knew this was not a request or a suggestion – it was an order. The taller man gave

CHAPTER TWENTY-ONE

a small nod and both men returned to their seats inside the car. Fleming paused, letting a tiny smile flicker at the corners of his mouth, before sliding into the vacant back seat. Alone.

"So, gentlemen," began Fleming, once inside the car with the doors shut behind them. His voice was soft, quiet and controlled. He licked his thin lips. "We are now nearing the end of a very long and winding road, are we not?" He patted the briefcase beside him as he spoke and managed a small laugh. "Our journey's end."

The taller man turned slightly in his seat and laid his eyes briefly but longingly on the briefcase. He kept one hand on the steering wheel and one hand resting loosely inside his overcoat pocket. Fleming casually glanced at the man in the passenger seat, noticing that he, too, had one hand shrouded inside his overcoat pocket.

"And now we have our prize," continued Fleming, letting his eyes flicker back to the briefcase. He paused for a second and listened intently. Still no sirens. Still no flashing lights. Still no thud-thud of the helicopter overhead. The smile grew on his thin lips. "It's a wonder that you haven't tried to take it from me," he said, looking back up at the two men in the front of the car. "I know I would have." The smile danced playfully on his lips.

The taller man broke his hungry gaze from the briefcase and briefly glanced at his smaller companion in the front passenger seat. In that split second, Fleming snatched both pistols from under his overcoat, grasping one in each hand, and rapidly fired one shot from each simultaneously. The bullets easily found their targets. They tore into the back of each man's head, exploding with a mixture of blood, gristle, bone and brain. The bullets exited through their foreheads and smashed through the front windscreen, shattering it into a thousand pieces.

Isabel's screams filled the night air. But there was no one around to hear her. Fleming calmly stepped out of the car, wiping the blood splatters from his face with a clean, crisp handkerchief. He walked back to the Mercedes and, ignoring Isabel's panic ridden cries for help, he pulled open the driver's door and shot Petrov directly in the centre of his forehead.

Petrov slumped forwards onto the steering wheel, his face resting heavily onto the car horn.

Without pausing for breath, Fleming turned his attention to Vasiliev who was frozen to the spot in the passenger seat. Unable to move, his face wide-eyed and terror stricken, Fleming pumped another pullet into his left temple.

Isabel's screams, mixed with the Mercedes' blaring car horn, echoed around the deserted forecourt. And were very quickly joined by a cascade of deafening sirens. Fleming snapped his head around to face the approaching noise, looking over the roof of the car to see a stream of police cars heading his way. The unmistakeable thud-thud-thud of the police helicopter zoomed in once again from above, this time accompanied by a powerful searchlight sending an arc of light dancing over the pavement towards Fleming and the Mercedes.

With no time to lose, Fleming pulled open the rear passenger side door and grabbed hold of Isabel by the arm. He dragged her from the car and pulled her towards the doors of the open warehouse. Isabel gave little or no resistance.

Fleming kicked the padlock and chain out of the way before wrenching open the door and pushing Isabel inside into the darkness.

* * *

Time: 2.05pm
Date: 9th November 2008
Location: Metropolitan Police HQ, London

DC Amanda Cassidy perched on the edge of DS Cooper's desk and held a folded piece of paper between her fingers.

"So, what's it worth Cooper?" She let the piece of paper dangle, temptingly, in front of DS Cooper's face and raised her perfectly manicured eyebrows. "Drinks? Dinner?"

DS Cooper let a smile creep across his lips. "Well. Let's see what comes

CHAPTER TWENTY-ONE

of it first, shall we?" He made a grab for the piece of paper, but DC Cassidy flicked it out of his reach.

"You're all talk, Cooper, all talk." She gave him a wink, and then let the paper fall from her fingers and land on Cooper's desk, narrowly missing his mug of tea. Pushing herself off the corner of his desk, she began to saunter back across the office towards the door, casting a flirtatious glance back over her shoulder. "If you need me, you know where to find me…"

Cooper gave a small chuckle and nodded. "Thanks, Amanda." He picked up the piece of paper and unfolded it – revealing a telephone number written in neat handwriting. A contact number at Vauxhall Cross, as promised.

If anyone knew who Isabel Faraday was, the spooks would.

* * *

Time: 3.05pm
Date: 9th November 2008
Location: Avenue du Petrell, Paris

Jack's car screeched to a stop only inches away from Fleming's Mercedes and he jumped out. Even from where he was standing he could clearly see both Vasiliev and Petrov's lifeless bodies slumped forwards in the front of the car, Petrov's slumped over the steering wheel. Jack went over to the driver's side, reached in and pulled the body backwards, killing the blaring horn.

His gaze then rested on the other car, parked just in front of Fleming's Mercedes. He didn't need to approach any closer to know that the occupants inside will have met the same grisly end as the two Russians in the Mercedes. One of the doors was open and a lifeless arm was hanging out, knuckles scraping the rough tarmac, blood dripping from the fingertips.

Sergeant Boutin dashed to Jack's side, taking hold of his arm and trying to guide him back towards the patrol car.

"It is not safe, Monsieur. You have no body protection and no weapon. You must wait for my colleagues."

Jack shrugged the Sergeant off and quickly surveyed the scene in front of him. He didn't care about body armour, and he cared even less about guns. He had to act fast. He knew that. Every second he lost was a second Fleming gained.

He decided to take control. "Take up your positions!" he shouted, trying to raise his voice above the cacophony of slamming doors, screeching sirens and overhead helicopter blades. The French police had arrived in force, and armed officers were now spilling out from patrol cars all around him. "But do not fire! I repeat…do…not…fire! We have a young woman hostage inside this building! Under no circumstances are you to fire without my express authorisation!"

Sergeant Boutin shouted what Jack hoped was an accurate translation.

"It is OK, Inspector." The Sergeant had seen Jack's worried expression. "They will wait for your orders. Now please…come with me." He took hold of Jack's arm once again and managed to lead him back towards the safety of their squad car. "This warehouse is not used. There is no electricity. And no lighting. No power at all inside. And there is no way out – other than through that door there." Sergeant Boutin nodded his head back towards the front doors of the warehouse which Fleming had pulled firmly shut behind him. Sergeant Boutin paused before turning back towards Jack. "What should we do now, Inspector?"

Jack allowed his gaze to rest on the warehouse doors.

One way in.

One way out.

"We wait," he replied, slowly. "We wait."

*　*　*

Time: 3.05pm
  Date: 9th November 2008

CHAPTER TWENTY-ONE

Location: Metropolitan Police HQ, London

"You're sure?" DS Cooper frowned into the telephone receiver. "You can't tell me anything?"

"Nope, sorry." On the other end of the phone, MI5 officer Alex Cresswell sounded apologetic. "Highest security level clearance on this one. I don't have access."

"Why would she have such a high security level clearance?" Cooper could almost hear Cresswell's shrug on the other end of the line. "As far as we know, she was just someone who worked in an art shop."

"If you want to know more, you'll have to take it higher. To the top. Tindleman."

"Charles Tindleman?"

"Yep. He's the only one who can gain access to this lady's details, I'm afraid. Complete system lock-out."

Cooper thanked Cresswell for his efforts and hung up.

Isabel Faraday.

MI5

Where was all this leading?

* * *

Time: 4.05pm

Date: 9th November 2008

Location: Avenue du Petrell, Paris

The minutes ticked by, each one seemingly slower than the last. Jack had been given a thick bullet-proof vest and Sergeant Boutin demanded that he wear it. It felt heavy and cumbersome but Jack pulled it on as instructed. There had been no sounds coming from within the warehouse. No movement. No voices. No nothing.

There was nothing to suggest that there was anyone inside at all. Yet they *had* to be in there. They had been seen going in…and they had not been seen to come out.

One way in.

One way out.

The armed police officers had spread themselves out and were now covering the entire circumference of the warehouse and its grounds. Most were positioned at the front, training their weapons on the one and only entrance – and the one and only exit. Fingers hovered steadily over triggers, waiting for further instructions. Other officers were deployed around the back of the warehouse, even though according to Sergeant Boutin there was no means of escape or entry there. The rear courtyard saw a handful of officers resting against a high-backed fence, training their weapons along the passageway which linked the front to the back. Some had climbed up onto a neighbouring garage, kneeling on top of its corrugated roof, guns cocked and ready.

Police tape had been wound round both vehicles that contained the dead Russians, the bodes remaining in situ until the scene of crime officers could go about their work.

And so they continued to wait.

Jack nervously chewed his bottom lip. As the minutes ticked by he felt more and more uneasy. Something wasn't right. He could feel it. Fleming had taken Isabel into a warehouse with no visible means of escape. And he had callously killed each and every one of his accomplices, destroying his one and only potential escape route. Why would be do that? What was he planning? The man didn't strike Jack as being stupid.

After an hour, Jack made a decision. He couldn't stand around waiting any longer, he knew that. They had no choice but to penetrate the building. Sergeant Boutin had earlier pointed out to him a small ventilation grate towards the rear of the building. It was small, barely big enough to pass through, but it would have to do.

After some persuasion and discussion, Sergeant Boutin authorised three officers to slip through the ventilation grate into the narrow shaft that led inside. Each wore heavy protective clothing and carried torches attached to their headgear. It was a tight fit, with barely enough room to shuffle

CHAPTER TWENTY-ONE

along on their bellies, but inch by inch they made their way inside as silently as they could.

The last thing Jack saw were the soles of the men's boots disappearing from sight into the darkness beyond. He held his breath – and waited again.

***

Time: 3.00pm
    Date: 9th November 2008
    Location: MI6 HQ, London

Charles Tindleman stared at his computer screen and felt the sickness start to spread from the inside. All colour was draining rapidly from his face, leaving him with a pale, green-tinged pallor. He re-read the email alert once more – but each time he read it, it told him the same. Unauthorised access attempt. Unauthorised access attempt. Unauthorised access attempt.

Somebody had been trying to access Isabel Faradays details. And repeatedly. Tindleman knew that if he dug deeper he would be able to find out who. And when. And most probably why. All of which made him feel even more nauseous.

The who and the when didn't really matter.

But the why.

That did matter.

That was what bothered him.

And scared him.

Closing the email alerts down from the computer screen, Charles Tindleman's eyes rested on the glass vial sitting on the corner of the desk. It had sat there for an hour now, teasing him. Testing him. Taunting him. Had the others received the same call? Tindleman continued to stare at the vial until he knew he couldn't delay it any longer. Reaching forwards, he grasped the vial tightly in his hands and closed his eyes.

THE PHOENIX PROJECT

* * *

Time: 4.10pm
  Date: 9th November 2008
  Location: Avenue du Petrell, Paris

The wait was agonising. Silence was replaced by yet more silence. Jack glanced at his watch for what felt like the millionth time. The men had been gone seven long minutes, and not a sound had been heard. Sergeant Boutin gave him a worried look and just as Jack was about to open his mouth to voice his concerns, there was a shout from the front of the warehouse. Jack sprinted along the passageway around the side of the building, arriving to find the front warehouse doors wide open. One of the officers who had crawled in through the ventilation grate was now talking animatedly to his colleagues on the front forecourt. He was out of breath and clearly agitated.

"What's he saying?!" Jack's heart was thumping wildly inside his chest as he turned towards Sergeant Boutin. "What's happened?!"

"He says that they have found her!" translated the Sergeant, somewhat breathlessly, a smile starting to form on his lips. "They have found the girl! She is inside, and she is all right."

Jack instantly felt a huge tidal wave of relief wash over him, and, closing his eyes, he leant back against a nearly patrol car to steady himself. But Sergeant Boutin had not finished.

"The girl is OK, but there is no sign of the captor." The Sergeant's words caused Jack's eyes to snap back open. He found himself watching two armed officers emerging through the open warehouse doors and between them they half carried, half dragged a woman whom Jack could only assume was Isabel Faraday.

Jack pushed himself off the patrol car. "Quick! Get her out of here!" he barked, grabbing a flashlight and training its beam over their heads and towards the darkness of the now open warehouse. "We still have a suspect at large inside this building. Almost certainly armed. And definitely

CHAPTER TWENTY-ONE

dangerous."

Jack waited while Isabel was ushered across the forecourt and pushed into the safety of a nearby squad car, which immediately reversed away at speed. After they were gone, he turned towards Sergeant Boutin and without a word the two men jogged over and stood either side of the gaping warehouse doorway. Then slowly before them a steady stream of armed officers filed into the building, each brandishing a loaded pistol. After the last one had disappeared inside, Jack peered cautiously around the doorframe.

The warehouse was now awash with light. Huge arcs of brightness from the officers' flashlights danced and jigged over the floor and walls. Jack very quickly realised that the place appeared to be empty.

He edged into the warehouse and watched as the search unfolded before his eyes. Officers combed the building from top to bottom, finding it to be largely empty except for a piles of crates and boxes stacked along the sides and rear of the building. Jack's eyes followed as the search moved in a methodical fashion, officers already beginning to climb up on top of the crates to sweep their flashlights behind to check for any signs of Fleming. There appeared to be none.

If Fleming was still there, he remained hidden and out of sight.

Just as Jack was about to turn and leave, a terrible gnawing sensation eating away at his insides, he heard a sudden cry from the back of the warehouse. Officers immediately stopped their own searches and began to rush towards the sound. Urgent commands were yelled out in French, their voices bouncing off the empty metal shell of the building. Jack found himself following the crowd, his heart beating faster and faster the closer he got to the crates at the back of the warehouse. The stream of officers before him clamoured over the crates, Jack bringing up the rear. As he climbed over the last crate and dropped down behind it, he saw a large circle of officers surrounding something on the floor.

Sergeant Boutin fought his way out from the middle of the pack of jostling bodies. His expression was grave.

"They've found a body," he said, his voice low, taking Jack by the arm.

"Thank Christ for that," Jack replied, making a move forwards, wanting to see Fleming for himself. Sergeant Boutin placed a hand against Jack's chest, gently forcing him to stop. He slowly shook his head.

"They've found a body – but it's not him. It is not your man."

***

Time: 4.14pm
Date: 9th November 2008
Location: Avenue du Petrell, Paris

Fleming allowed himself a small smile. He took in a deep breath and filled his lungs with the cool, crisp late afternoon air. It felt good. It felt so very, very good. He let his pace lessen slightly, his shoulders and arms relaxing, swinging happily by his sides as he strode along the pavement.

He could still hear the gentle thud-thud-thud of the helicopter overhead, and the wailing sirens and shouts from the warehouse. But they were becoming fainter and fainter with every stride, until eventually he couldn't hear them at all.

His plan had gone without a hitch.

He adjusted his hat and straightened his jacket, making sure that the shiny buttons were correctly fastened. The policeman's uniform fitted him perfectly. He patted his pocket where his pistol was stowed and gripped the metal briefcase tightly as he silently paced deeper and deeper into the Paris streets….and out of sight.

***

CHAPTER TWENTY-TWO

Time: 11.00 am
Date: 10th November 2008
Location: Metropolitan Police HQ, London

DS Cooper angled his computer screen so that Jack had a clear view.

"I ran her name through the computer for you, just like you asked – and you'll never guess what it's thrown up." DS Cooper paused, making sure he had Jack's full attention. "Miss Isabel Victoria Faraday," he announced, reading from the screen in front of him. "Been under MI5 and MI6 surveillance since the age of 5. I've had the guys over at Vauxhall Cross look her up for me, but no one's any the wiser as to why. Maximum level security clearance." DS Cooper watched as Jack's eyebrows arched. "Apparently she was under the direct control of none other than our own Charles Tindleman. He was the only one authorised to access her details. I've pulled all her files but its showing up nothing. A bit fat zero. A dead end. All entries and details deleted, just when Tindleman decided to top himself." Jack's eyebrows arched even further, and DS Cooper continued. "She's on the system, but that's all. The only person who had access to her files was Tindleman himself. And he's dead."

Jack nodded, thoughtfully, rubbing his fingers over the week's worth of stubble pricking his chin. He'd brought Isabel back late last night, and the questions still kept mounting up. He stared at Cooper's computer screen. There was more to Isabel Faraday than met the eye, of that he was sure.

Charles Tindleman – head of MI6

Malcolm Liddell – Chief Superintendent Metropolitan Police
Both knew Isabel Faraday.
Both seemed to want to protect her.
Both were now dead.
Jack got up from his desk. There was somewhere he needed to be.

* * *

Time: 11.30am
Date: 10th November 2008
Location: Metropolitan Police HQ, London

Detective Inspector MacIntosh gently pushed open the door into Chief Superintendent Liddell's office. Penny hovered, cautiously, behind him.

"I'll let you know when I'm done," he said, giving her a brief smile as he stepped into the room and closed the door behind him. Penny gave a nervous nod and seated herself back down at her desk.

Jack looked about him and saw that the place looked the same as it always had done on the handful of occasions that he had been summonsed before the Chief Superintendent. And the same as the last time he had stood in this very spot. The last time Chief Superintendent Liddell had been seen alive.

The same chairs were still arranged symmetrically around the same neat and tidy desk, two either side and one in the middle. Jack sniffed the air – it smelt stale and stuffy. He moved towards the desk, taking his time to walk around the back and pause at Liddell's heavy leather chair. The scene of crime officers had finished with the place now. They had combed the room for evidence – for clues – for any sign as to what had happened. They had bagged up what they needed and left. Most of what they had taken away was sitting on Jack's desk upstairs in the investigation room – piles and piles of polythene bags which needed to be examined and re-examined, tagged and re-tagged, categorised and re-categorised – in the vain hope of providing the smallest clue as to why the man did

CHAPTER TWENTY-TWO

what he did.

Jack let his eyes fall down onto the desk itself. Liddell's computer and monitor had been taken away to be forensically examined, leaving behind a small outline of dust to show where it had once sat. All that remained on the desk itself was a tall, chrome pot which housed a number of pens and pencils, a thick jotter pad, the telephone console and a small photo frame. Jack leant forwards, reaching out to touch the edges of the frame. It had been laid down on its front, masking the photograph from view. Jack lifted it up slightly and peered underneath. He could make out the happy, smiling faces of what he presumed were Liddell's family – happy faces that continued to smile and laugh despite the horror that had taken place inside this very room. Faces from the past – faces oblivious to the present.

Jack let the photo frame rest back down on the desk and let his eyes carefully roam once again. He noticed a large, dark stain on the wood in front of him, and further patches on the floor beneath. Jack didn't need to ask himself what they would be. The forensic guys had tried to clean up after themselves as best they could, but human blood was very hard to shift. It seeped down into the very grain of the wood, into the very fibres of the carpet, casting its indelible mark and remaining there as a constant reminder of what had come to pass.

Jack reached into his pocket and pulled out a transparent polythene bag. He unfolded it and held it out in front of him. The bag contained a photograph of the Chief Superintendent lying unceremoniously face down on his desk, blood seeping out from the gaping wound to his head. It was clear to Jack, and anyone else, that half of Liddell's head was missing.

From his other pocket, Jack pulled out a smaller polythene bag – this one containing just a small scrap of paper with the words "Please Forgive Me" written in Liddell's neat handwriting. The message had been found on the Chief Superintendent's desk, just at the edge of the river of blood flowing from his head. The sides of the paper were tainted dark red.

Please Forgive Me.

Please Forgive Me.

Please Forgive Me.

Jack sighed and placed both bags back into his pocket. What was Liddell seeking forgiveness for? For killing himself? For blasting a crater in the side of his head and spilling his brains on the office furniture? Jack shook his head. He knew there had to be more to it than that.

Instead of placing the calls to the ports and airports as he had promised, Liddell had chosen to telephone Fleming. That they already knew. Jack had listened to that very conversation courtesy of Penny. And shortly after that conversation had ended, Liddell had ended up dead. There would be an investigation, an inquiry, a post mortem and an inquest. But Jack knew, as did everyone else in the building, that the Chief Superintendent had taken his own life. With his own hand. The only thing that none of them knew, was why.

Jack sighed and took another look around the room. There had to be something else. Something the forensic guys had missed. Something he himself had missed. Something that tied Liddell to Isabel….and to Tindleman.

Just at that moment the door opened, and Penny popped her head into the room. Jack nodded a friendly greeting, knowing how she would be feeling inside. She tried to avoid looking over at the desk – instantly remembering what she had seen when she had returned to the office that fateful afternoon.

After nervously walking the streets for an hour or so, unable to concentrate on her shopping, she had decided to go back to the office. She needed to find out if Liddell had discovered his conversation with Fleming was not as private as he had intended. She had let herself back into the office and instantly saw that the mobile phone lying on her desk was still switched on and the line was still connected through to the Chief Superintendent's office. Her heart began to quicken. Maybe he hadn't come out of his office yet. Maybe he had actually put in the calls to the ports and airports as he was supposed to. Maybe Jack had been wrong about him. Maybe. Maybe. Maybe.

Penny edged over towards the internal door that separated her from the

CHAPTER TWENTY-TWO

Chief Superintendent's office. She placed an ear up against the smooth wood, held her breath and listened. But no matter how hard she tried, she couldn't hear a sound. Nothing at all. No voices. No movements. No nothing. Nervously biting her lip, she held her head even closer to the door and listened again.

Still there was nothing.

She glanced over her shoulder and noticed that the Chief Superintendent's overcoat was still hanging up on the coat stand. He was still in his office. Somewhat relived, Penny gently knocked at the door – the sound of her tapping barely audible over her breathing. There was still no sound or movement from within, so she knocked again – louder and more confident this time.

Still there was nothing.

Gripping the cold metal handle tightly in her hand, Penny pushed the door open – and only just managed to stifle the heart rending scream that welled up in her throat.

Penny shook her head to rid herself of the gruesome image that now floated through her mind. She fixed her eyes steadily onto the carpet in front of her feet. Jack looked up as he saw the door open, noticing that Penny was avoiding looking anywhere near Liddell's desk – where she had been the first one to discover his lifeless body slumped over in a pool of his own congealed blood.

"The Area Commander is here, Sir. They're all waiting for you upstairs," she said, her voice small and shaky.

Jack nodded and walked back around from behind the desk. He followed Penny back out into the outer office, closing the door behind him.

"Thank you," he said, lightly touching her arm. "Thank you for what you did. It can't have been easy."

Penny turned towards him and frowned slightly, her pale drawn face looking far older than its years. "For what I did? I...I don't quite understand........"

"For the telephone call," explained Jack. "When I phoned you from Paris, telling you what I suspected about the Superintendent, I didn't ....well, I didn't know if you would believe me. I didn't know if you would listen to me, or help me. So, thank you for trusting me."

Penny's frail shoulders gave a small shrug. "I…I wasn't sure at first. I thought….I hoped that you were wrong. "She cleared her throat gently. "But I guess that you must have been right after all……I just didn't think it was possible……." Her voice tailed off as the vision of Liddell's blood-soaked body filled her mind again.

Jack stepped forward and squeezed her arm once again.

"Anything is possible, Penny. Anything at all."

*　*　*

Time: 2.00pm
Date: 10th November 2008
Location: Charles Tindleman's office, MI6 HQ, London

The doorway was barred with "Police – Do Not Cross" tape.

"They haven't done a formal forensic sweep yet," said DS Cooper, snipping the tape with a small pair of scissors. "Other than removing the body, they've left the place exactly as it was. I told them that you would want to be the first to have a look around."

"Good man." Jack ducked under the flaps of tape and stepped into the inner sanctum that was the personal office of the head of MI6. "I can see I'm training you up well."

"Aren't you supposed to be somewhere right now?" DS Cooper followed Jack into Charles Tindleman's office. "I thought the Area Commander was in town and had asked to see you?"

Jack grimaced and waved the comment away. "He can wait. I've got far more important things to be doing."

"What was the Chief Super's office like?" asked DS Cooper, standing at Jack's side as the two officers glanced around the room.

"Pretty much the same as this," replied Jack, letting his eyes take in the scene before him. "Nothing out of place. Everything as it should be. Except

CHAPTER TWENTY-TWO

for Liddell lying in a pool of his own blood with half his head missing of course."

DS Cooper's eyes widened in surprise. "He wasn't......?"

Jack smiled and shook his head. "No, no, he wasn't still there. I feel sorry for his PA though, Penny. She was the one who found him. Walked right in on him. It's really shaken her up, poor woman."

"You think they're all connected? The Chief Super, Tindleman, the others?"

Jack raised his eyebrows. "Can't think for a moment why they should be.... but then again, how many people do you know kill themselves with cyanide pills these days? It's not your most obvious form of suicide aide. It's all very.... very...."

"Soviet," concluded DS Cooper, breaking away from Jack's side and heading towards Tindleman's large, glass fronted bureau behind his desk. "That was what they used to do wasn't it? Soviet spies? Carried cyanide pills around with them and swallowed them before they could be interrogated and made to disclose any Russian secrets."

Jack gave a small laugh. "And both Liddell and Tindleman were well-known, high-ranking Soviet spies."

DS Cooper just shrugged and glanced back at Jack over his shoulder. "I'm just saying.... that's what they used to do."

"Mmmmm." Jack walked over to Charles Tindleman's desk in the centre of the room, stopping in front of it. "Except Liddell made doubly sure by putting a bullet through his brain."

"Why would he do that?" DS Cooper left the bureau and made his way over to join Jack at the desk. "I mean, take the pill – if indeed he did take one – and then shoot himself as well?"

"Maybe he didn't like the idea of death by cyanide poisoning. Maybe he didn't think it would be quick enough. If push came to shove, I know which method I would be choosing."

"So, what was Tindleman doing with one?" DS Cooper frowned, and watched Jack reach into his pocket. "I mean, I heard on the grapevine that he probably took his pretty much the same time as Liddell took his – and those in Moscow too. And the one in the States. All within minutes of each other, that's what's being said. The press are gonna have a field day with this one when it gets out."

Jack brought out two pairs of latex rubber gloves from his pocket and threw a pair at DS Cooper. "Got to make sure we are good little girls and boys whilst we're in here, Cooper. Don't touch anything without these on." Jack snapped on his gloves and immediately cast his eye over the desk, in much the same way as he had done in Liddell's office only minutes before. Again, nothing seemed out of place.

There were the usual desk-top items – a few pots of pens and pencils, a desk diary, a calendar, two notepads, a telephone console and the computer monitor and keyboard. Nothing had yet been taken away for examination. The pathologist had been to wrap up the chair in protective polythene to preserve whatever forensic material that may be left on it – after Charles Tindleman was lifted out of his seat and placed into a body bag.

But Jack wasn't interested in the chair.

Slowly, he sniffed the air. The room didn't smell as stale or musty as Liddell's had. But it still had its own unique, unmistakeable aroma. Jack knelt down next to the desk and pulled out the wastepaper bin which was tucked neatly underneath. Inside were the charred remains of what looked like paper – lots and lots of paper. Most had been turned into blackened strips of charcoal, curled up at the ends, nestling in amongst a bed of powder and ash.

Most of it, but not all of it.

Jack tipped the bin on its side and took a closer look, shaking the contents gently to reveal several glimpses of white. His nostrils filled with the sweet, acrid aroma of burnt paper. Careful not to disturb the paper too much, Jack brought out a small pocket knife – a seemingly useless Christmas present not so long ago, but which was now proving very useful indeed – and selected a tiny pair of tweezers. He used them to push away the burnt, blackened contents and reveal more of the white beneath. Taking a fresh polythene evidence bag from his pocket, he gently used the tweezers to pick up a tiny fragment of unscorched paper. Jack glanced at it momentarily

CHAPTER TWENTY-TWO

before placing it inside the bag. He then extracted several other pieces of half-burnt, half-charred paper, and placed them inside their own bags for later examination.

Whatever Charles Tindleman had been doing in the moments leading up to his death, he had wanted this evidence destroyed. Jack motioned to DS Cooper that their search was done. Perhaps he had thought shredding was too risky, and opted for fire – fire being the ultimate destroyer.

But the fire had been incomplete

The fire had left something behind.

* * *

Time: 3.00pm
Date: 10th November 2008
Location: Vauxhall Bridge, London

Fleming stood his collar up high around his neck, and pulled his wide-brimmed hat down firmly over his brow. The chill wind was whipping up along the Thames and ruffling the flaps of his raincoat. He tightened the belt a little – but not so tight that the pistol strapped to his side would be seen.

He turned his face away from the bitter wind and looked out across the slate grey water. It swirled beneath him, dark and murky, most uninviting. How many secrets lay buried at the bottom of its depths, he thought to himself. Undisturbed. Undetected.

Vauxhall Bridge was quiet. The cold wind and blustery showers successfully deterring most people from venturing out on foot – opting instead for cars, buses and taxis. The traffic crept painfully slowly along the tarmac behind him, nose to tail, bumper to bumper, the chill air clogged with heavy petrol fumes.

Fleming looked paler than usual. And thinner. His cold grey eyes were tinged with tiredness. He hadn't managed much sleep since returning from France – there had been too much to do.

He leant forwards and rested against the cold, damp concrete of the bridge. His body ached. His bones creaked. His brain thumped beneath his skull. He felt as though his whole body was beginning to shut down. He brought out a folded newspaper from beneath his arm. The front page was awash with pictures of the austere faces of Chief Superintendent Liddell and Charles Tindleman, followed by in depth reports of how their bodies had been found and the police investigations that were now underway into why they had chosen to take their own lives in such dramatic circumstances.

Deeper inside the newspaper there were pictures of Dimitri Federov, Sergei Ivanov and Austin Edwards – more unexplained suicides, more police investigations, more speculation. Scotland Yard was already working closely with the FBI and CIA, according to the reporter.

Speculation was rife on the links between all five suicides. Money laundering, drug smuggling, sado-masochistic rituals and paedophile rings, to name but a few. The list was ever growing. Fleming afforded himself a small smile.

Speculation. Speculation. Speculation

No one was even close.

Towards the bottom of page 3 was a grainy black and white picture of Fleming himself, taken Fleming guessed from the CCTV cameras at the police station in Paris. The picture wasn't great. Fleming wasn't even looking at the camera. It was just a smudgy outline of a man, his features blurred, his identity unknown. It could have been anyone.

The reporter asked for anyone with any information as to the whereabouts of this man to call Scotland Yard direct, or Crimestoppers anonymously. A list of contact telephone numbers followed. Fleming managed another smile. Information on his whereabouts was unlikely as he had covered his tracks well. They would never catch him. Not now.

He re-folded the newspaper and tucked it back underneath his arm. He then reached into his breast pocket and drew out a small glass phial. Popping off the lid, he tipped the small capsule into the palm of his hand. He stared, unblinkingly, at it for some time, oblivious to the traffic around

CHAPTER TWENTY-TWO

him.

What had gone through the minds of the others, he wondered, when they were in this very position. What thoughts had run through them as they contemplated the unthinkable, yet considered the inevitable? Had any of them whispered a silent prayer of forgiveness? Had any of them prayed for salvation? Had any of them considered not going through with it at all?

Fleming continued to stare at the tiny capsule, gently picking it up between his thumb and forefinger. Here he was now, the last man standing. After all this time, he was the last link in the chain. Now it was his turn to face his demons. Now it was his time.

They had failed; they had all failed.

The papers. Still missing.

The girl. Still alive.

Everything was still out there.

But the money. Fleming cast a brief glimpse down at the briefcase by his feet. At least he had the money.

As if in slow motion, Fleming raised the capsule to his lips. The noise from the traffic behind him sounded distant and far away. He took no notice of the honking of horns, the revving of engines, the gentle click-click of windscreen wipers. The rain was coming down faster now, splattering against his raincoat and beginning to run down his face.

He closed his eyes and smiled.

He was ready.

* * *

Time: 3.00pm
Date: 10th November 2008
Location: Vauxhall Bridge, London

DS Cooper sighed and pulled on his handbrake yet again. The traffic was getting worse as the day wore on. The thick grey clouds overhead were now squeezing out large fat raindrops which were now thudding heavily against his windscreen, aided by the stiffening breeze. Few people were bracing themselves against the elements today – most were tucked up in cosy taxis or cars, sitting and waiting for the slow line of traffic to wind its way across Vauxhall Bridge.

Cooper had left Charles Tindleman's office along with Jack after they had done a quick sweep, not really knowing what they were looking for. Jack had wanted to head back to the station on foot. The Area Commander was waiting for him, and no doubt there would be a grilling in the offing, so Jack being Jack had decided to take the longest route possible back to the station. Cooper afforded himself a quick smile.

While sitting in the snail like procession of traffic, Cooper saw a brief movement out of the corner of his eye and turned his head towards the window. Through the stream of raindrops trickling down the side of the glass, he could just make out the figure of a man standing on the pavement in the middle of the bridge. He seemed to be hunched up against the wind, staring out across the Thames.

DS Cooper continued to watch him. Today did not look like the day for taking a pleasant stroll across the water. He watched and wondered if the man was a thinker, or a jumper. There were sometimes cases of people jumping over the side of the bridge, plummeting into the cold, murky depths below. Searching for some form of salvation, or maybe just a way out. DS Cooper hoped today was not one of those days.

He continued to watch the man, his car engine ticking over silently as the traffic lights on the bridge ahead changed to red. The man had one hand inside his raincoat pocket, but the other held up to his lips. He seemed to be holding something in his fingers, but DS Cooper was too far away to see what it could be. Whatever it was, it was something very small.

The man had his eyes closed. Maybe he was thinking. Maybe he was praying. His hand hovered in front of his lips, his mouth opening slowly. DS Cooper continued to watch as right before him, in one continuous swift movement, the man brought his right hand back over his head and quickly threw whatever he had been holding out into the choppy grey

CHAPTER TWENTY-TWO

waters of the Thames.

* * *

CHAPTER TWENTY-THREE

Time: 4.00pm
  Date: 10th November 2008
  Location: Metropolitan Police HQ, London

Jack leant back in his chair and surveyed the scene. He had commandeered a briefing room on the top floor and turned it into a makeshift investigation room. No one seemed to mind. In fact, he doubted whether anyone really knew. No one was paying him very much attention anymore, as all hell was breaking loose downstairs. The Area Commander was prowling the corridors, barking questions and demanding answers that people just didn't have. The press were constantly beating down the doors outside, wanting to know whether the country was at risk from a terrorist threat, wanting to know if the suicides were linked to something more sinister. Something that would help them sell more newspapers. Wanting to know. Wanting to know.

Jack was happy to let them argue the point downstairs, away from him. He needed time to think and more than anything he needed peace and quiet. And he was happy that he was being left alone to do just that. The powers that be seemed to have forgotten about him, and that was just the way he liked it.

Thankfully, the room was empty and he manoeuvred several tables into one long line down the centre. He then distributed the various evidence bags from both scenes of crime across the tables – Liddell's office and Charles Tindleman's - and then placed photographs of Isabel, Mac and

CHAPTER TWENTY-THREE

Andre in amongst them, together with the other suicide victims.

All he had to do now, was work out what linked them. For he was sure there was a link – somewhere. In the very centre of the tables he placed the grainy black and white photograph of Fleming. Jack was certain he was the main man, the key to everything.

Just then, DS Cooper walked into the room and shut the door behind him. He raised his eyes questioningly at Jack.

"How's it going? Any breakthroughs yet?"

Jack gave a tired smile. "Not yet, but I'm working on it."

"I just walked in. Traffic on the bridge was a nightmare. People are asking what you're up to downstairs. And where you are."

"I bet they are."

"And the Custody Sergeant downstairs says that Andre chap wants to talk to you. Just you. On your own."

Jack looked up, sharply. "He's decided to talk?"

DS Cooper shrugged. "Not sure. I think the Custody Sergeant is under pressure to release him – what with everything else that's been going on lately. And he's not under arrest yet."

"Over my dead body." Jack jumped to his feet. "He's not going anywhere."

* * *

Time: 4.05pm
Date: 10th November 2008
Location: Interview rooms, Metropolitan Police HQ, London

Andre had been mute ever since he had slipped into the police car in Paris. Refusing to answer questions, refusing to confirm or deny any details. He had been checked over by the police doctor before leaving France, and later again by a psychiatrist courtesy of the Metropolitan Police. He had been passed fit and well by both.

Jack eased himself into a chair behind the small wooden table in the centre of the interview room. It creaked underneath his weight.

"So, Andre," began Jack. Keeping his voice light. "It is all right if I call you Andre, isn't it?" He paused, waiting for a response which never came. Jack shrugged to himself and carried on. "Someone tells me you have something to say."

Andre lifted his head and gave a brief nod. His eyes flashed over to the tape recorder sitting on top of the table. Jack noticed the glance and immediately held up his hands.

"No tapes, Andre. This is just between you, and me. OK? Whatever you tell me in here goes no further. No tapes. No records. No nothing." Jack paused. He knew this was not strictly true, but figured Andre would swallow it. "You're here as a witness, Andre. Nothing more than that. This was explained to you when we left Paris. All I want you to do is tell me what you know – about Isabel. About anything. And help me to find Fleming."

Andre slowly nodded his head and lowered his gaze to his lap. There was a long silence which echoed around the walls of the small interview room. Jack could hear the clock softly ticking on the wall in the background. There were muffled voices from outside in the corridor, the occasional sound of a door slamming, but other than that there was nothing. Just silence.

After what seemed like an eternity, Andre looked up and caught Jack's gaze. "It wasn't their fault, you know."

"Whose fault?" replied Jack, returning the steely gaze but keeping his voice light.

"Isabel's. Mac's. They had no idea what they were involved in."

"Involved in?"

Andre paused. "What I am about to tell you, Detective Inspector, has already led to the deaths of too many people. It has to stop. It must stop. Now."

* * *

Time: 4.30pm

CHAPTER TWENTY-THREE

Date: 10th November 2008
Location: Investigation Room, Metropolitan Police HQ, London

DS Cooper snapped on the overhead lights. The room was instantly bathed in harsh, fluorescent lighting which made him squint. The day had already turned to a murky, foggy dullness outside, so Cooper shifted away from the window. Rain was now falling in heavy curtains, washing away the sludge and slush that had been lining the roads, cleansing the streets of the dirty brown mush that always seemed to follow snowfall in London.

Sitting at the investigation table, DS Cooper eyed the bags of evidence Jack had lined up in the centre. Bag after bag, clearly labelled, clearly identified. Methodical. That was DI Jack MacIntosh. He picked up a photograph of Isabel and drummed it against the side of the table. Who was she? DS Cooper shared Jack's unquiet suspicions that all was not as it seemed with the seemingly ordinary Isabel Faraday.

Just then, Cooper's eyes fell on the latest edition of the Evening Standard that Jack had been reading earlier, noticing the half-drunk mug of cold coffee sat by its side. Cooper reached over and straightened out the front page. His eyes scanned the leading story – the leading story that was on all the local and national newspapers up and down the country. There seemingly was no other news worthy of reporting on this cold and dismal day in November.

"The Famous Five". The press went at the story like a ravaging wild cat, scavenging food in an inhospitable terrain. The Met's Press Office was saying very little, muttering about a formal press conference in due course, but the FBI seemed to have no concerns in making their voice heard. "Coordinated efforts are being made to get to the bottom of the apparent suicides spanning the USA, the UK and Russia", and "working tirelessly to confirm the identity of the rogue FBI Agent John Fleming…." were quotes from a "reliable US Government official."

DS Cooper scanned the rest of the front page, his eyes finally resting on a small grainy photograph of Special Agent Fleming nestling in the bottom left hand corner. It looked like a shot taken from the CCTV footage from the Paris police station yesterday, not the best in quality but the features of the supposed FBI Agent could be clearly seen. Even the paleness of his skin seemed to be enhanced by the poor quality reproductive film.

Cooper's eyes searched Fleming's face – he could make out the narrow eyes, the smooth almost translucent skin, the dark hair peppered with flecks of salt-like spray. A row of perfectly straight white teeth appeared through his taut smile. Those lips. That smile. The narrow face and protruding nose.

Cooper frowned. He had seen that face before. And recently. He glanced up at the window, hearing and watching the fat rain drops slamming against the windowpanes in a never-ending rhythm.

The rain.

The bridge.

The man on the bridge.

Cooper raced from the room and headed for the stairs.

Fleming was here.

Fleming was in London.

* * *

Time: 4.30pm

Date: 10th November 2008

Location: Interview rooms, Metropolitan Police HQ, London

Jack stared long and hard at the table in front of him. Again, the soft tick ticking of the wall clock was the only sound in the room. "That's quite some story, Andre," he said, eventually. "Quite some story indeed."

Andre shrugged. "I said I'd tell you the truth. I didn't say you would believe me."

"I'm not saying I don't believe you...." Jack paused, feeling as though that was exactly what he *was* saying. "It's just quite a lot to take in…"

"You're a clever man, Detective Inspector," replied Andre, holding Jack's gaze without blinking. "I'm sure you can manage."

CHAPTER TWENTY-THREE

"This.... this organisation of yours? It was called the Phoenix Project?"

"It wasn't mine – it was Kreshniov's baby."

"And you're sure about the dates?"

"Positive." Andre paused, and inched forwards in his chair, closer to Jack. "Poborski and Kreshniov controlled everything. The Phoenix Project belonged to them. When it all went wrong, they both wanted to take their revenge on the others who were left – especially Poborski. He was hung out to dry after the experiment went wrong. He was the fall guy, the one who was going to take the blame, be made to suffer if and when it all went up in smoke. The payment he was supposed to receive after the experiment? That was never paid. The other members of the Project closed ranks and reneged on the deal. He got nothing. He'd been the go-between, securing the steady stream of investment funds from the Russians. Without him and the Russian money, the Phoenix Project would never have got off the ground. They knew that, and so did he. Poborski felt like he deserved something. He felt he was owed."

"So, this Poborski. He wanted what? Publicity? Revenge? What?"

"Money," laughed Andre, smiling at Jack's bemused expression." Poborski wanted Isabel's money."

"*Isabel's* money?" Jack's frown deepened. "Why Isabel's money?"

"Because when the money wasn't paid to him after the experiment, the Project members paid it to the Faradays instead. Every last penny."

"Why on earth would they do that?"

Andre smiled again and tapped the side of his head with his forefinger. "Think, Detective Inspector. "Think."

Jack frowned even further. He didn't like the game Andre appeared to be playing. "I'm not here to be messed around, Andre. If you've got something to tell me, spit it out. Otherwise, I've got better things to be doing with my time."

"You really don't have a clue, do you?" Andre's smile danced playfully on his lips. He was enjoying being in control. "You really have no idea?"

Feeling more than a little exasperated, Jack rose out of his chair, letting the wooden legs scrape noisily across the concrete floor. "So tell me. What the hell is it that I don't understand? But you'd better be quick, because I'm out of here." Jack turned and made for the door.

"Your friend - Fleming? You ever find out who he really was?" Andre's raised his voice a notch, and saw Jack's body hesitate before reaching the door. "Once you found out he wasn't, and never had been, FBI?"

Jack half-turned, glancing back over his shoulder towards the still seated Andre. "No. He could have been anybody."

"Indeed," replied Andre, another smile dancing over his lips. "But John Fleming wasn't just anybody. John Fleming is, and always has been, Karl Poborski."

The interview room door crashed open and DS Cooper burst in, his breathing rapid and his eyes wild. "Guv, its Fleming."

Jack looked up sharply, snapping his eyes back and forth from DS Cooper to Andre. "We were just talking about him."

"He's here," continued DS Cooper, throwing a copy of the Evening Standard down onto the interview room table and stabbing a finger at Fleming's grainy image. "He was on Vauxhall Bridge when I drove back. I'm sure of it."

* * *

Time: 7.00pm
    Date: 10th November 2008
    Location: Aeroflot Check-in desk, Heathrow Airport

Karl Poborski walked quickly through the airport concourse, pulling his cap down firmly over his head, the peak shielding his eyes. He arrived at the Aeroflot check-in desk – there was no queue.

He placed his ticket and passport on the counter, and one small suitcase onto the conveyor belt.

"Good evening," greeted the Aeroflot check-in girl, her hair scraped back neatly off her heavily made up face. "The 21.45 service to Moscow?"

Poborski gave a curt nod of the head. "Yes" he replied, in perfect Russian.

CHAPTER TWENTY-THREE

He noted the girl's name on her pin badge was "Natalie."

Natalie smiled and glanced down at his open passport. "Mr Chevchenko, your flight will be boarding in approximately 45 minutes. Please proceed to gate 12 immediately. Did you pack your suitcase yourself, sir?"

Poborski again nodded curtly, and managed a tight-lipped smile. He scooped up his passport from the counter and slipped it back inside his jacket pocket.

"You have one item of hand luggage?" Natalie nodded at the briefcase sitting at Poborski's feet. "Did you pack that yourself, Sir?"

Poborski also glanced down at the metallic silver briefcase resting by his side. He afforded himself another small smile; but a smile that didn't quite reach his cool eyes. "Yes, I did."

Natalie completed her security questions and then handed Poborski his boarding card. "Please proceed directly to passport control and then to gate 12. Have a nice flight. Mr Chevchenko."

Poborski took the boarding card, picked up the briefcase, and then abruptly turned away from the desk heading towards security and passport control. There was a small queue of people waiting patiently in line, and Poborski slipped in unnoticed at the rear. He gripped the silver briefcase tightly in his hand.

As he waited he glanced around the airport concourse. There were several armed police officers strolling through the thinning evening crowds. Poborski watched them but they didn't appear to be looking for anyone in particular. He noticed the positioning of the CCTV and security cameras; one was directly above his head, monitoring the progress of the passport control queue. Several others faced the check-in desk he had just vacated. Poborski looked up, directly into the face of the camera above him. He watched the red light blinking; but he felt safe. He felt secure. Nobody was looking for him, not Karl Poborski. Not even Ivan Chevchenko. They would all be looking for John Fleming.

But John Fleming no longer existed.

John Fleming had never existed.

The queue moved steadily forwards until it was Poborski's turn to pass through the security personnel. He handed his passport over to the passport control officer, and waited. The officer took the passport in his outstretched hand and immediately flipped to the back page. Turning the passport on its side to look at the photograph, the officer then looked up and caught Poborski's eye.

"Please remove your hat, Sir," the officer said, nodding at Poborski's cap which was still pulled firmly down on top of his head.

Poborski reached up and slowly withdrew the hat. His hair was now an even shade of light brown, his eyes a dark chocolate. Amazing what can be done with a small tube of hair dye and tinted contact lenses. Fleming was no more; Poborski had been reborn. Or maybe Chevchenko. For now.

The passport control officer looked back down at the passport in his hand, and, after what seemed like an eternity, gave a quick nod of the head and waved Poborski through.

Poborski gratefully took back his passport and headed for the baggage screening queue. His heart was beginning to thump a little harder inside his chest. He had passed the first two hurdles, now for the final one. He placed the silver briefcase onto the conveyor belt and emptied his pocket of change and mobile phone into one of the plastic trays. With one last lingering look at the briefcase, Poborski walked through the electric scanner.

The scanner remained silent and no one approached him. Poborski walked to the end of the conveyor belt and waited, carefully controlling his breathing so as not to draw any unnecessary attention to himself. Tiny beads of sweat began to form on his top lip as he watched the conveyor belt slowly chug into action.

Poborski watched the baggage screening officer's every move. He was a middle aged man, with a bushy brown beard that Poborski thought he could see remnants of a hurried cheese sandwich nestled in amongst the wiry curls. The buttons of the man's regulation blue uniform shirt were straining across his more than ample frame as he sat perched on an uncomfortable-looking high stool. His stomach flopped over his belt, resting on his thighs like a child's rubber ring. Reaching to the side, he

CHAPTER TWENTY-THREE

tapped the keys on a keyboard with short, stubby fingers, as he watched Poborski's briefcase advancing through the scanner on a small square black and white TV monitor.

Poborski nervously shifted from one foot to the other while several more beads of sweat formed on his brow. He slowly glanced over his shoulder to scan the available exit routes behind him. Just in case. Things were taking too long. The briefcase had been inside the x-ray scanner for longer than Poborski thought necessary – something must be wrong.

Looking over his shoulder once again, Poborski looked about for the best escape route in case he needed to run. There was a fire escape next to the disabled toilets behind him…..he could make a run for that…..if he had to……and maybe lose them on the stairs.

Poborski's mind was beginning to whirr, while his heart was beating so fast that he was sure someone must be able to hear it. Suddenly there was a loud clunk which made him visibly jump. Whipping his head back round to face the conveyor belt, he saw the silver briefcase had arrived at the end and was sitting directly in front of him. The baggage screening officer was busy wiping his glasses with a piece of tissue, before pushing them back onto his pink, chubby face. He didn't even acknowledge Poborski let alone his briefcase.

With a deep breath, Poborski retrieved the briefcase together with his mobile phone and loose change. Without looking back, he strode out across the departure lounge and headed for gate 12.

***

CHAPTER TWENTY-FOUR

Time: 7.00pm
 Date: 10th November 2008
 Location: interview rooms, Metropolitan Police HQ, London

"So, what was he after?" Jack watched as Andre methodically tore off small sections of the polystyrene cup that he held in his hands. "Fleming. Poborski. Whatever or whoever he is."

"I already told you," replied Andre. "Money. He was always just after the money."

"And to destroy the documents," added Jack. "The Phoenix Project data. He raced halfway around the world chasing after those papers. And he killed for them, according to you."

Andre managed a smile, but shook his head. "Poborski never wanted the papers, Inspector. Yes, he killed people along the way, but it was never about the documents for him."

"Hang on, but you told us Shafer and Stuart…..Mac….arranged to intercept the papers; a move masterminded by you, I hasten to add. The Phoenix Project papers were on their way to him, to Poborski – over at M16. He was posing as Fleming. Then he ended up chasing them halfway across France. Of course he wanted the papers!"

"He wasn't chasing the papers, Inspector."

Jack frowned and leant back in his chair. "But he must have been. As soon as they went missing he gave chase. He……" Jack stopped mid-sentence, realisation slowly dawning like a warm summer sunrise. "He was chasing

CHAPTER TWENTY-FOUR

the girl, wasn't he? It was Isabel he wanted."

Andre gave a smile and nodded. "The penny drops, Inspector. Congratulations. He needed her; he needed Isabel to get to her money. And he needed her in Paris, for that was where the bank was. So I arranged Mac to bring her and the papers to me." Andre gave a quiet sigh and avoided Jack's eyes. "It was all part of the plan."

"The plan?" Jack tried to get into Andre's line of vision, but Andre refused to look up. "You knew Poborski….or should I say Fleming……you knew he was following them?"

Andre shook his head. "He didn't need to follow them. He already knew where they would be; that they would be coming to me. It was all arranged, but…"

"But you had to make it look like they were being followed, or being chased," cut in Jack. "Isabel had to think someone was after her, or more importantly after the papers."

Andre conceded with a curt nod.

"And you double crossed them. Isabel and Stuart?" Jack waited for a response, but none came. He pressed on. "They trusted you. They thought you were on their side, they thought you were actually helping them. But all the time….. you were working with Poborski to get to the money,."

"No!" Andre raised his head with a jerk, his eyes flashing angrily at Jack. "It wasn't about the money – not for me. Yes, I wanted revenge, but I wasn't interested in the money. Poborski was welcome to that. I just wanted the Project to collapse – for there to be none of them left."

"Looks like you succeeded." Jack brought out a copy of the London Evening Standard. The front page was covered in photographs of the "cyanide five" as they were being dubbed. "Ivanov, Federov. Edwards. They were all members of the Phoenix Project?"

Andre nodded.

"And this…this pact?" Jack turned the paper towards Andre. "This was all part of the plan too?"

Andre nodded once more. "Edwards was a NASA scientist. And was Kreshniov's link to NASA and the US Government. Both Ivanov and

Federov were involved in securing the funding to finance the Project in Russia. There was an agreement between them all. All members of the Project had to take the oath – if the truth about the Project was going to be made public, the real truth about the accident, then everyone had a cyanide capsule which they would take the minute they got the call. The minute they got the order." Andre paused, looking again at each of the five photographs in turn. "If the call came through you were expected to end it. Immediately. No questions. No exceptions. Poborski must have made the call. "

"And he got to walk away with all the cash, no questions asked. And no one from the Project alive to stop him."

Andre nodded again.

"Except you." Jack tilted his head to one side and fixed his eyes on Andre. "You were a member of the Phoenix Project, weren't you? How come you never got the call? Didn't you take the same oath as the rest of them?"

Andre tore his eyes away from the newspaper and met Jack's inquisitive gaze. "That was never part of the plan."

"Oh yes, I forgot, "replied Jack, not covering up the hint of sarcasm that skipped into his voice. "The plan. You and Poborski were in this together, and were going to ride off into the sunset with a shed load of money weren't you? Isabel's money."

Andre opened his mouth to reply, but Jack held up his hand and cut in.

"Except your so-called plan hasn't gone all that smoothly, has it? Poborski seems to have disappeared with all the cash leaving you here to answer all the questions."

"I was never interested in the money" replied Andre, flatly. "I told you that."

Jack closed his eyes and exhaled loudly. "So what about Shafer? What was his role in all of this?"

Andre shifted in his seat and shook his head, his gaze falling into his lap. "Nothing. He wasn't involved. He was just.."

"Used?" Jack tapped his biro on the edge of the table. Andre was beginning to test his patience.

CHAPTER TWENTY-FOUR

"In the wrong place at the wrong time," finished Andre, hotly.

"I'll say," retorted Jack, letting a sarcastic laugh escape his lips. "He was a good man, by all accounts."

Andre looked up sharply. "I didn't know he was going to be killed. If I had known what Poborski was capable of I would never...."

"You involved an innocent man in your...whatever it is you want to call it. An innocent man who ended up dead. You can't distance yourself from that Andre. Simon Shafer, a British intelligence officer, ended up dead because of what you did."

Andre didn't reply. He simple stared at the stone floor.

"And what about Kreshniov?" Jack carried on. "You know where we can find him?"

"Kreshniov?" Andre slowly raised his eyes from the ground to meet Jack's. "You'll never find him. Not until he wants to be found." Andre held Jack's gaze for a moment longer before glancing down at the pad of paper in the middle of the table. "You haven't written much down, Inspector."

"You haven't given me much to go on," replied Jack, curtly. He threw the pen down onto the blank pieces of paper. "What exactly do you expect me to write?"

Andre gave a shrug and rested back into his chair, the aged wood creaking beneath his weight. Jack sighed and then shook his head; he was tired of this.

"When you think of something useful to tell me, like where Poborski or Kreshniov might be, then let the officers outside in the corridor know." Jack rose to his feet and headed towards the door. "Until then, I've got better things to be doing with my time."

* * *

Time: 8.00pm
    Date: 10th November 2008
    Location: Metropolitan Police HQ, London

To quote DS Cooper, the press were, indeed, having a field day.

The daily newspapers, from the tabloids right across to the broadsheets, reported on nothing else. Page after page of speculation. The "famous five" as they had now been quickly dubbed, had their faces splashed in amongst the newsprint repeatedly from cover to cover. No other story seemed to get a look in. Investigative journalists were queuing up to delve into the backgrounds of each and every one of them – trying in vain to come up with a common thread, a common denominator, to link all five together and thereby try to explain why they all met their end in the same unconventional way at almost exactly the same time.

But try as they might, each and every one failed. There were no conceivable links; nothing to join the unfortunate victims together.

So speculation was the order of the day. Without cold hard facts, the press resorted to luke warm supposition dressed up as being potential explanations. And there was plenty of that to go around. High up on the list was an international terrorist cell – each member of the "famous five" intent on bringing the civilised world as it was known crashing to its knees in one single catastrophic terrorist attack. Some of the more adventurous tabloids even went on to suggest that M15 and M16 had infiltrated the cell and the apparent suicides were nothing more than authorised executions.

Of course the security services declined to comment one way or the other, which further fuelled the fire over their potential involvement. The Prime Minster himself felt forced to hold various ad hoc press conferences to reassure the public that there was no cause for concern, but he declined to comment on anything specific.

Jack leant forwards with his elbows on his desk, and buried his head in his hands. His desk looked like a bomb had hit it, and he had no idea when he last slept. He didn't even know exactly what day it was.

This case was getting to him.

Andre was getting to him.

Just then there was a knock at the office door, and a PC's head appeared around the corner.

"Message for you, Sir." The young PC strode over to Jack's paper-strewn

CHAPTER TWENTY-FOUR

desk and handed him a note. "Downstairs couldn't get through to your office line."

Jack nodded and took the proffered piece of paper. His gaze shifted back to his desk, noticing that the telephone was buried underneath several files and a faint beeping noise was emanating from it indicating that the receiver was off the hook. "Thanks."

The young PC nodded, turned and left the room. Jack flipped open the folded piece of paper, and read the message. "Please call Pierre Macron, Manager of La Premiere Banque National – urgent. 00331-5543221."

* * *

Time: 8.00pm
Date: 10th November 2008
Location: Heathrow Airport, London

Poborski glanced up again at the flight notice board – the 21.45 service to Moscow was being delayed by 45 minutes because of a technical problem. He nervously crossed and then uncrossed his legs, shifting uncomfortably in his seat. The departure lounge was quite empty, not many people waiting for the last service to Moscow on a cold winter's night. Departures came and went for destinations such as New York, Tel Aviv, Montreal, New Delhi. But Poborski had to wait.

He wanted to be on the plane and out of here. He did not like waiting. He felt like he was being watched. The longer he sat here the more opportunity there was that things could go wrong. His plan had run like clockwork so far, no hitches. No trouble getting to the airport, no problems checking in or getting through passport control. The briefcase had even managed to get through the scanner without alerting suspicion. Things were going as smoothly as he could have hoped – except for the delayed departure.

He glanced nervously around him once again. Even less people around now. He decided to move to a nearby coffee bar, noticing that there was a small, enclosed booth at the very back, almost hidden from view. It would be quiet and dark in there. He would wait there until his flight boarded.

**

Time: 8.05pm
    Date: 10th November 2008
    Location: Interview rooms, Metropolitan Police HQ, London

Jack stepped back into the interview room. Andre had been taken for a cigarette break and some fresh air by one of the junior officers, so the room was empty. Walking over to the interview table, he pulled his suit jacket from the back of the chair and slipped it on. In his haste to leave before, he had left it behind.

Turning to go, Jack's eyes fell on the table top. On the other side of the table, where Andre had been sitting, Jack saw his notepad. Tipping his head to the side, Jack could see various scribblings and doodles on the top sheet – nothing that seemed to make much sense or was seemingly of any interest. What made Jack look underneath the top sheet he would never know. But something made him do it.

In the centre of the page beneath was a small question mark. Next to the question mark Andre had written in simple neat handwriting:

"We learn from failure, not from success."

Frowning, Jack swept the notepad up and slipped it into his pocket. He still had the telephone message from the Manager of the Premiere Banque National in his hand, and wondered what was so urgent.

Jack left the interview room in search of a phone.

**

Time: 9.00pm
    Date: 10th November 2008
    Location: Heathrow Airport, London

CHAPTER TWENTY-FOUR

Poborski pushed his coffee cup to the other side of the table and massaged his temples. Only another ten minutes to go. The tannoy had announced that flight 401 would be ready for boarding in ten minutes, the technical problems having been finally resolved and not taking as long as anticipated. Only another ten minutes until he could breathe again. He wanted to be sat on that plane, only then would he feel safe.

Poborski reached down under the table and pulled the silver briefcase up onto his knees. His eyes started to gleam, greedily. Gently he ran his hand over the top, caressing it as if it were an object of desire. His thin lips broke out into a strained smile; not long now.

Quickly looking up to check he was still alone and not being watched, Poborski snapped open the briefcase locks. He would just have a quick look, just a little. Nothing much, just a little peek at what he had worked so hard for. What he had waited so long for, what had brought him so far.

Slowly, he raised the lid of the briefcase and held it open. Even in the relative darkness of the coffee booth he could see the faint gleam of fresh currency. The case was stacked full from side to side, the top layer almost at the brim. Poborski breathed in deeply through his nose, letting the familiar aroma of cash fill his nostrils.

* * *

Time: 8.15pm
   Date: 10th November 2008
   Location: Metropolitan Police HQ, London

Jack leant against the front desk and nodded his thanks to the custody sergeant for lending use of the desk phone. The phone call to Pierre Macron had indeed been most interesting. Jack afforded himself a small smile.

"Hey, Guv?" Jack turned at the sound of his name and saw DS Cooper pushing through the double doors leading from the interview rooms. "Andre's being put to bed for the night in one of the cells."

Jack nodded and motioned for DS Cooper to follow him upstairs. "We can carry on with him tomorrow. And someone else will be joining us shortly too. I'll fill you in over a coffee."

"He handed me this." DS Cooper held a white envelope out towards Jack and they climbed the stairs. "It's for Isabel."

Jack stopped, sharply, mid stride and turned round to see the envelope. He took it from DS Cooper and looked at the name carefully printed on the front. "Isabel" was all it said.

"Any idea what's inside?" Jack turned to continue their journey to the top of the stairs.

"None." DS Cooper jogged up the last few steps and followed Jack towards the canteen. "Just told me to make sure she got it."

Jack nodded and slipped the envelope inside his jacket pocket. "OK, we'll get it to her. Firstly, though, I need a coffee. And secondly, what do you know about this?" He held out his notepad with Andre's doodles and scribbles and the "we learn from failure, not from success" inscription.

DS Cooper took the notepad as they entered the canteen and walked over to their usual table in the far corner. "I've never heard of it – but I can find out."

Jack nodded at his partner and went to get the coffees. "You do that, Cooper, you do that."

* * *

Time: 10.05pm
Date: 10th November 2008
Location: Runway, Heathrow Airport, London

The cabin lights dimmed in readiness for take-off. Poborski relaxed back in his seat and closed his eyes. It was nearly over; it was very nearly over. The cabin crew were making their way along the aisles, checking seatbelts had been securely fastened. They then positioned themselves for performing the pre-flight safety demonstration.

CHAPTER TWENTY-FOUR

Poborski had seen it many times before and carried on relaxing in his seat, his eyes firmly closed. With any luck he might sleep the whole way back to Moscow. As he lay back he placed both his hands protectively on the silver briefcase resting on his lap.

The aircraft's engines roared into life and began to taxi along the runway, bouncing over the uneven tarmac, slowly making its way to the holding area to await its turn in the queue for take-off.

The flight crew continued their safety demonstration – the use of the overhead oxygen supply in the event of sudden changes in cabin pressure, and how to inflate the individual bright yellow life jackets in the event of landing on water. Poborski gave a small chuckle to himself. If they landed on water, the first thing he would save would be his briefcase.

With the safety demonstration at an end, the flight crew walked along the aisle and took their places ready for take-off. Except the aircraft didn't take off. It didn't move. After a few more seconds the cabin lights sprang back into life, bathing the aircraft in artificial light. Poborski sensed the change and opened one eye. He felt the aircraft's engines slow and eventually cut out, leaving the cabin in silence.

"Ladies and Gentlemen." The pilot's voice crackled over the plane's tannoy system. "This is Captain Hackerley speaking. I am afraid there is a small administrative matter that needs to be taken care of on board before we can be on our way. Please remain in your seats. I apologise for this further short delay."

Both of Poborski's eyes now snapped open, and he straightened up in his seat. Instinctively he pulled the silver briefcase closer to his chest. He heard the sound of the cabin doors being opened at the front of the aircraft; someone was coming aboard.

Poborski began to sweat. He glanced nervously over his shoulder to check the rear exit. Two flight attendants stood guard in front of the locked door. Turning his head back round to the front, Poborski's heart almost stopped beating. Before him, two uniformed, armed police were striding down the aisle, heading his way.

"Karl Aleksey Poborski," spoke the first officer as he arrived at Poborski's side. Poborski noticed the officer gripped his semi-automatic weapon tightly in his hands. "I am arresting you on suspicion of theft, murder, kidnapping and false imprisonment. You do not have to say anything, but it may harm your defence if you do not mention when questioned something that you later rely on in Court. Anything you do say may be given in evidence." The officer paused and continued to fix Poborski with a hard stare. "Do you understand?"

Poborski's mouth was dry. His breathing became shallow and rapid. He was trapped. There was no escape. Slowly he began to nod.

"Cuff him," barked the officer, nodding towards his colleague behind him. "And take control of that briefcase."

* * *

CHAPTER TWENTY-FIVE

Time: 2.05pm
   Date: 11th November 2008
   Location: Green Park Parade, Cambridge

Isabel drew her legs up underneath her and settled back against the soft cushions of her sofa. She nursed the hot mug of coffee in her lap, but knew that it would be left to go cold. Just like all the others. She couldn't eat. She couldn't drink. She had barely slept. Her front room now almost looked like it should. Books had been placed back on the shelves, drawers replaced back in the sideboard, magazines neatly stacked on the coffee table. Anything broken had been quickly thrown away. Isabel didn't want any reminders of what had happened in here. Who had been in here. Why they had been in here.

   Everything, that was, except the photograph sitting on the mantelpiece. Its glass had been cracked, sending jagged spidery patterns out across the surface. The frame was snapped at the corner, the wood chipped and splintered. But Isabel had dusted it down and placed it back on the mantelpiece, and she now stared at the picture as if searching for some kind of answer. It was her favourite photograph – one of only a treasured few that she possessed. It showed her fifth birthday, and she was sitting astride a small tricycle in the back garden of their family home. The old sprawling apple tree in the background was groaning under a dearth of shiny red fruits. Mum was holding onto her hand, making sure she didn't topple sideways. Dad had a hand on Mum's shoulder, smiling his usual cheeky lop-sided grin. The three of them together, smiling for the camera.

Isabel had always wondered who took that photograph – who was actually behind the lens.

She closed her eyes and let her head rest back against the cushions behind her. She felt sleepy, even though it was just after lunchtime. She couldn't sleep at night; she didn't feel safe. The police had been wonderful, straightening out her house for her, replacing her door and window locks with new ones, even arranging for a security light to be fitted outside her front door. But she still didn't feel safe. She jumped at the slightest noise. She left the TV on day and night, didn't open the door to anyone.

Mr Taylor had been round to see her, which was nice. He had brought her a huge bunch of flowers, which now sat in the corner of the room on the small nest of tables, its leaves now beginning to wilt. She had only reluctantly let him in after checking and double checking through the spy hole in her front door. He had been very sympathetic, told her to take as much time off as she needed, that her job would be waiting for her when and if she wanted to come back. Isabel had smiled gratefully and had given the usual expected responses, even offering him the obligatory cup of coffee and a biscuit. But she had been relieved when she finally shut the door behind him and could return to her silent, solitary existence. She didn't want to be with anyone. She didn't need to be with anyone. She was better off on her own.

Isabel had opened a small window in the front room to let in some crisp, fresh air – to try and remove the smell of someone else being in her house. It wasn't a real smell, obviously - she knew that. It was something only she could detect, a feeling that had worked its way into the very being of her house, and no amount of fresh air could displace it.

In the distance she could hear the far away voices of children outside, playing in the nearby school playground. Shouts and cheers, laughter and songs. They sounded so happy and carefree. Life was carrying on as normal – for everyone it seemed, except herself. For her, time had stood still, time was frozen, just like the snow and frost dusted ground outside.

Isabel had been so deeply immersed in her thoughts that she had not

CHAPTER TWENTY-FIVE

heard the footsteps outside of her front door. She jerked upright at the sound of the sharp tapping at the door, almost sending her coffee cup flying across the carpet.

She waited, holding her breath; waiting to see if the person would knock again. Sometimes they did, sometimes they didn't. The seconds ticked by. There was no sound. Isabel started to relax back against the cushions.

Rap rap rap

Whoever it was had not gone away.

Rap rap rap

Louder and more insistent this time.

Isabel's stomach tightened and her heart began to race. She thought about getting up to look out of the window, to see who it was, but then there would be the risk that the caller would see her curtains move, see them twitch, and would instantly know there was someone at home. Better to stay still. Better to stay quiet. They would soon give up and go away. They always did – eventually.

Rap rap rap

Even harder this time

They were not going away.

Isabel made to get up off her sofa, intending to move towards the back of the flat, out of sight, but she had barely got to her feet when she heard the letterbox creak open.

"Isabel?" said a voice. "Isabel? I know you're in there."

Isabel edged out into the entrance hall, slowly peering around the edge of the door frame towards the front door. She could see the letterbox propped open with a hand. There was a face up against the opening, she could see their eyes peering through.

"Isabel? Open up, please. Let me in…...it's me. "The voice paused. "It's Mac."

* * *

Isabel led Mac into the front room without saying a word. She sat back down on the sofa with her back facing him, curling her legs back underneath herself. Mac edged into the room, hovering cautiously by the door. He could almost taste the tension in the air. Neither of them spoke.

Mac's eyes swept the room, taking in the recently re-stacked books, straightened picture frames, neatly re-arranged magazines. There were empty places on the sideboard where there had once been ornaments or other mementoes of a life. There were empty spaces on the walls, once home to pictures or photographs – now all gone; only a faint outline to suggest their previous presence. Mac eventually broke the tense silence.

"I spoke to DI MacIntosh, Jack, yesterday." He tried to keep his voice light. Isabel didn't respond. "He told me that he'd offered you witness protection – a new identity, a fresh start somewhere else." Still Isabel didn't respond; not even hinting she had heard. Mac sighed and stepped further into the room, lowering himself slowly down onto the sofa next to Isabel. She seemed to visibly flinch and edged further away from him, continuing to face the window. "You don't have to live like this, Isabel, "he continued, softly. He desperately wanted to touch her, to reach out and hold her, reassure her that everything would be OK. But he daren't. "You don't have to live in fear; you don't have to jump six feet in the air every time someone comes near you. You don't have to keep yourself locked up in here…." He gazed around the room once again. "You can go away, start again somewhere new. Somewhere fresh. No one need know anything about you. You could start to forget….."

"Forget?!" exploded Isabel, suddenly turning round and facing Mac. Her eyes flashed with a heady mixture of anger and hatred. "You think I can forget about….about…?" Isabel couldn't find the words she so desperately wanted, so merely shook her head and returned to staring out of the window. "You just have no idea, do you?" she breathed.

"Not unless you talk to me, no" replied Mac gently. "Why won't you accept the help the police are offering? Why won't you let them protect you? They can get you a new house, a new job, a new name, everything. You don't need to worry about anything. No one could ever find you."

Isabel shuddered. "I don't want a new name, a new house, a new job.

CHAPTER TWENTY-FIVE

I already have a name. My name is all I've got left." Isabel glanced up at the battered photograph on the mantelpiece. "It's all I have left of them." Isabel swallowed hard, and turned round to face Mac once again. Her eyes took on a softer tone, and were no longer blazing with anger. Instead they welled up with thick, salty tears. "I like my home. I like my job. I like my life. I don't want to have to start all over again somewhere else, somewhere new. All I know is right here. If I go….I'll have nothing."

"I could help you," offered Mac, gently. He inched closer to Isabel.

Isabel visibly stiffened. "I don't need your help," she snapped. "Don't you think you've done enough…all of you?"

Mac frowned. "I…I don't understand….I…"

Isabel once again flashed her angry eyes to Mac. "All the lies, all the deceit. But you know the worst thing about it all? The very worst thing?" She paused, her voice catching. "I actually believed you. You had me taken in, almost from the word go. I can't believe I fell for it so easily." She closed her eyes and sighed deeply, her lips almost twitching into a smile. "But all the time it was about the money. Just the money. It wasn't about them at all…" Isabel nodded at the photograph on the mantelpiece. "You never knew them. You never even met them. Neither of you had. You both lied to me to get to them. To get to the money. That was all you wanted from me…..their money."

Mac opened his mouth to speak, but Isabel held up her hand and cut him short.

"Why did you have to do it? Why did you have to bring them into it?" Isabel's voice cracked, and her cheeks were now streaked with tears, her eyes red and swollen. "They were all I had left. My memories. Now that has been ruined, ruined forever. You made me think they were alive, that I would eventually get to see them again; that the past 20 years had all been a dream and I was about to wake up. Do you have any idea how that made me feel? That my parents were actually alive after all?" Isabel took a breath and paused, wiping the tears from her cheeks with the back of her hands. The anger had now subsided from her voice. "Why couldn't you just say you wanted money? Why didn't you just kidnap me and make me hand it over? Anything. Anything would have been better than this. Why create so many lies, so much deceit? Why?"

"I never lied to you, Isabel." Mac's voice was firm and even. "Never. I never knew about the money. I swear."

"Yeah right," Isabel sniffed, giving Mac a scathing look. "Sure you didn't."

"It's the truth." Mac tried to catch Isabel's eye, but she refused to acknowledge him. "I believed him too. Andre. He told me your parents were alive, and I believed him. But I never knew about the money, I swear to you. I thought it was all about the papers."

"Sorry, but I find that pretty hard to believe right now."

"I didn't know, I really didn't." Mac shook his head and dropped his gaze. "Everything I told you was the truth. Every bit."

"He's right, Isabel." Jack MacIntosh appeared out of nowhere and leant against the doorframe. "He's telling you the truth."

***

Time: 2.15pm
 Date: 11th November 2008
 Location: Green Park Parade, Cambridge

Jack sat down opposite Isabel, perching himself awkwardly on the edge of the low coffee table. He fixed Isabel with his eyes.

"Sorry to intrude, but you left your front door open."

Isabel looked up, held Jack's gaze for a few seconds before switching her eyes to Mac. Then, without a word to either of them, she switched her gaze back to looking silently out of the window once again.

"I'm still not moving," she said, flatly, her fingers playing absent mindedly with the frayed cuffs of her woollen cardigan. "I don't want your new identity, your new house, your new job, none of it. I just want to be left alone."

"That's fine, Isabel. That's not why I'm here." Jack tried again to make

CHAPTER TWENTY-FIVE

eye contact. "In fact, you don't need police protection at all. None of it. We've got him. Fleming that is…..or Karl Poborski as he is really known as. He'll be no threat to you now."

"He's what?? He's Poborski?" interrupted Mac, his eyes widening. "Karl Poborski?"

"The one and the same, "nodded Jack, still trying to catch Isabel's gaze.

"You're sure?" Mac shook his head in disbelief. "Who told you that?"

"Andre", replied Jack. "Apparently he's known Fleming's real identity all along."

"Andre?" Mac's eyes widened even further. "Andre told you? How come he…….?"

Jack held up a hand and shook his head at his brother. "Now isn't the time to go into details, Stuart. I just came round to let Isabel know that Fleming…. Poborski….was in custody. That he poses no further threat."

Mac ignored his brother's attempts to keep him quiet. "How did you catch up with him? Where was he?"

"He was picked up at Heathrow last night, attempting to board a flight to Moscow. Travelling in the name of Ludwig Chevchenko. Dyed hair, tinted contact lenses, fresh clothes, false passport. Pretty good disguise by all accounts."

"How did you know he would be there?" frowned Mac. "Was he being followed all the way back from Paris?"

Jack shook his head. "No need. I had an interesting call from the Manager of the bank in Paris yesterday." Jack couldn't help but let a small smile play with his lips. "There was a little piece of gadgetry in his briefcase…..something to let us know where he was, day or night."

"A bug?" Mac raised his eyebrows. He instantly thought back to the bugs fund in Marie's apartment and on Andre's watch.

Jack gave a small nod. "Well a tracking device to be exact. Useful little things sometimes."

"And the money?" Mac glanced across at Isabel, who was still staring blankly out of the window. "He still had Isabel's money?"

"No money to find." Jack also let his gaze rest on Isabel, noting how she appeared not to be listening.

Mac's face dropped, and he nodded, ruefully. "He already stashed it somewhere else, did he? I guess it'll never be found now." Mac pushed himself off the sofa and walked over to the window, gazing out into the deserted street. "Crafty bugger."

Jack continued to shake his head and gave another small smile. "There wasn't any money there to find, because he never had it in the first place."

This time it was Isabel who cut in. "What do you mean he never had it in the first place?" She dragged her gaze away from the window and looked at Jack. Her eyes let him know she had been listening all along. "I was there. I saw him take it."

Jack nodded. "I know." He paused before continuing, leaning forwards to hold Isabel's enquiring gaze. "When I arrived in Paris and discovered Fleming…Poborski…. had impersonated my identity to the French Police, and then disappeared with you, I noticed on the CCTV recordings that he had made a phone call from the front desk just before you both left. Since no one had used the phone since, I simply re-dialled the number. The call went through to the Première Bank Nationale. I spoke with the manager of the bank and got him to divulge what Fleming had asked for. Then it all clicked into place." Jack paused again, looking at Isabel's tired face, He tried another half-hearted smile. "Fleming was never chasing the documents, Isabel. He was chasing you. He wanted your money and needed you to gain access to it. That was all he was ever after. Andre confirmed it all, and explained how Poborski came out of hiding in Russia, took on the guise of Special Agent Fleming and followed you to Paris. He made it look like he was following the papers, but really he was following you. And your money."

Jack quietly rose from the coffee table he was still perching on, and slipped onto the sofa next to Isabel. He reached out and gave her arm a small squeeze. He felt her instantly flinch under his touch. "I got the bank manager to swap the briefcases, replace yours with a dummy one full of fake money. There was a top row of real money, just to make it look authentic, but the rest was just rubbish. Banks like this one always have

CHAPTER TWENTY-FIVE

dummy cash at the ready, for just this kind of thing."

"But how did the tracking device get inside?" It was Mac's turn now. "You arrived at the bank just after we did, and after Fleming had already left. We watched him go."

Jack turned to his brother who was still leaning against the window sill. "The tracking device was an added extra, something even I wasn't aware of at the time. These high security banks have all manner of security devices at their fingertips these days, as you might expect. This particular vault has the best security system throughout France, maybe even throughout Europe. No losses, no robberies, no thefts or attempted thefts have been made in the last twenty years. Probably the safest place in the world."

Jack paused and turned back to face Isabel. He noted how her eyes were softening slightly. "When your parents first deposited their money in the vault, there was no fingerprint analysis, no DNA system locks in place. But as the technology advanced over the years, the bank updated its security systems. Introduced fingerprint scans for all cash withdrawals; DNA samples of all account holders to be collected and linked into the system. High security systems for a high security bank. Your parents couldn't have chosen a better place."

Isabel was still facing Jack. Her eyes misted over and she gave a small nod of recognition. "I remember my parents' solicitors asking me for a blood sample a few years ago, and some fingerprints. They said it was for security reasons at the house; if it was ever broken into. I wasn't living there, so they wanted my DNA and fingerprints on record." Isabel's voice wavered. "And all the time it was for this."

Jack reached out again and touched Isabel's arm. This time he noted she didn't flinch. "Included in the additional security features of the bank was a rule that where large amounts of money were withdrawn, anything over £100,000, a small tracking device was automatically fitted as standard. Even though the bank had swapped the briefcase for dummy cash, the manager had the foresight to still place a tracking device inside. And I'm glad he did."

Mac frowned. "He never checked? Fleming? Poborski. He never looked in the briefcase and saw it was fake money?"

Jack shrugged. "Maybe he did, maybe he didn't. A quick look inside and everything would look normal, the top layer being real cash."

"Where is he now?" asked Isabel, her voice sounding so fragile it could break.

"He's in custody at our station at the moment. He's due to be interviewed later today, with hopefully charges brought soon after. He'll be remanded in custody, Isabel, so you don't need to worry. There will be no question of him being allowed bail." Jack felt Isabel sag slightly next to him. "I don't think he was ever going to come after you to hurt you, Isabel. Not once he had the money. That was all he wanted."

Isabel looked up, holding Jack's gaze. She gave a small nod and wiped away a moist tear from her eye. "Thank you." She then let her gaze fall on Mac and her eyes took on a confused, almost distrustful glaze.

Jack intervened. "Stuart knew nothing about the money Isabel." He looked at his brother and gave a small grimace. "He's telling the truth, for once in his life. Going after the money – that was all Poborski. Andre knew of the plan, but Stuart….." Jack broke off and raised his eyebrows at his brother. "Well, Stuart I think was taken for a bit of a ride."

"Where is he now?" asked Mac, his face dark and his voice sounding hollow.

"Like I said," replied Jack. "Fleming…Poborski…...he's with us at the station…"

"No, I mean Andre," interrupted Mac. "Where's Andre?"

"Andre is with us too, seeing if he can help us with our enquiries."

Mac nodded. "Is he in trouble?"

"Andre?" Jack considered it for a moment. "Well that's up to him. There's a lot we still need to know, a lot of this whole thing doesn't make a lot of sense, and Andre can provide answers…..*if* he is willing to help."

"You really have got him?" Isabel's voice although still quiet, had a firm edge to it. She wiped her cheeks free from tears and tucked a wayward strand of hair behind her ear. "He's…. he's not still out there?"

"We really have got him, yes." Jack gave her a reassuring smile. "He's not

CHAPTER TWENTY-FIVE

a threat to you anymore. Thanks to Stuart's call."

"My what?" Mac whirled his head round to face his brother. "What call?"

Jack allowed himself a rueful chuckle and fixed his brother with a knowing look. "You never were a good liar, Stu, even when you were little."

"I don't know what you mean." Mac avoided Jack's eyes, and looked down at his feet.

"The phone call you made to us, about Fleming and Liddell. It got patched through to Liddell's PA, and she then passed it on to me...."

Mac continued to look at this feet, noting how frayed his shoes were looking. He shrugged. "Still don't know what you mean. I never made any call."

Jack laughed again. "You used your real name, Stu. It couldn't have been anyone else."

* * *

Time: 2.15pm
   Date: 9th November 2008
   Location: Café Bleu, Rue Saint Pierre, Paris

"I'll see you outside." Mac nodded his head towards the door of the café. "I won't be a minute, just need the toilet."

Andre sighed but nodded his agreement. "Don't be long." The café was now bustling with customers and Andre was happy to be leaving. He headed outside while Mac threaded his way through the queues of people waiting at the counter.

Mac pushed open the door of the men's toilets, grateful that they were empty. He quickly slipped inside the nearest cubicle and pulled out his mobile phone.

"Metropolitan Police headquarters, London," he whispered into the mouthpiece. "And make it quick." He waited a few seconds, drumming his fingers impatiently on the back of the cubicle door. "Yes, I do want you to connect me. Quickly, I haven't got much time."

After what seemed like an eternity, but was only a few seconds in reality, there was a small click and a pleasant sounding voice filled the earpiece.

"Metropolitan Police headquarters, how may I help?"

"Hello, yes," Mac spoke quickly, trying to keep his voice low. "I need to pass on some information. About Chief Superintendent Liddell and Special Agent Fleming."

"May I have your name please?" came the reply.

Mac hesitated, momentarily caught off guard. "My name? It's….er……it's Mac."

"Mac?" The receptionist paused. "Is that your first or last name?"

"It's short for MacIntosh. Stuart MacIntosh."

* * *

CHAPTER TWENTY-SIX

Time: 2.30pm
Date: 11th November 2008
Location: Green Park Parade, Cambridge

"How much of the letter did you read?" asked Jack. "The one Shafer wrote?"

Mac shrugged. "I'm not sure. The first couple of pages maybe; perhaps a bit more. It was difficult. We were sitting in the middle of a busy café; there were people all around us. Andre was getting nervous; he didn't want us staying in there very long. He pulled the flash drive out and we had to leave."

"Hmmm," mused Jack. "And that was where you read about Fleming and Liddell? In Shafer's letter? What else did he say?"

Again Mac shrugged and shook his head. "Like I said, it was difficult. We only read the first few pages. Shafer was basically warning us that Fleming wasn't FBI and that he wasn't really after the papers, that he was after Isabel. And he said that Liddell was involved too, and we shouldn't trust him. He was bent. Shafer reckoned Liddell knew all about Fleming, knew he wasn't FBI."

"Did he mention why? Why he thought Liddell was involved?"

"I think he might have done, later in the letter. We didn't get a chance to find out. We didn't read the rest of the letter. I think maybe Shafer did know more; I think he was trying to tell us, but he never got the chance." Mac broke off, his mind flooded with the horrific pictures of his friend lying dead in a cold Paris gutter. "Fleming made sure of that. It was

Fleming, wasn't it? Who killed Simon?"

Jack nodded. "Probably. But there was nothing in the letter, the bits you managed to read, which told you why Fleming and Liddell were connected?"

Mac shook his head. "No. Shafer seemed to go off track…..he started talking about Kreshniov, saying that he knew that he wasn't dead. That it had all been faked and that he knew exactly where he was and what he was about to do. And who he really was."

"He didn't say anything more specific than that?"

"I think he was about to but Andre pulled the plug – the café was getting too busy. He wanted to get us away, somewhere quieter. I never got to see the rest of the letter."

"So, the flash drive?" Jack raised his eyebrows at his brother. "Where did it go?"

Mac shrugged once again. "I guess Andre kept it."

Jack looked down at his watch. They needed to be getting back. He reached into his pocket and threw his car keys at Mac. "Go wait in the car. I'll be out soon." Mac shrugged and turned to leave.

"I am really sorry, Isabel," he said, casting her an apologetic look. "I really am."

"Andre told me about your parents," said Jack, once the front door had closed behind Mac.

"He's a liar," snapped Isabel, whipping her face back round to look out of the window once again. "I think we've established that. My parents died in a car crash."

"You don't believe him?" questioned Jack. "You don't believe this Phoenix Project ever existed?"

"Do you?" Isabel's voice was hard and jagged. She glared round at Jack. "Hasn't all this just proved to you what a huge pack of lies this all was?"

Jack shrugged. "Andre hasn't really told us the full story; I know that much. As for the rest….? Andre, Poborski – they are very clever individuals. The plan they hatched to get to your money was pretty sophisticated. It took a lot of planning. And a lot of patience. They

CHAPTER TWENTY-SIX

knew what they were doing."

"But you can't possibly believe them, it's absurd...."

Again Jack shrugged. "Do I think the Phoenix Project actually existed? At the moment, no I don't. I've run background checks on everyone. Karl Poborski did exist, and worked for NASA. He was last heard of in 1986; no records of him after that date. Same for Boris Kreshniov. He is recorded as having worked for NASA and was Chief Executive of PRISM – but again no records for him after 1986. Except we do have a death certificate for him certifying his death in Moscow in 1987. As for Gustav Friedman – records show him working for NASA in the late 70s and early 80s – but he died in 1986. Andre Baxter doesn't exist at all, anywhere." Jack paused and gave a deep sigh. "If I am going to be persuaded that this Phoenix Project actually existed then I'm going to need something more. At the moment, I have nothing."

Isabel nodded, but remained quiet. Her eyes strayed towards the mantelpiece, resting once more on the photograph of her parents.

"I'm sorry, Isabel, I really am." He watched as she blinked back the tears. "I don't think Andre did know them; I think you are right. They did die in a car crash in September 1986."

Isabel nodded, wiping a stray tear away from her cheek. She tried a half-hearted smile at Jack. "I know. I know."

Jack made to get up again. "I'll see myself out." He hesitated while rising from the sofa. "I don't think Andre really meant to cause you any harm. Both he and Fleming…Poborski…. they were out for the money. Unfortunately, this meant you had to be caught up in it too."

Isabel nodded again, but returned her watery gaze to the window.

"But he did ask me to give you this though." Jack paused by the coffee table, pulling a small white envelope out from his jacket pocket. "I'll leave it here." He left the envelope on the top of the mantelpiece, next to the photograph of Isabel's parents. Nodding slowly to himself, Jack turned and left.

An icy wind followed Jack into his car as he slipped into the driver's seat.

"Do you think she believes me? About the money?" Mac rubbed his hands together and waited for Jack to start the engine to get some warmth into the car. "That I didn't know?"

Jack gave a small shrug, but nodded his head. "I think so. Probably. I think everyone's been lied to at some point in this case."

"He had me fooled, that's for sure. I mean the papers, the documents. I *saw* them. At least I *thought* I saw them – they all looked so real."

Jack let the engine idle for a while, turning the heater up to full whack to get rid of the iciness inside the car. "Apparently some clever computer software was all it took. It seems our Andre Baxter is a dab hand with computers – would have been easy for him."

"Maybe," shrugged Mac. "But it still doesn't make much sense to me."

"I guess it isn't meant to. Con men rarely make sense."

Mac continued to shake his head slowly from side to side. "No, I don't believe that. I've known Andre for years. And I've known Simon for years. Simon definitely had pictures of Andre on his desk that day, the day I got the sack from the post job at M15. Someone was after him, I could tell. And Simon helped him disappear."

"But did you really?" cut in Jack, now fastening his seatbelt and looking to pull out into the road. "Know him, I mean. He told you he was Gustav Friedman – but I think we've established that was a lie. Friedman died in 1986."

"So why was his picture on Simon's desk? Why was he asked to track him down? It doesn't make any sense."

Jack joined the traffic and headed back towards the M11 southbound. Fog was now beginning to sink through the cold afternoon air, and cars were crawling along with headlights peering into the gloom. "You said yourself, Andre could hack into any computer network in the world. Maybe that was all he was doing. No secret Project, no secret experiments. Just him stealing someone else's cash and getting caught."

"What about the necklace? How did Andre just happen to have the other part of it, and it was an exact fit?"

"Just leave it, Mac," sighed Jack, craving a cigarette. He reached down and fumbled in the side of the door for a stick of chewing gum. "You're

CHAPTER TWENTY-SIX

lucky you've got out of this without any charges yourself."

"There's more to this, and you know it, Jack." Mac turned and started looking out of the passenger side window, watching the street lights blink weakly through the heavy fog.

Jack folded the gum into his mouth, wincing at the taste. Although he wanted to tell Mac to let it drop, Jack had a gnawing feeling in the pit of his stomach that his brother was right.

Isabel heard the car pull away. She walked over to the window and pulled the heavy curtains across to block out the dreariness of the late afternoon fog. Walking back to the comfort of her sofa, Isabel found herself looking at the photograph on the mantelpiece. She dropped down and snuggled up to the soft cushions while imagining herself to be back in the garden, five years old, without a care in the world. It had been her birthday, the day that the photograph had been taken. She remembered riding her tricycle, ringing the little bell on the handlebars, pedalling round and round the garden, shrieking with delight as her birthday cake was brought out to the garden table. Her mother and father were laughing…….

Isabel looked away to break the memory. Her eyes came to rest on the small white envelope sitting next to the photograph. Pausing only for a moment, she reached forward and picked it up. Something Andre wanted her to have. Isabel turned the envelope over lightly in her fingers, almost letting it slip through to the floor – not sure if she wanted anything from the man who had made such a fool of her. Anger and shame welled up inside her like a well stoked fire.

She was almost ready to toss it into the waste paper bin, but curiosity got the better of her. Gently breaking the seal, Isabel peered inside the envelope to see three small pieces of what at first glance looked like card. But they weren't card – they were photographs.

Reaching inside the envelope she slipped the photographs out and turned them over to face her. She immediately froze. Staring back at her was an exact replica of the photograph she had been looking at for so long – the photograph sitting only a few feet away from her on her very own mantelpiece. The same laughing, smiling expressions of her mother and father; her own grinning smile sitting atop a little red tricycle.

The same photograph.

The exact same photograph.

Isabel felt her hand shake as she turned the photograph over. There was an inscription on the back, slightly faded now due to age, but still legible.

"To our dear Gustav. Summer 1985. Much love, your good friends Christopher, Elizabeth and Isabel."

Quickly, Isabel flipped the photograph back over, checking she wasn't dreaming. It was definitely the same photograph, staring back at her. She hurriedly looked at the other two photographs beneath, her heart beginning to pound in her chest. The next photograph was a similar pose – she saw herself still perched proudly on her tricycle, grinning from ear to ear. Her mother was still holding her hand, with the same happy and carefree smile adorning her lips. But it wasn't her father that was standing next to her with his hand upon her mother's shoulder; there was someone else in the picture instead, taking her father's place. Her father must have been taking the photograph this time. The man standing at her side was smiling into the camera. His clear pale grey eyes pierced the camera lens. His hair was long and wavy, the tips just brushing his shoulders. A neat, cropped beard hugged his chin. Small, wire-framed spectacles perched on the end of his narrow nose.

Recognition washed over Isabel instantly.

She remembered her birthday more vividly now. It was as if memories that had been lost for so many years, locked away in a dusty drawer, had now been unlocked and allowed to flood her mind. She could remember this man coming to see her mother and father, helping to get the birthday party food ready, helping to bring out the birthday cake to the table in the garden, helping to blow up the balloons and hang up the streamers. She remembered.

She checked the final photograph. Her hand was now shaking uncontrollably, unsure of what she was going to find. She was sitting alone on the grass, a large plaster covering one knee. Memories hit her like a tidal wave – she had been pedalling her tricycle down a slight incline towards

CHAPTER TWENTY-SIX

the back of the garden, close to her favourite climbing tree. Her mother was busy taking the plates back into the kitchen after their birthday tea. She was pedalling faster and faster, picking up more and more speed, the pedals whipping round out of control. She let go of the handlebars, hoping that would make it stop – but the tricycle toppled over and she had fallen with a painful thud onto the grass below. A pedal caught her knee, drawing blood.

Then a hand appeared at her side, helping her to her feet. A pair of strong arms swept her up into the air and carried her inside the house. She had buried her face in his shoulder length hair, her arms clinging tightly around his neck, feeling the soft bristles of his beard prickling her tear stained cheeks.

Isabel let the photographs tumble from her grasp. She had known it when she had met him. She had known they had met before. The person who had been staring out at her from the photograph was the very same person who had been behind the camera of the picture she had treasured for so many years.

Andre.

A man she had known as Uncle.

* * *

Time: 1.00pm
Date: 7th November 2008
Location: Flat 7, Rue de Bougainvillea, Paris

"It's good to see you at last, Isabel." Andre handed Isabel a steaming cup of hot coffee, which she accepted gratefully. "Good to see you here, safe and sound."

"I'm still not sure why I'm here," she said, drinking deeply from the cup and instantly feeling the warmth spread throughout her chilled body. "Or what any of this is about."

Isabel looked up and studied the man before her. His grey eyes were

323

piercing, yet kind looking. The skin around them had started to crinkle, giving his face a warm and lived-in look. She felt instantly comfortable in his presence. It was uncanny; a man she had never met before made her feel like she had known him for years. She took another long drink from the cup and pushed the thought from her mind.

* * *

Time: 5.30pm
 Date: 11th November 2008
 Location: Metropolitan Police HQ, London

Jack sat for a moment, drumming fingers on the steering wheel. It had taken them hours to negotiate the M11 and then the M25 through the advancing fog that had seemed to follow them south. Mac had jumped out, muttering that he needed some space to "sort his head out". Jack murmured something in return and let him go. He was now parked in the car park of the station, but made no move to get out of the car.

Something was bothering him.

Jack released his seat belt and then reached for his mobile phone. His call was quickly connected.

"Cooper? It's me."

"Hey, stranger. Where have you been?"

"Around." Jack looked out the side window of the car, watching police officers come and go through the back entrance. "I'll fill you in soon. Have you had any luck with that quote? The one Andre wrote in my notepad?"

"Not yet, Guv. I've had to sit in with Poborski most of today, but the guy isn't saying a word. I'll start searching now though."

"Thanks, mate. Anything you find out, let me know. I'll catch up with you later."

"OK, no problem. Hey. Before you go, is it true?"

"Is what true?" Jack rubbed his forehead with his fingers, feeling a nicotine deprived headache coming on.

CHAPTER TWENTY-SIX

"Your brother…. that you found your brother again? Everyone's talking about it."

Jack breathed out heavily, watching his breath mist the windscreen in front of him. "I'll catch you later, Cooper."

* * *

Time: 5.30pm
Date: 11th November 2008
Location: Green Park Parade, Cambridge

Isabel sat alone in the dark, staring at the photograph. She had been rooted to the spot, not even turning on the lights when the room began to slowly sink into darkness as the sun went down.

Uncle.

Her eyes bore into the photograph once again, searching the face she had once known so well. How had she not realised? How had she not recognised him? It was all coming flooding back to her now like tidal wave after tidal wave. She could almost feel his sturdy, strong arms around her as he carried her back into the house for her mother to nurse her wounded knee.

Uncle.

Isabel instinctively reached down and touched her knee, where she knew a faint scar was still visible where the sharp pedal had cut viciously into her skin. Her mother had the lightest touch. She had swept Isabel into her arms and stroked her face, caressing her softly while the tears flowed down her rosy cheeks.

Just as the tears were flowing again now. Isabel's heart ached as she looked down at her mother's carefree and smiling face. She lightly traced her finger over her mother's features, desperately wanting to feel her loving touch once again.

I miss you Mum.

THE PHOENIX PROJECT

***

Time: 6.00pm

Date: 11th November 2008

Location: Investigation room, top floor, Metropolitan Police HQ, London

The fog that had followed Jack and Mac back from Cambridge had descended in earnest, and now the whole city was enveloped in a blanket of suffocating white. Jack leant against the window and peered out across the rear car park. He could barely see any of the cars parked below – the fog seemed to have sucked the life out of anything it touched.

Wearily pushing himself away from the window, he returned to the tables arranged in the centre of the room. Driving back from Isabel's flat, the gnawing feeling in the pit of his stomach had given way to a cast iron belief that something was not right. Cooper had been to work and methodically arranged all the Phoenix Project evidence, such as it was, into some sort of order.

But something was definitely not right.

Nothing made any sense.

Jack reached forwards and picked up the plastic evidence bag that contained the papers found in Charles Tindleman's waste paper bin. Having found a few charred pieces of paper in the bottom of the bin, Jack had decided to place the entire bin into evidence.

You never know.

There was a lot of charred ash, but some of the papers still had some sections legible to the naked eye. Jack tipped the bag on its end, dislodging some of the contents. What had he been burning? What was so important that needed eradicating from memory before eradicating yourself from human existence?

The scene of crime officers had stated that Tindleman's office had still smelt of charred ash and burning paper when they came to process the scene. The ash had even still been warm to the touch in parts. Whatever

CHAPTER TWENTY-SIX

he had been burning, whatever he so desperately needed to destroy, he had done so only seconds before ending his own life.

Jack picked up a nearby magnifying glass and shook the evidence bag again. Most of the papers were burnt beyond recognition, their contents charred to the deepest blackness, or smothered in such a deep smoky brown colour that their words had been lost forever.

He gently opened the bag and, picking up a pair of tweezers, began moving the fragments around. Bit by bit he checked over the contents. Nothing seemed even remotely legible. Some typeface could possibly be seen underneath the charring on some of the pieces, but they had been rendered illegible by the extreme heat. Some papers, Jack thought, seemed to show what looked like diagrams or drawings. But again, they looked so damaged they were incomprehensible.

Jack reached down to the bottom of the bag with the tweezers. Moving some heavily charred pieces of paper aside, there appeared to be several other pieces which had much less visible smoke and fire damage. Maybe the intense fire had burnt out, not having enough energy to engulf everything in its path.

Maybe Tindleman had run out of matches? Or maybe simply run out of time.

Gently, Jack brought one of the pieces out of the bag, carefully pinching the corner with the tweezers, his hand seeming to shake with concentration. He didn't want the paper to disintegrate into powder before his eyes. Placing the paper down onto a piece of clean blotting paper, he brought the magnifying glass over the top.

The edges of the paper were a burnt orange; but the words in the centre were clearly visible.

* * *

CHAPTER TWENTY-SEVEN

Time: 6.15pm
 Date: 11th November 208
 Location: Metropolitan Police HQ, London

The custody sergeant at the front desk sighed. It had been a long day and his shift was not over yet. Remembrance Day was usually a quiet affair on the streets on London, but not even the National Day of Remembrance had stopped the usual influx of hardened criminals – the shoplifters, the car thieves, the pub brawls, the domestic violence incidents, the knife attacks, the drug dealers. For them it was just another day, another day in their life of crime. All the custody cells were full.

Reaching for the telephone, the custody sergeant dialled Jack's extension.

"DI MacIntosh? It's Sergeant Wiltshire, custody desk. Your chap is still not speaking."

Sergeant Wiltshire could hear Jack's exasperated tone at the other end of the line. "Yes, OK. Will do." He replaced the receiver and turned to his computer screen.

Karl Poborski was playing dumb.

Arrested at 10.05pm last night. Read his rights. Provided with food and drink. Advised of his right to silence and right to legal assistance.

Nothing.

No reaction.

Nothing at all.

Sergeant Wiltshire updated the custody record. An extension had been

CHAPTER TWENTY-SEVEN

granted to detain Karl Poborski for a further 48 hours.

Maybe tomorrow he would start to talk.

But the clock was ticking.

* * *

Time: 6.30pm

Date: 11th November 2008

Location: Metropolitan Police HQ, London

Jack opened the makeshift incident room door and peered out into the corridor. As luck would have it, DS Cooper was passing by on his way to the canteen.

"Cooper? You busy?"

DS Cooper stopped in his tracks and turned to look back over his shoulder. "Why, you got something?"

Jack shrugged. "Maybe, maybe not. Just wanted someone else to run their eye over something. See what you think." Jack ducked back inside the room, and DS Cooper turned on his heels and followed.

"Shut the door." Jack nodded at the open doorway. "I'd like to keep this under wraps for the time being."

DS Cooper did as he was bade, intrigued by the secrecy. He joined Jack at the side of the incident room table, noticing the various collections of plastic evidence bags lined up in neat rows. Jack was nothing if not methodical.

"Take a look at this. Tell me what you see." Jack pointed at the nearest evidence bag that contained the charred paper remains.

DS Cooper frowned, momentarily, but then took the proffered magnifying glass from Jack's out stretched hand and began to peer at the blackened papers. "Just a bunch of burnt paper, Guv," he murmured. "Are these from Tindleman's office? From his bin? Not much left from what I can see." He raised his head, quizzically. Surely Jack hadn't called him in here just to get his opinion on a bag of barbecued letters.

"Well, that's what I thought too," replied Jack. "At first." He nodded at the three pieces of charred remains sitting on the white blotting paper. "Now have a look at those."

DS Cooper moved his attention to the blotting paper, leaning over to take a closer look. He held the magnifying glass more closely over the small fragmented pieces, chewing his bottom lip as he concentrated.

Although quite badly damaged around the edges, a section of type face in the middle was clearly visible. "….an existing child, Isabel Faraday…in the protective custody of…." DS Copper looked up, raising his eyebrows at Jack. Jack merely nodded. DS Cooper turned his attention to the second, slightly larger piece of burnt paper. It was less damaged, more words were visible, just over three lines. "…. From the members of PRISM….to be termed the Phoenix Project. Experiment due for launch under Space Shuttle Explorer…. Launch date 21st September 1985. All necessary tests to be completed by……" DS Cooper hesitated and let his eyes flicker to the third piece of paper. This one was smaller than the rest, but still had one line of words visible through the scorch marks. "Boris Kreshniov to oversee the Explorer operations. Karl Poborski to be ultimately responsible for…."

DS Cooper stood upright and let out a low whistle.

"My thoughts exactly," nodded Jack. He reached forwards and pinched the edges of each of the three pieces of scorched papers with the tweezers, and returned them to the evidence bag. "How do three pieces of paper, each containing the words Isabel Faraday, The Phoenix Project and Boris Kreshniov, find their way into the waste paper bin of the head of M16?"

* * *

Time: 10.00pm
   Date: 11th November 2008
   Location: Metropolitan Police HQ, London

Karl Poborski barely flinched as his cell door was slammed shut behind him. He looked around his 10' x 6' space and shrugged to himself. He had been in worse situations. The custody sergeant had just informed him that his detention had been authorised for a further 48 hours. He had given the sergeant nothing, not even a flicker of a reaction.

He would say nothing.

He would speak to no one.

He would take his secrets with him.

They were trying to force a solicitor on him, to persuade him to talk. But it would be a waste of time. Call who you want, he had told them. It will be your time and money you are wasting, not mine. The duty solicitor was due tomorrow, but Poborski knew it would make no difference.

He would say nothing.

Laying down on the thin, threadbare mattress, Poborski could feel the flat metal bed beneath. There was one thin, scratchy blanket provided to keep away the chill. Yes, he had certainly been in worse places than this. The Russians knew how to interrogate prisoners. There were no regular custody reviews, no medical check-ups, no meals provided or toilet breaks. You were left in a hole to rot. Until you spoke. Or until you died.

Karl Poborski pulled the scratchy blanket over his body and closed his eyes.

Yes, he had been in worse places than this.

* * *

Time: 11.00pm
   Date: 11th November 2008
   Location: Metropolitan Police HQ, London

It was late, but Jack knew he would never manage any sleep if he didn't make this call now. He had told DS Cooper to head off home; they would be making an early start the next day. Andre Baxter had some talking to do. And so did Poborski. Jack unlocked the door of his car, the key sticking in the frozen lock. The door groaned as he pulled it open and slid inside its icy interior.

His call went to voicemail.

"Hi, PC Daniels. Its DI MacIntosh here. About what we were talking about in the canteen before. I need some more help. I need you to find out about anything you can on the Space Shuttle Explorer programme in the 80s. Call me."

Jack tossed his phone onto the passenger seat and started the engine. It too seemed to groan and protest in the sub-zero temperatures. Pulling out of the car park, careful not to slide on the ice that was already forming on the tarmac, Jack headed towards home. It was a short journey, not long enough for the heaters to make any headway in warming the interior of the car; Jack's breath still billowed out in puffs of wispy white as he pulled up outside his flat.

Jack jumped out of the car and hurried inside. He needed sleep, but knew it's presence probably wouldn't grace him much tonight. Forcing his front door key into the lock, Jack shouldered the door open, looking forward to at least a shot of single malt whisky to warm his insides, even if sleep was to evade him.

He pulled himself wearily up the two flights of stairs to his flat, and he stumbled into the front room, rubbing his tired eyes, his heart leapt into his throat at the vision of a figure silhouetted by the window.

"Jesus!" Jack grabbed the door frame for support and felt for the wall light, snapping it on and bathing the room in a warm glow. "What the hell are you doing here?"

Mac dangled a set of keys from his finger. "You said to let myself in anytime?"

Jack exhaled loudly, his heart rate slowing. "For Christ's sake, Stu, you nearly gave me a heart attack."

"Sorry," grinned Mac, sheepishly. "I didn't think you would be home this late."

Jack waved his brother's apologies away and walked over to the sideboard nearby, pulling two glasses towards him. "Joining me?" He

CHAPTER TWENTY-SEVEN

nodded at the bottle of whisky.

Mac raised his eyebrows and nodded. "Yeah, sure. I don't want to keep you up though." He glanced at his watch, noticing the time.

Jack shook his head and poured two generous measures of the amber liquid. "I don't expect to get much sleep, as usual, so……. Cheers." He handed Mac one of the glasses and raised his own in a gesture of greeting.

Mac accepted the glass and took a small sip, letting the fiery liquid burn his throat as he swallowed. "You still having them then?" He eyed his brother with concern.

"Having what?" Jack avoided Mac's questioning gaze and slumped into the armchair by the window. He took a long swig from his glass, savouring the heat as he swirled the liquid around his mouth. He closed his eyes, knowing his brother would still be searching for him with his eyes.

"You know what," replied Mac quietly, sitting himself down on the small sofa opposite. He stared down into his glass. "The dreams. The nightmares. You still having them?"

Jack's body stiffened slightly, and the muscles in his face tightened and his jaw clenched involuntarily. He shrugged. "Sometimes."

Mac took in his brother's unshaven and tired appearance. "Looks like more than just sometimes to me," he muttered. "Always the same one? The same one as before?"

Jack paused and opened his eyes. He caught his brother's gaze but then looked away and shrugged. Another mouthful of hot liquid burned his throat, giving him a much needed anaesthetic.

"You still seeing that shrink?" Mac persisted.

"She wasn't a shrink." Jack shot his brother a fierce look, an edginess entering his voice. "She was a psychotherapist."

"Whatever. You still seeing her?"

Jack shook his head. He had begun weekly counselling sessions with the police force's own therapist a few years back – when the dreams, the nightmares, had started to become too much. But after a while he had stopped going. Too much analysis of the mind felt uncomfortable.

"Go back and see her – it's nothing to be ashamed of if you're not coping."

Jack shot him another look. "It's fine. I'm fine. It's nothing." He paused, remembering his vivid dream of the night before. "I found our dead mother hanging from a light fixing when I was 4 years old. What else can I say? It happened. I've dealt with it."

Although Jack knew he really hadn't dealt with it at all.

Just at that moment, Jack's mobile phone began to ring. He reached inside his jacket pocket and flipped it open. "Yes?"

It was Isabel. "Is Mac with you?"

Mac.

Jack found it odd hearing his brother's childhood nickname used once again. It had been so long since he had last heard it. To him, he had always been Stuart, or Stu. But Mac? Mac had been what the other schoolboys had called him, what the other schoolboys had taunted him with. And eventually what his street name had been when he had fallen in with the wrong crowd after various foster families had tried but given up on him. The street gangs had been happy enough to pick up the pieces and take him under their wing. "Mac" had survived on the streets. "Mac" would always survive on the streets. But not Stuart.

"Well, is he?" Isabel's voice jolted Jack back into the present.

"Yeah, he's here," replied Jack, trying to focus his mind through the fog of tiredness and whisky. "Look, Isabel, it's late. Can't it wait until tomorrow?" Jack looked at his watch. Tomorrow was nearly today.

"He knew them. He knew my parents."

Jack rubbed a hand over his face, and frowned. "What do you mean? Who knew them?"

"Andre."

"Isabel," Jack sighed. "We've been through all this…. I don't think he did…"

"He did. I know it." Isabel cut in. "I have proof."

"Proof? What proof?"

"Meet me at the station, first thing in the morning. And bring your brother. You need him to tell you where they sent the papers."

CHAPTER TWENTY-SEVEN

* * *

Time: 3.15am
   Date: 12th November 2008
   Location: Kettles Yard Mews, London

Jack thrust open the window at the front of his second floor flat and braced himself against the sudden rush of icy cold air. It was late. Or early, it depended how you viewed it. He didn't know how late; he'd stopped looking at his watch hours ago. But sleep evaded him. It danced playfully around in front of him, teasing him, seducing him even – but it still evaded him all the same.

Stuart seemed to have no such trouble finding sleep – he lay sprawled on the sofa under a blanket, lightly snoring, oblivious to Jack's turmoil.

Outside it was quiet; the only sound being an occasional car or taxi passing by underneath his roadside window, or a distant car alarm or police siren singing through the heavy darkness. Jack perched himself on the window ledge and scanned the view outside. Rows and rows of tiled rooftops spread out in front of him, chimney pots rising like totem poles, the occasional treetop poking through. It was a view he liked. He enjoyed looking out, watching the darkness, watching the shadows; imagining those that lived inside were sleeping soundly in their beds, oblivious to the world outside – oblivious to those who were wide awake and watching. Always watching.

Jack found it calming. Life was going on all around him; nothing stopped; nothing changed. He cradled a fresh mug of tea on his lap, watching the steam rise from the mug as it hit the cold night air. He sipped it, grateful for its warmth. He had toyed with the idea of adding a shot or two of Glenmorangie, spying the almost empty bottle by the side of Mac's sleeping body. But his head was already far too cluttered. And the shots he had shared with Mac earlier had done nothing to beckon sleep.

He glanced down at his notebook, lying open in his lap. He hadn't progressed very far.

Faraday
Prism
Phoenix Project
SS Explorer
Fleming/Poborski
Kreshniov
Andre
Tindleman/Shafer
The Russians

All entries followed by a question mark.

How one linked to the other Jack was no closer to working out.

He exhaled, quietly, not wanting to wake his sleeping brother. His warm breath sent small wispy puffs of condensation swirling towards the open window.

His brother; Stuart, Mac – how did he fit into all this? They hadn't seen each other in how many years? And yet here he was, sleeping on his sofa. Drinking his whisky.

The Faradays. Were they alive? Were they dead? Were they resting in a remote cemetery in the Kent countryside as Isabel had been led to believe for all these years…or….

The more Jack thought, the more confusion fogged his brain. He pushed himself off the window ledge and soundlessly pulled the window shut behind him. The room was now icy cold and he shivered as he went to pass by the sleeping mound on the sofa. Stuart. A twinge of childhood memories gripped his heart. Being separated from Stuart after their mother's suicide had affected them both severely; something Jack wasn't sure could ever be made good again. Foster families had tried to keep them together, but Stuart's behaviour meant that they had to be separated. No amount of counselling could deal with the hurt and rejection they both felt. Jack picked up the near empty bottle of whisky and took a generous swig. Cluttered brain or not, he needed this.

And it was better than a cigarette.

Turning to walk back to his bedroom, Jack paused and instinctively

CHAPTER TWENTY-SEVEN

drew the blanket up around his sleeping brother's shoulders. He was still his baby brother; he still needed Jack.

Just at that moment Jack's phone chirped; an incoming message. He frowned as he glanced at the screen and saw that the message was from PC Trevor Daniels. Opening the message, Jack noted the time as 03.17 – what was PC Daniels doing sending messages at this time of night? Or was insomnia rife through all levels of the police force?

"Result on the Phoenix Project," the message read. "Article left at front desk. Urgent."

That was it. Nothing more. No elaboration. No explanation. Nothing.

Jack closed the message and took both the phone and the remnants of the whisky into his bedroom.

Phoenix Project or no Phoenix Project, he needed to salvage some sleep.

* * *

CHAPTER TWENTY-EIGHT

Time: 7.45am
  Date: 12th November 2008
  Location: Metropolitan Police HQ, London

"You need to see these." Isabel thrust three worn photographs towards Jack as he and Mac dragged themselves out of Jack's car. Jack's desire to sleep last night had not been enough; whether it was the whisky, or the memories of their mother, something had kept him from peaceful slumber. Even Mac, who had seemed to sleep soundly, looked as though he hadn't had a wink.

Jack hesitantly took the proffered pictures, glancing down at them momentarily.

"Isabel…" Jack made to walk past her, into the rear of the police station. "Now really isn't a good time. We need to go and chat with our friend Andre; this will have to wait. And Poborski is due to be interviewed this morning. The custody clock is ticking." Jack's mind was upstairs in the makeshift incident room; the evidence bag with the charred papers from Tindleman's office were waiting for him.

Isabel moved sideways and blocked his entrance; holding her hands up in front of his chest. "No, you don't understand," she said, urgently. "These aren't just any old pictures, family snaps, - you really do need to see them. Now."

Jack paused, looking into Isabel's eyes and seeing the urgency flowing through them like electricity. He recognised the haunted look that clouded

CHAPTER TWENTY-EIGHT

her. He glanced back at Mac, who was following him up the path to the rear entrance of the station. He just merely shrugged in response.

"Really," she repeated her voice calmer now. Her eyes pleaded with Jack. "You need to see them. He gave them to me. Andre."

Jack looked back down at the pictures in his hand. The one on the top he vaguely recognised – similar if not identical to the one he recalled seeing on Isabel's mantelpiece back at her flat. He opened his mouth to say something, but Isabel cut in.

"Read the back. There's an inscription." She paused while Jack turned the photograph over. "He knew them, Jack. Andre really *did* know them."

Jack read the inscription, written in small, neat handwriting, and felt his mouth turn curiously dry. He flicked through to the next photograph, and recognised the face of the man almost as instantly as Isabel had done.

"Where did you…?" began Jack, all thoughts about confronting Andre with the evidence bag upstairs momentarily slipping from his mind.

"They came from Andre," explained Isabel, relaxing her tense shoulders now she knew she had Jack's full attention. "They were in the envelope you left for me." She paused. "He must have kept them all this time."

* * *

Time: 4.00pm
Date: 26th June 1985
Location: The Glade, Church Street, Albury, Surrey

Isabel reached out and took a huge buttercream biscuit from the plate and ran back out into the garden. Her tricycle sitting beneath her favourite tree, and she ran gleefully towards it. She plonked herself down on the grass under the shady branches and bit hungrily into the biscuit. She sighed, happily, to herself and crunched her way through the rest of the biscuit, smearing buttercream on her fingers and cheeks.

Being 5 was great.

Isabel couldn't imagine being any happier than she was right now. As she chuckled to herself and finished her biscuit, she heard her mother's voice singing out across the garden.

"Isabel....! Isabel......!"

Isabel spied her mother standing by the back door, looking out across the patio towards the trees at the bottom of the garden.

"It's time for presents!"

Isabel yelled with delight and skipped her way back towards the house, where she saw her mother, father and favourite uncle all waiting to greet her on her very special day.

"This is the best day ever!" she shrieked as she ran into her mother's side and hugged her tight.

And there he was.

Standing right next to her; his own pale grey eyes gleaming and laughing.

Uncle.

Her favourite Uncle

Andre.

***

Time: 7.50am

Date: 12th November 2008

Location: Metropolitan Police HQ, London

Jack dragged his feet across the lobby towards the front desk; Mac and Isabel hung back. His eyes stung from the brightness of the fluorescent strip lights buzzing overhead. Frowning from the brightness and sleep deprivation, Jack caught the attention of the Custody Sergeant behind the front desk.

"You have something for me?" Jack's voice sounded thick and heavy. He rubbed his throat, the memory of the warm lubrication of the whisky from the night before was a distant memory. "From PC Daniels?"

Sergeant Wiltshire nodded and reached underneath the counter.

"Yes, young lad was most insistent that you have it. Can't think why."

CHAPTER TWENTY-EIGHT

The Sergeant gave a small laugh as he proffered what looked like a piece of paper and a magazine towards Jack. "Seems to be one of those farfetched American magazines – someone claiming to have been abducted by aliens or something."

Jack waved off the explanation and took the folded piece of paper and magazine from the desk sergeant's hand. It did look like one of the sensationalist magazines, so popular over in the States. He gave it a cursory glance and was about to read the attached note when Sergeant Wiltshire continued.

"And you're wanted in the interview rooms – Karl Poborski is to be interviewed this morning whether he likes it or not. Something about getting an interview strategy together."

Jack nodded and stuffed the magazine in his back pocket. "Cooper, can you show Mac and Isabel upstairs to the canteen. Get them a coffee. Then we need to go sort out Poborski."

* * *

Time: 8.30am
Date: 12th November 2008
Location: Metropolitan Police HQ, London

"Ok so you go and handle Poborski. I'm going to pay our friend Andre a visit." Jack drained his mug of coffee and reached for his chewing gum. "What time is the duty solicitor coming?"

"'Bout 9.30 I think," answered DS Cooper, finishing the rest of his takeaway egg and bacon toasted sandwich he had managed to pick up from the deli around the corner. "Don't reckon it will be a very long interview by all accounts…..he's still refusing to talk."

Jack shrugged. "See what you can do. All we can do is ask the questions. If he chooses not to speak then so be it. We have enough on him for the theft of the cash at least."

"And you? How are you going to tackle Andre?"

Jack picked up the photographs Isabel had given them and cast his eyes over them one more time. "Well, he *certainly* has some talking to do. I can't help but feel our friend Andre is playing us. I'm just not sure what the game is."

DS Cooper nodded and rose from his chair. He picked up his notebook which contained the list of questions he and Jack had decided Poborski needed to be asked; the draft interview strategy and expected time line. "Well, looking at this, I'm guessing I will be done in about 20 minutes if he "no comments" all the way through.

Jack nodded. "I'll catch you later. I'll be in interview room 1 if you care to join when you're finished."

Both DS Cooper and Jack headed their separate ways down towards the interview rooms.

***

Time: 8.30am
Date: 12th November 2008
Location: Canteen, Metropolitan Police HQ, London

The canteen was busy. Mac and Isabel managed to find themselves a spare table in the far corner, away from the hustle and bustle of officers settling down to a hurried breakfast or their dinner, depending what shift they were on. An enticing smell of sizzling bacon, sausages and eggs wafted through the canteen, making their stomachs growl. Mac had got Jack to order him a full breakfast; two slices of toast, eggs, bacon, sausages, hash browns and baked beans. Plus a large mug of milky tea. He tackled it, hungrily, stuffing a large forkful of hash browns and beans into his mouth.

Isabel nursed a black coffee and pushed around a slice of toast and jam on her plate. She wasn't hungry. Her body needed food, she knew that. Her stomach was growling with hunger but she couldn't face eating. She felt as though her whole life had been turned upside down, and her insides

CHAPTER TWENTY-EIGHT

felt ragged.

"Did you always trust him?" Isabel's voice sounded small and lost amongst the noise sweeping through the busy station canteen. "The whole time you knew him, you always trusted him?"

Mac paused, his hand hovering before his mouth, the fork loaded with scrambled eggs and sausage. A few baked beans dripped down into his plate.

"You mean Andre?" He lowered his fork back down onto the plate and reached for his mug of tea.

Isabel nodded, her haunted eyes seeking Mac's. "Yes, you never once thought he lied to you?"

Mac took a large gulp of his milky tea and then shook his head. "No, never. I trusted the guy 100%. He helped me when I needed it most."

Isabel's eyes lowered and she resumed nudging the slice of now cold toast around her plate once again. A congealed blob of raspberry jam fell over the side onto the table. "What about the papers?"

"What papers?"

"The papers Andre posted, while we were at Marie's flat. You didn't think that was odd? The courier turning up in the middle of the night? I saw him hand them over. Told the courier to hurry."

Mac shrugged and picked up his fork again. "Not really. He said he was posting them to keep them safe." He thrust the fork into his mouth again and savoured the taste of the creamy scrambled egg and meaty sausage. "I believed him."

"But who was he sending them to?"

* * *

Time: 2.45am
Date: 9th November 2008
Location: L'Apartament Blancos, L'Avenue du Soleil, Paris

Andre opened the door to the flat before the courier had a chance to knock. A heavily clad courier in motorcycle leathers filled the doorframe.

"Rapide." Andre handed the courier the envelope. "Aussi vite que vous pouvez – en Angleterre."

Isabel watched from behind the door to the kitchen as Andre pulled out a bundle of notes from his back pocket. He handed the notes to the motorcycle courier who merely nodded and stuffed them inside his backpack. With a curt nod, the courier turned and left.

"Rappelez – rapide!" called out Andre as the motorcyclist disappeared into the darkness.

***

Time: 9.00am
Date: 12th November 2008
Location: interview rooms, Metropolitan Police HQ, London

Jack flung open the door to Interview Room 1, sending it crashing into the wall behind. From the gouge in the plasterwork, this was something that had been done many a time before. He strode over to the table in the centre of the small, stuffy room and threw the series of photographs Isabel had given him in front of Andre. Andre stood up from the chair he had been seated at and merely raised an eyebrow at the dramatic entrance.

"How about you start by telling me the truth?" thundered Jack, pushing Andre forcefully back down into his seat. "Right here…. Right now." Jack's eyes flashed with anger; he hated being lied to above anything else. "You sent these pictures to Isabel. I need you to tell me why."

Andre reached out and calmly picked up one of the photographs. Isabel was on her tricycle; Mrs Faraday was smiling at her side. Andre let his eyes sweep across the photograph until he saw himself with a protective hand on Mrs Faraday's shoulder. He stared deeply into his own eyes – where he saw a man full of hope, full of happiness, full of belief, staring back at him. A man looking forward to the months ahead, excited at the

CHAPTER TWENTY-EIGHT

prospect of what they were about to embark on. But within months of this picture being taken, the family he had grown to love so much, the family he had come to treat as his own, would be ripped apart. Forever.

"You knew them…. The Faradays. And you knew Isabel." Jack paused, waiting for a reaction from Andre. There appeared to be none. "I need you to start from the beginning and tell me everything you know. And I mean everything this time. You let a poor girl believe her parents were still alive only to shatter her hopes less than 24 hours later. Why did you do that? Why did you need to do that? That girl is a mess right now, because of you. How did you know the Faradays?" Jack placed his hands on the table and leant forwards, fixing Andre with his eyes. "You need to start talking….and fast." His voice was calmer now, but his hunger for the truth was only just beginning. He watched as Andre continued to stare at the photograph in his hand. He watched as Andre's eyes flickered with recognition, and something else……. Was that remorse? Guilt? Sadness? Reaching into his jacket pocket, Jack dropped the evidence bag from upstairs onto the table. "And while you're at it, you can tell me another thing – how did the papers that you had in your possession, the papers everyone was chasing their tails around Europe for, how did they end up being burnt to a crisp in the office of the head of M16? Burnt only minutes if not seconds, before he takes his own life?"

Andre dropped the photograph that he was holding in his hand. Jack didn't wait for him to respond.

"I want to know *how* you knew him. *Why* you knew him. And how *your* papers ended up next to *his* dead body? "

***

Time: 9.15am
   Date: 12th November 2008
   Location: Interview room 3, Metropolitan Police HQ, London

"The time is 9.15am and we are in interview room 3 at Metropolitan Police

HQ. This interview is being conducted by myself, DS Cooper. Also present is….." DS Cooper passed and nodded at his colleague next to him.

"DC Amanda Cassidy." DC Amanda Cassidy straightened her skirt and tucked a stray lock of her jet black hair behind her ear.

"Please state your full name for the tape." DS Cooper nodded across the table at Poborski, who was staring down at his lap, making no eye contact. He remained silent. "Please state your full name for the purposes of the tape," repeated Cooper, his voice taking on a slight edginess. Again, Poborski refused to make eye contact and remained silent.

"For the purpose of the tape, the suspect has refused to answer." DS Cooper opened his notebook on the table in front of him. "From our records we are interviewing Karl Aleksey Poborski, date of birth and address unknown. Also present is Mr Poborski's solicitor. Please introduce yourself for the tape." DS Cooper nodded at the young woman sitting by Poborski's side, looking apprehensive. He reckoned she must be a trainee solicitor, or at least only newly qualified, as she looked terrified.

"Miss….Miss Eleanor Horscroft. From Ableman and Greene Solicitors." The young solicitor's voice was faint and quiet; DS Cooper could detect a tremble in her soft tones.

"Thank you. Today's date is 12th November 2008 and the time is now 9.18am. We are interviewing Karl Poborski in the presence of his solicitor on the suspicion of theft, murder, kidnapping and false imprisonment. I will remind you that you do not have to say anything, but it may harm your defence if you do not mention when questioned something that you later rely on in court. Everything that you do say may be given in evidence. Do you understand?"

Poborski gave no indication as to whether her had heard or understood. He remained with his eyes lowered, and he remained silent.

* * *

Time: 9.25am
    Date: 12th November 2008

CHAPTER TWENTY-EIGHT

Location: interview rooms, Metropolitan Police HQ, London

"I've told you already – I knew the Faradays from the Phoenix Project." Andre stared past Jack, avoiding looking at the Detective Inspector's enquiring eyes. "We've been through all this before."

"Ah yes, the Phoenix Project," thundered Jack. "Evidence of which I have yet to see." Jack was still standing in front of the table, too agitated to take a seat. "Now…how about we start this again. With the truth."

"I've already said……"

Jack slammed his fist down onto the table in front of Andre, and leant in until his face was only inches from Andre's. "I said the truth! I have a young woman upstairs who has been to hell and back over the last few days – one minute her parents are dead, the next they are alive. Now they are dead again. Which is it, Andre? Which story is she to believe?"

Andre looked up and held Jack's piercing gaze. Jack noticed his eyes were glassy. "They didn't die in the car crash back in 86. That was a setup…it was faked." Andre paused, and dropped his gaze back down to the picture of the Faradays. "It wasn't them."

* * *

Date: 25th September 1986
    Time: 22.07pm
    Location: 25 kilometres outside Lyon, Rhone Valley, France

Andre checked his watch for the thousandth time. The seconds were ticking by so slowly; time seemed to have turned and seemed to be crawling backwards. Poborski's voice echoed around his head.

"Make sure there are no mistakes." The voice was cold. Unemotional. "This has to be perfect."

There was a light drizzle in the air, the dampness clinging to Andre's face as he waited.

Waited.

Waited.

The moon slipped gratefully behind the thickening clouds which were bubbling up in force, and turning the night sky into a dense inky blackness. Andre edged out from underneath the trees which had been affording him much needed cover for the last half an hour. They were late. The drenched leaves on the overhanging branches skimmed his head, sending fat raindrops bouncing and trickling down the back of his neck. He shivered and looked up at the hill in front of him. The road was deserted, snaking its way up and out of sight, disappearing into the murky darkness. They had chosen this spot well.

Andre nervously checked his watch again. Come on. Come on. Come on. Don't let me down.

"This has to be perfect." The voice echoed through his head once again. "Make sure there are no mistakes……no mistakes….no mistakes."

Just as Andre was contemplating the unthinkable – that they weren't coming at all – a set of headlights blinked into view. They headed steadily down the hill towards him. Andre stood rooted to the spot, his pulse quickening, and feeling the drizzle turn into heavier droplets of steady rain.

The headlights stopped a few metres away from him, and then the lights died, plunging the road back into darkness. Two figures emerged from the front of the battered dark coloured van, both hunched against the rain that was now cascading from the clouds above. They headed towards him.

"Where's the car?" asked the first figure. Andre did not know his name; did not want to know his name. That had been the deal. No name; no questions; no problems. Andre noticed that the man had a matted black beard that hid his lips from view.

Andre nodded towards the dense undergrowth behind them. "In there."

The bearded figure nodded, curtly, and headed towards the trees. Andre didn't know what else to do, so followed on behind. A few moments later they emerged, pushing a dark coloured vehicle into view. The tyres crunched noisily over the stones and gravel by the side of the deserted road. Andre glanced nervously over his shoulder, expecting the sound to

CHAPTER TWENTY-EIGHT

draw attention to them – expecting someone, anyone, to appear out of the gloom and discover them.

"Open the door," barked the bearded figure, brushing roughly past Andre as he headed back towards his van. Andre stumbled over to the car and fumbled with the driver's door handle. Behind him he heard muted voices, then the sound of something heavy being dragged from the van, landing with a soft thud on the muddy tarmac.

Andre turned, his stomach tightening at the sight of the body bag lying prostrate on the ground. The rain splattered noisily against the heavy duty plastic. A second figure now emerged from the darkness, grabbing hold of one end of the body bag and dragging it away from the roadside and towards the protection of the trees – towards Andre and the car they had just dragged out of the undergrowth. Again Andre did not know the man's name. Again, it was part of the deal. This one, however, was clean shaven. Andre could see his thick lips grimacing as he struggled with the weight of the bag.

The zip was quickly undone, its raw sound cutting through the wind and rain like a finely sharpened knife. A lump formed in Andre's throat. He stood transfixed, unable to move, his hair plastered to his forehead by the rain which was running in rivets down his face, dripping from the end of his nose, his ears and chin.

The body bag was now fully open. Andre saw flesh. Lots of flesh. The flesh was deathly white, even in the night time gloom. An arm. A hand. A glimpse of a face. Andre swallowed hard again. He was glad the night sky was as dark as it was, glad the moon had stayed away. Glad the rest of the body was swathed in shadows.

"Here, take this," commanded the bearded figure, holding up a limp arm from the body bag and gesturing for Andre to take hold of it.

Andre had to force his feet to move forwards, they felt like they were held fast in quick sand or cement. They obeyed, albeit slowly. He bent down and gingerly took hold of the pale arm. It was male. Curling, thick hairs covered the forearm. There was a large hand, with neatly clipped fingernails. It was surprisingly heavy. Andre had expected the arm to feel light, with all life extinguished, but it weighed heavily in his hands.

"Come on quickly, we must be quick." The clean shaven figure had taken hold of the dead man's feet and was already lifting them up and out of the body bag. Andre noticed the dead man was wearing carefully pleated trousers and a pair of expensive looking, shiny brogues. Well-polished, well looked after.

Andre gripped the pallid arm more firmly, closing his fingers around the cold, pale flesh. He tried to look away as he pulled the man's torso from the bag. He didn't want to see his face. He didn't want to see his eyes. Andre grunted as he heaved with both hands – helping to lift the man's upper body high into the air, free of the bag. Then he and the clean shaven figure stumbled awkwardly over to the car with their cargo. After resting briefly against the bonnet, they heaved the body into the driver's seat, pushing his stiff legs underneath the steering wheel and placing his lifeless hands in his lap. The dead man's head lolled forwards, his chin resting on his chest.

"Belt him up," barked the bearded figure, nodding at Andre before turning back towards the body bag behind them.

Andre reached inside the car and pulled the driver's seat belt down and round the dead man's upper torso. He couldn't reach the seat belt socket on the other side of the seat. He pulled harder on the belt, trying to reach further around the body, but still couldn't make it reach far enough. Andre grimaced as he lent further and further inside the car, his face now only inches from the dead man's cheeks. Andre closed his eyes, refusing to look. He mustn't see the eyes; he mustn't see the eyes.

He pulled fiercely on the seat belt and fumbled blindly with the clasp, searching with his fingers for the socket. He clenched his teeth, forcing his eyes shut even tighter. The smell was beginning to waft up into his nose. A smell he had never smelt before. A smell he never wanted to smell again. It was sweet, yet rotten at the same time. Nausea filled his senses.

At last Andre found the seat belt socket with his fingers and snapped the clasp tightly into place with a welcoming "click". He paused, his breath coming in short, sharp rasps. He could feel the raindrops at the back of

CHAPTER TWENTY-EIGHT

his neck mixing with his sweat. As he paused inside the car he heard the sound of grunts and grimaces nearby, then the car seemed to move and rock from side to side.

Snapping open his eyes, Andre immediately felt the bile erupt in his throat. In front of him, on the passenger seat, barely inches from his own face, two more pale, pallid eyes stared out at him. The eyes belonged to another deathly white, harrowed face, almost identical to the one now sitting in the driver's seat. Her mouth was slightly open; her lips heavily made up with scarlet red lipstick, slightly parted. Her tongue lolled lifelessly between a set of pearly white teeth.

Andre pushed himself out of the car, scrambling away from the bodies. He caught sight of a second empty body bag behind him.

Inside the car now sat a man and a woman, both fully clothed, yet the life had been squeezed out of them many days before. The bearded figure slammed the passenger side door shut, the clean shaven man pushing Andre out of the way to do the same with the driver's door. With both doors shut, both bodies were now finally encased inside their metal tomb.

Andre stumbled further backwards, until he eventually reached the van's bonnet. He clutched the cold metal to steady himself, his legs no longer having the strength to support him. He turned his face up towards the heaviness of the night sky, welcomed the feel of the cold sting of raindrops on his skin. Nausea continued to coarse through him like a fast flowing river. He turned to the side and retched.

The sound of the van's doors opening behind him made Andre turn around.

"Thank you," spoke a hushed, gentle voice. "We couldn't have done this without you."

Andre looked into the face of a woman – her hair neatly pulled back from her delicate features, a red headscarf wrapped around her to protect her from the cold and rain. She reached out and placed a hand lightly on Andre's arm, gently squeezing.

Andre nodded; he had nothing left to say.

Just then a man appeared at his side, offering his own hand. Andre took it, and shook it slowly.

"You have taken such a risk for us," said the man, his voice low. His face had a haunted, pinched look, and his soft brown eyes did nothing to conceal his anguish. "We can't thank you enough."

Again, Andre merely nodded.

"They said you would need these." The man reached into his jacket pocket and brought out a fistful of jewellery and two watches, placing them into Andre's quivering hands. "And these." The man slipped two wallets out of his rear trouser pocket, placing them on top of the jewellery.

"Look out for Isabel for us, won't you?" pleaded the woman, stepping forwards, tears beginning to well up in her eyes. "Look after her. Watch out for her. And one day, tell her…..tell her why we….why we had to do this?" The woman's voice hitched and broke, the tears now streaming down her cheeks. She pulled a handkerchief from her sleeve and buried her face.

Christopher Faraday placed a comforting arm around his wife's shoulder, and steered them back towards the waiting van.

While the moon still languished behind the heavy storm clouds, Andre leant inside and released the handbrake. Between the three of them they managed to push the car towards a break in the undergrowth. The two bodies, now dressed in the Faraday's jewellery and engraved wristwatches, bounced and juddered as the car rumbled over small rocks and boulders, quickly gathering speed as is headed down the ravine below.

Andre and the two men stood back and watched. The car had soon disappeared from sight. All that could be heard was bumping and scraping as the car sped towards the bottom. After what seemed like an eternity, Andre heard the final sound. An earth shuddering explosion as the car reached its final destination, coming to rest on the jagged rocks below. Andre saw the bright yellow and orange fire ball erupt through the murky night, and knew that the job had been done.

* * *

CHAPTER TWENTY-NINE

Time: 9.45am
Date: 12th November 2008
Location: interview rooms, Metropolitan Police HQ, London

"How did you do it?" Jack leant forwards, his elbows digging into the hardwood table, fingers laced together under his chin. He needed a shave; the bristles pricked an untimely reminder into his skin. He fixed Andre with a long stare, wanting to get in behind those pale grey eyes; eyes that he was sure knew so much, and were hiding even more.

Andre closed his eyes momentarily, blocking out the detective's penetrating gaze. He leant back in his creaking chair, and breathed in deeply – seeming to be savouring the silence. Then he snapped his eyes open.

"Two mortuary assistants from the local pathology rooms," he said, finally, meeting Jack's stare.

"Names?"

Andre shook his head, slowly and deliberately. "No names. That was the deal. I had an acquaintance who worked at the local hospital…he knew someone, who knew someone…. Who knew someone else. I had no idea who they were; they had no idea who I was. It was better that way."

Jack nodded, thoughtfully. "And the people in the car?" Who were they?"

Andre shrugged. "Two unidentified bodies – maybe homeless, no one really knew. Certainly no family or friends to collect them from the mortuary."

"And you placed them inside the car…. The Faraday's car…..and put identifying items on them such as watches, jewellery, rings on fingers. And left items like wallets, driving licenses, inside the car before......" Jack paused. "Before rolling them down a ravine."

Andre gave a slight shudder, then nodded. Just thinking about that night made him feel like he was back there on the rain drenched road, with mud and puddles splashing up his legs as he pushed and strained to get the car moving. He could almost taste once again the mixture of raindrops and sweat trickling down his face and seeping into the corners of his mouth as the car lurched further towards the edge of the ravine. Remembering the heaviness of the bodies, the coldness of their skin. How the deathly pallor of their faces seemed to gleam even in the absence of any moonlight. And the eyes.... Those staring, haunting eyes, so cold and lifeless.

Andre shook his head sharply to rid himself of the unwanted memories.

"Who identified them?" questioned Jack, although he half expected the answer he would get.

"I did," replied Andre, regaining his composure. "After we had finished at the ravine....I went back home and telephoned the police to report them missing." He paused, refusing to let any more memories of that night invade his thoughts. "It wasn't long before a patrol car passed by and saw the flames. The car was identified as belonging to the Faradays, and the police put two and two together. Then they contacted me."

"And you went along to identify the bodies," finished Jack. "You told the police it was them, the Faradays. You identified two complete strangers as being your friends."

Andre nodded, slowly. "They had no other next of kin. I was the closest they had."

"Convenient", muttered Jack, pushing himself away from the table and leaning back in his chair.

"They were already dead...the bodies I mean. Nobody killed them." Andre dropped his gaze to his lap. "No one knew who they were."

"They would have had family, or friends, somewhere. What gave you the right to take that away from them?"

Andre looked up sharply. His eyes were as hard as ice. "It had to be done.

CHAPTER TWENTY-NINE

Poborski was after the Faradays; he was insistent they should be killed. He was obsessed. He was nervous about the information they had, what they knew about the Project and what went wrong. Information that would destroy him. And they also had his money."

"Ah yes," nodded Jack." The money. I wondered when we might get around to that. How did Poborski know about the cash the Faradays had?"

"Everyone knew; it wasn't a secret. Everyone in the Project, that is. After the accident, the Project founders turned on Poborski and Kreshniov. They wanted someone to blame for the mistakes, they needed someone to take the rap for the disaster that the Project had now become. The Russians were coming down heavily on the Project founders – they had invested a lot of money in the experiment, and had just seen it all go up in smoke. Someone needed to pay. The Project founders had to back track fast. They refused to give Poborski his agreed bonus – he was meant to get $1m after the experiment was complete – but they refused. Instead they gave it to the Faradays in the hope it would buy their loyalty, buy their silence. They wanted to persuade them to stay in the US under careful watch of the Project founders. But the Faradays just took the cash and disappeared."

"With your help," added Jack, not taking his eyes from Andre. "Let's not forget that."

Andre gave a curt nod. "It was too risky just to try hiding, taking on a different identity. People would still be looking for them. Poborski would still be looking for them. The best thing was if they could disappear…. Permanently."

"Again, with your help," repeated Jack.

Andre shrugged and a small smile flickered across his lips. "Dying is easier than you think."

"And Poborski never suspected that you double crossed him?" Jack's question hung in the air like a hangman's noose. " He believed that you had caused the car crash that had killed the Faradays; he never once thought that they might still be alive and well?"

Andre repeated the shrug. But the smile had gone from his lips. "I don't think so. If he had, I don't think I would still be here today, do you?"

Jack nodded to himself. "Possibly not." His mind was now racing; pieces of this bizarre story were now slotting into place. Some at least; but not all. "And Kreshniov? Did he know of your little plan with Poborski?"

"Yes, he knew," nodded Andre.

"So, if the Faradays didn't really die in that car accident, where are they now?" Jack fixed Andre with a cool stare. "And while we're at it, I've got bodies stacked up here left, right and centre. You need to start telling me why. Let's start with Chief Superintendent Liddell."

* * *

Time: 10.00am
    Date: 12th November 2008
    Location: Interview Room 3, Metropolitan Police HQ, London

"Where were you on the evening of 9th November?" DS Cooper stared across the interview room table at Karl Poborski, but was met with no response.

"Were you in the region of L'Avenue du Soleil in Paris?"

Again, zero response.

"I put it to you that on the evening of 9th November 2008 you fatally stabbed a Simon Shafer, experienced MI6 secret service officer, with the intent to end his life. What can you tell me about that?"

Again, no response from the other side of the table.

"I also put it to you that you kidnapped and falsely imprisoned a Miss Isabel Faraday, keeping her against her will. What can you tell me about that?"

Again, DS Cooper's questions were met with no response from Karl Poborski.

Cooper paused and looked sideways at DC Amanda Cassidy. She gave a half smile and shrugged in response. They both glanced up at the clock on the wall above the tape machine; they had been questioning Poborski

CHAPTER TWENTY-NINE

for 45 minutes and the man had not uttered a sound. Not even a breath.

"We have evidence to link you to both crimes, Mr Poborski, you would be most wise to answer our questions now while you have the chance." DS Cooper put down his pen and closed his notebook. They weren't getting anywhere.

"Detective, my client does not have to answer your questions, as you are well aware." Miss Eleanor Horscroft's faint voice echoed around the bare walls of the small interview room. She picked nervously at the hem of her tailored suit jacket. "I think we have established that he does not wish to say anything, therefore I request that this interview be terminated."

DS Cooper fixed the young solicitor with an amused look. This was the first time he had heard her speak since announcing her name for the purposes of the tape at the beginning of the interview. He noticed how her cheeks were tinged red and she continued to pick at the lining of the sleeve of her suit jacket, her gaze lowered to her lap. Shaking his head to himself he raised his eyebrows at DC Amanda Cassidy and she nodded in agreement.

"Interview suspended at the request of Mr Karl Poborski's legal representative. The time is 10.04am." Cooper leant across and clicked the off button on the tape recorder. He rose from his chair and fixed Poborski with a penetrating stare. "Maybe some time back in your cell will allow you to rethink, Poborski. We've got you for another 2 days. This is not over yet."

Poborski's head shot up and, for the first time that morning, Cooper noted that Poborski was listening.

"Oh, did they not tell you?" DS Cooper allowed another small smile to creep across his lips as he made his way towards the door. "We've been authorised to keep you for up to 96 hours. Enjoy your cell."

With that, he opened the door and allowed DC Amanda Cassidy to exit in front of him.

* * *

Time: 10.15am
Date: 12th November 2008
Location: interview rooms, Metropolitan Police HQ, London

"Chief Superintendent Liddell and Charles Tindleman were related by marriage." Andre took a sip from the Coke can he had been handed; the polystyrene cups of bitter tasting coffee had long been discarded. "Liddell's wife, Catherine, was Charles Tindleman's sister. They spent a lot of time together in and out of work."

"OK, I didn't know that," nodded Jack, sipping his coffee and wincing at the taste. "Continue."

"Back in early 1985, both Liddell and Tindleman were on a fact finding mission to the USA. Liddell was an up and coming Detective Inspector, a bit like yourself DI MacIntosh. Tindleman was a rookie MI6 agent, still wet behind the ears. They were sent to the USA to evaluate the relationship between the western world and the Eastern bloc. Remember this was the 1980's – the Cold War was still frosty, although beginning to thaw. The Iron Curtain was still hanging, although looking a little frayed around the edges. There was still a lot of secrecy and mistrust. Thatcher's Conservative Britain wanted to promote strong ties with the USA, so Liddell and Tindleman found themselves sent over as kind of ambassadors if you like – representatives of the Metropolitan Police and the Security Services. A new, young and fresh-looking approach."

Jack nodded at Andre to continue.

"It was mostly a promotional exercise, something for the headlines back home. Nothing more than a publicity stunt for the Government really. Liddell and Tindleman were treated like royalty by the Reagan administration. They were taken on tours of all the main political and security establishments – the Pentagon, the White House. They shook a lot of hands. Drank a lot of coffee.

"One of their tours was to the NASA headquarters in Washington DC, and also to the Kennedy Space Centre. Space exploration was big business at this time, and the USA were at the fore front of this new and exciting world. Their space programme was worth billions of dollars. Something many Americans were immensely proud of.

"Whilst at NASA HQ they are said to have met the acquaintance of Boris Kreshniov. Over the course of a few drinks, a proposal was put to Liddell and Tindleman. They would be given unprecedented access to highly confidential and top secret information concerning space exploration, something even the British Government wasn't even aware of yet – in return for a small favour. They were asked to act as arbiters – to run an independent eye over the Phoenix Project data and give their opinion as to its authenticity. In return, not only did they get unprecedented access to top secret intelligence information, something which would have appealed to Tindleman, they also got to share a tidy $1m between them. This was Poborski's touch – his little sweetener for them."

Andre could see Jack's face developing a frown. He held up a "bear with me" hand and carried on.

"The Russians were nervous about investing so much in the Project. They wanted independent verification; someone not connected to the Project or to PRISM. They wanted someone to confirm the data was correct and that the experiment was viable. So, as far as Poborski was concerned, independent verification was exactly what they would get. He would make sure of it. And who doesn't trust the British?"

Andre could see Jack's face remained unconvinced.

"The respective Mrs Liddell and Mrs Tindleman were high maintenance ladies," continued Andre. "Used to a certain kind of lifestyle. Their husbands had good jobs, but progress up the career ladder was slow. And with interest rates being what they were, money was always in short supply. The offer from the Project was more than a little enticing. Both Liddell and Tindleman needed to climb high in their respective ranks, and they felt honoured to have been chosen to be involved at such a high level, involved in such an historic event. Just think what it would do to their careers when the experiment was a huge success – they could say they were there at the very beginning, at the very epicentre.

"So they agreed. Neither knew the first thing about the data they were being asked to examine. But that didn't matter; that was not what they were asked to do. All they had to do was verify that the data was authentic; had not been tampered with in any way. Poborski assured them that everything was in order and that the experiment could not fail. All safety checks had been completed successfully many times over. What could go wrong? So Liddell and Tindleman signed on the dotted line and collected a cool half a million dollars each.

"After the accident, they were wracked with guilt. Poborski contacted them and told them that under no circumstances were they to breathe a word to anyone about the experiment or the existence of the Project. *No one must know.* Not even their families. If they did, they would be killed; it was that simple. Neither Liddell nor Tindleman needed much persuasion to keep quiet. They were just as keen to keep the Project and its subsequent disastrous experiment hidden from the outside as the rest of the Project founders.

"Both men would receive pictures through the post of their families – innocent pictures of them out in the garden, outside the supermarket, filling up with petrol, walking the dog, picking up the children from school. They got the message loud and clear. Both Liddell and Tindleman put up and shut up. But they would be looking nervously over their shoulders for the next 20 years."

Jack shook his head, slowly. "And they killed themselves, all these years later? Because of something they did two decades ago? I don't buy it. Why couldn't they have just admitted what they had done, or continued to deny it, keep quiet like they had been? Killing yourself seems a little extreme….."

"They were led to believe the truth was about to come out. Everything they had done was going to be made public knowledge. Poborski must have convinced them that the game was up."

Jack still shook his head. "But killing yourself? I still don't see how two fully grown, intelligent men would decide to end it all like that rather than face the music. I just don't get it."

Andre leant forwards, his elbows on the table, resting his chin on his hands. "Honour," he said simply.

CHAPTER TWENTY-NINE

"Honour?" Jack made a face and let a smile shadow his lips. "Where are we now? In a Jackie Chan movie?"

"Both Liddell and Tindleman were military trained. Look into their backgrounds, you'll see that they both spent time in the forces – both in the SAS, Special Operations. They were trained to put their country, their unit, their comrades, first – before themselves. Honour." Andre paused, watching Jack closely. "If the truth had ever come out, what they had done, they would have felt nothing but shame. Shame would have come crashing down on their careers, and their families. Shame and contempt. As they were acting outside of British Government control, outside of any approval whatsoever, there would be no one there to help them. No one to support them. Nowhere to hide. There could be no hastily arranged cover up, no hush-hush deals behind the scenes to stop the news leaking out. They would have been on their own and hung out to dry. They would have been a liability.

"The shame would have been unbearable for such proud men. Men who had been trained to honour and obey at all costs. To take their own lives would have been the only thing to do. The only *honourable* thing to do. The only true way out."

Jack sighed. "And they killed themselves, on who's say so? Poborski's?"

Andre nodded. "I imagine he would have put in the call right after he got his hands on the cash. He was intent on exacting his revenge on everyone associated with the Project – from those at the very top, to those at the very bottom. He wanted them all to pay for how they had treated him, how they had made him live underground for so many years, how they had denied him his rightful share of the money. How they had cast him aside like the weakened runt of the litter. His hatred for his former partners festered away inside him for many years, growing bigger and more poisonous by the day – like a cancer steadily growing, steadily spreading until it was all consuming. He knew that if he told them that the data was about to be made public, the shame would be too much to bear. They had all lived in fear of the truth being told for so long, that when the time came they would actually be glad to do it. They would even welcome it. Poborski knew this; he was a clever man. Never underestimate what he is capable of, Detective. He knew that with that one call, he could be free."

* * *

Time: 10.45am
   Date: 12th November 2008
   Location: Metropolitan Police HQ, London

"How did you get on?" Jack walked into the office and saw DS Cooper sitting back at his desk. "With Poborski."

DS Cooper shook his head, ruefully. "Nothing, Guv. Didn't even confirm his name. Absolute silence the whole way through."

"Typical." Jack sat down heavily at his own desk and sighed at the fresh mountain of paperwork that had accumulated in his in-tray. Not only that, other files had appeared on the desk space next to it. "At least Andre can't keep quiet."

"Anything useful?"

"Well, he's certainly filling in the gaps." Jack pulled out his notepad and flicked through a few pages until he got to where he needed. "The phone calls. Something struck me. Andre is suggesting it was Poborski who made the calls to everyone to take the pills. I need you to do some digging."

"Sure thing, Guv. It's not like re-interviewing Poborski is going to take us far."

"Get hold of the phone records for Poborski – see who he called. Also take a look at those for Tindleman, Liddell and the others. See who it was that called them too."

* * *

Time: 11.15am
   Date: 12th November 2008

CHAPTER TWENTY-NINE

Location: Interview rooms, Metropolitan Police HQ, London

Jack locked eyes with Andre. "Just supposing this is all true…supposing I believe what you are telling me. Something still doesn't make sense to me. The data."

Andre held Jack's gaze. "What about the data?"

"Why send it back to the UK? Why were the papers on their way to Tindleman? If all they wanted to do was bury the truth, sending the only set of papers that evidenced what had happened directly to them - surely that was just playing into their hands? Once they had them, they would destroy them?"

Andre tore his eyes away from Jack's penetrating stare. "The papers were never going to make it to Tindleman. He would never have had the chance to destroy them."

"Ah yes, the briefcase in the black cab." Jack gave a rueful smile. "Whose gem of an idea was that? Leave a briefcase in the back of a black cab as bait, and then set the trail in motion all the way across to Paris. Genius."

"No one was supposed to get hurt," said Andre, darkly. "Things started to go wrong; Poborski started to deviate from the plan. Shafer was never meant to be harmed, never meant to be involved in Paris. Tindleman sent him there; I had no idea he was coming."

"Really?" A small laugh caught in Jack's throat.

"Really. He was only meant to lose the briefcase. Nothing more. Sending him over to Paris…" Andre paused and shook his head. "He was never meant to die. He was a good man. He didn't deserve that."

"So why was he killed? And by whom?"

Andre shrugged. "He found out information he shouldn't have. Maybe he had been doing some digging around on his own, stumbled on something. He found out that Fleming wasn't who he said he was; wasn't FBI. I don't know how he did it – but Simon was always a good agent, a good investigator. It doesn't surprise me that he found out Fleming was a fraud." Andre paused, thinking back to the café where he and Mac were sitting reading Shafer's last words. "He wanted to warn us who Fleming really was. That he was really Poborski."

"Which you already knew," cut in Jack.

Andre nodded in acknowledgment. "Yes. I knew. But Simon put everything down in writing – probably his worst mistake. Poborski must have found out what he knew – he had bugs everywhere; it wouldn't have been difficult. And when Simon came to see us, outside Marie's flat – Poborski must have been waiting for him. Killed the man before he could say anything else." Andre closed his eyes, momentarily, trying to rid himself of the vision of Shafer's body lying lifeless on the cold, rain drenched street in Paris. He shivered.

"He really had no idea that you were working with Poborski? That you already knew Fleming was a fraud?"

Andre opened his eyes, the vision from Paris evaporating. "I don't think so. He was trying to warn us."

"And got himself killed in the process."

"That was not meant to happen," fired Andre, angrily. "Poborski changed the rules. I didn't know what to do anymore. I had to get the papers out of his way – in case he changed his mind and intended to destroy them too. I didn't know he had been bugging us….bugging me. Once I found out…the plan had to change."

* * *

Time: 2.25am
   Date: 9th November 2008
   Location: L'Apartament Blancos, L'Avenue du Soleil, Paris.

Andre parted the heavy drapes with his hand and looked once more out into the deserted street. *Where are you? Where are you?*

He avoided looking at the alleyway where he knew Shafer was lying cold and stiff. There was nothing more he could do for the man now. He had to focus. He had to concentrate on what next step to take. Poborski was out there, he was sure of it. He had just left his calling card. But what

CHAPTER TWENTY-NINE

his next move would be, Andre couldn't tell. The plan was unravelling before his eyes.

Andre stepped back into the room and closed the drapes. There was only one thing he could do. With his mind whirring, he knelt down and retrieved the briefcase from under his rucksack. Swiftly opening it, Andre brought out the contents – a bundle of papers and CD ROMs. Without stopping to think further, thinking would only complicate matters, he reached into the bureau by his side and rummaged for an envelope. Marie being Marie, the bureau was well stocked and had everything he needed. He quickly found a large brown envelope and sellotape.

Stuffing the papers and CD ROMs into the envelope, Andre hurriedly printed the recipient's name and address on the front. Charles Tindleman, MI6 Headquarters, Vauxhall Cross, London. Pausing only to write a small note on a spare scrap of paper, Andre quickly sealed the envelope with strips of sellotape.

He only hoped he was doing the right thing.

Pulling out his mobile phone he quietly punched in the number. It was answered immediately. "It's me. I need something couriered fast. Right away." Andre nodded. "I'll text you the address."

* * *

Time: 11.30am
Date: 12th November 2008
Location: interview rooms, Metropolitan Police HQ, London.

"But why send them back to M16?" pressed Jack, the ever present frown still furrowing his brow. "I still don't understand. You again sent them back to the very people who wanted them destroyed. The first set were on their way to M16, then hijacked by the black cab. They end up in your possession again in Paris....and then you send them back again? It doesn't make any sense."

Andre rubbed his eyes. "I thought Tindleman might have had a change of heart. He was always the weaker of the two – him and Liddell. I thought maybe he wouldn't have the courage to carry it through when the time came, and that once he got the papers he might……" Andre sighed. "I put a note in with the papers. I pleaded with him to look after them, not to destroy them – to do the right thing. I told him Shafer had been killed, that it was Poborski who was deviating from the plan. I hoped he would see sense and do the right thing."

"Well, he didn't, did he?" said Jack, flatly. The newspaper with the headline "the famous five" was still sitting on the table in front of Andre. A square photograph of Charles Tindleman stared back out at them. Jack nodded his head towards it. "He did as he was told."

Andre nodded. "I made an error of judgment. Tindleman did what he had wanted to do all along – erase the past; burn it; destroy it. Then destroy himself."

Jack pointed at the newspaper headline, his finger tapping each of the photographs in turn. "Dimitri Federov. Sergei Ivanov. Austin Edwards. Charles Tindleman. Chief Superintendent Liddell. The Famous Five. Then there was you, Poborski and Boris Kreshniov. That was it? That was everyone in the Phoenix Project?"

Andre looked at the photographs in the newspaper and then glanced up at Jack. "Yes. All those still alive, yes. There was a chap called Grant Williams, head of security control. But he died not long after the Project was disbanded – cancer. And Earl Calderwood, he was in the programming department. He was killed in a car crash a few years later."

"So the Project is now completely defunct? Nobody left?"

Andre shook his head. "No one except Kreshniov and Poborski."

"And you", repeated Jack, fixing another stony stare on Andre. "You're still here."

Andre shrugged non-committedly and returned Jack's stare without blinking. "It would appear so, yes."

"And the papers?" Jack questioned. "Where are they now?"

Andre frowned. "They were destroyed. In Tindleman's waste paper bin – you said so."

CHAPTER TWENTY-NINE

Jack smiled, the lines around the corners of his tired eyes creasing. "One set was destroyed by Tindleman, yes. We have the remnants of it here." He nodded to the plastic evidence bag of charred papers sitting on the corner of the table that Jack had brought in with him. "But there was another set, wasn't there?" Jack paused, watching Andre carefully. "So where it is?"

Andre returned Jack's questioning gaze with a blank expression. He said nothing.

"Come on Andre. I know it exists. You have another copy. Of course you do. Something this important? There was never going to be just the one copy, was there? Where is it?"

Still Andre's mouth remained tightly shut. His expression betrayed nothing.

"What have you got to lose?" Jack leant forwards in his chair. "You've told me everything else so far – maybe if you told me where these documents were I might be able to help you." He continued in a low voice. "You're in quite a spot of bother right now – kidnapping, false imprisonment, conspiracy to steal, conspiracy to murder......"

"Murder?" Andre's voice snapped. "I didn't kill anyone."

"Dupont and Shafer ended up dead." Jack let the statement hang in the air. "Not to mention the rest of them." He waved his hand at the newspaper in front of them. "Aiding and abetting a suicide is still a criminal offence you know."

Andre snatched the newspaper from the table and flung it across the room, where it bounced off the wall and landed by the door. "That was not part of the plan, I've told you that. Poborski changed the plan, not me."

"So you keep telling me, Andre," cut in Jack, a smile creeping over his lips. "But what if I don't believe you?" He eyed Andre carefully, watching as the man's temperature began to rise. "You helped each other disappear 20 years ago, stayed in touch for the best part of those 20 years, hatched this little plan....in the course of which 7 people have now died." Jack held his hands up and shrugged. "How else am I meant to see it?"

"I didn't kill anyone!" exploded Andre, a tiny bit of phlegm flicking from the corner of his mouth in his anger. He thumped the table in front of him

"That was Poborski! You know it was! He strayed from the plan. He made the calls. He….."

"So you keep saying," interrupted Jack. "But at the moment all I have is your word for it. And absolutely nothing to back it up." Jack paused and held Andre's angry stare in his gaze. "Problem is…..you're here with me now, and he's not. What am I to think?"

"That's low" shot back Andre. "That's really low, even for you guys. So you're blackmailing me now, right?"

Jack spread his arms wide and shrugged. "I'm just saying Andre. How can I believe anything when you won't show me the papers to back it all up?" He cocked his head to one side. "Think about it some more. I'll be back."

Jack got up and scraped his chair noisily across the hard concrete floor. "But don't take too long." He paused and turned round while reaching for the door. "I've got Poborski in custody across the way, and he's just dying to tell me everything he knows."

With that, Jack headed out of the door.

"I've changed my mind – I want a lawyer!"

Andre's words fell against the echo of the slamming door.

* * *

CHAPTER THIRTY

Time: 12.00pm
Date: 12th November 2008
Location: Kettle's Yard Mews, London

Mac hadn't seen the teddy bear in years, but as soon as he saw it the memories came flooding back. It looked just the same. Oversized, fluffy, floppy head which lolled to one side; huge brown eyes that followed you around the room; and the fur, so soft and just waiting to be cuddled. Mac had been inseparable from his teddy bear.

Inseparable until that day.

He had only been 4, but that day was embedded into his memory like a diamond cutting into glass. He remembered the car that had been the one to take him away – it smelt funny inside, and he didn't want to go. He didn't want to leave Jack. He didn't want to leave his brother. He had fought all the way, refusing to sit still and kicking out at the seat in front of him, screaming at the top of his lungs.

Mac picked up the teddy bear and brushed its fur with his hand. Still so soft. And Jack had kept it all this time. Mac knew he hadn't been the best behaved boy in the world, and for that he was sorry. But he had only been a little boy of 2 years old when their mother had died, and their father…..well, they had never had a father either.

Mac didn't remember much about their mother, and for that, maybe, he was grateful. He wasn't sure. Would he be in a better place if he had remembered her? Mac didn't remember where they went after Mum died.

He vaguely remembered living in a large house, where he and Jack had shared a bedroom. There had been lots of children there, too, that he did remember. Lots of children. Lots of noise. Although he didn't remember too much about it, Mac knew that he hadn't liked it very much.

Then there was a quiet house. This one he did remember. It was their first foster family and they lived somewhere quiet, in the countryside. Mac could remember seeing fields, with cows and sheep. He had never seen cows and sheep before, and was fascinated by their sounds and their smell. But it was from there that he had been taken. That was where the car had come to take him away. To take him away from Jack.

Mac placed the teddy bear back on the wooden chair in Jack's bedroom. He hadn't been an easy child; of that he was certain. When he was older, various social workers had given him labels such as "destructive", "rebellious", "attention-seeking" and even "violent" at times. "Delinquent" was also a popular term. He did remember the other foster families who tried their hardest to help him after he had been separated from Jack. And when he thought of them, he felt remorse and shame. He had been such a handful for them, no wonder he only ever lasted a few months in any one place. No one wanted him. No one could handle him. No one could change him.

And that was how he had ended up in an approved school at age 13, then quickly advancing on to youth detention for the rest of his teenage years. It wasn't something that he was proud of.

Mac sat down on Jack's bed and looked about him. His brother seemed to be doing all right for himself, but lived a sparse and empty kind of life. He saw no evidence of any female company, and from what he had learnt about his brother during the last few days, he seemed to live a solitary existence.

But then again, so did Mac.

Two apples from the same tree.

Yet one was more diseased than the other.

Looking at the small bedside table which housed a glass of water, a packet of paracetamol and a book on The Police and Criminal Evidence

CHAPTER THIRTY

Act, Mac saw a small black and white photograph sitting in a plain silver-plated frame, almost hidden by the small bedside lamp. Mac pulled it out and saw an attractive young woman with a flawless complexion staring back out at him. Soft looking, dark eyes and a warm smile lit up her whole face.

Mac didn't have a picture of their mother. He didn't really remember her. But he knew that this was her. And Jack slept with her by his side night after night. Mac didn't like to think what state his brother's headspace must be in. Finding your mother's dead body swinging from a light fitting when you were 4 years old must mess you up in some way.

Hence the shrink.

Or the psychotherapist as Jack called her.

Maybe they both needed one.

* * *

Time: 12.30pm

Date: 12th November 2008

Location: interview rooms, Metropolitan Police HQ, London

"You know what I really don't understand?" sighed Jack, loosening his tie and sitting back down opposite Andre. The clock was ticking; he knew they wouldn't be able to hold Poborski much longer without the extension being granted, and Andre could up and walk out any time he liked. "Why wait so long? For this so-called revenge? We're talking twenty years – that's a heck of a long time to wait."

Andre cleared his throat and took another sip of the lukewarm coffee in front of him. "Where's my lawyer?"

"It's in hand," bluffed Jack. "But technically you don't need one as you're not under arrest. You can get up and go any time you want."

Andre put down his coffee. "It was me who wanted the papers. Not Poborski. All he was interested in was the money. But I wanted the data, because the data holds the truth. The data doesn't lie. And one day I wanted the truth to be known." He took another sip of coffee. He winced at the bitterness it still held. "I thought that if I held all the papers, all the information about the Project, then one day I could put it to good use. It is still plausible, you know? This kind of space exploration. This kind of space experiment. Probably more so now. You only have to read the scientific journals these days to see that space science is moving towards potential colonisation of other planets at an alarming rate."

Andre's voice tailed off; his eyes took on a wistful, almost dreamlike look. "It is still possible. We could still do it. Everyone else at the Project wanted the data destroyed. Buried. Treated as though it had never existed. But I couldn't let that happen. Too much had gone into making it possible. That data had to be kept alive, at whatever cost."

"What had Poborski been doing, all this time?" Jack's voice cut into Andre's thoughts. "Where has he been?"

Andre blinked and looked up. "He went to ground, after the accident. Disappeared. The Project founders cut him loose and told him never to return; unless it was with the missing documents they knew I had taken. I made them nervous. They didn't know what I was going to do with the data. They didn't know where I was, and more importantly for them they didn't know where the data was."

"So where did you go?"

Andre dismissed the question and carried on. "Poborski was told to get Tindleman and MI6 involved, to search for me. To find the data. That was how Simon got involved. Tindleman gave him the task of tracking me down; which he did."

"But he never turned you in...why was that?"

Andre shrugged. "I can be quite persuasive."

"I bet. And then?"

"I died." Andre looked back up into Jack's gaze. "I told you before; dying, it's easier than you think."

"So you *were* Gustav Friedman – but then became Andre Baxter. Overnight."

"It maybe took a bit longer than overnight, but essentially yes. My so-

CHAPTER THIRTY

called death made the Project founders call off their search for the data. They assumed it had died with me. Instead they turned their attentions to the Faradays. They were another loose end that needed dealing with. Poborski was told to ensure that they were never heard of again."

Jack nodded. "The car accident that never was."

Andre gave a curt nod. "I had to protect them – the Faradays. I couldn't let them die – they were too valuable."

Jack rubbed his unshaven chin, thoughtfully. "Yet more who die, but don't actually die. It's becoming a bit of a habit."

Andre frowned. "What do you mean?"

"Well, there was you, turning into Andre Baxter. The Faradays...who turned into goodness knows who. And let's not forget our friend Kreshniov."

Andre's head jerked up, his eyes fixed on Jack. "What about Kreshniov?"

"Well, he disappeared too, didn't he? Supposedly died...but probably didn't. You don't have a lot to say about him. Plenty about Poborski, plenty about the Faradays - but not about him. Why is that, do you think?" Jack eyed Andre, curiously. "What is he? Some kind of enigma?"

Andre stifled a chuckle. "Not an enigma, no. Although he might be quite flattered at that label." He paused, letting a ghost of a smile flicker over his lips. "Kreshniov made sure his tracks were covered. News of his death filtered back to the Project founders – I'm not sure many were convinced, but...nobody could find him, and in time people stopped looking. They took the death certificate as a comfort that he was at an end."

"What do you think happened to him?" pressed Jack, interested to see the smile still played on Andre's lips.

"Me?" Andre raised his eyebrows in surprise. "I don't think I thought too much about him. I was too busy disappearing myself."

"Quite," murmured Jack. "So, the Faradays...what truly happened to them?"

Andre shrugged. "Went into hiding, much like me. Contact was not encouraged."

"And Poborski? He didn't know that the Faradays didn't die in the car accident?"

"No, he thought it was them. He thought he had done what was asked of him. We did a pretty convincing job."

"So then what did he do? Poborski?"

"He could afford to wait and exact his real revenge. The money, *his* money, was left to Isabel in a trust fund – but the legacy would not be paid out until after her 26th birthday." Andre shrugged. "Poborski was a patient man. He could wait. But he never forgot."

"And Isabel?"

"I watched her grow up at her Aunt's house." Andre managed a warmer smile as he let the memories back inside his head. "They had a place not too far from Isabel's family home. I made sure they had enough money. I would send packages to her Aunt, to make sure she was being cared for, looked after. It was what I had promised to do." Andre's thoughts returned to the gloomy, rain-drenched night where the Faradays lives had ended; the promises he had made to both Elizabeth and Christopher. "I lost my parents when I was young, too. Have no family to speak of. I needed to make sure she was OK. One orphan to another.

"And then she grew up; left her Aunt's house and moved away. It was harder to keep an eye on her after she moved on. I thought she might move back into the family home, but she didn't. Instead, the Trustees of her parents' estate let the house out to long term tenants, and Isabel moved away completely. Without her Aunt, I found it hard to stay close to her. I had no way of knowing what she was doing, what she was thinking. I found it difficult to keep my promise. I needed someone to get close to her; to get inside her little world. To act as her protector. I couldn't do that myself, it would raise too many questions....so I employed someone to befriend her." Andre swirled the remnants of the now stone-cold coffee in the bottom of the polystyrene cup. "His name was Miles."

Jack's head jerked at the mention of the name.

"Miles?"

Andre nodded, looking up from his coffee. "He was someone I had worked with for a while. Nice guy, Trustworthy. I asked him if he would

CHAPTER THIRTY

help me out, and he agreed." Andre paused and held up his coffee cup. "Any chance of a refill?"

Jack ignored the request. "This Miles….did he know anything about the Phoenix Project? Anything about her true family?"

Andre shook his head, and gave a small laugh. "No…I don't think he would have believed me, do you?" He shook his head again. "No, I didn't tell him anything about Isabel's real family. I just asked him to look after her, to become her friend. Protect her. I made up some cock and bull story about her being a long lost niece, and I wanted to make sure she was doing OK, settling into a new area, new job. Stuff like that. He didn't question me. He thought he was doing me a favour." Andre paused. "And, of course, he was being paid."

"So, what changed? You let Isabel start a new life in a new place……what made you turn everything on its head?"

Andre's gaze dropped to the table. "Poborski," he said, simply. "Poborski contacted me out of the blue. He knew Isabel was approaching her 26th birthday and the trust fund money would be accessible."

"He knew how to contact you?" questioned Jack, raising an eyebrow. "Even after all this time?"

"We kept in touch, sporadically. He knew my death was a fake. We used PO boxes and anonymous email addresses, keeping tabs on each other. We only knew the bare minimum about each other, not enough to know where we were located, but enough to keep in touch. We both needed something from the other; he needed me as his route to Isabel, I needed him as the route to the Project and the final set of data."

"So, you used each other?"

"Possibly. We were never friends, we didn't particularly like each other, but we needed each other." Andre gave a small smirk. "Would have made the perfect marriage."

"Back to Isabel….how did she get embroiled in this…in this farce of a race across Paris?"

Andre sighed and looked at his watch. "Inspector, I am getting rather tired of all this. When is my lawyer arriving? When am I free to leave?"

375

"When I say so, "replied Jack, gruffly. "When you have told me everything."

"But I have been very candid with you, Inspector," smiled Andre. "Surely you have enough to go on by now? And I really do need to see my lawyer. All these questions, Inspector. You do know they are inadmissible without my lawyer present?"

"Your partner across the way there, Poborski, has been most enlightening, I don't hear him squealing for a lawyer to be present" replied Jack, letting his own smile play with his lips. "I think you have a little more to give me."

Andre sighed and acquiesced. "Poborski hatched the plan. He wanted the money and he needed Isabel to get to it. He was going to get to her, with or without my help. I felt that the only way to protect her would be to go along with his plan – at least I would be on the inside. I would know his moves; I would know his plans. I could make sure that Isabel would come to no harm. He wasn't interested in her, it was just about the money. Once he had that, he would leave her alone. He would be gone. I was sure of that. He didn't care if the truth about the Phoenix Project came out, or if it died a death. Once he got his money he would disappear back to Russia, or wherever he desired, crawl back under the stone he had been living under for the last twenty years, I didn't care. Create himself a new identity…and be gone." Andre spread his fingers in the air, enacting a puff of smoke.

"You never once thought he knew? That you had double crossed him? About the Faradays?"

"I sometimes worried he might find out, that the car accident was a fake. That the Faradays weren't really dead. I felt that the quicker he got his money, the quicker he would be gone."

Jack exhaled loudly and stretched his arms above his head. "Back to this Miles chap," he said. "Where is he now?"

Andre shrugged. "Went off backpacking not so long ago. I haven't seen or heard from him since. He and Isabel were getting close….very close." Andre paused. "I hadn't bargained for that. It made me nervous. It wasn't

CHAPTER THIRTY

part of the deal. If Poborski's plan was going to work, then Miles needed to be gone – so I gave him some money and suggested he go travelling. And he went."

"You paid him off?" said Jack, raising his eyebrows. "You paid him to disappear?"

"No, no...not like that," Andre shook his head. "I just gave him an incentive to go. I knew it would be an offer he couldn't refuse."

"Getting to be a bit of a habit this, isn't it?" breathed Jack, folding his arms in front of his chest and fixing Andre with a cool gaze. "Disappearing. Next thing you know; they end up dead or under a different identity."

"Miles went travelling, that was all," retorted Andre. "I've not seen or heard from him since."

Jack continued to hold Andre's gaze for a few moments longer, then reached into his jacket pocket.

* * *

Time: 1.30pm
   Date: 1st October 2008
   Location: South Africa

The sun was riding high in the pale blue sky, its incessant heat beating down onto the uneven tarmac below. Cicadas chirped merrily from the tinder dry bushes that lined the roughly hewn road. He needed to find shelter from the sweltering sun....and water. He needed to find water. He wiped his forehead with the back of his hand, feeling the sweat run off him as if he was turning on a tap. He had been walking since the early morning, since dawn had broken across the village. His legs felt like lead. Each step he took made him feel as though dead weights had been strapped to his ankles. His feet were itching maddeningly inside his heavy walking boots. He dragged them forwards, often stumbling over the uneven path. Each time he did so he kicked up a plume of dry dust.

He shifted his backpack higher up onto his shoulders. He had only brought necessities with him, but even those were weighing heavily on him now. He had left the rest of his things back at the boarding house in the village – and right now he wished he had left himself there too. It hadn't looked quite so far on the map. The hills hadn't looked quite so steep. The scenery hadn't looked quite so barren and devoid of shade. He had been walking for six hours non-stop; his water bottle had long since been emptied. But he was nearly there. Surely he had to be nearly there?

He was sure the next village was just over the brow of this hill – and with it, the ocean. The cool, lapping waters would soothe his hot and bruised feet. The dust and dirt would be washed away in the crystal clear tide. He would rest under a shady tree, his weary legs thankful for the soft sand beneath him. The vision refreshed him somewhat and he quickened his pace despite the discomfort.

Right now he was glad Isabel had not come with him. She would never have managed this long hike. Never. Miles grimaced and forced himself onwards, one tired foot in front of the other, his head bowed under the intense midday heat. He vowed to splash out on a taxi back to the boarding house.

With the chirping of the cicadas in the bush rows, the heavy dragging of his boots through the hard dust below, and his harsh rasping breaths, Miles did not hear the sound of the car behind him. The driver had cut the engine and was letting the car free wheel gently down the incline, almost devoid of sound.

Miles had at last reached the brow of the hill and was now half jogging, half stumbling down the other side. The view was breath-taking. The dry barren landscape of the past six hours now gave way to lush green trees and a sparkling indigo sea. As the waves gently rippled on the tide, snow white foam danced atop the crests and broke soundlessly onto the sandy shore.

It was paradise.

A cooling breeze now caressed Miles' sunburnt face. He was here, he was finally here. He had finally made it. He closed his eyes and lifted his head up towards the cloudless sky.

CHAPTER THIRTY

Paradise.

The knife sliced cleanly and silently through his neck like it was hot butter. It made no sound. Miles uttered no sound as he dropped to the dusty floor like a discarded rag doll. Two rough hands dragged his body from the roadside, pulling him out of sight into the bush. A single shot to the temple finished the job.

* * *

Time: 12.45pm
Date: 12th November 2008
Location: interview rooms, Metropolitan Police HQ, London

"Was his name Miles Sanderson? Born December 1985. 6 feet, 1 inch, short dark hair, brown eyes?" Jack's gaze retuned to Andre. "Muscular build, birthmark on his left thigh?"

Andre's eyes took on a confused look. He nodded, slowly. "Sanderson, yes. That was his surname. I..I'm not sure about his date of birth, or any birthmark"

Jack carefully unfolded a 12" by 15" colour photograph onto the table in front of them. "Miles Sanderson," his voice low and controlled. "Found dead six weeks ago in a remote area of coastal South Africa."

Andre's eyes dropped to the photograph to see the body of a young man lying prostrate on a piece of rough wasteland. Throat cut, bullet hole to the left temple. Flies beginning to feast hungrily on the dried, congealed blood around his mouth.

"So, tell me," continued Jack, ignoring Andre's sickened expression. "How did you know Isabel would take the bait? Go to the restaurant? Go to the flat and let herself in with the key? Bit risky wasn't it? What if she just didn't go?"

Andre dragged his eyes away from the photograph and stared at the wall above Jack's shoulder. "It was a risk, yes. But I knew if I could get her to the restaurant then she would go through with the rest."

"But how could you be so sure?" pressed Jack. "What if she just didn't want to go? Your whole plan rested on her going to meet……meet this Miles." Jack stabbed a finger at the photograph.

Andre paused, still staring at the wall and refusing to drop his gaze back to the photograph. "I had a back-up plan…but I knew I wouldn't need it. I knew how she felt about him…Miles." Andre's eyes lowered slightly from the wall, to reach Jack's gaze. "She was pretty hurt when he left without her. There was unfinished business between them – if she knew Miles was back in town and wanted to see her, I knew she would go."

"But all the while he was lying dead in a bush, halfway around the world."

Andre's eyes flashed with anger. "I didn't know that, did I?" he growled. "I had no idea." His eyes flickered down, back towards the photograph. "I didn't even know where he had gone. I thought he was heading to Australia."

"Well, *someone* knew where he was," said Jack, raising his eyebrows.

"I'm telling you, I had no idea where he was. South Africa, you say?" Andre looked back up at Jack. "I didn't kill him. Why would I? He was a good friend to me."

"Funny that," continued Jack. "Some of your "good friends" seem to have a very short life expectancy. Take Shafer, for instance. You keep telling me how much of a good friend he was. And wasn't Dupont a "good friend" also? Now Miles. See a pattern emerging anywhere?"

Andre covered his face with his hands. "It's the truth, I swear. Miles was a good lad. I never laid a finger on him. I never wanted him dead. I sent him away so he wouldn't get involved. I thought it would be safer."

"*You* may never have wanted him dead, but someone else did." Jack's voice was devoid of emotion. He was tired, and needed to bring this to a close. And soon. "Someone knew where he was, where he was heading. And that someone had him killed."

"But…"

Jack got up from his chair and began walking towards the door. "I'm tired of this, Andre. Let's see what your good friend Poborski has to say." He paused with his hand on the door handle. "Maybe you need some time

CHAPTER THIRTY

to think. I know you're keeping something from me. I *will* be back."

* * *

Time: 1.35pm
  Date: 1st October 2008
  Location: South Africa

With the body dragged into the bushes, out of sight, the car swung around and waited – its engine idling in the hot, still air. The driver's door creaked open and the driver silently beckoned to the assassin holding the blood stained knife to get back inside.

Once the door was closed, Karl Poborski pulled away from the edge of the dirt track and headed away from the lapping shores of the ocean.

* * *

Time: 4.00pm
  Date: 12th November 2008
  Location: Metropolitan Police HQ, London

Back in his office, Jack slumped back in his chair, listening to the wood groaning beneath him, seemingly in sympathy with his creaking bones. It was getting late. He needed some rest but his brain kept ticking over and over, refusing to hush. He had left Andre to stew a while ago now, and he had not been back. He had left the less than attractive pictures of Miles' mutilated body on the interview room table; he could only wonder what was going through Andre's mind right now.

And Poborski was still refusing to talk. They had him for another 48 hours before they needed to charge him. There was still time to break his silence. Jack let his weary eyes rest on the steadily growing pile of paperwork and files in front of him; his in-tray was more than overflowing. He had neglected his other cases badly over the last few days – but decided another day couldn't hurt.

Pushing himself up from his chair, he reached for his jacket which was hanging over the back. He needed food. And sleep. But he was unsure which was his main priority. And in his back pocket was the magazine PC Daniels had passed to him earlier in the day, and Jack had not had the chance to look at it yet. Maybe a quick bite to eat in the canteen and he could have a quick browse. As he made to leave, the telephone on his desk began to shrill. Momentarily considering whether he should ignore it or not, Jack reached across the sea of loose papers and extracted the handset.

"DI MacIntosh," muttered Jack, holding the receiver under his chin while he shrugged himself into his jacket. "Uh-huh." He nodded and reached for the notepad he kept for telephone messages, surprising himself that a spare pen was nearby. "Give me their number and I'll ring them back when I get a chance." He stifled a yawn with the back of his hand and quickly scribbled the number down. Replacing the receiver back underneath the pile of paperwork, Jack ripped off the top sheet of the notepad and stuffed it in his pocket.

It was then that he paused, his body frozen rigid. His eyes remained focused on the now empty notepad. He had pressed so hard with the pen that he could see the imprint of the phone number on the next sheet. Reaching forwards, Jack pulled the notepad closer.

He ran a finger over the faint imprint of the telephone number and frowned. He had seen something like this before somewhere….and recently. All thoughts of catching a few hours' sleep evaporated from his mind and he bolted from the room in the direction of the stairs.

* * *

CHAPTER THIRTY-ONE

Time: 4.10pm
Date: 12th November 2008
Location: investigation room, top floor, Metropolitan Police HQ, London

"Cooper, you still here?" Jack paced up and down the investigation room, his heart thudding in his chest. He gripped the phone tightly in his hand, trying to stop himself from shaking. "Come upstairs – the investigation room on the top floor. Quick as you can."

As he waited, Jack unwrapped another stick of nicotine gum and grimaced as he forced it into his mouth. He could do with a cigarette, right now; he needed one. No sooner had the vision of the cigarette packet entered his head, DS Cooper entered the room and the vision was gone. Jack rubbed a hand over his unshaven chin and smiled to himself ruefully.

"Just in time, Cooper, just in time." Jack threw the empty gum wrapper into the nearby bin and motioned for his colleague to follow him to the investigation table. "Tell me what you see."

Jack nodded at the plastic evidence bag he had extracted, placing it on its own in the centre of the table. Cooper looked quizzically at Jack before leaning closer to the table and examining the bag.

"Looks like the note found in Liddell's office." Cooper picked up the evidence bag and saw the note inside. "Please forgive me", the note read, written in small neat letters. "His suicide note."

Jack nodded and reached forwards, taking the evidence bag out of DS

Cooper's hand. "Indeed it is." He placed the bag back down on the table and picked up another, handing it to a bemused DS Cooper. "Now tell me what you see here."

DS Cooper slowly took the second bag from Jack, eyeing his superior officer curiously. Glancing down at the bag he recognised the contents straight away. "It's the note you found outside your front door."

"Correct again, Cooper. Correct again." Jack took the bag back and placed it next to Liddell's suicide note. "Now tell me what connects them." He nodded down at both bags on the table, unable to disguise the small smile that crept over his lips.

Intrigued, Cooper again leant forwards over the table. He looked from one to the other, noting the similarities at once. "Well the paper looks about the same size, and both are written in black ink. The same ink even. Looks like a fountain pen. Maybe even the same paper."

Jack was nodding before Cooper had even finished speaking. "Bang on Cooper – but that's not all." Without saying another word, Jack removed both pieces of paper from their protective bags and placed them side by side. One was indeed the suicide note, written by Liddell moments before he took a gun to his head. Both Jack and DS Cooper again saw the small, neat handwriting in thick black ink….. "Please forgive me". The other was the note Jack had found under a milk bottle outside his front door……..28th January 1986. 25th February 1986. The same neat handwriting. The same thick black ink.

But it wasn't the handwriting that had caught Jack's attention. He lifted the milk bottle note and placed it directly on top of Liddell's suicide note. The pieces of paper were an exact match. Same size. Same dimensions. Same thickness.

But that was not all.

The person who had written the two dates on the milk bottle note had pressed down so hard that its indentation could be seen on the note underneath. Jack lifted the top note up slightly so DS Cooper could see. And there it was. A faint indentation of the two dates clearly visible on Liddell's suicide note underneath. Faint, but definitely there.

CHAPTER THIRTY-ONE

The two notes had been written on the same pad of paper.

By the same person.

By Chief Superintendent Liddell.

"Well I'll be dammed," breathed DS Cooper.

"Liddell was trying to warn me," said Jack, returning both notes to their protective plastic bags.

"Warn you?" DS Cooper frowned. "Warn you about what?"

"I'm not sure, "mused Jack, "but he was trying to give me a clue, right? He was trying to tell me something." Jack tapped the bag containing the milk bottle note. "He wrote this note and left it outside my house. It has to mean something."

"But we checked the dates out. We got Daniels to dig into it for us. The first one was easy – no secret as to what happened then. But the second?" DS Cooper shook his head. "He came up with nothing. Nothing happened on 25th February 1986. Nothing at all. Nada."

"Or so we thought." Jack pulled out the UFO America magazine from his back pocket. "Daniels found this for me…..I didn't think it was significant until I looked at the dates. Here, take a look." He threw the magazine at Cooper who caught it deftly in his hand.

DS Cooper looked at the front cover. It was indeed one of the sensationalist UFO magazines that did the rounds over in the States. PC Daniels had pinned an extract from one of the articles to the front and outlined it in thick red permanent maker pen. He had also added a sticky post-it note, "p61" printed in his neat handwriting. Cooper looked up at Jack who merely nodded at him to read it.

The article started with several "eyewitnesses" who had reported seeing a strange craft in the night sky over the American state of Utah. The UFO believers were convinced it was a surveillance craft from outer space, sent from another planet to undertake testing on the human race. A NASA spokesman denied it was anything to do with them. The American military also denied that the aircraft belonged to them, confirming they had no operations, covert or otherwise, within the area on the night in question. There were several small blurred photographs, some showing a series of bright lights moving slowly across the sky, another seeming to show a large aircraft-shaped object flying low across the horizon as if it was coming in to land.

Someone even claimed to have found unidentified moon-rocks in their back yard, another saw scorch marks on the grass where the aircraft would have landed. Several claimed to be able to smell strange odours emanating from other unexplained holes in the ground. The stories piled up thick and fast.

But Jack wasn't interested in those.

His interest lay in the date of this so-called extra-terrestrial visitation.

A date that PC Daniels had circled, once again in his thick red marker pen.

25th February 1986

"Well, I'll be dammed, "breathed DS Cooper. "25th February 1986."

Jack nodded. "And look further, down at the bottom. In the margin."

DS Cooper's eyes scanned down to the bottom of the article, and saw in a small footnote by the margin, that there was a small annotation cross-referencing this article with another in a sister publication. An article that was entitled "The Rise and Fall of the Phoenix Project."

* * *

Time: 4.15pm
Date: 12th November 2008
Location: Parliament Square, London

Dusk had well and truly started to take hold while Mac and Isabel sat in near total silence underneath one of the large trees surrounding the Square. The bench was cold and icy, but neither seemed to notice. Traffic around the Square was slowly creeping its way home, exhaust fumes from stationary taxis and buses clinging to the fog that was rapidly descending as the temperature plummeted.

"Will you be all right getting home?" Mac turned towards Isabel, noticing

CHAPTER THIRTY-ONE

how much smaller she looked, as if she was shrinking before his very eyes. "Why don't you stay over somewhere?"

Isabel blinked but shook her head. "I'll go home – but just not yet."

They had been sitting in the Square for about an hour, nursing takeaway cups of coffee from a nearby shop. Isabel had initially shown interest in the statues inhabiting the Square, walking from one to another, Mandela to Churchill, Churchill to Lloyd George, touching the frozen bronze work. The statues were now encased in darkness, towering above them and casting heavy shadows across the Square.

But Isabel found it peaceful. In amongst all the traffic noise, it still felt peaceful and tranquil. She glanced sideways at Mac who was sitting slumped on the bench, huddled inside his jacket to try and keep out the cold. The air felt moist and damp from the fog, but there was still an underlying chill that threatened further snow.

"Don't lose touch," she murmured, her words barely audible above a passing double decker bus.

Mac turned his head to look at her. "Sorry?"

"I said don't lose touch." Isabel afforded a weak smile to Mac. "With your brother. Now you've found him again. Don't let him go. Family are everything."

* * *

Time: 4.25pm
   Date: 12th November 2008
   Location: Metropolitan Police HQ, London

Jack headed out of the rear doors into the car park, fishing his mobile phone from his pocket. He punched in PC Daniels' number; it was answered almost immediately.

"It's me," said Jack, as soon as the call was connected, his heart racing. "I need a copy of that magazine. The one with the Phoenix Project article."

"No can do, "replied PC Daniels. "The article was pulled at the eleventh hour, never published. Some kind of injunction."

Jack's heart rate faltered. "What?"

"It was never printed. Never appeared in the magazine – or anywhere else."

"Then get me the authors – whoever wrote it. I need to speak to them!" Jack paced up and down beside a patrol car, glancing across to the other side of the car park where two officers were huddled together having a quick cigarette break. Jack rubbed his eyes and looked away; his cravings beginning to rumble.

PC Daniels paused before replying. "Can't do that either, I'm afraid." His voice was like a dead weight to Jack's ears.

"Why not?" Jack looks at the magazine in his hands again. "All I need is their names. The name of the sister publication is here. All I need is a few minutes to talk to them. If they can verify the existence of this Phoenix Project...."

"They can't." PC Daniels' voice was flat.

"Why the hell not?"

"Because the article's authors were both killed in an unexplained road accident soon after the injunction was served."

* * *

Time: 4.15pm
    Date: 12th November 2008
    Location: Metropolitan Police HQ, London

DS Cooper frowned. And rubbed his eyes. The artificial light overhead felt like it was burning into his retinas, and the glare from the computer screen in front of him added to the discomfort.

None of this made any sense.

He had the telephone records of Liddell, Tindleman, Edwards, Ivanov

CHAPTER THIRTY-ONE

and Federov displayed in front of him. Each of them had received a phone call in the moments before their suicide – and each from the same number. Andre had told them it was Poborski who had made the calls, who had given the orders to die. But when Cooper had checked Poborski's phone, he had also received a call from the same unregistered number. It looked like he, too, had received the call to end it all.

Gathering up the paperwork, Cooper went in search of Jack.

* * *

Time: 4.30pm
   Date: 12th November 2008
   Location: interview rooms, Metropolitan Police HQ, London

Jack threw open the interview room door, making Andre flinch, DS Cooper following on close behind. "25th February 1986. Tell me what you know." He thundered towards the table where Andre sat quietly sipping a fresh cup of coffee. "Now!"

Andre looked up at Jack's flushed face and smiled. "Goodness, Inspector – you do look a trifle flustered." He nodded at the chair opposite him." Maybe you would like to sit down?"

Jack remained standing. "And maybe you would like to quit clowning around and stop wasting everyone's time. Tell me what the hell has been going on here….and I mean the truth this time. No more bull shit." Jack nodded at DS Cooper to close the interview room door. "And we can start with 25th February 1986."

* * *

Time: 5.00pm
   Date: 12th November 2008
   Location: Parliament Square, London

Isabel pulled the door shut on her small VW Polo and raised a hand at Mac who was bending down to peer in the passenger side window. She leant across and wound the window down, her face being met with an icy blast from the gathering breeze.

"Take care, Isabel," he nodded. "If you're sure you won't stay, make sure you drive safely."

"I will." Isabel nodded, gratefully, and gave Mac a smile that almost met her eyes. Almost. "And thanks for listening."

Mac shrugged. "No problem. Anytime."

"Say thank you to Jack for me too. You've both been so kind. And understanding."

Mac raised his hand again and stepped back, letting Isabel wind the window back up and encase herself in her metal box, protecting herself against the bitter cold outside. She raised a gloved hand and gently pulled away from the roadside, slipping into the heavy stream of crawling traffic.

Sighing, Mac headed in the opposite direction, towards Jack's flat.

Family.

The only family he had was Jack.

Isabel had urged him not to lose touch with Jack, now that he was back. Mac instinctively thought of the tattered teddy bear sitting in Jack's bedroom all this time, and it gave him a strange feeling inside.

Maybe this time he wouldn't.

∗ ∗ ∗

Time: 4.30pm
    Date: 12th November 2008
    Location: interview rooms, Metropolitan Police HQ, London

"The Faradays returned to earth in the dead of night – out in the desert in Utah, away from prying eyes. 25th February 1986." Andre watched as Jack slowly paced from one end of the small, stuffy interview room to the other.

CHAPTER THIRTY-ONE

"NASA have no recorded flights at that time, Andre," replied Jack, shaking his head. "Anywhere in the US. I've checked." Jack remembered PC Daniels' authoritative list of NASA recorded flights for the month of February 1986 and secretly thanked the young rookie for his obsessional hobby. "There was nothing recorded after the Challenger disaster the month before."

Andre's lips curled into a smile. "You have been doing your homework, Inspector. I'm quietly impressed!" He paused for a second, fixing Jack with smiling eyes. "But you are missing the point."

Jack frowned. "The point?"

"NASA don't have any recorded flights for that day, Inspector, for one simple reason."

"And that is?"

"It wasn't a NASA controlled flight." Andre paused while he gauged Jack's reaction. The Detective Inspector was giving nothing away, so he carried on. "The Faradays were returned by a Russian shuttle. They had been on a Russian space station, after all. They had been scheduled to return a few weeks earlier, a rescue flight launched on 28th January…..but events overtook that rescue attempt. So the Russians stepped in."

Jack's eyes darted up to meet Andre's. "Challenger? That shuttle was meant to go and rescue the Faradays?"

Andre gave a curt nod. "Challenger was due to host a number of experiments during its mission – including classroom lessons beamed back to earth by the first civilian school teacher to ride up into space. But NASA and the US Government had also added the Faraday rescue mission to its list of duties." Andre paused and lowered his gaze. "When that became impossible, an alternative plan had to be arranged."

"And nobody saw anything? On the 25th February when the rescue flight landed?" Jack shook his head. "I find that quite hard to believe."

Andre merely shrugged. "Well I don't think their eventual return went *completely* undetected…….." Andre let his eyes lower to rest on the rolled up copy of UFO America poking out of Jack's back pocket. "But whoever did see something that night…no one took them seriously. Just some crazy

UFO spotter." He gave Jack a knowing smile.

Jack pulled the magazine out of his pocket.

"And it was such a shame no one ever got to read that article…what was it going to be called again?" Andre tapped his head and made a show of trying to recollect. "The Rise and Fall……something like that?"

Jack pointed the rolled up magazine threateningly at Andre. "Do you know something about this? The authors of the Phoenix Project article?" He approached the table and held Andre's gaze. "Do you know how they both managed to die so suddenly?"

Andre feigned surprise. "I *do* hope you are not suggesting I had anything to do with that, Inspector……."

"Well did you?" thundered Jack. "It's very convenient for the authors to both suddenly die…. Another road accident was it? What was it they were about to say? What secrets were they about to spill?"

Andre's lips drew into a tight smile. "Gosh inspector, it sounds like you are almost starting to believe the Phoenix Project was real…."

"Stop playing games, Andre…."." Jack returned the magazine to his pocket, his brain was starting to whir, piecing things together.

"Indeed I shall, Inspector. In fact, I believe I have helped you folks more than enough. And if I'm not mistaken I am here merely as a witness and am free to leave at any time." Andre made a show of getting to his feet and retrieving his jacket from the back of his chair. "As much as I would love to stay and chat, I really do have better things to do. And it is getting *so* late, and my lawyer still hasn't turned up, so……." He gave Jack a forced smile and starting heading towards the door.

"Stay right where you are." Jack's voice was hard and firm. "I'm not done with you yet."

"But *I* am done with *you*, Inspector," replied Andre, continuing towards the door.

"Andre Baxter…..Gustav Friedman…..whatever it is you call yourself these days," continued Jack. "I am arresting you on suspicion of perverting the course of justice, assisting an offender, conspiracy to murder, and aiding and abetting a suicide. And that's just for starters. Now sit back

CHAPTER THIRTY-ONE

down."

Andre froze in his tracks, and Jack pushed roughly past him.

"Read him his rights, Cooper…and don't let him out of your sight."

CHAPTER THIRTY-TWO

Time: 8.30pm
 Date: 12th November 2008
 Location: Metropolitan Police HQ, London

Jack leant against the front desk, stifling a yawn. He still badly needed some rest. Stretching his arms out behind his back, Jack heard his creaking bones agree with him. Looking over to the far side of the reception area, he saw Andre huddled against the bank of telephones on the wall, nursing the telephone receiver protectively towards his ear.

"You don't believe him?" DS Cooper nodded his head over towards Andre, and handed Jack his first umpteenth cup of coffee of the day. "About the plan? With Poborski? You think he was in on the whole thing from the beginning? Killing Shafer – that was all planned too?"

Jack shrugged and took a sip of the coffee, wincing at both how it scalded his lips and how the bitterness attacked his tongue. "I don't know. He's hiding something for sure." Jack continued to watch as Andre shifted from one foot to the other and glanced nervously over his shoulder. "I don't know why but I have an uneasy feeling about our friend Andre."

"You think he's lying?"

"Not entirely…. but." Jack paused and swallowed the rest of the acrid coffee, throwing the paper cup in a nearby bin. Slowly the fogginess of his sleep-deprived brain was lifting. "This Project…this Phoenix Project. I need to see for myself that it existed. I need that evidence in my hand. I need those papers……" Jack's voice tailed off and he rubbed his eyes with

CHAPTER THIRTY-TWO

palms of his hands. "He knew Isabel. And he knew her family. And I mean, *really* knew them. Why was that if this Phoenix Project didn't exist?"

"You want me to stand over there with him?" DS Cooper nodded over at Andre once again. They both stood and watched as Andre finished dialling the number into the keypad and cradled the receiver close to his chin. "See who he's calling?"

"No, "Jack shook his head. "If we believe the Phoenix Project actually existed, then everyone in it is dead and Poborski's in custody. Who else is there left for him to call?" Jack turned away and made to walk towards the stairs. "Leave him alone for a few minutes, take him back to the cells when he's done. He's probably calling his Mum, or his sister or something."

"Thought he was an orphan…and an only child?" DS Cooper continued to watch Andre through the steam rising from his coffee cup.

Jack shrugged again. "In that case, maybe he's calling his lover, his banker or his priest. Maybe all three in one. I couldn't care less so long as he tells me where the rest of those bloody papers are. And soon. Ring me when he's back in his cell." With that he turned and hauled himself wearily up the stairs towards his office. The overflowing in-tray on his desk was calling.

Andre turned slightly and caught the questioning gaze of DS Cooper, who was still watching him intently while sipping his coffee. Andre hurriedly turned away, holding the mouthpiece close to his chin, and cupping his mouth away from prying eyes.

"It's me," he breathed into the mouthpiece. "I need a favour." He paused momentarily as two police officers passed by behind him. "I'm a little tied up. Can you take a book back to the library for me, its overdue? Yes, that's the one. Dracula. " There was another brief pause while he listened to the rely, and then gave a sharp nod. "Yes. Same place. Top shelf." After hearing confirmation from the other end of the line, Andre abruptly hung up.

Turning round, he came face to face with DS Cooper who was now standing only inches behind him. Andre recoiled a little, his eyes flashing back to the telephone receiver. "Detective, you made me…"

"Jump?" finished DS Cooper, raising his eyebrows and nodding at the telephone. "Sorry. Finished your call?"

Andre nodded and allowed himself to be led back in the direction of the cells.

* * *

Time: 10.45pm
Date: 12th November 2008
Location: Metropolitan Police HQ, London

Jack rested his head in his hands before dragging the next file from the towering in-tray. Each time he turned his back, someone seemed to add something more, another file, another memo. Something else that needed his attention, something else that needed urgent review. With the new Chief Superintendent finding his feet in his new post, Jack knew that the knock on his door was coming soon, and the first thing on the agenda would no doubt be this groaning backlog of cases. His desk was cluttered with scribbled notes and messages, but he was getting close to the bottom of the pile…..for now.

"Jack?"

Jack looked up to see DS Cooper walking into the office, looking tired and somewhat dishevelled. His shirt tails were untucked, his tie long since confined to his own desk drawer opposite, and several spots of coffee splattered on the front of his trousers. His eyes looked heavy and in need of sleep.

"I'm glad I caught you, I was about to call."

Jack frowned and looked at his watch. It was nearly 11pm. DS Cooper saw the look that crossed Jack's face.

"I know what time it is, but believe me – you will want to hear this." DS Cooper thrust a piece of paper at Jack. "Read it."

Jack took the paper from Cooper's outstretched hand and looked down. He instantly recognised it as the quote Andre had given them earlier. "We

CHAPTER THIRTY-TWO

learn from failure, not from success," muttered Jack under his breath. "What's this all about?" Jack looked up at DS Cooper, a slight frown darkening his brow. He glanced back down at the quote once more; at the words that had been bothering him ever since Andre scribbled them on Jack's notepad.

"Dracula." said DS Cooper, simply, taking the piece of paper back from Jack's hand.

"Dracula?" Jack shook his head as the frown deepened. "What do you mean, Dracula?"

"It's where the quote comes from." DS Cooper's tired face managed a small smile. "It took me a while, but I found it."

"And?" Jack shrugged his shoulders. "I need to know this at nearly midnight, how?" Jack made a move to get up from his desk, tossing the final file back into the in-tray. If he was lucky he might be able to get home for a few hours' sleep before the sun came up. DS Cooper blocked his path and held up the piece of paper once more.

"Seriously, you need to hear this, Jack. It's not just about the quote."

"Then what is it all about? Look, we're all tired here, we all need to get some sleep…."

DS Cooper cut in. "You want to know where the papers are, right? The second set? Andre's set; the ones that he has had all along?"

Jack eyed DS Cooper, cautiously. "Yes," he nodded. "But we don't know where…."

"Yes we do," cut in DS Cooper.

"We do?" Jack's frown deepened even further. "How?"

"Andre."

"Last time I heard, Andre wasn't talking. Clammed right up. Demanding on a lawyer. Couldn't or wouldn't tell us anything, I don't know which. I don't even care which. If those papers exist, then he's not going to tell us where. He's protected them for the last 20 years, he's not going to stop now."

"I think he's already told us." DS Cooper's voice was calm and even.

"He's what?"

"Told us. Where the papers are." DS Cooper held Jack's confused gaze for a few seconds then took him by the arm, guiding him away from his desk and towards the door. "That quote you gave me – it's from Dracula – Bram Stoker's Dracula."

"Yes, yes, you just said." Jack reached for his overcoat which was hanging on the back of the office door. "So how does that tell us where the papers are?"

"I overheard Andre's phone call. Remember when he demanded his right to his phone call?"

Jack nodded, his stomach tightening. "He wasn't calling his priest then?"

DS Cooper shook his head, slowly. "I don't know who he phoned but it definitely wasn't his priest. Whoever it was, he told them to pick up a library book for him. Dracula."

"He told them to do what?"

"To pick up a library book for him, one that needed to be taken back. It was overdue. He gave them the book title. I thought it strange at the time…….."

"So, he uses his one phone call to ask someone to return an overdue library book?" Jack hung his overcoat back on the door.

"Except I don't think he was really asking them to return it. He was asking them to go and get it; to keep it safe. That quote Andre gave you?" DS Cooper held up the piece of paper with the quote on again. "He was just playing with you; testing you. He knew it was a quote from the book. He knew that book was the one and only clue to where the documents were….*if* you were clever enough to know where to look."

Jack took another look at the quote in DS Cooper's hand and exhaled loudly. Images of his brother filled his head.

* * *

Time: 11.50pm
    Date: 11th November 2008

CHAPTER THIRTY-TWO

Location: Kettle's Yard Mews, London

"It was a way we used to communicate," said Mac. "A bit childish, I know. Probably a million other ways far easier, far safer. But we kind of liked it. Bit of an adventure trail. A mystery. Probably read too many adventure comics when we were kids." Mac looked up and took another sip of the whisky he held in his hand.

"So, you would hide the information you wanted to pass on…..you'd hide it in the pages of a book?" Jack eyed his brother, cautiously, and a smile played on his lips. "But you hated books as a kid."

Mac nodded, and smiled ruefully. "I know."

"And it worked?" Jack raised his eyebrows, speculatively, taking hold of the whisky bottle and pouring another measure into his own glass.

"Maybe not 100% of the time, but mostly, yeah. All we needed to do was give the book title and a location. And it was always the top or bottom shelves. Simple really."

* * *

Time: 10.50pm
  Date: 12th November 2008
  Location: Metropolitan Police HQ, London

Jack's head cleared in an instant. The fog of exhaustion that had been engulfing him lifted like a stage curtain at the theatre. His eyes met DS Coopers and they both came to the same conclusion. "The crime scene photos from Andre's flat."

Taking the stairs two at a time up to the top floor investigation room, Jack burst in and snapped on the overhead lights. The room was instantly bathed in harsh fluorescent lighting.

"The scene of crime guys, they must have taken photos of Andre's flat. They must have covered every inch." Jack headed to the table that still housed all the plastic bag evidence. "Where are the pictures?"

DS Cooper hurried over to his side and began pulling at the polythene bags, searching for what they needed. It wasn't long until his hand closed on the scene of crime photographs from Andre's flat. Jack grabbed the bag and tipped the contents onto the table in front of them. They both rummaged through the photographs, knowing what they were looking for. The scene of crime guys had been thorough; there seemed to be hundreds of photographs. Literally hundreds. They pored over pictures of Andre's flat – the entrance hall, his desk, his sofa, his bedroom, his wardrobes, his bathroom, his kitchen; even pictures from inside the fridge.

And then Jack saw it.

He picked up the small square photograph and strode over to the far wall, pinning the photograph to the investigation room pin board. DS Cooper joined him, and they both stood back, looking at the picture.

"Well, I'll be dammed," muttered Jack, rubbing his chin, thoughtfully.

Andre's bookcase.

The bookcase was crammed full of books, one next to the other, all manner of shapes and sizes. Jack reached into a nearby drawer and pulled out a magnifying glass. He trained the magnifying glass over the top of the photograph, scanning the shelves.

"What did he always say?" muttered Jack, narrowing his eyes as he scanned the grainy book titles. "They always used the top or bottom shelves…."

Jack paused the magnifying glass at the right hand end of the top shelf. Both he and DS Cooper peered closer. And then closer still

And there they saw it. The thick oblong spine of a dark red book.

Dracula.

* * *

CHAPTER THIRTY-THREE

Time: 5.00 am
Date: 13th November 2008
Location: Metropolitan Police HQ, London

"Sergeant Boutin says the room is already sealed and under guard." DS Cooper replaced the telephone receiver in its cradle and looked up as Jack re-entered the investigation room. "They will make sure no one enters, or touches anything, until you manage to get over there. You're on the first Eurostar service at 6am."

Jack nodded, thoughtfully. "We get the book…..we get the evidence." He threw a bacon sandwich wrapped in greaseproof paper into DS Cooper's lap. "Get that down you, think we've earned it this morning."

DS Cooper caught the sandwich and grinned. "Then all this…. hits the fan." He took a large bite out of the sandwich, letting a dribble of melted butter run down his chin. Speaking with his mouth full, he watched as Jack perched on the corner of the investigation table and start to devour his own sandwich. "You reckon the papers will actually be there? That there will be something to prove the Phoenix Project existed?"

Jack shrugged, concentrating in his sandwich. He wasn't sure what to believe anymore. Did he truly believe the papers would be there to reveal the world's best kept secret, its greatest ever deception? He couldn't say. But if they were there, the consequences would be enormous. If they unearthed a space experiment on this scale which had been kept out of the public domain for so long…. who knew what the outcome would be.

"If you had asked me a fortnight ago I would have laughed in your face," Jack eventually replied, swallowing the last of his sandwich and throwing the scrunched up ball of greasy paper into the nearby bin. "But now…" Jack shook his head. He thought back to the huge files PC Daniels meticulously kept, documenting space travel and exploration over the last half century. The references made to a secret club, a secret society…. references made decades ago.

"You think we can prove it?" DS Cooper nodded at the investigation table, still littered with evidence bags.

Jack leant behind him and pulled out the nearest evidence bag. Reaching inside he brought out another photograph – the one of Isabel sitting astride her red tricycle on her fifth birthday. "This is where it all starts." He jumped off the table and pinned the photograph next to the one of Andre's bookcase. He gazed into the eyes of Andre, standing next to Isabel and her mother. "This…is where it all began."

"Think we should tell our friend that we know where his papers are?" DS Cooper joined Jack in looking at the pin board. "Or surprise him later?"

"Mmmmm," Jack murmured, nodding to himself. "I think we should pay him an early wake up call. Let him know that the truth will be told."

**

Time: 5.10am
Date: 13th November 2008
Location: Metropolitan Police HQ, London

Jack paused outside the Custody Suite, cell number 3. There was no officer standing guard outside the door, and the corridor itself was empty. He frowned slightly and pushed the heavy door open. The cell was empty, save for an empty coca cola can and a tray of half eaten sandwiches from the night before. Jack heard footsteps behind him, and looked back outside into the corridor.

"You looking for your man?" asked a young officer, striding towards the

CHAPTER THIRTY-THREE

door and nodding at the empty interview room. "He's gone to answer an early morning call of nature. PC Williams took him a few minutes ago."

Jack waved his thanks and retraced his steps back up the corridor. He thought about getting a fresh cup of coffee while he waited, but decided instead to go and see what was holding Andre up. He wanted to speak to him before he headed off to catch the train.

Jack had managed to slip home during the night, for a change of clothes and a quick shower. He felt fresher but knew he didn't particularly look it. He ran his hand over his ever growing stubble, and could still feel his eyes prickling with lack of sleep. He reached the end of the corridor that led to the men's toilets, and saw PC Williams standing outside.

"Our man inside?" enquired Jack, nodding at the entrance door to the toilets.

"Yes, sir," replied PC Williams, glancing down at his watch. "Been in there a few minutes, complaining of a stomach ache."

Jack nodded and went to stand next to PC Williams. The minutes ticked by, slowly. Jack glanced at the wall clock behind him, and the noticeboard covered in memos, information sheets, internal newsletters and such like. Half of which Jack was sure he must have been handed before, but had consigned to the bin within seconds of receiving them. Notifications of promotions, transfers, retirements. New internal procedures. Fire drills. Health and Safety Awareness courses. Up and coming legislation changes. And details of the annual staff Christmas dinner.

Jack sighed and glanced back at the wall clock. He caught PC Williams' eye, watching the young officer look down at his own watch and shrug.

"OK, he's had long enough," announced Jack, roughly pushing open the men's toilet door. "Stomach ache or no stomach ache."

Jack stood fixed to the spot and looked around. There was no one at the urinals. There was no one at the wash basins. There was a row of five cubicles on the far wall and Jack kicked open the door on each and every one.

Nothing.

No one.

Empty.

*　*　*

Time: 11.15am
Date: 13th November 2008
Location: Flat 7, Rue de Bougainvillea, Paris.

A leg weary DI Jack MacIntosh slowly pulled himself up the stone steps to Andre's apartment. He had managed a couple of hours sleep on the train, but it had been fitful at best. He had left the station in a scene of complete turmoil and good old fashioned panic. The entire building had gone into high alert, all doors in and out locked. Officers were hurriedly placed on guard duty on all entrances and exits, including windows. Corridors were checked inch by inch, rooms searched, cupboards emptied.

But Jack knew that it would all be in vain.

The search would find nothing.

Andre was gone.

The door to Andre's apartment was sealed with blue and white striped French police scene of crime tape, the strands criss crossing the door frame, refusing to permit entry. Without pausing, Jack sliced his arm through the tape and pushed open the door. The French police officers stationed on either side of the entrance didn't flinch and paid him no attention.

Jack walked into Andre's apartment and headed straight through towards his front room. It was exactly how the crime scene photographs had portrayed it. Small. Dark. Full of books. There was a large blank space on the writing desk – Andre's computer and associated paraphernalia had been seized long ago and were currently languishing in the police station technology support room.

But Jack wasn't interested in Andre's computer.

He turned and faced the heavy bookcase leaning against the far wall behind him. It looked so much larger than in the photographs. Gazing up

CHAPTER THIRTY-THREE

at the rows upon rows of books and publications, Jack could almost hear the shelves groaning under the dead weight. Thick dust lined the edges of the shelves, giving the air a dank, musty smell.

Jack stepped closer and trailed a finger along the spines of the books in front of him, cocking his head to one side to read their titles. Some he had heard of, some he had not.

20,000 Leagues Under the Sea, by Jules Verne.

A Brief History of Time, by Stephen Hawking

Black Holes & Time Warps, by Kip Thorne

Solaris, by Stanislaw Lem

The Andromeda Strain, by Michael Crichton

Have Space Suit, Will Travel, by Robert Heinlein

NASA

Pausing, Jack's gaze rose to the top shelf, where the dust appeared to be much thicker. He noticed a small set of steps at the side of the bookcase and dragged them over to the right hand side of the shelving. Reaching into his back pocket, Jack brought out the crime scene photograph of Andre's bookcase. He had neatly circled a thick red tome towards the very end of the shelf. Jack glanced from the photograph back up to the top shelf of the bookcase, and stuffing the photograph back in his pocket he began to climb.

Dust particles began to tickle the insides of his nose as he moved closer and closer to the top of the steps. He tried to hold his breath as he trailed a finger along the spines of the books facing him. Judging by the amount of dust and dirt which fell from them, the books must have lain up there undisturbed for many years. Books which hadn't even been opened for a decade or more, never mind read. None of them even flicked through; none of them disturbed at all. All living in a peaceful sleeping slumber.

All except one.

Jack halted, sharply. His fingers hovered, uncertainly, over a thick red book with a wide spine and gold lettering. This book was different. Its spine was almost free from dust, the title of the book spelt out in thick, ornate gold spidery lettering. The gold from the lettering shone out, almost glinting in the gloom around it. Jack noticed that the space in front of the spine was also, unusually, dust free. Unlike the rest of the shelf.

Jack placed his hand on the top of the book and gently pulled it forwards. He could now see the front of the book and the title jumped out at him.

Dracula, by Bram Stoker.

Jack pulled the book further forwards and held it in his hands. It was lighter than he had expected. It was a large, thick book with ornate gold embossed corners and edging. Yet it felt curiously light.

Jack climbed back down the steps, holding the book like you would a newborn baby. He had been thinking of this moment during the entire journey across the channel earlier today, wondering what it would feel like when he finally held it in his hands. Wondering if it would still be there.

But it was still there.

And now he had it.

With his mind racing and his heart thumping. Jack carefully opened the book.

**

Time: 4.30pm
  Date: 13th November 2008
  Location: Metropolitan Police HQ, London

Andre flattened his body against the outside wall until the voices had disappeared. He rubbed his newly shaven chin, feeling the smoothness of the skin underneath his freshly manicured fingers. It felt different. It felt strange. But it felt good. He let his hands run over the top of his head, smoothing back the neatly gelled hair – now a dark shade of brown, almost black.

He then removed his glasses and inserted a fresh pair of tinted contact lenses – the transformation was now complete.

Andre bent down and snapped open the small leather briefcase by

CHAPTER THIRTY-THREE

his feet. He reached inside and brought out a handful of passports and identification cards. He searched quickly for the appropriate ones, slipped them inside his expensive-looking suit jacket pocket and replaced the rest back where they had come from, snapping the briefcase shut.

Straightening up against the wall, he readjusted his tie and fastened the suit jacket over his waistcoat. He then stepped away from the wall and marched confidently around the corner of the Metropolitan Police HQ and thrust open the front doors.

Andre noticed a large number of police officers manning the front doors and standing by the stairs and other internal doors. A smile crept across his lips; looks like somebody is missing, he thought drily to himself. Heading over to the main reception desk, Andre felt many pairs of eyes watching his every move.

"Mr Jonathan Hutchinson," he announced, in a new clipped Home Counties accent, flashing a smile at the young WPC manning the desk. "Defence solicitor to see Mr Karl Poborski."

A puzzled and slightly fraught look crossed the young WPC's face, as she turned to consult the registration book in front of her. "Oh, sorry, I wasn't aware he was due to see a solicitor again this afternoon. I thought he had already had a visit earlier today." She flicked quickly through the papers in front of her, and then turned to the computer screen next to her. "My apologies, we are a bit all over the place at the moment. One of our detainees has absconded, and its thrown everything out of sync."

"Oh really?" murmured Andre, his face taking on a surprised expression. "How unfortunate."

The WPC gave a wan smile, and started tapping away at the computer keyboard. "Sorry, I won't keep you a moment."

Andre gave a sly glance over his shoulder and saw the officers standing guard at the front doors were paying him no attention at all.

"Look," said Andre, bringing his gaze back round to the WPC before him. "I'll let you in on a little secret." He leant forwards over the desk and kept his voice low. "He hasn't actually asked for me to be present, but I know him well. I've represented him a few times before." Andre slipped a small rectangular laminated business card across the desk towards the WPC and flashed her another pearly-white smile. He noted that she picked it up and glanced at the name.

Jonathan Hutchinson, Hutchinson, Reed & Stone Solicitors. It gave an address in the West End.

"He can be a slippery little bugger," continued Andre. "When he wants to be." He paused for a moment or two, to make sure that he had the WPC's full attention. "I bet he's making your lives a misery here. Not cooperating. Not answering questions. Being facetious. Making demands." Andre watched as the WPC gave a small, slow nod.

"You could say that," she replied, rolling her eyes towards the ceiling. She slid Andre's business card back across the desk. "Driving the detectives mad. Can't get anything useful out of him. And now this." She waved her hand at the reception area.

Andre nodded, sympathetically, and glanced down at his watch. "And I bet you have either got to charge him or let him go soon, too."

Again the WPC nodded, glancing back at the computer screen. "Mmm-mmm, within the next few hours. He's had two extensions already."

"Well, how about I go and have a little word or two with him? Maybe I can persuade him to open up a little – give you guys a little help?" Andre flashed another smile.

"You think he'll listen to you?" The WPC raised her eyebrows and gave a disbelieving look.

"Within the hour I'll have him singing like a canary," chuckled Andre, giving the WPC and even wider, even whiter smile. "I personally guarantee it."

The WPC frowned. "And why would you do that, Mr Hutchinson?" She nodded at the business card still resting on the desk. "You're supposed to be his defence lawyer."

Andre smiled ruefully and leaned in a little closer to the WPC. He held her gaze for a moment or two longer and then winked.

"Well let's just say I'm fed up to the back teeth with the guy – he's got away with murder, quite literally, for far too long. Time he got what was

CHAPTER THIRTY-THREE

coming to him. Help us both out." Andre paused. "Just let me in with him. Ten minutes will do. I'll just slip in and out, no bother. No one else need know. We can just keep it between ourselves…" Andre managed another wink.

The WPC paused for a moment, her gaze straying back to the computer screen next to her. "Well, I should really call it in….have DI MacIntosh speak to you first, but he's just got back from France. I think he's upstairs, so…..."

"Time's ticking away." Andre glanced over his shoulder once again. Still the officers by the front entrance were not paying him any attention, standing with their backs to him and facing the doors. "You give me ten minutes now, and your DI MacIntosh will have the surprise of his life when he comes down. He will find Poborski can't talk fast enough." Andre paused again and held the WPC's gaze. "And I'll come by later on and whisk you away for a thank-you dinner for two." Another smile.

The WPC felt her cheeks begin to colour and burn, and she started chewing on the end of her biro giggling like a schoolgirl.

"OK, Mr Hutchinson, you've got ten minutes. I'll walk you down."

The WPC emerged from behind the front desk and led Andre down a corridor he already knew well. "Ten minutes," confirmed the WPC, as she pushed open the door to interview room number 5. "Come see me when you're finished."

Andre nodded, flashed another smile, and watched as she turned away, heading back up the corridor towards the front desk. As she disappeared from view he turned towards the officer standing guard outside the interview room.

"Couldn't pop and get us a couple of coffees, could you?" he asked, pulling up his briefcase and tucking it under his arm. "Got a lot to get through here." He tapped the briefcase with his hand. "Something warm and wet might loosen his tongue a little."

The officer nodded and headed off in the other direction, towards a set of stairs that lead up to the canteen. Once he was safely out of sight, Andre entered the interview room and closed the door behind him.

***

Time: 4.35pm
 Date: 13th November 2008
 Location: Interview Room 5, Metropclitan Police HQ, London

"Well, well, well," smirked Karl Poborski as he watched Boris Kreshniov cross the cold concrete floor of the interview room towards him. "So the rumours were true. I'm impressed. How did you manage it? The escape I mean….everyone here is talking about it. You have created quite the disturbance."

Kreshniov ignored him and placed his briefcase down in the centre of the shabby table where Poborski was sitting. Poborski sat up straight, his slim fingers playing with the solid gold cuff links chained to his expensive shirt sleeves. His expensively tailored suit jacket hung from the back of his chair.

"I'll be out of here soon myself," Poborski continued, a thin smile playing on his lips. "Just have to sit it out for another few hours, and then they will have to let me go." He eyed Kreshniov with smiling eyes. "You've done me a favour actually. They are all far too busy trying to find out how you got out to be bothered to continue interviewing me…and the clock is ticking…tick..tock..tick..tock."

Kreshniov hovered by the table and snapped open the briefcase locks. "You think you are so clever, don't you?" His voice was tense. "You think you're invincible. Karl Poborski. The man who can't be touched."

"Now, now," mocked Poborski, the smile on his lips breaking out into a wide grin. "Let's not fall out. After we have been playing so nicely together, too."

"You lied to me," barked Kreshniov, his eyes flashing with red hot anger. "You said no one else would get hurt. You were only interested in the money."

"And so I was," replied Poborski, his eyes still dancing with laughter. "And still am."

CHAPTER THIRTY-THREE

"So why did you kill Shafer?" Kreshniov's voice cracked slightly as he remembered his dead friend. "What threat was he to you?"

"Oh, he was a big threat, Boris, my friend. A big threat." Poborski's voice darkened, laughter no longer dancing around his tone. "He was far too clever, that was his downfall. He just wouldn't let it go. Found out too much about me. He would have turned us both in to his MI6 friends given half a chance. He needed to be silenced. I had no choice."

"There is always a choice," whispered Kreshniov, his voice barely audible. "We all have a choice."

"And my choice was to look after number one," announced Poborski, breezily. "You have a problem with that? Once we get out of here, we can think about how we can finish off the job."

"Finish off the job?" Kreshniov caught Poborski's gaze. "What do you mean finish off the job? It's over, Karl. It's well and truly over."

Poborski held Kreshniov's stare, and slowly shook his head. "It's not over Boris, and you know that. We've just hit a temporary blip, that's all. They've got nothing on either of us. Once we get out of here we can finish the job properly. They still think you are Gustav Friedman – the man who never existed. Boris Kreshniov, they still think is lying dead and buried in a Russian cemetery." Poborski let another smile dance over his lips. "And me. Well, DI MacIntosh blew my cover a little earlier than expected.….but I never did really like being FBI." The smile broadened. "We can still do it, you know, Boris. We can still get the money ….." Poborski's words were cut short.

"The money?" Kreshniov took another step closer to the table. "You're still after the money?"

Poborski nodded slowly and deliberately, a greedy gleam crossing his eyes. "Of course. Did you think I would just give up? That money is mine, Boris. You know it. I know it. I've waited twenty years to get my hands on it, I'm not going to give up that easily." Poborski's face tensed. "I won't stop until I get what's mine. And you are going to help me."

Kreshniov closed his eyes, breathing deeply and evenly. The muscles in his shoulders relaxed, the tenseness which had enveloped his body upon seeing Poborski again suddenly now evaporated. He slowly opened his eyes and scowled.

"I'm not going to help you," said Kreshniov, his voice relaxed and firm. "I told you – this is over."

"You *will* help me," snapped Poborski, phlegm flying out of the corner of his mouth in a sudden burst of anger. "You *will*. You owe me. You are my only link to the girl – she has the money and I need to get to it. You have what you wanted – you've got your precious papers. Now it's time for me to get what I want. We had a deal, Boris. You have no choice."

"Oh yes I do, Karl," replied Kreshniov, a small smile flickering onto his lips. "And I've already made my choice. I won't help you. I won't let you get close to Isabel, and I won't let you get to her money."

There was a prickly, stony silence for a moment as Poborski digested what he had just heard. His anger now turned to laughter. Slowly, he brought his well-manicured hands together and started clapping. Short, sharp claps, interspersed with cold laughter.

"That's good," he laughed, pretending to wipe away tears from his eyes. "That's very good. You almost had me going then. "The clapping stopped abruptly. The laugher subsided. Poborski's face darkened further. "You will do as you are told, Boris. You will find the girl, you will lead me to her and you will help me get what is rightfully mine."

"And if I don't?"

"Then you will be seeing your friend Shafer much sooner than you bargained for." Poborski flashed a menacing look. "And as for your friend Isabel….." He made a cutting action across his throat with his hand. "I'm sure she would like to finally meet up with her long lost lover…..Miles? Was that his name?" Poborski made a show of trying to remember the dead man's name. "I think that was it. Hard to make out what someone is saying when their throat is filling up with blood…"

Kreshniov ignored the caustic sarcasm in Poborski's voice. He rested his hands on the table and leant forwards so that he was only inches away from Poborski. "Isabel doesn't have the money, Karl." He leant in even closer, tapping the briefcase with one hand. "I do."

CHAPTER THIRTY-THREE

* * *

CHAPTER THIRTY-FOUR

Time: 4.35pm
  Date: 13th November 2008
  Location: Metropolitan Police HQ, London

The book lay open in the centre of Jack's desk, all other files and paperwork hastily brushed to the side.

Jack was sat slumped in his chair, his head resting in his hands. The book had weighed heavily in his hands the whole journey back across the channel, and it weighed even more heavily sat here on his desk.

But Jack's heart felt even heavier.

He had pinned so many hopes on it, on finding the book. Once he had the book, the papers and everything else would fall into place. All the answers would be there. No more questions. No more theories. Just answers.

DS Cooper rushed hurriedly into the office. "You're back!" he exclaimed, rushing over to the table. "You got the….." He stopped dead in his tracks, his eyes falling on the open book in front of Jack.

"Yes, I'm back," sighed Jack, raising his head from his hands. "And yes, I got the book."

Jack pushed himself up from his chair and turned the book round to face DS Cooper's expectant face. The book was not really a book at all. It was nothing but a shell. From the outside, from the shelf, it looked like a regular book – the front and back covers were intact. Even from the outside the pages looked perfect and unblemished. But inside, once

CHAPTER THIRTY-FOUR

opened – all that could be seen was a large square depression cut out of the pages to leave a deep recess.

A recess which was perfect to hide anything away from prying eyes.

A recess perfect for hiding the Phoenix Project papers.

But a recess that was empty.

"Shit." Cooper pulled across another chair and sat down heavily. "Someone got to it first?"

"So it would seem," nodded Jack, pushing himself up from his chair and wandering over to the window that looked out onto the car park. He gazed out into the gloom, wanting to look anywhere but the hollowed out book on his desk. He had stared at it the whole way back across the channel, and now it sickened him. "See if you can get a trace on the number Andre called from the phones downstairs. I want to know who he spoke to. It's a long shot, but…" Jack shrugged and made his way back over to his desk.

DS Cooper nodded and made to get up. "Oh and before I forget, the FRU have been on the phone downstairs. Want to know if you've had a look at the file they sent over?"

Jack raked a weary hand through his unkempt hair and shook his head. "Sorry. Forgot all about them; what with all that's been going on. Tell them I'll call them back."

DS Cooper nodded and went to disappear back through the door. "Oh, and the front desk say that Poborski has his solicitor with him again."

"Fabulous," murmured Jack, and waved a hand at the departing Cooper.

Jack slumped down into his chair, once again, hearing and feeling it creak beneath his weight. His desk was again as untidy and unkempt as his hair. The files he had managed to clear yesterday had been replaced by others. Once again his in-tray was stuffed to bursting point with messages and memos, each vying for his attention but none achieving it. Empty coffee mugs, stained with week-long remnants of dark brown liquid lined up at the edge of the desk.

Jack closed Andre's book and placed it to the side. There was no point keep looking at it, it wouldn't change the fact that the papers that were once hidden inside were now gone. With a sigh, he turned his attention to the file sitting neatly and squarely on the very top of the towering pile that was his in-tray. It had been sent over in an envelope marked "URGENT"; the envelope itself lying crushed in the wastepaper bin under the desk. Jack reached for the file and flicked it open, sighing heavily. He'd forgotten all about the Facial Recognition Unit. The FRU. They were a new unit, set up only a few months back, working on computer generated facial recognition.

Everyone at the station had been asked by their superiors to assist the FRU in compiling their database and putting their newly installed software to the test. In any serious investigation, the senior investigating officer was to forward photographs of suspects and witnesses to the FRU to help them develop their techniques. Jack had dutifully complied and sent them copies of all the photographs he had in the Faraday enquiry, from the early family photographs of Isabel and her parents, to the mug shots of the deceased Russians.

And then he had forgotten all about the FRU.

But the FRU had not forgotten about him.

The first page Jack opened contained a dossier of the photographs used, and a catalogue of the techniques the unit had put into operation. Jack skimmed through the next few pages, speed reading through the technical jargon which meant nothing to him. He turned another page, skimmed some more, stifled a yawn.

Then halfway down page 9, he froze.

* * *

Time: 4.40pm
   Date: 13th November 2008
   Location: Metropolitan Police HQ, London

WPC Gillian Lockwood glanced up at the wall clock opposite the front desk. She started to bite her bottom lip, nervously. He's had his 10 minutes now and she should really go down and shoo him out. But maybe he was

CHAPTER THIRTY-FOUR

getting results and everyone would thank her at the end of the day?

She decided to give him another 5 minutes and busied herself going through the pile of telephone messages that littered the desk in front of her. Sergeant Wiltshire would be back soon anyway and she would go and show Mr Hutchinson the door then.

* * *

Time: 4.40pm
Date: 13th November 2008
Location: Metropolitan Police HQ, London

"How accurate is this…this test, or whatever it is that you do?" Jack pressed the telephone receiver close to his ear, the file still open at page 9 in front of him. He was breathing hard and felt his heart pounding in his chest like a sledgehammer. He paused, listening to the reply at the other end. "And you're sure about that?"

Just then, DS Cooper flew into the room, his face flustered. "Guv, I got your message……"

Jack held up a hand to silence his partner, pointing at the phone in his hand. He reached down and put the call on speakerphone. "Listen to this."

"We run a series of facial recognition software programmes," spoke the FRU operative. "Only after a positive result on one test do we move onto the next. Your photographs passed all 5 programmes with one positive result in each."

There was a long pause. DS Cooper frowned at Jack, but then followed Jack's gaze to page 9 of the opened file on his desk. He edged closer and looked at two photographs that were side by side, staring out from the blank paper. DS Cooper recognised one immediately – below the caption was "Andre Baxter". It was the mug shot they had taken from him when he had been brought into the station.

The second photograph, however, DS Cooper had never seen before. And neither had Jack.

"The second photograph…. where did that come from?" Jack asked the question that was hanging on DS Cooper's lips.

There was a pause and rustle of paperwork on the other end of the phone line. "Uploaded by a PC Daniels, so it says here."

"And…the result? There's no mistake?"

"The two subjects in the photographs,' continued the person from the FRU," are one and the same person. No question. No doubts. It's a 100% positive match."

Jack raised his eyebrows at DS Cooper and they both stared back down at the two photographs in the file. The caption below the second photograph stared back out at them.

Boris Kreshniov.

Andre Baxter is, and always had been, Boris Kreshniov.

* * *

Time: 4.42pm
Date: 13th November 2008
Location: Metropolitan Police HQ, London

"Thank for holding the fort, Gill." Sergeant Wiltshire opened the side hatch and let himself back in behind the front desk. "It's a madhouse out there right now."

"No worries, Guv," replied WPC Lockwood, picking up her mobile phone and making room for Sergeant Wiltshire. "I've tried to put these phone messages in some kind of order but there's so many of them….mostly media I think."

Sergeant Wiltshire grimaced and took hold of the pile of telephone messages. "They can wait. Looks like they are setting up camp outside in time for the early evening news anyway. Anything else I need to know about?"

WPC Lockwood shook her head. "Not really. Just a Mr Hutchinson, a solicitor, has come in to have a chat with Poborski. They're in interview

CHAPTER THIRTY-FOUR

room 5. He's had about 15 minutes, I told him he could have 10."

Sergeant Wiltshire nodded. "OK, thanks Gill. Let's leave them a while." He glanced up as an officer came through the front double doors, momentarily giving a preview of the congregation of media vans and reporters setting up on the police station front steps. "It's a circus out there."

* * *

Time: 4.45pm
Date: 13th November 2008
Location: Metropolitan Police HQ, London

Jack snatched up the telephone receiver again and punched in the numbers as quickly as his shaking fingers would allow. DS Cooper had gone back downstairs to see if Poborski's solicitor had finished with him.

"C'mon, c'mon," he muttered, irritably, twisting the telephone coil impatiently around his fingers as he waited for PC Daniels to answer the call. "Pick up, pick up, pick up…."

PC Daniels answered the call on the tenth ring. "Hullo?" It sounded to Jack as though the young PC had been disturbed from a deep sleep, but Jack had no time to feel sorry for him.

"Daniels? It's Jack…Jack MacIntosh."

"DI MacIntosh? Sir. What can I do for you?" PC Daniels sounded much more awake. "I was only thinking yesterday that……"

Jack cut in sharply; there wasn't time for niceties. "Tell me again about PRISM."

"PRISM?" PC Daniels sounded unsure. "I'm not sure, I…"

"PRISM," repeated Jack, trying to hide the impatience in his voice. "You told me it was a spin-off from NASA….some secret organisation……. stood for something like Protection Research….."

"Primary Research for International Space Management," finished PC Daniels. "But it wasn't secret. It was a committee set up to oversee NASA's involvement in international space projects. To try and coordinate regulations throughout the space industry…worldwide. It was Government financed, all above board."

"And Kreshniov?"

"A member of PRISM. Ex KGB Space Scientist. Thought to have headed up the Phoenix Project, if that ever existed."

"Did you ever stumble across any photographs of him? Kreshniov? In any of the research you did?"

PC Daniels paused. "Now you come to mention it, no. There were never any actual pictures of him that I could find. There was meant to be one kicking around somewhere, but I'll be blowed if I could find it. He was a bit of an enigma."

"Indeed."

"Disappeared in 1986, meant to have died in Russia in 1987. Never been heard of since."

"Until now," Jack breathed, and cut the call.

* * *

Time: 4.50pm
Date: 13th November 2008
Location: Metropolitan Police HQ, London

"Do you still have the personal effects of Andre Baxter?" Jack leant over the front desk to catch the attention of the custody sergeant. "The stuff we took from him when he came in?"

Sergeant Wiltshire nodded and pulled a folder out from under the counter. After leafing through the first few pages he came to what he wanted.

"Booked in, right here." He turned the folder towards Jack, so Jack could see the list of items for himself. He let his finger trail down the list. Money in various denominations, penknife, mobile phone charger, wallet, two sets of keys, phone…..but it was the last entry he was interested in.

CHAPTER THIRTY-FOUR

One Sony Flash Drive.

"I need that – the flash drive." Jack tapped the entry on the folder. "Right away."

"I'll get it booked out to you," nodded Sergeant Wiltshire, taking the folder back. "It might take a while, there's a bit of a commotion going on outside." He inclined his head towards the front doors. "The media circus are in town."

Just then DS Cooper came flying through the double doors leading from the interview room corridor. "Jack! Quick, it's Fleming.......Poborski....you need to see this."

* * *

Time: 4.52pm
   Date: 13th November 2008
   Location: Metropolitan Police HQ, London

Jack burst through the double doors, with DS Cooper following in his wake.

"Where is he?" barked Jack, striding down the corridor towards the interview rooms.

"Interview Room 5." DS Cooper almost jogged to keep up. "All hell is breaking loose, its chaos."

Their footsteps echoed as they quick stepped along the corridor floor, and once they rounded the corner they were immediately confronted by a flurry of chaotic activity.

All hell was, indeed, breaking loose.

A hastily erected cordon surrounded the door to Interview Room 5. Two scene of crime officers hovered in the background, dressed from head to toe in white protective body suits. They clutched evidence bags in their hands, waiting for the nod to begin their work.

As Jack and DS Cooper arrived, the senior police pathologist Dr Philip Matthews, emerged from the interview room, removing his white latex gloves with a snap. He looked grim. Catching sight of Jack, Dr Matthews gave a brief nod in his direction. Jack glanced down to the gloves in his hands – they were heavily blood stained.

Jack opened his mouth to speak, but Dr Matthews held up his hand.

"Gunshot to the head. Single shot. Dead before he hit the floor."

"Weapon?" asked Jack, arriving at the side of the senior pathologist, and raising his eyebrows more in hope than anything else.

Dr Matthews shook his head and ran a hand over his balding crown. "Nothing at the scene. Our guy just simply blew the man's brains out – then disappeared." The pathologist made a gun shape with his right hand and forefingers, and then waved his hand up in the air as if the weapon itself had simply disappeared into thin air. He was a tall man, having to stoop as he exited the interview room. His wiry frame made his expensive dark grey suit hang awkwardly off his shoulders. But Jack liked the ageing pathologist; he knew he could rely on him.

Jack nodded and watched as the two scene of crime officers received the go ahead to enter the room.

"Catch me later, Jack," said Dr Matthews, stepping aside. "After I've had a chance to do the PM. I'm not sure it'll tell us a great deal more, but I'll let you know." With that, the pathologist made his way back down the corridor, away from the bodies now filling the tight, narrow space.

Jack stepped towards interview room 5, stopping outside the door – careful not to cross the threshold and contaminate the scene. His eyes focused on the hardwood table in the centre of the room, a large pool of glutinous blood already covered the top of the table and was slowly dripping down the table legs onto the floor.

The man's head lay slumped unceremoniously in the centre of the bloody puddle, a single bullet hole clearly visible in the left temple. His eyes stared emptily across the table towards Jack.

"He had a visitor, Sir," said a young police officer, coming to stand at Jack's side. "WPC Lockwood at the front desk let him in. Said he was his defence solicitor, and that he knew him."

Jack turned and caught a glimpse of a tearful WPC talking to a senior

CHAPTER THIRTY-FOUR

officer. She was gesticulating with her hands, in between sobs, trying her best to describe the man who had breezed in and out of the building in less than 15 minutes.

"He gave her this card," carried on the young PC, handing Jack a small, rectangular, laminated card. "Said his name was Jonathan Hutchinson."

Jack took the card, but only gave it a cursory glance. He knew it would be fake. There was no such lawyer by the name of Jonathan Hutchinson. And there would be no such law firm by the name of Hutchinson, Reed and Stone.

With one last look back at Karl Poborski's lifeless eyes, Jack slipped the card into his pocket and began walking back towards the doors. He nodded at DS Cooper as he passed by.

"Andre? Or should I now say Kreshniov?" DS Cooper raised his eyebrows and inclined his head back towards the bloodied interview room.

"Has to be," murmured Jack, stepping aside as the two mortuary assistants arrived with a body bag and stretcher.

"Where do you think he will be now?" continued DS Cooper, following Jack back out into the reception area.

Jack shrugged, and shook his head. "With Andre…..Kreshniov……who knows?"

"DI MacIntosh?"

Jack turned round at the sound of his name, to see the custody sergeant waving a piece of paper at him.

"I have the flash drive you wanted." The custody sergeant leant across the desk and handed Jack the flash drive, Jack scribbling his signature on the desk sergeant's clip board to acknowledge receipt.

With a nod of thanks, Jack slipped the flash drive into his pocket and turned to head back upstairs he had a feeling the place was going to turn into a media circus, and he for one did not intend to be a part of it.

* * *

CHAPTER THIRTY-FIVE

Time: 12.35pm
  Date: 14th November 2008
  Location: Metropolitan Police HQ, London

Jack leant back in his chair, stretching his arms above his head. Both the chair and his shoulders creaked in unison. At least he had managed to get home last night for some much needed sleep, and sleep had come surprisingly easily too. Once the furore about Poborski's murder had died down, there was no point in hanging around for the fall out. Jack had sneaked out through the rear car park and set off for home on foot, avoiding the gaggle of newspaper reporters camped out on the front steps of the station. The new Chief Superintendent had made a short statement and refused to answer any questions, ensuring that the reporters would camp out overnight.

Once at home, Jack found Mac sound asleep on the sofa and dragged his duvet out from the bedroom to cover his brother. As he stood and watched Mac slumbering, he felt a pang of, what was it? Guilt? Sorrow? Love? Their lives had started out in exactly the same way, but the paths they had then taken had differed dramatically. Letting Mac sleep soundly under the warm duvet was the least he could do. Jack found some blankets in a cupboard and settled himself down to sleep.

"You sure it was Andre….Kreshniov…..that shot Poborski?" DS Cooper nodded at the photograph sitting in front of him on Jack's desk. Jack's gaze rested on the faces in the picture once again. The faces stared back at him.

CHAPTER THIRTY-FIVE

Isabel's eyes dancing with delight on her 5th birthday; her mother's eyes full of love and happiness; a young Boris Kreshniov smiling and laughing at the camera.

Jack gave a snort and rolled his eyes at the ceiling – the fluorescent lights above blinking intermittently. "Course it was him. Who else is left?" Jack studied the photograph again, looking deep into Andre's eyes. Into Boris Kreshniov's eyes. He saw the same twinkle. The same secretive, furtive look. Eyes that hid so much. Eyes that were still hiding so much more.

Sighing wearily, Jack pulled out the flash drive from his pocket and dropped it onto his desk next to the photograph. The flash drive contained the whole story – or at least, as much as anyone knew. As much as Shafer had known. Shafer had found out Andre's secret, had stumbled upon the fact that he was really Boris Kreshniov. How he had managed to find this out, nobody knew. No one but Shafer, and he would take that to his grave. By all accounts, Shafer was a remarkable MI6 agent. And a remarkable man.

The flash drive had contained a warning. A message. Shafer had been trying to warn Isabel and Mac that not only was Fleming not really FBI, and was actually Karl Poborski, but that Andre wasn't who he claimed to be either. Jack remembered Mac telling him about being in the café and looking at the contents of the flash drive – but Andre had shut the computer down before they had got to the end of it. It now began to make sense. Andre would not have wanted his secret unearthed so early in the plan.

Just then the telephone on Jack's desk began to ring. Jack glanced at it, buried as always under a pile of paperwork, but ignored it. After a few rings it fell silent. Moments later, the telephone on DS Cooper's desk began to ring instead.

"DS Cooper?" Cooper snatched up the receiver before it had completed its second trill. "Yes, he's here." DS Cooper flashed a look at Jack who was frantically shaking his head and waving his hands across his face. "You want to speak to him?"

There was a pause as DS Cooper listened to the voice on the other end.

"OK, I'll tell him." He replaced the receiver and turned to Jack. "Something's come through for you downstairs – something from the South African police? They've got some kind of video surveillance footage for you? CCTV?"

Jack nodded and yawned, leaning back in his chair once again. "I'll go down a bit later on."

DS Cooper caught hold of his partner's gaze and raised his eyebrows. "I think you might want to take a look now, Guv. They reckon they have something you might want to see."

* * *

Time: 1.05pm
    Date: 14th November 2008
    Location: Metropolitan Police HQ, London

"Get onto the Great Northern Bank, the branch on George Street," barked Jack. "Ask them to check the Faradays' account….NOW!"

DS Cooper snatched up the nearest telephone receiver and began to dial frantically. Jack turned back to the computer screen in front of him and studied the images playing out before him. The pictures were not great; black and white, and somewhat grainy. But they were good enough. They showed him exactly what he needed to see.

Reaching out, Jack clicked the mouse and made the whole video run once more from the beginning.

Footage from the Harbour Lodge Boarding House, Mahutu village, South Africa, 1st October 2008, started to play. The video camera had been placed behind the reception desk – if you could call it that. The reception area was a small room with two large double doors that opened out onto the street outside. There was one person behind the small wooden desk – the proprietor, Mr Mahlangu, Jack guessed. He could just make out the top of the man's head, a large balding patch only visible to the camera viewer.

CHAPTER THIRTY-FIVE

Mr Mahlangu, the owner of the boarding house, had set up the video camera behind the desk after two recent opportunistic robberies. The boarding house was his livelihood; his only source of income to support his wife and five children. He was not going to be robbed again without recording the criminals in action. The local South African police were so laissez faire, and most were in the pockets of the local gangs and criminal fraternity, Mr Mahlangu didn't trust them.

At precisely 3.17pm two figures walked into the reception area of the Harbour Lodge Boarding House. One approached the desk, while the other hung back by the entrance. Jack watched as the first man engaged Mr Mahlangu in a short conversation. After a minute or two, the man reached into his jacket pocket and pulled out what appeared to be a wallet, and began extracting a series of notes. Jack leant forwards, closer to the screen, trying to see through the greyness of the film. He watched as the man put the bundle of notes down on the desk in front of Mr Mahlangu and then slid a small piece of paper across to him.

He then turned to leave.

Jack paused the video with a click of the mouse. He glanced down at the typed written statement he held in his hand, faxed through from the local South African Police. They had interviewed Mr Mahlangu and the man's memory had been nothing short of spectacular. He had remembered his two visitors clearly; describing them perfectly, even down to the shininess of their shoes.

Maybe this was something to do with the fact that two complete strangers had walked in off the street, completely unannounced, paid off a customer's bill in cash, and had also left a healthy wad of notes for the "inconvenience".

Jack glanced back at the computer screen. The man who had just handed over the cash was frozen in time, hovering in the middle of the entrance lobby, turning to leave but staring right up at the camera as he did so. His eyes met Jack's. Jack stared back into those all too familiar eyes. He wore the same tight-lipped expression on his thin face; the same immaculately tailored suit clung to his sinewy frame; the same glint in those cold, grey eyes.

Karl Poborski had just settled Miles' boarding bill in full. No doubt because he knew that Miles would not be returning, mused Jack, an image of the young man's mutilated body flashing into his mind. According to Mr Mahlangu, Poborski had told him that there had been a family tragedy and Miles was flying directly back to the UK. Poborski had given him another bundle of notes to cover the cost of sending Miles' luggage, such as it was, to the address on the piece of paper. There was enough money to cover first class air freight home, plus a more than generous tip. Mr Mahlangu was told to keep the change, a sum which equated to more than three month's takings for the small boarding house.

Mr Mahlangu had done as he was bade, but he had the foresight to keep the piece of paper Poborski had given him. Jack looked back at the witness statement in his hand, and the photocopy attached to it.

28 Halfpenny Lane, Bagshot.

Jack rubbed his chain, feeling the ever present stubble pricking his fingers. It wasn't so much that Poborski had paid for Miles' rucksack to be shipped back to the UK – what concerned Jack more was the second man in the grainy video clip. Jack flicked his eyes back to the computer screen and focused on the man still standing by the entrance doors.

He was casually dressed, with a baseball cap and sunglasses on. He was leaning against the door frame, his face turned to look back out onto the street outside, while Poborski did the "business" with Mr Mahlangu. His face was turned away from the camera, obscuring his features. It was only when Poborski turned to walk away, the job having been done, that the second man changed position.

Jack clicked the mouse and let the video footage carry on. Poborski turned away from the desk and headed towards the open door. Even though he now had his back to the camera, Jack had no doubt at all that those thin lips would be curled into a smile. Poborski continued towards the door, heading towards the second man; and it was then that Jack saw him.

It was only the briefest of glimpses, but that was enough.

CHAPTER THIRTY-FIVE

With a quick nod of the head, Poborski walked out of the door into the glaring South African sunshine.

Boris Kreshniov turned and followed.

Jack raised his head and looked over at DS Cooper, who was just hanging up the phone. Cooper met Jack's gaze and slowly shook his head.

"The account was cleared several days ago," said DS Cooper. "All funds withdrawn."

Jack let out an audible sigh. He already knew the answer to his next question, but he asked it anyway.

"Any record of who withdrew it?"

DS Cooper shook his head once again. "They won't give out that kind of information without a warrant, but they were able to tell me that it would have to have been one of the nominated trustees."

Jack nodded.

Of course it would.

* * *

Time: 1.15pm

Date: 12th November 2008

Location: Interview rooms, Metropolitan Police HQ, London

"I knew the money wouldn't be at the Paris bank vault. I had most of it moved a while ago. Poborski was on a wild goose chase from the very beginning."

"You moved it?" Jack leant back in his chair and chewed the end of his pen while he listened.

"Well, Mr & Mrs Faraday did, "replied Andre. "And me. We were all Trustees for the account. No one could withdraw or move any funds without our signatures."

"Until Isabel came of age….." said Jack.

Andre shook his head. "Even when she turned 25, Isabel still needed the Trustees permission to remove the funds. She would only have individual access to the account when we signed away our Trusteeship." Andre paused, and then added. "Mr & Mrs Faraday wanted the money to be doubly protected, they still didn't trust anyone."

"Apart from you," commented Jack, eyeing Andre carefully.

Andre gave a small nod. "Apart from me, yes."

"So when did you move it?"

"A while ago, I'm not quite sure of the date." Andre paused and matched Jack's careful gaze. "I left a small amount in there, in the Paris account, just to keep the account open."

"Any reason for the move?" asked Jack, raising his eyebrows questioningly.

Andre merely shrugged. "No, not really. It was just easier to have it all in London."

* * *

Time: 1.20pm
Date: 14th November 2008
Location: Metropolitan Police HQ, London

Of course it was.

Jack knew the real reason the money had been moved. In London it was more accessible. In London it would be right where he wanted it. In London, Boris Kreshniov could finally get his hands on what he had been after all along.

"Tell me," mused Jack, still looking at the grainy images of the Harbour Lodge Boarding House. "Imagine you are a master of identity fraud. What would you do with $1m of stolen cash?"

"I'd make myself a new identity and disappear," replied DS Cooper, without hesitation. He walked over and joined Jack at the computer monitor. Together they both watched the grey images from the Boarding House play out once again.

"Exactly," breathed Jack. "Exactly."

CHAPTER THIRTY-FIVE

***

Time: 3.30pm
   Date: 14th November 2008
   Location: Beverly Hills Hotel, Los Angeles, USA

The hotel receptionist tapped the keys, lightly, on her keyboard; her long manicured fingernails gleaming with a shiny coat of perfect peach.

"And how many nights will you be staying. Mr Orlande?" She looked up and gave Boris Kreshniov a wide smile, her pearly white teeth glinting in the hotel's soft lighting. Her lips were dark and full, their redness a stark contrast to her porcelain features. She reminded him of Marie, in a way.

When she had been alive.

***

Time: 7.00pm
   Date: 9th November 2008
   Location: Flat 5, Rue de Bougainvillea, Paris

He looked back over his shoulder and nodded, contentedly, to himself. The room looked as it always had done; neat, tidy, everything in its place.

The body could not be seen straight away from a casual glance, hidden behind the luxurious white sofa in the middle of Marie's lounge. He went over and gave her one last look. It was a shame. She had been quite nice; until he had realised she had double crossed him with Poborski. Once he knew that, her fate had been sealed.

Bending down at her side, Kreshniov tucked a stray hair behind her ear and stroked the side of her cheek with a gloved hand. Beautiful. So beautiful, really. Her porcelain white skin hid the fact that her life had been extinguished, her scarlet red lipstick still covered her plump, fleshy lips. They were still soft and pliable to the touch. In time she would stiffen and death would take hold of her features, casting her in stone for eternity.

Kreshniov leant forwards and arranged the chiffon scarf around her neck to hide the developing bruises, the evidence of her means of death.

"Goodbye, Marie." He whispered, giving her cheek one last stroke. "You should never have trusted him."

Straightening himself up. He glanced around the room one more time before heading for the door. He needed to get going. He was only meant to be collecting his wallet from his flat on the floor above. They would be waiting for him.

Pulling the door shut behind him, Kreshniov didn't look back.

* * *

Time: 3.30pm
    Date: 14th November 2008
    Location: Beverly Hills Hotel, Los Angeles, USA

"Just the one," replied Kreshniov, returning the smile. "I have some business to attend to."

"One night in our Penthouse Suite," confirmed the receptionist, entering the rest of the information in the hotel's computer. "Of course, Sir. Have you any luggage?"

Kreshniov glanced down at the briefcase sitting on the luxurious pile carpet beneath his feet, leaning against his ankle. He afforded himself a small, secret smile. A knowing smile.

"Just the one….but I'll take it up myself." He gave another smile at the receptionist and a stony glare at the loitering bell-hop nearby.

"And how will you be paying, Sir?" asked the receptionist, turning the hotel log book forwards him.

"Oh, I shall be paying cash," smiled Kreshniov, filling in his details with large spidery handwriting. He gave another sideways glance at the briefcase by his feet. "I think that's best, don't you?"

He returned the hotel log book to the receptionist and winked.

"Have a nice stay with us here at the Beverly Hills, Mr Orlande." The

CHAPTER THIRTY-FIVE

receptionist handed him his key accompanied by another wide, well-rehearsed smile.

* * *

CHAPTER THIRTY-SIX

Time: 8.20am
 Date: 15th November 2008
 Location: 28 Halfpenny Lane, Bagshot, Surrey

Number 28 Halfpenny Lane was on a quiet looking street. Each side of the road had tidy looking detached and semi-detached houses, neat and well-tended gardens, with immaculately swept front paths and driveways. It was a shady street, the pavements lined with leafy oak and horse chestnut trees.

Number 28 was towards the far end, tucked away in a corner. Its front garden was neatly kept, with a circular flower bed in the middle of neatly clipped grass, and a thick waist high hedge circling around the edge.

Jack checked the address one more time from the photocopied paper in his hand. It was the right address. Slowly, he stepped forwards and pushed open the small metal gate. It creaked a little, the noise amplified by the sleepy silence of the street. He looked over his shoulder in case he could see if any of the neighbours were watching. He saw plenty of net curtains, but none were twitching.

He turned back and stepped through the gate. Carrying on up the garden path, Jack quickened his step. He didn't fancy engaging in too much conversation should anyone care to ask who he was and what exactly he was doing here. Hell, he didn't even really know whose house this was supposed to be.

The front door was solid wood and fitted with a Yale lock. Jack raised

CHAPTER THIRTY-SIX

his hand and pretended to knock, but after a few seconds he decided to make a detour around the side of the house. The garden path continued around the left hand side of the house, and Jack cautiously made his way along it. Once again he took a brief glance over his shoulder; still nobody in Halfpenny Lane was watching.

There was one small window along the side of the house, and another door. Jack paused by the window. It looked like it would be a window into a downstairs toilet or bathroom. He leant forwards and tried to peer inside, but the ridged glass gave nothing away. Without wishing to waste any more time, Jack made a decision. He dragged a nearby wheelie bin across the path and picked up a decent sized stone that was resting nearby. Without looking to see if anyone from Halfpenny Lane had woken up and begun watching, Jack hoisted himself up onto the top of the wheelie bin. He simultaneously felt the wheels move under his weight and the shoulder seam of his jacket rip. He swore under his breath but carried on.

The window was approximately 3 feet high and 3 feet wide, and was shut fast. Holding onto the window ledge with one hand to steady himself, Jack knelt on the top of the wheelie bin and shrugged off his suit jacket. He noticed the right arm was ripped away from the shoulder seam, exposing the frayed threads. Quickly, he wrapped up the stone in the jacket and smacked it against the window pane.

It rebounded immediately and nearly bounced out of his hand. Swearing again, Jack wrapped up the stone even more tightly and flung it at the window with so much force that he nearly toppled off the bin with the effort. This time the glass splintered upon impact, sending Jack's jacket and the stone sailing inside through the jagged opening.

"Shit," cursed Jack, out loud this time, struggling to retain his balance. As he drew his hand back through the jagged glass, a thin trickle of blood rolled through his fingers. He instinctively sucked the skin, the metallic taste of the blood filling his mouth. "Shit, shit, shit." He looked down and saw that it was only a small cut, although seemingly quite deep. He glanced back at the window and saw an ugly jagged pieced of glass protruding from around the window frame. He cursed again and then kicked at the glass splinters with his shoe.

With the window now relatively free from glass fragments, or as good as he could make it with a size 9 shoe, Jack got back on his hands and knees and began to crawl through the opening.

He had been right; the window did lead into a bathroom. It was a tight fit, but Jack manage to pull himself onto a ledge inside the window, sending bottles of half used shampoo, bubble bath and hair wax crashing down into the empty bath below. He swung his legs through and dropped down into the bath.

The bathroom smelt clean. There was a faint citrus aroma in the air. Jack also noticed that there was a new roll of toilet paper in the dispenser, and toilet bleach cleaner had recently been sprayed around the toilet bowl.

Stepping out of the bath, Jack's gaze rested on the sink next to it. Peering more closely, Jack could see traces of hairs around the plug hole and a pair of small scissors resting on the side. The blades on the scissors bore more traces of hair. Bending down, Jack reached into the wastepaper bin and retrieved an empty packet of black hair dye.

Dropping the box of hair colourant back into the bin, Jack turned and left the bathroom. Outside was a small hallway; to the right led to the front door. There was a thick heavy curtain pulled across the door, shutting out any trace of sunlight. To the left, the hallway led further into the house. Jack turned left and soon found himself in a small kitchen. Doors off from the kitchen led to a separate living room and dining room. All showed evidence of recent visitors. Empty cups and plates stood on the draining board in the kitchen. Food was still in the fridge. The TV was on stand-by in the living room.

Jack made a quick sweep of the downstairs rooms. The contents of the house appeared to be pretty standard. Nothing stood out as unusual. There were books on the bookcase, DVDs stacked up next to the TV. Magazines and newspapers were in a rack next to an armchair; Jack noticed the latest newspaper was dated yesterday 14th November. There were pictures on the walls; ornaments sat on shelves and in display cabinets. Cups, saucers and plates were stacked inside the kitchen cupboards; cutlery lay

CHAPTER THIRTY-SIX

in drawers. There were even coats and jackets hung neatly on coat hooks underneath the stairs.

With one last look at the downstairs, Jack turned and jogged up the narrow staircase. He didn't know how much time he had, but he knew what he was looking for.

Upstairs he found three bedrooms of varying sizes, all simply furnished. Clothing was hung in wardrobes; shoes stacked neatly under the beds. Clock radios blinked on bedside tables.

Jack opened and checked all the wardrobes and cupboards. Nothing.

He checked under the beds. Nothing.

He opened the chests of drawers. Still nothing.

Pausing on the small landing, Jack scratched his head. His finger was still oozing blood and starting to throb. Where would it be? Was it even still here? Maybe it had been sent somewhere else entirely, or even destroyed? Perhaps he was wasting his time looking for something that no longer existed. It had been a long shot after all.

Jack sighed and made to head back downstairs again. Then he paused. In between bedrooms one and two was a small narrow door. To Jack it looked like an airing cupboard. Stepping across the landing, Jack pulled the door open and sure enough there were several shelves crammed with layers of sheets, duvets covers, pillow cases and towels. The cupboard was jam packed. There didn't seem to be an inch of spare space anywhere.

Jack made to close the door, believing it to be another dead end, when something caught his eye. The bottom section of the airing cupboard housed the hot water tank, and filled most of the area. There was a narrow gap on either side for the pipe work.

But as Jack peered closer, he saw something. Something seemed to be wedged behind the hot water tank. He knelt down and reached into the dark cavity with his bleeding hand. He rummaged around blindly, unsure what he was touching and not really wanting to think about how many spiders may be lurking in the cobwebby depths, until he felt something. Closing his grip on it, he pulled it out.

THE PHOENIX PROJECT

* * *

Time: 12.55pm
 Date: 13th November 2008
 Location: Interview rooms, Metropolitan Police HQ, London

Andre slowly drummed his fingernails on the worn wooden table top. His voice was low and controlled. He avoided looking at the graphic photograph of Miles' mutilated body.

"Once I knew they were seeing each other…..I had to make him leave."

Jack frowned, deep furrows forming on his forehead like troughs on a dried up river bed. "But why? Isabel was a grown woman – what harm could it have done?"

Andre was shaking his head even before Jack had finished speaking. "I couldn't' allow it. I promised to look after her…."

"Didn't Miles take care of her?" cut in Jack. "They liked each other….didn't he keep her safe? I don't understand."

Andre's head shook even more violently. "No, I couldn't let it happen. It wasn't……it wasn't right."

"Fancy her yourself, did you?" challenged Jack, fixing Andre's cool blue eyes with a chilling stare of his own. "Was that it? Have designs on her yourself? Need to move the younger guy out of the picture first?"

"Don't be sick," exploded Andre, forcing his hands into fists and banging them so hard on the table that Jack's pen rolled off onto the floor. "She was young enough to be my daughter!"

Jack shrugged. "So what did you say to him? To Miles, I mean….to make him leave?"

Andre's mouth twitched in suppressed anger. "They weren't that serious about each other, it didn't take much."

"That's not the impression Isabel gave me," replied Jack, reaching down to pick his pen up from the floor. "She was heartbroken when he left."

Andre's hands began quivering again and he clenched them tightly

CHAPTER THIRTY-SIX

together to make it stop. "It had to be done," he breathed. "They couldn't be together."

* * *

Time: 9.00am
Date: 15th November 2008
Location: 28 Halfpenny Lane, Bagshot, Surrey

The rucksack was dirty. There was no telling how long it had been stuffed away out of sight behind the water tank. But Jack had no doubt who it had belonged to. He pulled on a set of latex gloves to preserve any forensic evidence that may be on or inside the bag; although fully aware that his unorthodox way of gaining entry to the property pretty much rendered any evidence inadmissible in court.

He unzipped the top of the bag and folded down the flaps. Peering inside he saw that there were a few items of clothing near the top – some t-shirts, a couple of baseball caps, a pair of shorts. Reaching in a bit further, Jack found an iPod, some batteries and a set of ear phones.

Along the side of the rucksack there was a separate inner compartment, which Jack carefully unzipped next. This section contained a few toiletries – some sun cream, insect repellent, shampoo and shower gel.

Jack re-zipped the bag. He wasn't interested in t-shirts, sun cream or insect repellent.

The last section of the bag to be searched was at the front. There was a small compartment, no bigger than a pouch or pocket really. Jack pulled back the zip and waited. He wasn't quite sure what to expect, what he would find. Reaching inside he pulled out a mobile phone, wallet and a small address book.

Jack turned the wallet over in his hand, and winced as the cut on his finger opened up. He could see an area of dark liquid spreading inside the latex glove. Turning his attention away from the pain, Jack focused back on the wallet. It seemed to be quite full, bulging even. He unpopped the press stud fastening and the wallet fell open. Inside there was a bundle of crumpled foreign currency notes – mainly South African. A few uncashed travellers' cheques. Some loose change. There was a UK driver's licence tucked away in the back. Jack looked at Miles' face as it stared out from the small square picture on the front.

Behind the driver's licence there were several other photographs. Jack pulled them out and studied them one by one. The first picture immediately made his stomach lurch. It was a picture of Isabel. A picture of her carefree face. She was smiling, laughing, seemingly without a care in the world. The photograph seemed worn around the edges, as if someone had handled it many times. As if someone had held it close every night before falling asleep.

Jack slid Isabel's photograph back into the wallet. Then he froze. In his hand he held two more pictures. But these were much older. The first was of a smiling baby with clear blue eyes twinkling out from a chubby baby face. A toothless grin; shiny red cheeks. A chin coated in dribble. Two cheeky dimples on either side.

Instinctively Jack turned the picture over. On the back he read the inscription.

"Our favourite picture of you! Aged 6 months 20th June 1986." Jack turned the photograph back over and stared once more into those clear blue eyes. He then turned his gaze to the second photograph in his hand, and his heart momentarily froze. His stomach tightened and lurched as if it was about to jump out of his mouth. His heartbeat quickened so much that he could feel it pulsating in his ears. He felt like his head was about to explode.

The picture he held in his hands was so familiar. Chillingly familiar. He had seen one just like it before, almost a mirror image. Two happy, smiling, doting parents, grinning out at the camera. A small child no more than 4 years old, sitting aboard a tricycle. And a family friend standing, happily, beside them.

Christopher Faraday had a caring arm around his wife; she had her head rested happily against his shoulder. Both were smiling into the camera

CHAPTER THIRTY-SIX

lens. But the child in the photograph was not Isabel.

It was a boy.

Jack's hands felt clammy inside his latex gloves. He no longer felt the painful throbbing from his finger; no longer noticed or cared for the blood accumulating inside. He held the photograph of the smiling toothless baby in his left hand, and compared it to the photograph in his right. It was the same child. It had to be. There was the same smile, albeit the child on the tricycle now had teeth. The eyes had the same cheeky twinkle, the cheeks were still chubby and red. The same cheeky dimples on each side.

Jack then pulled out Miles' driving licence again. He felt his mouth go peculiarly dry. He stared into Miles' clear blue eyes again – and then into the eyes of the child on the tricycle. And then into the blue eyes of the chubby baby.

He didn't need the FRU to tell him they were all an exact match.

With his hands now visibly shaking, Jack turned over the family photograph. Sure enough there was an inscription, once again in the same neat handwriting.

"21st December 1989 – 4th birthday with Uncle Andre."

Jack turned the photograph back over and looked at the happy family smiling back at him, and the grinning 4-year-old Miles. And the smiling face of the family friend.

Boris Kreshniov stared back out at him.

* * *

Time: 9.00am
Date: 15th November 2008
Location: Beverly Hills Hotel, Los Angeles, USA

The foyer of the Beverly Hills Hotel was bustling with a large group of Japanese businessmen, all congregating underneath the sparkling, glittering chandeliers near the check-in desks. They greeted each other with a firm handshake and slight bow, their ID badges swinging from around their necks, announcing their participation in the Fujitsu national management conference. The vast lobby echoed with their enthusiastic chattering.

But noise was good.

Crowds were good.

It meant Boris Kreshniov was able to slip into a quiet corner of the foyer bar, selecting a booth that shielded himself from the hub-bub of the Fujitsu checking in process. Kreshniov watched with amusement as neatly-dressed bell hops rushed back and forth, carrying heavy leather and Samsonite suitcases across to the foyer lifts.

Nobody paid any attention to Boris Kreshniov.

Or the man that sat opposite him.

The waitress brought them their two cups of coffee, strong and black, but her attention too was drawn to the melee taking place in front of the check in desks. She paid little attention to her only customers sitting in their private booth, whisking away the breakfast menu when both gentlemen indicated that just coffee was fine.

Kreshniov glanced up and took a long, hard, measured look at his guest over the top of his coffee cup.

"No hitches?" Kreshniov raised his eyebrows, questioningly.

"None." Austin Edwards gave a brief shake of the head and sipped his own coffee. His ample frame filled his side of the booth more than adequately, and he rested his forearms on the table as he leant closer towards Kreshniov. "It's as though I don't exist anymore," he smirked.

"Well, you don't." Kreshniov slipped a plain brown envelope across the table towards Edwards, taking a quick look around to see if anyone was watching. But nobody seemed remotely interested in two businessmen having a breakfast coffee together.

Edwards gave a small smile, his pale blue eyes glinting behind his new tortoiseshell-rimmed glasses that perched on his nose. His distinctive silvery hair had been lightly tinted with a touch of auburn, his eyebrows to match. His short, stocky frame had been elevated several inches by cleverly inserted heel wedges in his shoes, and an expertly disguised, yet

CHAPTER THIRTY-SIX

somewhat constrictive corset was holding his rotund middle section in check.

Austin Edwards looked, and felt, like a new man. He took the envelope and placed it in the seat next to him, on top of the early morning edition of the Beverley Hills Courier. He knew what would be inside. He trusted Kreshniov. Many didn't, but he knew that he could trust the extraordinarily brilliant scientist sitting opposite him. A man who hadn't yet changed the world, but Edwards had every faith in him that he ultimately would. Inside the envelope would be several more new identities Edwards could use to further disappear and enjoy the quiet life he so craved. Faking his own suicide had been a stroke of genius, orchestrated by the man opposite; the man who could make anyone disappear.

"And the book?" Kreshniov took another sip of coffee and nodded at the envelope that Edwards himself had brought with him to their breakfast meeting. Edwards slipped the somewhat larger and thicker padded envelope across the table towards Kreshniov and nodded.

"It's all there, as instructed. Your chap in Paris sent it by FedEx."

Kreshniov took the envelope, feeling the weight of its contents. He deftly slid his finger under the seal and flipped it open. He needed to see it for himself. Otherwise all of this would have been for nothing. Kreshniov didn't trust Edwards; Kreshniov didn't trust anyone.

While the two men drank their coffees, and waved away the waitress enquiring about re-fills, Kreshniov stared at the bundle of papers that he had slipped out of the envelope. The contents of his beloved Dracula lay in-between the salt and pepper shakers and the brunch menus. It had been a shame to have had to leave the book behind in his apartment, but it gave Kreshniov some perverse amusement to try and imagine the look on Detective Inspector MacIntosh's face when he opened the book to find it lay empty. For he knew that DI MacIntosh would have made the trip to Paris, to his apartment, to pick up the book that held the answers to so many questions.

Kreshniov let a small smile play on his lips as he lightly ran his fingers over the papers. The only existing set of Phoenix Project papers were safe and sound once more, under his watchful guard.

* * *

Time: 3.30pm
   Date: 15th November 2008
   Location: Metropolitan Police HQ, London

Jack held the photograph of a young Miles Faraday in his hand. A carefree little boy sitting aside his first tricycle, no doubt looking forward to the birthday cake and party games yet to come. Jack could make out a faint balloon pinned to the door of the house in the background of the picture.

Then he picked up the almost identical one showing Isabel astride her own tricycle – the pictures were chillingly similar. The only difference was the location. Isabel had been at home in the garden of her parents' house in Albury, Surrey. Jack had no idea where Miles' childhood home had been. France? Switzerland? Further afield?

Jack placed both photographs back down on his desk and sighed. The reason why Miles had been sent halfway around the world, ultimately to his death, was now crystal clear.

He could not be with the woman he loved.

Because she was his sister.

* * *

CHAPTER THIRTY-SEVEN

Time: 11.00am
Date: 16th November 2008
Location: MailBox Inc, Tottenham Court Road, London

It hadn't taken the investigation team long. A few well-placed phone calls to mail box companies across the capital, and the results had come back almost instantaneously. Various PO mail box addresses which had lain dormant and unused – fully paid up but never receiving any mail from anyone at any time. Initially the mail box companies were reluctant to speak and divulge any information on their customers, but as soon as they realised they were caught up in the scandal that had littered the national press for the last three days, they soon changed tack and couldn't be more cooperative.

The mail boxes had been opened to reveal exactly what Jack had expected. He afforded himself a small laugh as he pulled out the contents of the fourth box he had searched that morning.

"You had us all fooled, for so long," he murmured, unable to stop the smile forming on his lips.

Inside this particular mail box, just like all the others, Jack found a pouch containing several different shades of hair dye, a small set of scissors, comb and electric razor. A separate box contained a variety of coloured contact lenses, several different styles of glasses, even a few wigs. A final larger box spilled copies of forged passports, driving licenses and identification cards. Everything you needed to alter your appearance and identity in the shortest possible time.

Jack placed all the items into a cardboard box and carried it over to the cash desk.

"You'll need to sign for those," commented the cashier, turning a piece of paper towards Jack.

Jack nodded, well used to the procedure by now, and added his signature to the bottom. He then scooped up the box and went to re-join DS Cooper who was waiting on the pavement outside.

"Another?" DS Cooper nodded at the cardboard box in Jack's arms.

Jack nodded and tapped the box, "Yep, we got another one. How many does that make now?"

DS Cooper consulted his notebook. "This makes four across the capital this morning. And we've had calls in from Newcastle, Manchester and Birmingham with another possible half dozen or so between them."

Jack rested the box on top of his car, parked illegally on a double yellow line. He reached inside and brought out a handful of the forged passports.

Dimitri Chekov.

Walter Towzier

Franco Di Ablo

Harrison Chandler

"Where are you today, Boris?" whispered Jack, holding up each passport in turn. "Or, should I say, *who* are you today?"

* * *

Time: 2.45pm
    Date: 16th November 2008
    Location: Green Park Parade, Cambridge

Jack climbed the small steps up to Isabel's front door. The curtains were shut, and so were the windows. Two pints of milk sat outside on the doormat. He looked own at his watch. It was 2.45pm; the place looked deserted.

CHAPTER THIRTY-SEVEN

Jack reached up and pressed the doorbell, hearing the soft jingle-jangle echo behind the door. He listened, but there were no sounds of footsteps following on. Jack pressed the doorbell again. He had phoned in advance, leaving a message on Isabel's answerphone, that he would be calling by this afternoon. As he stood there he clutched the photographs of young Miles Faraday and the very dead Miles Sanderson in his hand.

Miles Sanderson.

Miles Faraday.

Isabel's Miles.

One and the same.

What he would say to her, Jack didn't really know. He hadn't thought that far ahead. How do you break it to someone that the person you had thought was your boyfriend, partner, lover – was in fact your brother? The brother you never knew existed. The brother who was now dead.

"No use standing there, son," called a voice from behind him. Jack jumped at the sound and turned to see an elderly lady walking past the bottom of Isabel's steps, a fluffy tortoiseshell cat tucked underneath her arm. She was dressed in a flowery, quilted dressing gown, dusky pink slippers on her shuffling feet, her hair encased in a pale blue hairnet.

"Sorry?" replied Jack, watching as the lady slowly climbed up the steps adjacent to Isabel's house, gripping the stone balustrade and pulling her heavy and tiresome legs up to the top. She paused to catch her breath on the top step and turned to face Jack. She smiled, her aged face crinkling and creasing.

"The young lady," she said, shuffling towards her front door, holding the cat closer to her body as she slotted the key in the lock and pushed the door open. "No use ringing the bell, she's not there."

Jack raised his eyebrows and glanced back down at the forgotten milk on the step. "No? Do you happen to know where she might have gone?"

The old lady began to shuffle across the threshold of her house, shaking her head as she did so. "Sorry, son, I don't get out and about very much anymore. Don't really see much of her to talk to. But she's nice enough. Takes my bins out for me every week. Can't manage so well these days, you see, not with my legs. I only saw her this morning, mind, because this one escaped across the way there." She began chuckling to herself and rubbed the cat's fluffy head with a gnarled hand. "I only opened the door to put the milk bottles out and whoosh she was gone…"

"You were saying the young lady had gone out?" Jack tried to steer the conversation back round to Isabel. "Do you know what time that was?"

The old lady pondered for a moment and stroked her cat underneath its chin. "Must have been after ten…yes, it was, because I had just finished watching that hospital programme. I do so like that in the mornings. Those doctors are so lovely. Look so much younger than they did in my day. Some of them look like they are barely out of school, dressed up in their little white coats…."

"After ten, you say?" interrupted Jack, trying not to let his impatience show.

"Yes, yes," carried on the old lady, leaning on the door frame for support. "Must have been nearer eleven now I think of it. I had just finished making my morning tea. I do so love a cup of tea in the mornings, and a few digestives…..I was just putting the empty milk bottles out, so yes, it would have been just before eleven, my dear….."

"But you don't know where she went?"

The old lady shook her head. "A taxi drew up outside and beeped its horn. Didn't hang about though. Just pulled up, put her suitcases in the back, and then they drove off….."

"Suitcases?" Jack frowned. "Did you see what make or colour the taxi was? Or what taxi firm it was from?"

"Sorry, dear, I'm not too good on motor cars. Never driven myself, you see. Never learned. My dear old husband, God rest his soul, always did the driving for us. I wouldn't know one end of a car from the other." She began to cackle, which then turned into a deep, throaty cough. She put the cat down in the hallway of the house and gripped the doorframe until the cough began to subside. "Must get along inside now, my dear. This cold and damp doesn't do much for my poor old chest."

With that, the lady stepped inside and closed her door. Jack paused for

CHAPTER THIRTY-SEVEN

a moment, his mind racing. He had telephoned at 9.30 that morning, to say he was coming this afternoon. Isabel must have received the message before she left.

Quickly, looking over his shoulder to check that no one was about, Jack bent down and reached underneath a little stone flowerpot next to the milk bottles. His fingers soon found what he was looking for, and he smiled ruefully to himself. People did still leave keys under their flowerpots.

* * *

Time: 1.05pm
Date: 16th November 2008
Location: LAX – Los Angeles International Airport

Flight BA365 to the Czech Republic was boarding. Boris Kreshniov let himself be carried along in the steady stream of people heading towards gate 27. He tightened his grip on his hand luggage, the Phoenix Project papers safely stowed inside. This was a bag he needed to keep within reach.

Kreshniov held his passport and boarding card in his other hand, and glanced down at his photograph as he waited patiently in line at the gate. Today he was Kyle Sansom, US businessman en route to Eastern Europe to secure a much needed trade deal between Prague and San Francisco, where he was the head of a biotechnical firm. Kreshniov allowed himself a small smile. He enjoyed making up his new identities, giving them not only a new appearance and new name, but new personalities, new jobs and new backgrounds.

And Kreshniov had particularly enjoyed this one. Kyle Sansom was a highly successful biotechnical scientist, who also had stakes in the San Francisco 49ers football team, and was planning to cross over into the world of baseball and give sponsorship to the San Francisco Giants. Another smile reached his lips as he presented his passport and boarding card to "Lydia", the smiling British Airways stewardess.

Yes, Kyle Sansom was an interesting guy. Kreshniov looked forward to playing him for the next 12 hours or so of the flight.

***

Time: 10.30am
 Date: 17th November 2008
 Location: Metropolitan Police HQ, London

Jack smiled as he walked past Penny's desk. "Just need to take another look at the room, I'll only be a few minutes."

Penny looked up from her keyboard and took out one of the earpieces from her headphones. "I don't think you'll find much," she replied, nodding towards the closed door leading to Liddell's office. "They've already been in to clear the room – the new Chief Superintendent moves in tomorrow. Carpet fitters are coming this afternoon."

Jack pushed open Liddell's office door and Penny returned to her typing. The room was almost empty. The carpet had been ripped up and rolled towards the far wall, awaiting collection. No doubt the new Chief Superintendent didn't fancy having a carpet with a faint outline of blood indelibly etched into its surface. Jack had to concede that this was probably a wise idea.

Liddell's old desk was stacked up against the right hand wall, three straight-backed chairs racked up neatly on top. Several filing cabinets nestled next to it.

Jack stepped back outside the room and nodded at Penny. "The contents of his desk?" he asked, raising his eyebrows as Penny removed her earpiece once again. "Are they still in the drawers?"

Penny shook her head and nodded towards several smaller boxes piled up on top of each other on an armchair behind the door Jack had just walked through.

"Mrs Liddell is coming to pick them up later." Penny's gaze lingered for a moment on the boxes, then she turned back to her computer screen and

CHAPTER THIRTY-SEVEN

resumed her typing.

Jack backtracked over towards the boxes. There was something intrinsically sad about seeing someone's entire life and career reduced to a few items crammed into some plain boxes. It seemed so cold. So impersonal. So empty. So final.

Jack flipped open the top box and reached inside. It contained several family photographs in heavy wooden frames – smiling faces, joyful expressions, a memory of times past of happiness and laughter. Beneath the photographs were some old paperback books and magazines.

Lifting the top box onto the floor, Jack began looking through the next one. This box seemed to contain the contents of Liddell's desk drawers. There was a personal organiser, a desktop diary, calculator, various items of stationery, ink bottles, post-it notes, even a box of paper clips. What Mrs Liddell would need a box of paper clips for, or indeed much of the contents of the drawers, Jack was unsure.

He lifted out the personal organiser and snapped open the popper stud fastening. If he was correct, what he was looking for should be in here. He was sure he had seen a glimpse of it before, when he was last summonsed to Liddell's office, but its significance hadn't registered. At the time he had thought of it as a mere doodle – something Liddell had scribbled down absent mindedly while talking on the telephone. We all did it. But now Jack was sure it meant something entirely different.

He began flicking though the pages. He saw the familiar entries in the A-Z telephone directory – doctor; dentist; the children's schools; various friends and family. There were notes on the calendar not to miss important anniversaries and birthdays, holidays and weekends away that had been booked, school parents' evenings and concerts. But Jack wasn't interested in these. He let the organiser fall open at the last page.

There it was.

A hastily scrawled telephone number with a small symbol scratched out in pen by the side.

A symbol Jack now came to recognise.

A prism.

THE PHOENIX PROJECT

* * *

Time: 12.00 midday
   Date: 17th November 2008
   Location: Liberec, Czech Republic

The mobile in his jacket pocket began to vibrate. Reaching inside with his free hand, he cursed under his breath. He had meant to turn it off; mobiles were so easy to trace these days.

Looking at the display screen, Kreshniov began to chuckle.

"You will have to do better than that, Detective, if you want to find me."

With that, Kreshniov rejected the call and switched the mobile off. He removed the back cover and slid both the battery and SIM card out. He was quietly impressed though, and a small smile remained on his tight lips as he slipped unseen into the throngs of nondescript people inhabiting this beautiful yet nondescript town. If Detective Inspector McIntosh had found this number then he was very smart indeed, and Kreshniov liked smart people.

Still allowing himself a silent chuckle, Kreshniov moved quickly towards a nearby alleyway. It was market day and the refuse lorries were in town. With a quick look over one shoulder to reassure himself that no one was watching, he slid open a large refuse container belonging to a café, and tossed the mobile inside, together with the battery and SIM card. He heard the satisfying clunk as the phone hit the bottom.

He then sauntered across the street and slipped into a vacant chair at a pavement café and watched the world go by. Kreshniov loved people-watching. He watched intently as market day shoppers browsed the stall holders' offerings, haggled for the best prices and chattered animatedly with fellow browsers alike. Since arriving yesterday, he had sat in this same seat several times and watched the same pantomime be played out in front of him. Yet despite his regular visits, no one seemed to recognise him; no one seemed to acknowledge him; no one seemed to see him. It was like he was invisible. Even after all these years, he was invisible.

CHAPTER THIRTY-SEVEN

And that was exactly what Kreshniov wanted.

Today, however, he had the added pleasure of seeing a refuse lorry reverse into the alleyway opposite. Two refuse workers jumped out of the passenger door and began dragging the wheeled refuse containers towards the rear of the lorry. One by one the bins were loaded onto the rear platform, and one by one the bins disgorged their contents into the cavernous hole at the back of the lorry.

Kreshniov watched as the lorry hungrily devoured the offerings.

Sorry to spoil your fun, Detective Inspector MacIntosh, smiled Kreshniov, as he ordered a fresh cappuccino from the young waitress, and closed his eyes while faint rays of European sunshine gently kissed his face.

* * *

Time: 1.30pm
 Date: 17th November 2008
 Location: Investigation Room, Metropolitan Police HQ, London

Boris Kreshniov.

Andre Baxter.

One and the same; interchangeable.

Jack held the two photographs in his hands, studying the faces staring back at him. It had been clever; almost too clever. Kreshniov was the master of disguise. First reinventing himself as Gustav Friedman, then as Andre Baxter. No one ever questioned who he really was. Nobody who knew the real Kreshniov had ever met Gustav Friedman, or Andre.

It was the perfect cover.

Almost.

Even Liddell and Tindleman seemed to have been kept in the dark, used like pawns in a game of murder, greed and deceit.

"You OK?" DS Cooper entered the investigation room and noticed Jack was sitting in near total darkness, the blinds drawn.

Jack merely nodded, not taking his eyes from the pictures. "They strung us a merry dance, the pair of them" he murmured, placing the pictures down on the table in front of him. "Then ended up trying to double-cross each other. Very nearly worked too."

"M16 are investigating Poborski right now," nodded DS Cooper, leaning against the table by Jack's side. "His name has come up as a hit on their systems already."

"I bet it has," mused Jack, wearily getting to his feet. "Bit late now though." He felt exhausted. He hated it when a case got the better of him, it made him feel drained.

"There was no way we could have known, Jack," said DS Cooper. "Kreshniov being Baxter. Poborski being Fleming. There was no way we could even have suspected."

Jack nodded. "I know." He knew it was the truth, but it didn't make him feel any better. He still felt as though he had lost. Lost the case. Lost the battle; let the bad ones get the better of him. And it wasn't a feeling that he enjoyed.

"So, what now?" DS Cooper nodded at the evidence boxes stacked up on the main investigation table. "They all going into storage?"

Jack's gaze rested on the boxes he had just spent the last hour packing up. He knew they had no further use for them anymore. Not really. Now that Poborski was dead and Kreshniov had disappeared, nowhere to be seen, there seemed little point keeping the investigation alive.

The new Chief Superintendent, about to move into Liddell's former office downstairs, had summoned Jack and told him as much. The investigation was to be wound down, closed, forgotten. There was nobody of interest still left alive. Jack had dutifully bagged up the evidence, made detailed inventories neatly listing everything in their possession, before carefully stacking them all away inside the boxes that now stood on the table before them.

It had been one of the shortest lived investigations of Jack's career. No sooner was the case opened, then it was forced to close. Forced by an unseen hand exerting its new found force and authority from the offices

CHAPTER THIRTY-SEVEN

below. Jack understood the reasoning behind the decision, and accepted it. But it didn't mean he had to like it. There was too much at stake, that much was obvious. Too much embarrassment for the department, the security services, the Government. Five suicides, including two prominent members of the security and police services; the murder of a suspect whilst supposedly in secure police custody, murdered in fact by an escaped prisoner also meant to be under police arrest at the time. It made grim reading.

Theories and explanations were splashed across the daily newspapers with increasing voracity. The press officers for M15, M16 and the Metropolitan police were under unenviable pressure to come up with immediate answers and conclusions, being bombarded with accusations of incompetence and corruption reaching up towards the highest levels. The press office had never been so busy.

The new Chief Superintendent had entered into a hot bed of fire. It had become his first mission to pour as much cold water on the fiasco as he could, to douse the flames before they destroyed everything in their path.

In short, the whole sorry episode had to go away.

It had to be buried.

Jack ran his hand over the final pile of papers which he had been nursing on his desk. The final bundle of evidence to be buried. He was reluctant to place them inside the final box. He couldn't quite bring himself to let go, to finally give in and admit defeat. His heart felt heavy. Although he understood the reason behind the decision to wind up the investigation, and in his sincerer and thoughtful moments he probably agreed with that decision, but he still couldn't help but feel beaten.

But most of all he felt he had let Isabel down. The quest to find out the truth behind the Phoenix Project and her parents. The evidence, he was sure, still lay within these boxes. Yes, they had pieced together the information Andre….Kreshniov….had imparted before his escape……but the all-important evidence was gone. Only Kreshniov had that. And the only remaining copy of the Phoenix Project papers was undoubtedly with him. Jack had so wanted to be able to hold that final set of papers in his hands, and then pass them into the only person who should truly have them….a Faraday. Isabel Faraday.

Kreshniov. Poborski. The Faradays. Miles. Isabel. PRISM. The Phoenix Project.

The answer lay within these boxes; Jack was sure of it. It always did. The answer, and therefore the evidence, lay amongst the pages and pages of typescript witness statements and photographs that Jack had just bound up and logged. It was buried….somewhere. And despite Jack's best efforts, he had failed to unearth it.

Failed.

Jack sighed and approached the investigation table, the final bundle of paperwork under his arm. He reached across and pulled the final open box towards himself, about to place the bundle on top and seal the box ready for storage. To finally bury the Phoenix Project and send it to its grave.

But then he stopped.

Glancing at the papers in his hands through bleary, sleep-deprived eyes, Jack's gaze rested on the document on the very top. It was the most recent statement from Charles Tindleman's PA, taken by DS Cooper only the day before. It had been more of an afterthought really; just a way to dot the i's and cross the t's. Making the evidence, such as it was, complete.

There wasn't much she could tell them. She hadn't been in the office when Charles Tindleman had taken his own life, or indeed when he had started the fire in his waste paper basket. She had been on her lunch break and out of the building, only raising the alarm when she returned to the office with her sandwiches and could smell the smoke.

Jack lifted the statement off the top of the bundle and skimmed the first page again. He wasn't sure why he felt compelled to do it again; he had already read it through a dozen times or more. There was just a feeling inside him that he was missing something, missing something so blindingly obvious that it should be jumping right out of the page at him. But it wasn't. Whatever it was, if indeed it was something, remained hidden.

CHAPTER THIRTY-SEVEN

The statement contained the usual information. Her movements on the day in question. Her relationship with Charles Tindleman. Her knowledge of his day to day routines. Her thoughts on his state of mind in the days leading up to the tragedy.

It was a thorough statement. All credit to DS Cooper's investigative and communicative skills.

But then he saw it.

The very thing he had missed so many times before.

* * *

CHAPTER THIRTY-EIGHT

Time: 2.00pm
　Date: 17th November 2008
　Location: Liberec, Czech Republic

Boris Kreshniov sipped at his freshly made cappuccino and tried not to smile. It had all gone surprisingly well, even by his own standards. And here he was, drinking coffee in amongst the other hundreds of tourists at any one of the many pavement cafes this town had to offer – he blended in well.

He could be anyone.

Literally.

He put down his cup and continued to read his newspaper. Karl Poborski's face stared back out at him. Apparently he had been found murdered in the Metropolitan Police HQ four days ago – a cold, calculated, clinical murder according to the reporter. Kreshniov smiled. He stared deeply into Karl Poborski's eyes while a faint breeze ruffled the paper. Kreshniov could still see the hunger in those eyes, the greed, the insatiable desire for money. Money that Poborski felt was rightfully his. Money that had been promised for so long, and then so cruelly denied to him.

The Phoenix Project.

Kreshniov let the newspaper rest back down onto the pavement café table.

The Phoenix Project.

It had been *his* dream. It had been *his* creation. *He* had been there at its

CHAPTER THIRTY-EIGHT

birth, its inception. *He* had fed it. *He* had nurtured it and cared for it. *He* had *loved* it.

And he had been there at its end. At its final demise. At its very death.

But its birth had been exhilarating.

The Faradays had come to his attention at the very beginning, and he knew immediately they were the ideal candidates to help him in his quest. He had befriended them and won their trust. He infiltrated their lives, gained their friendship, and most importantly gained their loyalty. He became their friend and mentor. Good old Gustav Friedman, head computer research scientist at PRISM. The Faradays could not know his true identity – they could not know he was Boris Kreshniov. *No one* could know.

It was then that Kreshniov created the Phoenix Project. With the Faradays on board, his lifetime's work was about to come to fruition!

Kreshniov took another sip of his cappuccino and this time did not try and hide the smile forming on his lips. He did not care who saw him. All they would see is who he wanted them to see. Another tourist, sitting at another table, drinking another coffee. He was invisible.

Kreshniov had wanted the Phoenix Project to succeed more than anything. As the head of PRISM he carefully handpicked his team for the covert, secretive experiment. He needed the very best. And he got the very best. Poborski was easy to recruit – having defected from the Eastern Bloc he was eager to make something of himself in the West. And he wanted money; lots of money. His links to Russia meant that the Phoenix Project had a source of finance.

The others had been useful, yet expendable in their own way. The two Brits, Liddell and Tindleman were in way out of their depth – they were needed for credibility purposes only – and once they had outlived their usefulness they could be tossed aside.

Edwards; he had been a useful asset. Kreshniov trusted him more than the others, which was why he had been allowed to live. Kreshniov patted the envelope by his side, still unable to be separated from the final copy of the Phoenix Project papers. They would go everywhere with him from now on.

Kreshniov had lived and breathed the Phoenix Project from its very inception. He wanted it to succeed more than anything...more than life itself.

And it so very nearly did.

When the disaster struck, Kreshniov was crushed. He could not understand what had happened, what had gone wrong. All the test data had been correct; all safety checks had been completed. It was impossible for the Phoenix Project to fail.

But fail it did.

And for Kreshniov the consequences were unthinkable. He did not care about the lives lost. He did not care about the Faradays, or the baby they had produced. All he cared about was himself. Instead of being hailed a scientific hero, with his name going down in history as the forerunner of space exploration and space habitation, he was going to be branded a failure. A nobody.

But he, Boris Kreshniov, could *not* let that happen.

Kreshniov was ready for the reaction of his fellow Phoenix Project members. He knew they would want to cast him aside, distance themselves from him – distance themselves from the disaster. But he was unprepared for them treating him as if he were of no importance at all, ignoring his voice, ignoring his thoughts. Treating him as though he did not *exist*.

Did they not know how much that hurt him? Did they not understand how much of his life's work was wrapped up in the Phoenix Project? How could they want to throw all that away? The Phoenix Project may not have been ready this time, but it *could* be. It *could* work again. All it needed was some refinement, some more testing, some more time. They were still on the verge of something truly remarkable, something truly spectacular; something of such international importance that it could not be just cast aside and forgotten. *Buried*.

But no one listened to Boris Kreshniov.

The other Phoenix Project members had wanted him out. Gone. They had vetoed the idea of the Project carrying on, instead wishing to bring it

CHAPTER THIRTY-EIGHT

to a swift and premature end. They did not want to listen to Kreshniov anymore. They did not trust him and they did not believe in him. Instead they closed ranks and shut the Project down. Evidence was buried. The Project *terminated*.

The Phoenix Project members were united in their desire to bury everything to do with the Project and its experiments. There couldn't be any risk of news of the disaster reaching the population at large. It had to disappear. But it was not only the physical evidence of the Phoenix Project that bothered them; there was the evidence that lived and breathed inside each and every one of them. Their own thoughts. Their own memories. That could not be erased.

So a deadly pact was formed. They would all live and keep the secret of the Phoenix Project safe with them; or they all died and took the secrets with them to their graves.

Kreshniov shifted in his seat and adjusted his sunglasses. The mid November sunshine was weak, but enough to dance over the terracotta flagstones in front of the café and rest on his skin. He could barely feel its warmth, but it gave a comforting illusion. He looked about him, watching as people went about their daily lives, oblivious to him and oblivious to what he had done.

His eyes lowered once more to the newspaper on the table before him. Karl Poborski still stared out at him with those same greedy eyes. A small part of him felt sorry for Poborski – a very small, miniscule part. They had both been cast aside by the rest of the Phoenix Project members; both acceptable casualties in the greatest disaster in space exploration history. It was inevitable that they would join together in the aftermath, there could have been no other outcome. Their initial loathing of each other soon morphed into a kind of mutual admiration, and then an unbreakable bond. Both became fixated on revenge – no matter what it cost, no matter how long it took. With Kreshniov's talent for creating fraudulent identities, they both were able to disappear and sink without trace – agreeing only to surface when they were sure their ultimate goal was in sight.

Ten years.

Fifteen years.

Twenty years.

It didn't matter how long it took.

They could wait.

Kreshniov still held Poborski's gaze in his eyes, staring out at him from the newsprint. The greed. It could always be seen in a person's eyes. They had both wanted the downfall of the other Phoenix Project members, but for completely different reasons. For Poborski it was obviously the money – money he thought was rightfully his, but had been denied him. For Kreshniov it was the destruction of the Phoenix Project members themselves; he wanted them to pay. Not in money. But in their lives.

So the final plan was hatched. They would obtain the final copy of the Phoenix Project papers, bring Isabel to Paris and thereby gain access to her family fortune. Poborski would get the cash, Kreshniov would get the documents.

And then they would disappear.

Forever.

Kreshniov knew that as soon as the Phoenix Project papers were out there, in the public domain, the rest of the Project members would carry out their deadly suicide plan. Kreshniov and Poborski had also undertaken to be part of the suicide pact; but Kreshniov gave a slight chuckle to himself as he took another sip of his cappuccino. That was never going to happen.

Kreshniov closed the newspaper, breaking Poborski's penetrating stare. He had resented Poborski's involvement from the outset and had never trusted him. As far as he was concerned, Poborski was one of the reasons that the whole project had failed. And the more time he spent with the man, the more Kreshniov's loathing for his ex-KGB associate deepened. So Kreshniov had decided to move the money. The transfer of the Faraday fortune was surprisingly easy. Julian Brownlow had unwittingly seen to that. Kreshniov was already a named Trustee on the Trust account holding Isabel's family inheritance under his assumed name of Andre Baxter. All it took was a friendly phone call to his good friend, Julian, Chief Executive of the Premier Capital Bank, and the deed was done.

CHAPTER THIRTY-EIGHT

* * *

Time: 5.45pm
   Date: 8th November 2008
   Location: L'Apartament Blancos, L'Avenue du Soleil, Paris

Mac was sleeping soundly on the sofa closest to the window, but Andre was confident he would not stir. The man had been without sleep for far too long; nothing was going to wake him tonight. Andre was wide awake and alone; having suggested to Isabel that she have a lie down in the small bedroom. Moving as quietly as he could, Andre pulled his laptop out of his holdall and switched it on. He hoped that gentle whirring sound as the laptop fired up didn't wake his sleeping companions. It didn't. Nobody stirred.

Andre glanced at the clock on the wall – 5.45pm. But 4.45pm in London. He hoped that there was enough time before the banks closed for business for the day. Pulling out his mobile phone, Andre quickly dialled Julian's direct number.

"Julian?" said Andre, trying to keep his voice as low as he could. "It's me, Andre." He paused while Julian Brownlow acknowledged the call. "Yeah, I'm fine. You know you said to call if I ever needed any help?"

It took less than five minutes.

A fresh deposit account at the Premier Capital Bank was opened in the name of Andre Baxter. Julian handled it personally while Andre remained on the other end of the phone. By the time he ended the call, his new account was set up and ready to receive new funds. There had been no need for the usual form-filling, or background security checks into his credit worthiness. No requirement to verify his identity with three forms of photo ID as would normally be the case. Julian had seen to all of that. It was the very least he could do, he said, for the man who had saved his bank's security systems and prevented him from being exposed to potential ruin. Whatever Andre wanted, Julian Brownlow was prepared to give him, no questions asked.

Julian trusted him.

Andre reflected for a split-second. There was a part of him that felt a little sorry for Julian. He liked the man. They had struck up quite a friendship over the many months they had been doing business together, and Andre did actually like the man.

But there was no room for sentiment anymore.

Andre reached into the side of his holdall and brought out the slim CD rom he had brought with him from his flat. He was glad he had hung onto it, and not sent it straight to Julian as he had promised. A brief whisper of guilt fleetingly washed over him, but he quickly brushed it aside. Julian would get the CD rom; eventually. He just had one thing to do with it first.

Andre inserted the disc into the laptop and waited for the programme to load. Again the laptop whirred into action, and Andre kept a careful eye on the slumbering Mac to check for any signs of awakening. With the CD rom quietly purring in the background like a contented cat, Andre opened up his new account details on the Premier Capital Bank website. The details of his newly formed account sprang onto the screen – current balance £0.00.

Andre clicked on the "change personal details" icon, and with the help of the security system busting CD rom programme, he was able to access his personal details within seconds. He was quickly able to change the name on the bank account, bypassing all encrypted security programmes that would normally prevent computer hackers accessing account details and making any changes. Accessing accounts and changing names was not a problem with the help of the CD rom. All were bypassed without so much as a hiccup.

Within three minutes, Andre Baxter's name had been erased from the newly created bank account, and indeed the banking system altogether. He no longer had an account with the Premier Capital Bank. He had *never* had an account with the Premier Capital Bank. As far as the bank was concerned, Andre Baxter did not exist.

Which of course, he did not.

William McArthur, however, did.

CHAPTER THIRTY-EIGHT

Navigating away from the bank's website, Andre swiftly accessed the Faraday Trust account at the Great Northern Bank. As he was a nominated Trustee, he had no trouble accessing the account details and arranging for the transfer of funds. With the touch of a button, William McArthur was a very rich man.

* * *

Time: 2.15pm
   Date: 18th November 2008
   Location: Liberec, Czech Republic

Kreshniov folded the newspaper and tucked it under his seat at the pavement café. He didn't need to read it anymore. He raised his hand and attracted the waiter's attention, ordering a fresh cappuccino to enjoy in the rest of the day's weakening sun. He leant back in his chair and raised his face to the sky – the weak sunshine with a very slight cooling breeze made for an exquisite mix. Life was good.

As his fresh cappuccino arrived, Kreshniov gave an involuntary shudder. The already weak November sun had slipped behind a cloud and was casting a chilled shadow across the bustling square. Something else accompanied the spreading shadow as it crossed the pavement café and crept over Kreshniov's pallid skin. What was it? Remorse? Guilt? Injustice? Kreshniov momentarily searched his soul; did he feel anything for Isabel and her family? The brother she never knew? Did he feel he had betrayed the Faradays? Betrayed Poborski and the others?

If his soul was seeking to let these alien feelings seep into his thoughts, they didn't last long. Kreshniov sipped his coffee. Isabel already thought her parents were dead. It was better left that way. She didn't need to know the truth; nobody did. And as for Miles. He was a casualty of war, plain and simple. Kreshniov's hatred for those who turned against him, for those who refused to believe in him, soon over took and suffocated any feelings of remorse.

Albert Dupont.

As Kreshniov leant back in his chair, the image of his former friend slipped into his head.

Albert Dupont.

As an investigative journalist he was always going to be a liability as a friend. To begin with, he had been useful. Very useful. When Kreshniov needed to find out anything about the state of the former Phoenix Project members, Dupont had been happy and willing to oblige. And the information he was able to glean was always 100% accurate. Kreshniov could rely on that.

But even Dupont outlived his usefulness. He had become too good at his job. His investigative nose for a good story, a cover up, meant he soon stumbled over the inconsistencies in NASA's exploration logs. He began asking questions; too many questions. He was working on tracking down the members of PRISM, and it was only a matter of time before he would crack open the secrets of the Phoenix Project. Dupont had signed his own death warrant the minute Kreshniov found out he had made enquiries with NASA HQ about the existence of a secret society.

Dupont needed to be silenced.

And Karl Poborski had been happy to oblige.

* * *

Time: 11.15am
Date: 8th November 2008
Location: Eiffel Tower, Paris

Poborski gripped the small hunting knife tightly in the palm of his hand. The base of the handle slid inside the sleeve of his jacket, safely out of sight. He glanced at his watch. It was time. He had to move now, quickly. They would be here at any moment, and he could not be seen.

Poborski strode purposefully across the plaza. He paid no attention to the hordes of tourists queuing at the South entrance to the tower. He was

CHAPTER THIRTY-EIGHT

oblivious to the clicking and snapping of their cameras, their shrieks of laughter, their joyful anticipation of climbing the structure which towered ominously over their heads. To Poborski, there was nothing and no-one around him.

He was alone.

He could see the journalist sitting on a low concrete bench on the opposite side of the plaza, just where Kreshniov had said he would be. He was alone, as instructed, sitting with his back towards the crowds, a rolled up newspaper held in his hands. Grey speckled pigeons pecked the ground around his feet, searching for the smallest specks of crumbs with their pointed beaks.

Poborski gripped the handle of the knife even more tightly, stretching his gloved fingers around the shaft. His footsteps made no sound on the pavement; no one seemed to see him as he lengthened his stride. It was as though he was invisible.

The attack was swift and clean. Within seconds it was over and Poborski melted away back into the laughing crowds. Dupont slumped forwards slightly, his chin resting on his ample chest, his scarlet red woollen scarf masking the gaping slit that crossed his jugular.

* * *

Time: 3.00pm
Date: 17th November 2008
Location: MI6 Headquarters, London

Olivia Green began to nibble at her bottom lip, looking worried. She glanced down at the statement in her hand, unable to stop it shaking and trembling in her grip. Jack smiled and reached out, gently patting her forearm.

"Don't worry," he said, warmly. "You haven't done anything wrong. I just need to go over some of the things you mentioned in your statement to DS Cooper."

Olivia nodded, and looked up through nervous eyes. "I...I don't know what else I can tell you," she said, her voice cracking. "I told him everything I knew."

Jack nodded and gently took the statement out of her hand. "I'm sure you did. I'm just interested in this bit here." He pointed halfway down the third page of the statement. "Where you say that Mr Tindleman asked you not to disturb him. It says here you believed he was attending to some paperwork?"

Olivia nodded, and dabbed her eyes with a damp tissue that she was nursing in her hand.

"But he had you to do his paperwork for him, didn't he?" continued Jack. "I mean, that's what you're here for. That was part of your job, wasn't it?"

Again, Olivia nodded. She put the damp tissue into the waste paper bin beneath her desk and tucked her neatly bobbed dark-brown hair behind her ears.

"So…" coaxed Jack. "What was he doing?"

Olivia gave a small shrug of her narrow shoulders. "I...I don't know. He just….he just asked me not to disturb him for the rest of the day."

"And this was…." Jack glanced back down at the statement in his hands. "About 11.00am?"

Olivia nodded, reaching for a fresh tissue from the box on her desk. "Yes I think so. I had just taken him his morning coffee."

Jack nodded, and looked back up into the PA's petite face. Although her statement gave her age as 26, to Jack she looked no more than a child. Her pale, porcelain skin was framed by smooth, straight dark chocolate coloured hair, cut into a neat bob. "And then…?"

"And...well, I left him to it. I didn't disturb him for the rest of the day, as he asked."

"Was that normal?"

"Normal?"

"Would he often ask you not to disturb him?"

Olivia paused for a moment, her eyes glazing over as she thought about her boss. Then she slowly began to shake her head. "Well, no….no it wasn't.

CHAPTER THIRTY-EIGHT

I...I don't think he has ever asked me not to disturb him before. He usually keeps his door open........I mean, kept his door open....It was unusual for him to keep it closed."

"What was it that he was doing...this paperwork?" pressed Jack. "What was it that he felt he couldn't ask you to do for him, as his PA?"

Olivia gave another small shrug of her petite shoulders. "I don't really know. It sounded like he was copying something."

Jack looked up sharply from the statement in his hands. "*Copying something?*"

Olivia nodded. "I remember now. I could hear the photocopier whirring before I went on my lunchbreak. And....and underneath the door I think I could see the light from the photocopier flashing through the gap. It was a bit strange, now I think about it........I usually do all his photocopying for him....he doesn't really know how to us the machine very well. I have the main photocopier out here." Olivia nodded at the large industrial sized photocopying machine in the corner of her office. "But he has a small one in his office. I don't remember him using it before." She paused and looked up at Jack, a worried look clouding her face. "Was that important? Should I have mentioned it to DS Cooper?"

Jack smiled and shook his head. "No, not at all. It's fine. Anything else you can remember as being a little bit odd, or unusual that day?"

"I....I don't think so....no."

"And you didn't see him at all after that? After he told you not to disturb him?

Olivia started to shake her head, then paused and swallowed nervously, resuming her lip biting. "He....er....after a while, just as I was putting on my coat to go for lunch, he handed me some envelopes to post." She looked up into Jack's eyes, her own starting to brim with fresh tears. "I....I'm sorry...I think I forgot about that."

Jack smiled again, feeling sorry for the poor girl. "It's all right, really. It's easy to forget things when you are in a state of shock." Jack had to remind himself that this poor girl had been the first one to find Tindleman at his desk, dead. "Do you remember if there had been anything unusual in the letters he asked you to post?"

Olivia considered Jack's question carefully for a few moments, and then slowly began to nod. "There was one envelope….it was a lot larger than the rest. Very thick. He doesn't usually send out anything quite that big."

"Go on," encouraged Jack.

"I remember….I thought it was a bit strange at the time……."

Jack nodded again, giving Olivia a reassuring smile. "What did you think was strange about it?"

"The address," continued Olivia. "The address to where it was being sent."

"And where was that?"

Olivia paused, and looked up into Jack's gaze. "To himself. He was sending it to himself."

* * *

CHAPTER THIRTY-NINE

Time: 4.00pm
Date: 17th November 2008
Location: Palace Mews Road, London

"Please take a seat, Inspector." Mrs Tindleman waved a frail looking arm towards an uncomfortable looking sofa. "Can I get you something to drink? Some tea, or coffee perhaps?"

Jack stepped across the living room towards the sofa, but remained standing. "No, thank you, Mrs Tindleman," he replied, softly. "I don't want to take up too much of your time."

"It's no problem," insisted Mrs Tindleman, already heading towards a door which Jack assumed led towards the kitchen. "The kettle has already boiled. It won't take a minute."

Jack smiled and nodded his head, slowly. "Then tea would be lovely, thank you." He watched as Mrs Tindleman left the room, noticing how stiffly she walked. Although she could be no older than her mid-fifties, her gait easily added another 15 years to her withered frame. Grief does that to you, mused Jack, watching the door to the kitchen swing shut behind her. He turned his gaze to the living room in which he stood; the floral curtains were closed, and didn't look as though they had been open all day. The room smelt a little musty as if not only the curtains but also the doors and windows had remained closed for some time.

The room was unnaturally tidy – nothing out of place. The photographs and picture frames on the mantelpiece were all correctly aligned in height order, and looked recently polished. The carriage clock in the centre was gleaming; its gently tick-ticking the only sound in the deafeningly quiet room.

There were no newspapers, no magazines, no open books. No cups, no plates. No shoes or jackets. Nothing to suggest that anyone was actually living here. It was as if time had stood still. And maybe for Mrs Tindleman, it had.

Jack edged closer to the mantelpiece and noticed several pictures of the late Charles Tindleman. Their silver-edged frames appeared to have been given an extra special polish, gleaming in the softness of the overhead light. Just as he reached out to take a closer look at what appeared to be a family gathering, maybe a wedding, Jack heard a gentle tinkling sound. He turned to find Mrs Tindleman leaning over the coffee table and pouring tea from a bone china teapot.

"That's very kind of you, Mrs Tindleman," he said, stepping away from the photographs and back towards the sofa. He sat precariously perched on the arm rest, and accepted the proffered china cup and saucer. Jack noticed she was unable to disguise her trembling hand, the cup rattling noisily inside the saucer. Jack looked up into her careworn face; she looked like she hadn't slept in days. Faint grey circles adorned the paper-thin skin below her puffy eyes, and unless Jack was mistaken it looked as though Mrs Tindleman had been crying.

"Are you sure you're all right, Mrs Tindleman," asked Jack, placing his cup and saucer back down on the coffee table, the tea untouched. "Because if there is anything I can do….."

Mrs Tindleman seated herself in an armchair opposite Jack and slowly shook her head. "I'm all right, Inspector," she said, wearily, her voice shaking in much the same way as her hands. "I have my son…" Mrs Tindleman broke off and looked away, blinking rapidly. She pulled out a small white handkerchief and careful dabbed her eyes. Her face looked pale despite the make-up she had attempted to apply that morning in an attempt to make herself feel normal. Her fair hair was pulled back rather harshly from her face and clasped in a hastily arranged bun at the back of

CHAPTER THIRTY-NINE

her head. Several wisps of hair hung down by the side of her wan cheeks, and the light overhead picked out the ever growing number of grey strands. She had always been a slender woman, but now looked gaunt and frail – as delicate as the expensive bone china tea service sitting in front of them on the coffee table. And just as liable to break.

"Was it my son you came to see, Inspector?" Mrs Tindleman turned back towards Jack and replaced the handkerchief in the pocket of her cardigan. Her pale eyes glistened with fresh tears.

Jack shook his head. "Not exactly, Mrs Tindleman. I was actually wondering if you remembered seeing something coming through in the post over the last couple of days? A large envelope. Quite thick?" Jack held his breath, wondering if maybe he had been a little too direct in his questioning. Maybe he should have approached it differently. He saw a small frown pass over Mrs Tindleman's face before she gave a shake of her head.

"I'm sorry, Inspector," she replied, her voice still strained. "I haven't really taken much notice of that kind of thing lately….." She let her voice tail off.

"No, of course not." Jack silently cursed at the insensitive way in which he had asked. "I'm sorry to have mentioned it." He made to get up, but stopped as Mrs Tindleman raised her head to catch his gaze.

"It's my son, you see, Inspector," she continued. "He was supposed to be coming over this afternoon to go through…..go through all the paperwork for me….." She paused, glancing over towards the front door as if she half expected her son to walk through just at that very moment. "But he hasn't arrived…."

Jack nodded, sympathetically, unsure what else to say. It had been wrong of him to have come unannounced like this. It had been too soon. Too raw.

"Everything of Charles' is in his study, Inspector." Mrs Tindleman focused her eyes back on Jack, fighting back the tears which were welling up at the mention of her dead husband's name. "You are more than welcome to go through and look for anything you need."

THE PHOENIX PROJECT

* * *

Time: 3.00pm
 Date: 18th November 2008
 Location: Liberec, Czech Republic

Kreshniov paid the waiter for his second cappuccino, leaving a generous tip. The waiter nodded his thanks, and removed the empty coffee cup. Gathering up the newspaper, Kreshniov made to vacate the table, ready to disappear into the anonymity of the bustling square.

Shafer.

Kreshniov paused. An image of Simon Shafer filled his conscience.

Yes, Kreshniov appeared to have a conscience. It was expertly hidden for the vast majority of the time, but occasionally, when his guards were down it managed to infiltrate his mind.

Kreshniov replaced the newspaper on the table and sat back in his chair, his usual expressionless features taking on an unnatural appearance. Was this sadness?

Shafer.

Shafer had been different. Shafer had been a friend, a true friend – in more ways than Albert Dupont had ever been. He had supported and helped Kreshniov when he had needed it the most, after fleeing the United States and the rest of the Phoenix Project, seeking oblivion. Shafer had helped Kreshniov settle into his new identity as Andre Baxter, and had ensured that any searches for him by M16 ended in his own death certificate.

Shafer had helped Boris Kreshniov to die. And for Andre Baxter to be born.

And he had demanded and expected nothing in return.

Kreshniov shivered, raising his clouded eyes towards the sky. The sun had crept out from behind the clouds, but failed to throw any warmth onto his skin. Visions crowded his mind of Shafer's lifeless body, lying there on a bed of damp leaves in a nondescript Paris suburb. It wasn't

CHAPTER THIRTY-NINE

meant to end like that.

Shafer was not meant to die.

Kreshniov could feel himself holding onto the body as the last gasps of life were ripped from him. At that precise moment, Kreshniov knew that Karl Poborski had changed the plan. In that split second, listening to Shafer whisper his final words, Kreshniov knew that Poborski too had to die.

Poborski had never been interested in the Phoenix Project. His one and only motivation had been money. Pure and simple. And at that exact moment, holding Shafer's bloodstained body, Kreshniov knew that he would do anything to get it. *Anything*. Including murdering their friends.

Shafer had been a risk. Kreshniov had always known that. Shafer was M16 and that made him "one of them." There had always been the risk that he would turn against them, divulge Kreshniov's real location; but Kreshniov had still trusted him. There had been something in the young Shafer's eyes, when they met for the first time all those years ago, something that told Kreshniov that he was a good man. A man of honour. A man of his word.

But honesty and trust meant little to Karl Poborski. He trusted nobody, and Shafer had been a risk too great for him to live with. Poborski had killed Shafer. Kreshniov had known that the minute he saw Shafer's body dead on the cold, damp Paris pavement. He may as well have signed his name in the dying man's blood.

And from that exact moment on, Kreshniov knew what he had to do. If Poborski could change the plan, so could he. There was no longer a joint partnership, a joint agreement. That had evaporated the very same moment the life had left Shafer's body.

But Kreshniov knew he had to act fast, Poborski had been one step ahead of him for too long. Now Kreshniov was acting alone; he felt free; he felt liberated; he felt in control once again.

Poborski had not done his homework. He had underestimated his fellow Phoenix Project founder. He had not truly appreciated who he was dealing with here.

No one got the better of Boris Kreshniov.

No one.

Shaking his head slightly, to get rid of the images of Shafer's final resting place, Kreshniov rose from the pavement café table. He looked down briefly at the newspaper resting on the edge. Karl Poborski's image stared back up at him, but Kreshniov barely noticed him. Turning his back, he walked away from the table and walked away from Karl Poborski.

* * *

Time: 4.10pm
  Date: 17th November 2008
  Location: Palace Mews Road, London

Jack silently closed the door to Charles Tindleman's study and looked around him. It felt strange, unnerving even, to be stepping into the private room of a dead man. He cast his gaze over to the large mahogany desk which swamped the room before him. There was a comfortable looking leather backed chair behind the desk and Jack felt that he could just see Charles Tindleman's plump frame nestling into it, dealing with his correspondence, working late into the night.

But now the room felt empty. Devoid of life. Jack felt like an intruder, as if he were walking on someone's grave. Without moving, Jack's gaze fell on the piles of paper strewn across the top of the desk. Much of it appeared to be papers and documents Charles Tindleman had been working on before his death. Several folders were still open, a single fountain pen resting on a piece of blotting paper.

Towards the front of the desk was a wire tray, home to a pile of what appeared to be the daily post. The letters were stacked up, several inches thick – Mrs Tindleman didn't appear to have been able to bring herself to deal with any of it, preferring to shut it away in Charles' study – shut it out of her life, shut it out of her grief.

Jack's heart began to beat faster. He could see instantly the envelope

CHAPTER THIRTY-NINE

that he was looking for. It was the only large A4 sized buff envelope in the pile, stuffed underneath all the others at the bottom of the wire tray. Jack inched himself closer to the desk, hardly daring to breathe. Could this be it? Could this really be it?

Reaching into the wire tray he gently pulled the envelope out, feeling how thick it was. With trembling hands, he turned the envelope over and his eyes rested on the address. The address written in Charles Tindleman's own distinctive handwriting.

This had to be it.

At last.

The missing piece.

* * *

Time: 3.10pm
Date: 18th November 2008
Location: Liberec, Czech Republic

William McArthur was now a rich man. Poborski's money was his; the Faradays money was his.

The Faradays.

Kreshniov tried not to think about Elizabeth and Christopher. He had singled them out at the very beginning as being ideally suited to helping him in his quest. But he had never quite intended to form as strong a bond with them as he ended up doing. By befriending him, they had invited him into their world and into their family. As Andre Baxter he had gained their trust, their friendship and their respect.

And in return he had become close to them; closer than anticipated. Closer than he had intended. Family outings, family gatherings, even family holidays. "Uncle Andre" was always invited.

So when he had suggested they go into hiding after the accident, to escape the Phoenix Project founders control, they had been easily persuaded. They had no idea that instead of running *away* from the

Phoenix Project founders, they were actually running *with one*.

Kreshniov had needed the Faradays in his control after the accident. The physical evidence he could deal with. He had one set of Phoenix Project documents in his possession, and he knew the only other set was at Phoenix Project HQ. He knew that eventually he would get control of all the papers, that was inevitable.

But there was one source of information and evidence that he could not control.

The information in the minds and memories of the Faradays.

If left unchecked and unmanaged, it was a time bomb waiting to explode.

The Faradays didn't die in the car accident in 1986.

But they did have to die.

* * *

Time: 2.00am
    Date: 1st January 2008
    Location: La Vigne Rouge Chalet, Cote D'Azur, France

The bodies lay side by side, as if in peaceful slumber. There was no sound from outside; nothing moved, nothing stirred. It was almost as if time had stood still.

Boris Kreshniov closed the bedroom curtains, shutting out the early morning sunlight. He turned and carefully wiped the blood from the blade of the slender kitchen knife against the already heavily bloodstained blankets, and then slipped it back into his jacket pocket. Then, trying not to touch the pools of dark, congealing blood which were seeping into the bedclothes, he gently lifted the necklace from around Elizabeth Faraday's neck. It wasn't easy – the necklace started to slip through his black leather gloves which were slippery and shiny with blood. Kreshniov lifted her head and tried to remove the necklace, the gaping wound from her neck was still oozing, her body still warm. But there was no life left inside the limp body, her eyes stared vacantly up towards the ceiling.

CHAPTER THIRTY-NINE

Kreshniov turned her face away from him, and gently pulled the necklace over her face and hair. He let her head drop back down on the blood-soaked pillow and held the necklace up to the faint light coming in through the curtained windows. He smiled to himself as he watched the silver pendant swing between his gloved fingers.

One half of a prism.

One half of *the* prism.

And Kreshniov knew who had the missing piece.

Having got what he wanted, Kreshniov made to leave the bedroom. He had already spent longer in the cottage than he had intended. The Faradays had put up more of a fight than expected. But now they both lay dead, side by side, and Kreshniov needed to move fast. He picked up two large canisters by his feet and began splashing the contents over the stained bedclothes. He made sure both bodies were drenched before making a trail behind him, out the bedroom door and onto the small landing. He continued down the steep, winding staircase towards the front door of the cottage, and then without turning round, Kreshniov struck a match and threw it over his shoulder.

CHAPTER FORTY

Time: 2.00pm
  Date: 25th May 2009
  Location: Albury Churchyard, Surrey

The headstones rose up out of the long grass, one of a long line of seemingly identical stones marking the final resting place of family, friends and loved ones. Jack knelt down and flattened the long tufts that had grown up around the sides of the simple granite headstone. He read the inscription silently to himself.
  "Elizabeth and Christopher Faraday – born 12th April 1950 and 15th November 1948 died 1st January 2008
  Like a Phoenix, you will rise again."
  At the end of the inscription, Jack noticed a small insignia. A small motif.
  A phoenix rising out of the fire. The fire in the shape of a prism.
  Jack turned and looked back over his shoulder. He nodded his head and motioned for Isabel to come forwards. She was hesitant at first, her feet unwilling to move or carry her forwards. But slowly she began to shuffle towards the graveside, and knelt down next to Jack in the cold, damp grass. She leant forwards and placed a single red rose on the raised earth – and a single tear trickled down her cheek.
  Jack stood up and took a few paces back, leaving Isabel alone with her grief. He watched as she got to her feet and leant across to a neighbouring grave, placing another single red rose in the shadow of the headstone. "Miles Faraday – born 21st December 1985, died 1st October 2008."

CHAPTER FORTY

Burying your parents for the first time was bad enough, but to have to do it a second time?

And your brother?

DNA had confirmed the bodies in the burnt out cottage were those of Elizabeth and Christopher Faraday; the fire had not consumed enough to make identification impossible. But the French police were no closer to knowing what had actually happened to them.

And then there was the headstone. Both of them.

The headstones had appeared during the middle of the night. No one from Isabel's family had requested them, and there was no clue as to who had ordered it.

Other than the person who paid for it.

William McArthur.

* * *

Time: 10.00pm
Date: 12th June 2009
Location: Kettle's Yard Mews, London

Jack sat down on the sofa and passed a can of cold Budweiser to Mac. Neither of them spoke as they watched the familiar beginnings of the BBC News at Ten.

"Today's top story – there are unconfirmed reports tonight of a multi-scale cover-up in the 1980s concerning a space exploration that went drastically wrong. Additional reports suggest the involvement of the ill-fated Challenger Space Shuttle. We have live reports tonight coming from Washington and NASA HQ."

Jack took a swig of the ice-cold beer and watched his brother do the same. The newsreader continued.

"NASA have so far made no comment, and the current US administration are denying any involvement. Here at home, MI5 and MI6 remain tight-lipped on any UK links to what had been dubbed the cover-up of the century. First we go live to our reporter Dan Ashman in Washington. Dan, what can you tell us?"

Jack muted the TV and took another mouthful of beer.

"You reckon the whole story is going to come out?" Mac leant forwards and picked up another slice of pizza from the box on the coffee table. "About Isabel? About the money? About all those who took the cyanide pills?"

Jack shrugged. "No idea. All I know is that the new Chief Superintendent is shitting a brick. I'm just glad I have a few days off." He too leant forwards and swiped a slice of the thick crusted pizza.

"And you think Isabel did the right thing?" Mac spoke while wiping a strand of stringy mozzarella from his chin. "Releasing some of the papers to the press?"

Again, Jack shrugged and took another swig of his beer. "It was her call. But in her shoes, I guess I would have done the same." After visiting Charles Tindleman's widow and finding the envelope in his office, Jack had handed all the Phoenix Project documents over to Isabel. It had seemed the right thing to do. Charles Tindleman had, indeed, made photocopies of all the papers Andre….Kreshniov….had sent to him. And that one last act of the head of MI6 had meant that the lasting legacy of the Phoenix Project would not be destroyed. Jack had thought about handing them to the new Chief Superintendent, but something had stopped him.

Isabel.

Everything in those papers belonged to her. It was her parents who had been at the centre of it all, her brother who had inadvertently been dragged in too. All three had died because of it. If anyone deserved to decide what became of the papers, then it had to be Isabel. When Jack had eventually found her, after she had vacated her Cambridge home and moved back into the family home in Albury, he had handed her the documents and told her to do with them what she felt was right.

If she wanted to keep them, fair enough. If she wanted to destroy them, fair enough. If she wanted them to become public knowledge, again it was her call.

CHAPTER FORTY

And it looked like she had chosen.

"She did what she felt was right, I guess." Jack handed his brother another can of Budweiser, noting that he had already drained his first. "And good on her, I say."

Mac accepted the can and snapped it open. "Will any of it come back on you?" Mac hesitated and took a sip of his beer. "On us?"

Jack shook his head and crushed his can in his palm, throwing it into the now empty pizza box. "I don't think so. Isabel was very clear on what information she wanted to make public, and what she didn't. I think we can trust her to be discreet."

"And Kreshniov? Will he ever be found?" Mac's words hung in the still, summer air.

Jack gave a small laugh and got to his feet, picking up the empty pizza box and heading across to the kitchen. He couldn't help but cast his mind back to the interview rooms.

* * *

Time: 7.05pm
    Date: 10th November 2008
    Location: Interview room, Metropolitan Police HQ, London

"And what about Kreshniov? You know where we can find him?"

"Kreshniov? You'll never find him. Not until he wants to be found."

* * *

Time: 10.00pm
    Date: 12th June 2009
    Location: Kettle's Yard Mews, London

Jack tossed a couple of empty beer cans in the recycling bin. "I think that will be up to him."

"And you?"

"What about me?" Jack half turned to look back at his brother while shoving the pizza box into the bin under the sink.

"You know. The dreams?"

Jack straightened back up and began filling the kettle. "I'm fine."

"No, you're not. I've been staying here for 6 months now and I can tell you're not fine, Jack."

"They come and go. The dreams. I can handle it." Jack fetched two mugs from the sink and busied himself with tipping coffee into them, avoiding Mac's gaze.

"I think you should start seeing her again," said Mac, simply.

"Start seeing who?" Although Jack knew full well who Mac was referring to.

"You know, that shrink."

"Psychotherapist," corrected Jack, opening the fridge for the milk.

"OK, the psychotherapist. I think you should start seeing her again."

Jack paused, the all too familiar memories of the dreams flooding his brain. It was true. He wasn't fine. He knew that. And he needed help. He knew that too.

"Just say you'll make an appointment to see her. See how it goes…"

"OK, OK, I'll make an appointment." Jack filled the mugs with boiling water from the kettle and brought them back over to the sofa. "Can we drop it now?"

"And I think we should go and see Mum."

* * *

Time: 3.00pm
   Date: 15th June 2009
   Location: Great St Mary's Church, Christchurch, Dorset

CHAPTER FORTY

For the middle of June, the day was dull and overcast. Maybe it was fitting, thought Jack, as he thrust his hands further into his raincoat pockets and followed the path through the churchyard.

"It's this way," called Mac, over his shoulder, heading down a fork in the path on their left.

Jack turned to follow, breaking into a jog to keep up with his brother. "How do you know it's down here?"

"Because, Jack, I've been here before. A few times." Mac nodded towards the far end of the path, close to a hawthorn hedge and old chestnut tree. "It's over there." He began striding towards the hedge.

"You've been what?" Jack quickened his pace and followed Mac, heading towards the end of the path. "What do you mean you've been here before?"

Mac stopped in front of the chestnut tree and lowered his eyes to the grass below. Before them was a patch of grass, overgrown and in need of a trim, marked with a simple wooden cross.

"Stella MacIntosh. Born September 18th 1942. Died April 5th 1971. RIP."

There was one small bunch of wilted roses lying on the tufty grass. "There she is." Mac glanced up at Jack and nodded his head down to where their mother lay beneath the earth. "There's Mum."

Jack felt a lump form in his throat and his pulse began to quicken. The image of their mother hanging from the light fitting filled his head as he gazed down at the small mound of earth and grass that was her grave.

"I never knew her, Jack. That's why." Mac knelt down and picked up the wilted roses. "I have no real memory of her."

Jack joined his brother and knelt down in the soft, damp grass by the graveside. He placed a hand on Mac's shoulder and gave it a squeeze. With his other hand he pulled out his wallet from his back pocket and flipped it open. Patting Mac on the back, he pulled out a small black and white passport sized photograph.

"Here, keep this." Jack handed the photograph of their mother's happy, smiling, carefree face over to Mac. "I guess neither of us really got to know her. Not properly."

"I think I'd like to stay for a while, in London.....with you." Mac held the photograph between his thumb and forefinger, staring at it, solemnly. "If that's OK?"

Jack smiled and straightened up, his knees creaking as he did so. "Of course, Stu. Stay as long as you like. Anyway, you need to be around. I need your help."

Mac got to his feet and slipped the photograph in his back pocket. "Help with what?"

"Well, it's all the station can talk about…..me and my long-lost brother. I need your back-up mate." Jack smiled at his brother and cast his eyes down at their mother's grave, before turning back towards the path. "Let's go get some lunch. I think I spotted a pub on our way in."

Jack and Mac turned their backs on the graveside and headed back out of the churchyard, listening to the chirp and call of the birds sitting on the hawthorn hedge. Mac tossed the wilting roses into a nearby bin by the churchyard gates, and made a mental note to place some fresh flowers on the grave before they left. Roses. He had a feeling mum liked roses.

"And the Phoenix Project? That's all over now?" Mac turned and waited for Jack to catch up.

"It's over….and it's not." Jack shook his head and headed out of the churchyard gates, in direction of the pub he could see at the top of the narrow lane ahead. "Let's go get a drink."

Following on, Mac pulled a packet of cigarettes out of his jacket pocket and tipped them in Jack's direction.

"Not for me, Stu," replied Jack, holding up his hands. "Day 279….and counting." He smiled at his brother and continued heading up the narrow lane towards the promised watering hole. As he did so, he considered Mac's last question.

The Phoenix Project. Was it over?

Kreshniov was still out there. And Kreshniov still had $1m of Isabel's money.

Jack knew he would not rest until he found it. The police investigation had been wound down and boxed up. Everything placed in storage to gather dust. After picking over the bones for several weeks, even the

CHAPTER FORTY

media had moved on to other stories. NASA had managed to cover-up the cover-up, and the security services here had licked their wounds and lived to fight another day.

The Phoenix Project was old news.

But Detective Inspector Jack MacIntosh never forgot.

One day he would find him.

It might take months. It might take years.

But one man couldn't hide forever.

Could he?

* * *

Message from the Author

Thank you for reading the first Detective Inspector Jack MacIntosh novel - The Phoenix Project.

I hope you liked it!

As an independently published author, I would be really grateful if you could leave a review. Visit my book page on either Amazon.co.uk or Amazon.com, and click "write a customer review":

www.amazon.co.uk/dp/B07HVXMDM5

www.amazon.com/dp/B07HVXMDM5

As an author I love hearing from my readers! Please get in touch by visiting my Facebook page:

www.facebook.com/michellekiddauthor.com

Or visit my website:

www.michellekiddauthor.com

and subscribe to my free email newsletter service - be the first to hear about new publication dates and exciting special offers!

Or enter the following into your search engine for newsletter sign up:

https://mailchi.mp/3fa8a1b2d32a/michellekidd

Or contact me via email:

michelle@michellekiddauthor.com

Once again, many thanks for reading!

Michelle Kidd
  2019

Printed in Great Britain
by Amazon